STATE
EMERGENCY

Sam Fisher is the pseudonym of thriller writer Michael White, author of the acclaimed international bestsellers *Equinox* and *The Medici Secret*. He lives in Sydney.

Visit his website at www.michaelwhite.com.au.

Also by Sam Fisher

Aftershock

STATE OF EMERGENCY

SAM FISHER

PAN BOOKS

First published 2009 by Bantam, an imprint of Random House Australia Pty Ltd

This edition published 2011 by Pan Books
an imprint of Pan Macmillan, a division of Macmillan Publishers Limited
Pan Macmillan, 20 New Wharf Road, London N1 9RR
Basingstoke and Oxford
Associated companies throughout the world
www.panmacmillan.com

ISBN 978-1-447-20150-2

1 3 5 7 9 8 6 4 2

A CIP catalogue record for this book is available from
the British Library.

Printed in the UK by CPI Mackays, Chatham ME5 8TD

Visit **www.panmacmillan.com** to read more about all our books
and to buy them. You will also find features, author interviews and
news of any author events, and you can sign up for e-newsletters
so that you're always first to hear about our new releases.

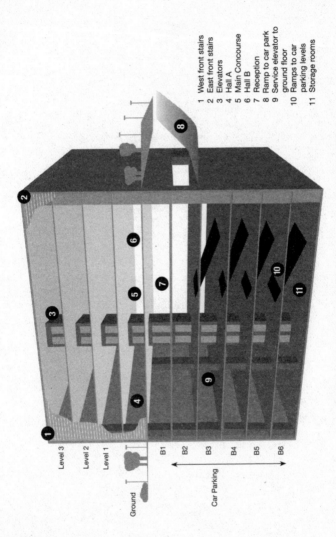

1 West front stairs
2 East front stairs
3 Elevators
4 Hall A
5 Main Concourse
6 Hall B
7 Reception
8 Ramp to car park
9 Service elevator to ground floor
10 Ramps to car parking levels
11 Storage rooms

Level 3
Level 2
Level 1

Ground

B1
B2
B3
B4
B5
B6

Car Parking

California Conference Center, Downtown Los Angeles, California

Part One

COME TOGETHER

1

Crete, Greece

To the tourists waiting at the entrance of Hotel Knossos, the coach seemed to appear out of nowhere. The rain was coming down in torrents, smacking out a heavy rhythm on the roof of the reception area. The huge shape that rounded a fountain in the courtyard looked like a giant beetle coming at them through the rain.

A cheer went up from the group. The coach was late and now they had less than an hour to reach the airport, almost twenty miles away. A few minutes later the passengers were all on board, their luggage stowed. The driver shouted something to one of the hotel staff as the doors hissed shut. With a hand-rolled cigarette dangling limp from his lips, the driver swung the big steering wheel and the vehicle nosed onto the mountain road.

The coach smelled bad. A blend of sweat and damp clothes and the fug of the driver's cigarette. There was also an animal smell, the smell of fear. The road from the hotel to the airport wound around treacherous hairpin bends. It was pockmarked with holes and irregular tarmac. All that could be seen through the curtains of driving rain was an empty void. A few feet to the right the cliff fell away to nothing.

But the driver had no fear. He swung the coach around the bends with the confidence of a man who had driven along these roads a thousand times and knew every bump, every ripple in the tarmac.

Outside, it was growing dark. An unnatural dark. Roiling storm clouds blotted out the last of the Greek daylight.

The driver cursed and braked sharply. The coach skidded, the tyres screeched. Great plumes of water leaped up the side of the vehicle. A woman screamed. Swinging the wheel dexterously hand over hand, the driver pulled the coach hard to the right and stopped an inch from a sheer wall of rock. A little white Renault, its headlights ablaze, edged past on the left. It left almost nothing between it and the edge of the cliff. The car accelerated away. The driver leaned on the horn.

The coach had stalled. The driver fired up the engine again, tugged on the heavy gearshift and swung the vehicle back into the centre of the road, around the next bend and on to a straight, narrow stretch. To the left, the passengers could see the lights of a village. White buildings nestled in a ravine. The view was blurred by the torrential rain. Twin shafts of yellow from the headlights danced in the murk. The driver pushed down on the accelerator. The speedometer nudged 60. To the right, the rock face flew by in a wash of grey.

The straight went on for more than a quarter of a mile, but up ahead the road curved sharply to the right. From there, a series of sharp turns led to a short tunnel cut into the rock. Beyond that stretched the long, slow descent to the highway and the airport.

The needle on the speedometer touched 65. Passengers exchanged nervous glances. An elderly man tried to get out of his seat to speak to the driver but his wife pulled him back. 'Don't be a fool,' she snapped. 'It'll only put him off.'

The headlights of a car appeared around the bend a hundred feet ahead.

The coach driver knew immediately there was nothing he could do. He tried easing his foot on the brake pedal, but there was no grip. The coach barely slowed. He pushed harder, knowing that too much pressure would send the coach aquaplaning to disaster.

The front left wheel hit a large bump in the tarmac. The driver tried to compensate, overdid it, and sent them too far right. The nearside wing mirror smashed against the rock wall. Lumps of glass and plastic shot along the narrow gap between the wall and the main body of the coach. A metal bolt ricocheted through a window two-thirds of the way along the coach and slammed into the right eye of the passenger in 23B, a young woman on her honeymoon. The bolt ripped through her brain, exiting close to her right ear and taking a large chunk of cranial bone and hair with it.

The driver panicked and slammed his foot hard on the brake. The rear of the coach almost lifted off the ground. The front suspension roared and the plastic front bumper hit the road and shattered. The back of the coach swung around as the vehicle aquaplaned on the wet tarmac. A wall of water shot up the side of the coach, which smashed into the car coming towards it. The car flew over the side of the coach and almost disintegrated as it landed on the road. The chassis separated from the body of the car and smacked into the rock wall before bouncing over the cliff.

The coach kept sliding along the road. The front of the vehicle collided with a knob of rock protruding from the corner. It spun around and thundered into the rock face side-on. A chunk of rock the size of a bowling ball broke away from the wall and rocketed through the windscreen, decapitating the driver and pulverising his head against the steel support behind his seat. The windows shattered and the passengers were thrown around like clothes in a dryer. The air was filled with the sound of crunching metal and screams.

Rebounding from the wall, the shuddering coach spun around. The back hit a rocky outcrop, sending the vehicle onto its side – and over the cliff edge.

2

The four choppers had blacked-out windows and one passenger each. They flew low over the ocean, ten minutes apart. Each of the passengers was given the full VIP treatment – champagne and canapés. But before boarding they had been told the trip would only be possible on the condition they signed a contract binding them under international law neither to speak nor write of anything they would see that day. Curiosity had won them over.

As each chopper landed, a black car docked with its door and its passenger was escorted into a waiting car. Like the choppers, the cars had windows made from polarised glass.

Still ten minutes apart, the cars arrived at a reception area and drove into a windowless hangar. There each guest was met by an official and an armed guard. They passed through a metal detector, and then were taken to a comfortable but windowless room. There was a coffee machine, sandwiches and cake. Soft sofas hugged three walls and a low table stood in the middle of the room. On top of this was spread a collection of glossy magazines.

Thirty minutes after the first guest had arrived, he was joined by three others. Two men in slacks and open-necked shirts appeared. They shook hands with the four guests and led the way to another, smaller room that looked like a college seminar room. The escorts left without a word.

3

Base One, Tintara

For 24 hours the world was gripped by images of a tour coach dangling on the edge of a promontory in Crete. They watched as rescue teams did everything they could to save the passengers. Mark Harrison was no different. Like millions of others around the world, he was glued to his TV screen. Unlike those millions, he could do something about it . . . almost.

The coach had lodged on a rocky outcrop 30 feet below the road. Beneath it loomed hundreds of feet of air.

The passengers had moved to the back of the coach to take the weight off the front end. The dead had been dragged along the central aisle, while the injured lay stretched out on the rear seats. A handful of survivors had managed to scramble through the shattered windows and onto the cliff, where they had been picked up by helicopters.

Emergency rescue teams had tried everything, but it was impossible to get into the coach without disturbing its precarious balance. Military choppers lowered massive metal jaws to clamp around the stricken vehicle, but the operation almost ended in disaster as the coach rocked wildly. After that, the rescuers backed off to work up a new plan.

Now the wind was getting up and, after a spell of clear skies, a storm was approaching. The choppers were grounded. In a last-ditch effort, a team of climbers abseiled down the cliff face, planning to secure cables around each end of the coach. These were connected to a massive haulage vehicle on the road high above.

The world watched as the sky turned an unhealthy black. The rain thundered down, drenching everything. A lightning bolt ripped across the sky, casting a horrid lemon light over the scene. The coach rocked in the high winds. Thunder smothered the sound of metal scraping on rock.

Harrison saw the first two rescuers reach the coach. One shuffled along a narrow ledge of rock with a two-inch-wide cable in one hand. A second lightning bolt hit the cable, sending over a million volts through the rescuer's body. He flew 20 feet into the air, his severed hand still gripping the cable.

Around the world, hundreds of millions of viewers gasped in unison. Nothing like this had been seen since two airliners had ploughed into the Twin Towers in New York City.

Harrison was alone in a white-walled room. He was sitting on the edge of a desk. He could feel his heart pounding. Without realising it, he was picking the skin around his right thumb.

A phone rang and he turned to answer it. 'They're all here, sir,' a voice said. 'Room 17.'

Harrison replaced the receiver and turned back to the screen, just as the coach lurched and slid away down the cliff.

4

Mark Harrison walked into Room 17. He was escorted by two men in black boilersuits. At a nod from Harrison, the men retreated from the room and closed the door behind them.

Harrison was wearing a dark blue suit and a white shirt without a tie. A few years back, one of his superiors had dubbed him 'Denzel' because of his striking resemblance to the Hollywood star. And indeed he did have something of the actor's commanding presence and air of authority. Aged 42, Harrison was six-foot-three and just shy of 200 pounds, without an ounce of fat on his broad frame. His hair was cropped short, and his face was taut and muscular, with narrow eyebrows and eyes the colour of burnt ash.

There were four people in the room – two men and two women. Harrison knew two of them personally, and the other two only by reputation. They were seated in a semi-circle, and in front of the group was a vacant chair and a small table. On this stood a jug of water, a glass and a remote control. On one wall of the room was a large flat-screen TV.

'Good morning.' Harrison placed a green folder on the table and looked at the four faces. His voice was deep, with just a hint of a Southern drawl to it.

One of the men leaned back in his chair. 'Mark bloody Harrison. I might have guessed.' He stood and the two men shook hands.

'It's good to see you, Josh,' Harrison replied.

One of the others, a Japanese woman in her early thirties with jet-black eyes and black hair cut into a bob, was shaking her head and getting up. 'Mark. You're well, I hope?'

'All the better for seeing you, Maiko.'

The other two in the room looked on, a little bemused.

Harrison sat down and folded his arms. 'I guess you all deserve an explanation.'

'That would be nice,' Josh Thompson said.

'First, I'd like to thank you all for agreeing to come here at short notice. The fact is you've all been brought here under false pretences. But –' and he raised a palm when he saw their frowns – 'let me assure you, it's for a very good reason.'

'So this is not a NASA training visit?' Maiko Buchanan said. 'That's what I was told.'

'No, it's not. Nor is it a seminar on a new encryption breakthrough,' Harrison added, looking at Josh. 'I think the best thing is for us to get acquainted. You've been here a few minutes. I guess you've chatted. Let me start at the beginning. A briefing, if you like.' He stood and picked up the remote, clicking it as he walked towards the screen on the wall. The lights dimmed.

'Peter Sherringham,' Harrison said, and a picture of the man sitting on the far right of the semi-circle appeared on the screen. He had curly sandy hair, blue eyes and a large mouth. Harrison glanced towards him.

'Born – Newcastle, England, March 1973. Now one of the world's foremost authorities on the manufacture, control and deactivation of explosives. An NCO in the British army from 1991 to 2004. Served in Northern Ireland, Afghanistan and Iraq. After retiring from the army, Peter founded Globex, now a leading specialist in commercial demolition.'

Pete Sherringham was sitting ramrod-straight in his chair. 'What's this all about?' he asked, with just a hint of irritation. He had a strong accent – working-class Geordie – but it was a soft, controlled voice, the voice of a man who was not easily rattled. 'I'm not complaining about the champagne, mind. But I get the feeling I'm not here to learn the details of a new explosive putty – as advertised.'

Harrison produced a brief smile. 'No, Pete,' he said.

Sherringham was about to respond when the screen changed and his face was replaced with that of a blonde woman with striking dark-brown eyes. He realised it was the woman sitting next to him.

'Dr Stephanie Jacobs,' Harrison continued. 'Born – Sydney, Australia, June 1975. Olympic 100-metre and 200-metre freestyle gold-medallist in 1996 and 2000. Completed medical training in 2001. Specialised in burns treatment. Became consultant at Royal North Shore Hospital, Sydney, 2007. Now heads an internationally renowned burns unit. Husband, SAS Major Edward Trevelyan, died in Afghanistan in 2009.'

Stephanie Jacobs sat calmly, legs crossed, hands in her lap, saying nothing. Her blonde hair was short, tucked behind her ears. She was wearing a smart suit that accentuated her perfect physique.

'Maiko Buchanan,' Harrison went on. 'Born – Kyoto, Japan, May 1974. Migrated with parents to Boston, Massachusetts, 1984. Engineering major at UCLA. A-grade soccer player, before being selected for fast-track programme at NASA. Has flown the space shuttle three times, most recently as mission commander.'

'Wow!' Maiko said, with a broad grin that lit up her small, pretty face. 'Sounds great – I hardly recognise myself!'

'Josh Thompson. Born – London, 1973. Olympic triathlon gold-medallist in Atlanta, 1996. PhD in cryptography, King's College, London, 2002. Served in the British SAS as an encryption expert until 2007. Retired with the rank of major. Published *The Theory and Practice of Cryptography*, 2008. Currently professor at Columbia University, New York.'

The others turned towards Josh, whose legs were stretched

11

out in front of him. He wore jeans and cowboy boots, a black T-shirt and leather jacket. His hair was dark and swept back. Prominent cheekbones made him look younger than his 38 years. He stood and gave a bow, and they saw what a large man he was, six-foot-five and broad-shouldered. As he sat down, he said, 'And what about you, Mark?'

At a click of the remote the screen changed. A picture of Mark Harrison appeared. They all read the CV.

Born: Houston, Texas, 1969

Rhodes Scholar, mathematics major, Oriel College, Oxford, 1987–1990. PhD in computer science

First African-American Oxford rowing blue

Head of new technology for IBM, 1991–1995

Served in the US Special Forces, 1995–2000. Retired with the rank of colonel

Fluent in Mandarin, Russian, French and Spanish

Marksman (Distinguished Expert Class)

Judo master (6th dan)

The picture clicked off and the lights came up.

'So,' Josh Thompson asked, 'now will you tell us why we're here?'

'I can do better than that. Follow me.'

5

Mark Harrison led them into a wide corridor. 'You'll have to excuse the cloak-and-dagger stuff,' he said. 'But I think you'll soon see the reason for it.'

Harrison ran his hand over a sensor pad on the corridor wall and a panel slid away, revealing a tropical vista. The four visitors were transfixed. The horizon was a line of statuesque palm trees rising above a swatch of jungle shrouded in mist. In the foreground stretched an expanse of turquoise water as flat as a mirror.

'We're on the island of Tintara, 1240 miles south-south-west of San Diego. And this is Base One. Follow me.'

The panel closed and Harrison walked quickly along the corridor. A door opened at the end and he led the four into a large room. A bank of plasma screens lined the wall to their right. Men in boilersuits were seated at control panels. Harrison strode past them to a massive window. Through the window, they could see a hangar 200 metres long and 100 wide. It was abuzz with human activity. Dozens of technicians were scurrying around, dwarfed by the two massive aircraft that dominated the hangar's huge space.

'Impressive, huh?' Harrison said, turning to the others.

The two identical machines looked like scaled-down but futuristic stealth bombers. Beside these was a line of brightly coloured ground vehicles. One looked like a bulldozer from the 22nd century, and next to it stood a tracked vehicle with a beautiful low profile.

In the centre of the vast space they could see a cluster of desks with what looked like ultra-thin flat-screen computer terminals. It took the visitors a moment to realise that the screens were images in the air – 3D holographic projections. The keyboards were also light patterns projected onto the desks. Most interesting of all, the computer operators were *talking* to the terminals – and the computers were answering back.

'Come, sit down,' Mark Harrison said, gesturing to the comfy chairs just back from the window.

'So, what's going on here?' the Australian, Stephanie Jacobs, asked.

'Something wonderful.'

'We'll have to take your word for that, Mark,' Maiko Buchanan said.

'Fair enough,' he replied. 'Have you ever watched a catastrophe unfold in the media and wondered why there isn't some special organisation that could go in and help?'

Harrison's four guests studied his face.

'Seven years ago I was watching TV when a news flash came on. A submarine was trapped on the ocean floor, just off Costa Rica. It was a civilian sub used by marine biologists. They were 2000 feet under water. Rescue teams could do almost nothing. It took three days for the US military to get involved. By the time they reached them, the five-man crew were all dead.'

'I remember it,' Pete Sherringham said. 'The *Montana*.'

'It was a turning point for me. I knew those men shouldn't have died. They could have been saved. I was angry. How could Western governments spend trillions of dollars each year on arms but not have a global specialist rescue organisation? How come we can precision-bomb Baghdad and get hundreds of thousands of soldiers into combat zones anywhere in the world, but we can't get to Costa Rica in time to save the lives of a group of scientists?

'I had a few contacts and I started calling in favours. It took me six months to reach the people with the power to make things happen, and another six months to persuade them to act. I envisaged E-Force as a multinational –'

'E-Force?' Josh Thompson broke in.

'Emergency Force. Simple, straightforward.' Thompson was nodding in assent. 'It's a multinational effort. The money is partly from governments – the G8 – and partly from cashed-up philanthropists, no names mentioned. A board of governors from six different countries liaises directly with contributing nations through the UN. E-Force is apolitical and non-military, as independent of government control as is possible in our age.'

'But that equipment,' Maiko Buchanan said, nodding towards the hangar. 'I've seen some pretty advanced stuff at NASA, but nothing like that.'

Harrison's eyes were alive with pride and excitement. 'No, you wouldn't have,' he said. 'Not many people have. You all know of DARPA, of course?'

'The US military research group?' Stephanie Jacobs offered.

'The Defense Advanced Research Projects Agency. There's an equivalent in Britain, ditto in Russia, China and so on. DARPA is an umbrella name for hundreds of research groups dotted around the USA. Each is financed by the Department of Defense and each works on technological projects that have military applications. Over the years, DARPA has given us the internet, stealth technology, lasers and countless advances in computers. The list is long. What happens is the military pumps billions of dollars into these research projects, and naturally they have first pickings of anything that comes out of them. Years later a technological breakthrough from DARPA filters through to the public. The average delay is about seven years.'

'But you said E-Force is non-military.'

'It is. Our technology doesn't come from DARPA. Back in the late fifties, when DARPA was established, some nervous congressmen didn't like the idea of the military having exclusive access to new technology. You have to remember this was at the height of the Cold War – McCarthy, reds under the beds. A small group of politicians created a secret offshoot of DARPA. They called it CARPA – the Civilian Advanced Research Projects Agency. The military had nothing to do with it. Didn't even know about it.

'CARPA survived, and thrived, in secret. Money was siphoned off to feed it, and like DARPA it has been responsible for some of the most important technological advances over the past fifty years. The thing that distinguishes the civilian branch is that the leaders of the organisation have a remit to spend at least half their annual budget on what they call "far future projects". DARPA isn't interested in looking too far ahead, but a large chunk of CARPA's money and energy goes into projects that are at least two decades beyond mainstream research. Some of this has been fed directly to organisations such as NASA,' Harrison said, glancing at Maiko Buchanan.

'All our equipment is from CARPA. The machines you saw down there won't be commonplace for at least twenty years. In fact, even the military won't have stuff like that for a decade. CARPA is our primary sponsor. They like to think of E-Force as their test dummies. Not a view I share, by the way. But I don't mind them thinking it in exchange for their technology.'

'So, what's the idea?' Pete Sherringham asked. 'You have an organisation of what, several thousand people? How do you operate? What's the infrastructure?'

'Good question. Yes, there's a large team at work here. This is Base One. We have smaller establishments in half a dozen key locations around the world. Over 1300 people are involved with E-Force. But at its heart it will always be a team of specialists. A small, elite group of gifted, super-intelligent, super-fit, highly trained individuals who will operate at the coalface. They will have all this behind them.' Harrison waved his hand towards the hangar. 'Ultimately, *they* will be E-Force.'

'You've suddenly started speaking in the future tense,' Josh Thompson said.

'Yes, I know. That's because I'm hoping that we will be that elite group.'

6

They all started talking at once. After a moment, Harrison put up his hands. 'Okay, okay. Controversial suggestion.'

'Are you serious?' Stephanie Jacobs asked. 'How could we possibly –'

'Of course I'm serious.'

The four guests were suddenly quiet.

'You're all perfect candidates,' Harrison went on.

'Except that we all have lives already,' Pete Sherringham retorted.

'I realise that. Look, no one expects you to give up your careers. After an initial three-month intensive training period, you will all return to your everyday lives and be . . . well, for want of a better expression, on-call.'

'Three months! How can I give up my research for three months?' Stephanie Jacobs exclaimed.

'I will take care of everything. Each of you has individual needs. Each of you will be remunerated in full for any financial losses, and you'll be paid handsomely for your time. Josh, I know your new book isn't out for six months. You can still work on the next one if you want to. We have peerless research facilities. Pete, your number two can run Globex for three months and you can be in constant touch with your managers from here. And Stephanie, the same applies. You have our resources at your disposal, and the everyday running of the lab can be managed. Maiko, there'll be no problem arranging a sabbatical from NASA for you.'

There was a heavy silence for a moment. Then Pete Sherringham spoke up. 'Okay, you seem to have all bases covered, Mark. But why should any of us agree to give up our time and jeopardise our hard-earned careers?'

Harrison looked around the table. He knew the answer. Each of the four were high achievers, determined and truly exceptional people. But he had studied their profiles. He knew, for example, that each of them had reached a point in their lives where they needed a new challenge. 'The decision is entirely yours,' he said. 'But there is one last thing I want to show you.'

He stood up and led them back to the seminar room where they had met. Harrison picked up the remote and flicked on the screen behind him. 'This happened just before I came in here to introduce myself,' he said.

The lights dimmed and the screen lit up. It showed the perilous scene on the Cretan mountainside. A rescue worker was making his way under the stricken coach when lightning struck. They all watched him fly through the air. Then, moments later, the coach began to slide. The camera followed it until it hit the rocks below and exploded.

7

Aldermont Correctional Facility, New York State

Mark Harrison was driven in silence through the prison gates. Twelve-foot-high grey fences stood to left and right. The view through the windscreen was swept with rain. *So different to Tintara*, he thought. He had got used to the sunshine and lush vegetation, and autumnal New York State just didn't cut it.

Letting his mind wander, he felt a familiar knot of excitement. His dream of creating E-Force was finally coming together. It was the culmination of his ambitions, a blend of all his talents, education and experience. Since growing up in Texas as a super-intelligent kid out of sync with his classmates and even his own family, he had been extraordinarily successful. He had savoured his time at university in England and had been extremely popular, becoming the President of the Oxford Union. After that, his career in IT had been a simple progression from one triumph to another, and then his switch to the US military had brought him immediate rewards.

He had been destined for great things, but no matter how much he achieved he always wanted more. It was clear to him now that something had always been missing, and that something was E-Force.

Mark cast his mind back over the meeting with the four people he most wanted as members. They had spent the night at Base One and he had shown them around the complex, trying, in his enthusiasm, not to go overboard. He had even attempted to play down the state-of-the-art facilities at Tintara. His guests had all left deeply impressed. He hadn't expected instant commitment, and of course none of them had signed up there and then. He hadn't pushed them. Better to let them mull it over.

He was confident about three of the visitors – Pete Sherringham, Maiko Buchanan and Dr Stephanie Jacobs. Josh Thompson was the problematic one. Josh was almost a celebrity – in some ways he had the most to lose.

And now, Mark thought, *here I am, hoping to enlist the vital sixth member of E-Force.*

When Mark was led into the cell he found Tom Erickson with his back to him. The light from a laptop cut through the gloom. The guard retreated and locked the door. Erickson spun his wheelchair and snapped shut the laptop.

He looked like a surfer except his legs were limp and twisted. Tom Erickson had marked his nineteenth birthday just a month earlier. His IQ had been recorded at 202 (four points higher than Stephen Hawking). He was wearing baggy jeans and an oversized Ramones T-shirt. His dark hair was lank and hung to his shoulders. His face was gaunt, but his dark eyes were alive and childlike.

It was a face Harrison knew from the cover of *Time* magazine, for Erickson was the most gifted computer hacker on earth. And it was this gift that had landed him here in Aldermont Correctional Facility with a six-year prison sentence. One year earlier he had been convicted of defrauding a private bank in Washington to the tune of $60 million. He had done it without ever moving away from his laptop.

Erickson was only ten when a truck had hit him outside his home in Baltimore. He had come so close to death that a priest had been called to the ICU. But he had survived, although his legs were rendered completely useless. Bedridden for a year, he had turned to computers and learned he had an intuitive understanding of them. He could almost merge with them. He played a hard drive the way Hendrix played a Strat – by instinct.

Tom's problems started when he hit puberty and began to resent his predicament. He could blame no one, but that only made it worse. He started to rebel against everything – his parents, school, but most of all some nebulous thing called 'authority'.

At his trial, public opinion had turned against Tom when he admitted he had robbed the bank simply because he could – because he wanted, as he put it, to 'fuck people around'. In a world in which money was more important than anything else, the trial had made Erickson infamous. National headlines dubbed him an 'Evil Genius' and 'Doctor Frankenstein of Cyberspace'.

He was no such thing, Mark knew. He was a kid with a great talent and no respect for authority. In other words, extremely dangerous but not inherently evil. 'I'm amazed they still let you near a computer,' he remarked.

Erickson looked Mark up and down. 'They think it's safe as long as I'm not online. Which *would* be true . . .'

Mark couldn't resist a smile. 'An odd thing to admit to.'

'Not really. Think you can prove anything? Good luck, man!'

'Okay, maybe we should start again,' Mark said. He walked over to Erickson with his hand out. The boy was reticent but took it limply, his long, thin fingers barely touching Harrison's.

'So what brings you to sunny Aldermont?'

'I have an offer I think will be mutually beneficial.'

'Don't tell me – another state-financed cluster-fuck. You have "government lackey" stamped on your forehead, dude.'

Mark looked confused.

'It goes like this,' Erickson sighed. 'The suits in Washington have got themselves in the shit again and will promise to knock a couple of months off my sentence if I solve their latest IT screw-up. You must know it wouldn't be the first time.'

Mark lowered himself onto the edge of the bed. The boy glared at him. *I can understand your frustration*, Mark thought. *Such wasted talent. It would make anyone furious with the world.* 'Well, I'm happy to say you couldn't be more wrong,' he replied after a moment. 'Take a look at this.' He handed Erickson a CD.

An image appeared on the boy's laptop. He looked disinterestedly at the screen, then frowned. His fingers skittered over the keys and his expression changed to one of sceptical curiosity. On the screen, a set of specifications and schematics flowed down as Erickson moved the mouse. Finally, he looked up, his head tilted slightly. 'Nice fantasy, Mr Government Man.'

'Reality.'

Erickson flicked a glance back at the screen. 'You're fucking with me.'

'No,' Mark said, folding his arms. 'What you have there is a spec for the most sophisticated computer ever built, a prototype quantum computer.'

'But we're – what – twenty years away from such a thing!'

'Clearly not.'

'Look, what's this all about? Assuming a quantum computer exists – which I doubt – what do you want me for?'

Mark told him the basic facts about E-Force. The boy stayed silent. When he had finished, the only sounds were from outside, a shout in the distance and the slamming of a heavy door.

'Okay,' Erickson said finally. 'So I wasn't that far wrong. You've hit a problem with your goody-two-shoes scheme. What you offering for my services? Three months for good behaviour?'

'You know,' Mark said, fixing his gaze on the strange kid in the wheelchair, 'for such an intelligent guy, you can be remarkably slow. I want you with us at Base One – permanently. Tom, I'm offering you a way out.'

8

Two weeks later

A conventional jet would take two and a half hours to get from southern California to Tintara. But the passengers leaving an isolated base near San Diego were not aboard a 747. A plane like theirs would not be in regular service for another couple of decades. It was a VTOLPA – a vertical take-off and landing passenger aircraft – one of only seven in the world. Known as the Hummingbird, it could carry 22 passengers and crew in considerable comfort at 40,000 feet, with an average cruising speed of mach 6, a little under 4000 miles an hour. This meant it could cross the stretch of the Pacific Ocean to Tintara in twenty minutes.

Maiko Buchanan, Stephanie Jacobs and Pete Sherringham hardly knew one another, but they now had common ground. Each of them had agreed to join E-Force. That first evening on Tintara, two weeks earlier, none of them had been able to express how they felt. It had taken time to sink in. So they had simply enjoyed a friendly dinner, drinks and, of course, the grand tour. Most importantly, though, they had all got on well.

Maiko had been the first to make a commitment. Mark had met her five years earlier at NASA, when he had helped with the agency's IT upgrades. Even back then, before Buchanan had her own mission command, he had been impressed by her abilities and commitment. But the thing he liked most about her was her open-mindedness. She could see the big

25

picture. This was the crucial reason he had invited her to join the team.

It was her ability to visualise that had made it so easy for Maiko to take the leap. That, and the fact the invitation had come at a great time. Her role at NASA had become a little nebulous. She was one of their most experienced pilots, but the sense of adventure was slipping from her grasp.

Maiko's life had been relatively uncomplicated until about six months before. She lived in Sugar Land, outside Houston, with her mother and her sixteen-year-old daughter, Greta. But her mother had now moved to a nursing home, and Greta was going through a rebellious phase. Maiko was still not sure what the root of the problem was, except that Greta was determined to reject her heritage wholesale and to be considered completely American, which of course she was. Maiko, though, still felt drawn to the country of her birth, the place where she had spent the first decade of her life. It was something Greta could not grasp, and Maiko disliked the fact that her daughter seemed to be ashamed of her family's roots. Greta had now moved in with her stepfather, Howard Buchanan, the man Maiko had divorced five years ago. Which left Maiko facing the prospect of living alone in her large house, going through the motions of a career that had peaked, and with no sign of a love life. It hadn't taken much to persuade her to pick up the phone.

The Hummingbird took off smoothly. Through billowing vapour from the engines, they could see the ground falling away. At 20,000 feet, the plane climbed on a steep diagonal before levelling off at cruising altitude. Once they were out over the Pacific, they felt a serge of acceleration as the engines thrust the craft forward to a comfortable cruising speed of mach 4.4.

Stephanie Jacobs peered out the window. She was feeling suddenly unsure of herself, isolated. *Have I made the right decision?* she wondered, then tried to smother her doubts.

Maiko had told her she had joined up because of good timing. Perhaps the same was true for her. Stephanie's lab in Sydney was relocating to a dedicated facility close to Avalon, a surf town 20 miles north. And as she watched the clouds rush by, she wondered for the first time whether perhaps Mark Harrison had actually known all about this. Perhaps it had informed his decision to contact her in the first place. *Never mind*, she thought. *It doesn't matter. I've made the commitment and that's that.*

'So, what made you say yes, Pete?' Maiko Buchanan asked. Stephanie Jacobs turned away from the window.

'Asked myself the very same question at least 20 times,' Pete replied. His strong Geordie accent sounded oddly quaint in this setting. He ran a hand through his thick sandy curls and fixed the two women with his intense bright-blue eyes. 'Our Colonel Harrison is obviously a very persuasive fella.' He smiled, but behind the nonchalance lay pain.

A month earlier, Pete had split from his second wife, Donna. She had wanted children, he hadn't. In his eyes, the world was a very nasty place, and bringing a new, innocent life into that world would have been cruel. He could never understand how intelligent people – who could see how corrupt the world had become – still chose to fill it with more people. He had loved Donna, but he had known that if he had let her have her way, he would never have forgiven himself.

'It's interesting there're only the three of us,' Stephanie said suddenly, snapping Pete out of his reverie.

'Not really,' Maiko replied. 'I never thought for a minute Josh Thompson would commit.'

'You know him, right?'

'Yeah, and he's a great guy, but he's his own man. He's also kinda famous now.'

Stephanie shrugged. 'I'm sure Harrison has a Plan B. To be honest, I thought Josh Thompson was a bit full of himself.'

27

Maiko grinned. 'He's certainly one for the ladies – so I'm told!'

They heard a sound from the direction of the flight deck and turned to see Mark Harrison approaching. Behind him a young, long-haired man rolled along in a motorised wheelchair.

'I'm glad you could all make it,' Mark said. He moved to one side as the youth came forward. 'This is Tom Erickson,' he added. 'Our IT guru.'

Peter Sherringham was the first to respond, shaking Tom's hand warmly. The two women looked stunned – they instantly recognised the infamous hacker.

'Well, I hope you're all enjoying the flight,' Harrison said, easing himself into one of the armchair-sized seats. He handed each of them a white envelope. 'Your contracts, and a down payment on your services.'

Pete was the only one to open his. He gave the contents a quick glance, but the others could tell he was pleased by what he saw. He folded the envelope and put it in his jacket pocket.

'I can't help noticing that there are only three of us from our first visit,' Stephanie Jacobs said.

'Yes. Regrettably, Josh Thompson has decided not to join us. But there are contingencies. Now, I wanted to just give you a quick briefing en route to Tintara. Once we arrive I want us to get straight down to business. Tom here will be overseeing every aspect of our computer systems. I can't emphasise enough the importance of this role. It's quite possible our lives will depend on Tom's talents.'

'Don't take this the wrong way, lad,' Pete interrupted, looking directly at Erickson. 'But aren't you supposed to be behind bars?'

'I was, until this nice man from E-Force came to visit,' Tom responded, nodding towards Mark. 'Looks like you're going to have to trust an old jailbird, dude.'

Mark handed each of them a leather folder. 'Basic stuff,' he said. 'Specs of the equipment, background info on the set-up.'

They flicked through sheets of data on the island and schematics of the base. Base One was the centre of operations, and for obvious reasons its whereabouts was a closely guarded secret. Tintara was little more than an atoll, three and a half miles long and 1500 yards across, girdled by pure white sand.

'This place is a freaking cliché,' Tom said, looking at an aerial photograph of Tintara. 'Palm trees, fantasy beaches, the works!'

'Yep, there's even a bar on the north beach run part-time by a couple of very enthusiastic technicians. They do a mean caipiroska,' Mark replied. 'There's almost nothing to see from the air, though. Some of the key buildings are on the surface, but camouflaged. As you saw on your first visit,' he added, turning to Pete, Maiko and Stephanie, 'a lot happens underground – we have living quarters, operations rooms and technical support, including an amazing complex of labs. The computer nexus is here,' he said, pointing out the location for Tom's benefit.

'We're over 200 miles from the nearest island – a long way from prying eyes. But, even so, security is tight. On missions, the aircraft are sealed against unauthorised access, and the skin of all vehicles and machinery has been coated with Camoflin.'

'Which is?' Maiko asked.

'Another wonder from CARPA. It's a paint that camouflages our equipment and blurs any photographs or video footage taken by nosy individuals. We use the same stuff for the buildings on the island. On the base, all access is controlled by retinal-scan technology. You each have quarters in the main accommodation area, here.' He tapped the map to show them.

29

'Now, as you know, nothing has been tested in the field yet and we won't be fully operational for three months. Once your training is complete, you'll return to your day jobs. But you'll be on-call to respond to any appropriate emergency. We'll be ready to tackle a broad spectrum of operations anywhere in the world. We can reach any point on the globe within two or three hours.

'Potentially, there will be five of us on a mission, but maybe not all at the same time. Tom will remain at Base One. As the computer expert, he'll be there to support us during a mission. Any questions?'

'How do you know if E-Force is needed?' Tom asked.

'BigEye, a set of satellites that monitors activity on the Earth's surface. Look in the file – pages 105 to 123, I think.' Mark paused for a moment. 'Okay, the training plan itself. You'll each be put through a core programme, which will involve an advanced survival course and instruction in how to use all the equipment at our disposal, including piloting the fleet of aircraft.'

Mark flicked a switch on his armrest and the cabin lights dimmed. A screen lit up in front of them. 'Just a quick survey of the equipment,' he said, and an image of a futuristic aircraft appeared on the screen. It was the Hummingbird. 'This is the plane we're sitting in,' he said. The image changed. 'And this is the Silverback. You three saw it on your first trip. We have four of these – John, Paul, George and Ringo. Top speed of mach 10. Crew of two. These can carry 500 pounds of equipment. They're designed to get one or two members of E-Force anywhere on Earth, ultra-fast.'

'You serious about those speeds?' Tom asked. He was shaking his head in disbelief.

'Yep,' Mark replied. 'All these planes are VTOL, for which they use conventional jet engines. But once they're at operational altitude, they shift to scramjets.'

'Scramjets?' Maiko said. 'We use them at NASA.'

'Of course. NASA's plane, the X-43A, is famous. Broke the air speed record in 2004. Mach 9.8. Our planes use a very advanced version of the same technology. Scramjets take in oxygen from the air at supersonic speeds and use it to burn fuel. They don't need to carry most of the propellant. They just suck up the oxygen as they move through the air. A bit like a whale eating plankton.'

The image changed again. This time a massive, almost spherical aircraft appeared. It was silver, with a flight deck high up on the sphere. It looked for all the world like a giant burger. 'The Big Mac,' Mark said. 'Our main cargo workhorse. It carries the heavy stuff; four-seater submarines, heavy digging equipment, winching machinery. We use the Big Mac to transport an array of equipment. This includes the Mole, a 2000-horsepower burrowing machine, the Cage, a protective framework for working in extremely unstable conditions, and the Firefly, a two-seater firefighting vehicle that can tolerate an outer-skin temperature of 1000 degrees Celsius for an hour. Aside from these, we have an assortment of heli-jets that can fly at mach 2, ground vehicles, boats and high-speed subs.'

The screen flicked off and the lights came up.

'You said there was a core programme,' Stephanie said. 'What else is there?'

'I was just coming to that. You'll have a further programme tailored to each of you. Those who've not had military training will be put through a course based on one used by the Green Berets. Those without medical training will be given a crash course in essential procedures.' Mark paused for a moment and looked into each of their faces. 'I won't pretend. It's going to be tough, very tough. Any questions?'

'Yeah, just one,' Tom said. 'I take it I'll be exempt from the hundred-yard sprint through mud and horseshit?'

9

The four men met in the flesh only rarely. Most of the time they merely shared pixels. Today's encounter was another of those virtual meetings.

At first glance, there was little that linked them. Granted, they were all overachievers. Two were politicians of significance, one was a resources billionaire, and the last a media mogul. All were aged between 50 and 70. One was very tall, six-foot-five; another very short, just five-foot-four. Two were fitness freaks and buff. One, the 70-year-old, weighed in at over 25 stone, with barely an ounce of muscle on him. The fourth was broad-shouldered with a paunch. Outward appearances, then, were entirely deceptive. Only one thing drew these four men together – money. They had met at a World Bank dinner for insiders, adjourned for brandy and cigars in a side room at Gleneagles one warm summer evening, and bingo – they had bonded.

At their next meeting, they decided what it was that they would do together. And at the same gathering they had shared a little black humour. They dubbed themselves Death, Conquest, War and Pestilence – the Four Horsemen of the Apocalypse.

Between them, these men were worth more than $100 billion. They controlled three of the most important sectors of 21st-century life – finance, the lifeblood of the world; the media, the neural net of the age; and the politics of the world's only superpower. At their meetings they each donned a tie with the colour of their attribute – pale green for Death, white for Conquest, red for War and black for Pestilence. It was probably a little OTT, but what the hell?

The Four Horsemen had a very simple agenda. Money was not just power, it was *everything*. Ergo, anyone who threatened their ability to make money was an enemy and must be stopped. At their third meeting in Cincinnati, soon after 9/11, they had joked about the old Wall Street war cry that it was not enough to win, you had to destroy your enemy. For them, the aphorism didn't go nearly far enough. The enemy must be utterly annihilated, their families destroyed, eviscerated, their corpses pissed on.

'So, what's the latest?' Death asked, his face large on three wall-screens, in Berlin, Shanghai and Dallas.

'We have to make a decision. Our friend the senator is growing more powerful by the day,' Pestilence responded.

'Very well,' Death replied.

'Is your plan really the only option?' Conquest adjusted his white tie as he spoke.

'You seem nervous.' Pestilence smirked. 'Most unlike you, my friend.'

'I'm not nervous – I just want assurances.'

'Oh, come now, Conquest. When is that ever possible? Nothing in life comes with assurances, does it? But at least we know we work for a noble cause. Human existence has shown there is no greater God than the greenback.'

'Yes,' chuckled War, his chins wobbling. 'Just take an L from gold and what do you have?'

The others stared at him stonily. They had heard it before.

'So, the plan,' Death said. 'You intend using the Dragon, I take it?'

'Who else?' Pestilence said. 'Actually, he's sorting out a minor irritation as we speak – that little shit, Gordon Smith.

But after that, he could begin preparations. Disposing of the senator will be an altogether trickier proposition.'

'So. When, exactly?' Conquest asked, and adjusted his tie again.

'Soon. Do I have unanimous approval?'

The others nodded in turn.

10

Museum of Modern Art, West 53rd Street, New York

'Champagne?'

Josh Thompson turned to see a smiling waiter holding a tray of drinks. He had arrived late. The event was the launch of the latest book by the art historian Anna Fitzgibbon, with whom he shared a literary agent, Carl Reed of Reed & Stringer. He noticed Carl accompanying a statuesque woman to a podium at one end of the room. A who's who of the New York literary and art scene were here to sip Veuve Clicquot, eat expensive canapés, and cheer the celebrated author. Away from the stage, they huddled in groups, sticking in the verbal knife in hushed tones.

Josh was finding it hard to engage. He didn't know many people here, but it wasn't that. It was the news on the radio as he drove to the museum. The city of Charleston, South Carolina, was facing the worst storm ever seen that far north. Hurricane Nell was hours away from the city and showing little sign of losing its potency. The Ashley River was at an all-time high and the levee was about to break. A city of over 700,000 people was facing imminent disaster. *It was New Orleans all over again*, Josh Thompson thought, as he made his way to the edge of the small crowd clustered around the podium.

Anna Fitzgibbon was a real pro, but Josh had never been interested in the minutiae of painters and painting. In many ways he was a down-to-earth character with simple tastes.

When it came to art, he could appreciate a good picture for its own sake. He didn't have much time for what his army buddies would have called 'arty-farty rubbish', and he couldn't care less how the artist had arrived at his or her revolutionary technique or what drugs were consumed while they painted their masterpiece.

Josh surveyed the room, the well-fed tuxedoed, the smug and the sequined. He drained his glass. *Right now the waves will be smashing into Old Charleston*, he thought. *The authorities would be doing their best to evacuate people. Brave volunteers would try to stand up to the unimaginable power of nature. At this very moment, people are dying.*

Later, after the speeches and the toasts and the backslapping, Josh found himself sitting alone on the front steps of the museum. It was an unseasonable balmy evening. From all around came the hum of the city, car horns, sirens, the pulse of millions of individual lives.

He suddenly felt very lonely. The press of those millions of people made little impression; it passed like a shadow. He'd always been comfortable with solitude – especially since Maggie had left him four years before. She always claimed that the SAS had ruined him, had turned him into an obsessive individual married to the army. But he knew this was only partly true. He was indeed an obsessive, but he hadn't been married to the army, he had been married to his specialisation – cryptography. He was a multitalented man and had excelled at many things, but what really obsessed him was the study of codes and ciphers, the arcane mathematical roots of the discipline.

And now he found previously unimagined pleasure in bringing that deeply intellectual work to the world through his popular books. *It was a shame*, he thought for perhaps the thousandth time, *that Maggie never understood that side of me.* Or perhaps it had been his fault for not illuminating his true drives and ambitions. He had a sneaking feeling his ex-wife would have liked being married to a bestselling author more than an SAS major.

'Gets a bit much after a while, doesn't it?'

Josh turned to see Tania Boreman, a writer friend from years back, lowering herself onto the step beside him.

'What's that?'

'Oh, the whole self-satisfied 'I love me' vibe. You know what I mean.'

He laughed and leaned in to kiss her on the cheek. 'It's good to see you again, Tan. What've you been up to?'

'You know. Still looking for the perfect man. Still trying to write the Great American Novel. The usual.'

'Well, you're not going to find either here.'

'Now really, what makes you think that?' She tilted her head to one side. 'Impress me, Josh Thompson. Take me somewhere cool and inspirational.'

Ten minutes later they were in a tiny subterranean bar called See Emily Play on 48th Street. They found a booth in a corner. The place had a 1960s mood to suit its name, complete with subdued lighting, big cushions on the floor of the booths, low tables, sounds courtesy of Soft Machine, Cream and Pink Floyd. A beautiful long-haired, long-legged waitress in a miniskirt and beads took their order.

'You seem troubled, Josh. Not your usual ebullient self,' Tania said, as their drinks arrived.

He shifted uncomfortably in his beanbag. His large and powerful frame was not well suited to squatting on a cushion.

'No, I'm fine,' he said, fixing Tania with his intelligent brown eyes.

She gave him a sceptical look, but Josh didn't change his expression.

'I don't feel I can talk about it.'

'Oh God! That's not fair. Now you *have* to tell me!'

He laughed, flashing his white teeth, and small wrinkles appeared at the corners of his eyes. 'Let's just change the subject, yeah?'

'Wimp!'

'Maybe.'

They had another drink and he started to relax. He enjoyed Tania's company. They had met at a writers group soon after he moved to New York, three years ago. They hooked up occasionally for drinks, dinner, sometimes for sex. No strings attached.

There was a lull in the conversation, and Josh suddenly said, 'It's Charleston – I can't stop thinking about it.'

For a moment, Tania looked lost. 'The hurricane? You serious?'

'Of course I'm serious. Why wouldn't I be?'

She shrugged. 'I didn't mean to sound . . . God, insensitive, I guess. It's just that it's the last thing I expected you to say.'

He felt anger rising and forced it away. Calmly, he said, 'Now you know why I didn't want to say anything. Forget I mentioned it. Another drink?'

'No. Yes – I mean yes to the drink. But Josh, don't get me wrong. I'm just a bit taken aback.'

He had regained his equilibrium. 'I know. It's dumb. I . . . I don't really know how to put it. It's just, sometimes I find it hard to simply . . . get on with things. Sometimes, I feel . . . I don't know . . . the weight of it all. The logical, hard-nosed part of me says, "Forget it – these things have nothing to do with you, just deal with your own problems." There're plenty of those, for Christ's sake!'

There was a silence between them for a moment. A Beatles track – 'Being For the Benefit of Mr Kite' – came on the sound system. Tania studied Josh's face as he looked into the middle distance, tapping a foot to the beat of the music. She had a lot of time for him. If it had been up to Tania, they would have taken their relationship a lot further a long time ago, but she always sensed that Josh was completely self-contained. He flirted and seduced, and he loved being popular. He was great fun to be around and he had an attractive energy, a *joie de vivre* that she found very sexy, but some sixth sense told her that no one could get really close to him, that he had higher priorities than intimacy or commitment to a woman. 'I understand,' she said at last.

'I'm not sure I do. I sound like a lunatic.'

'No, you don't.' She touched his hand and he wrapped his fingers in hers.

They had another drink and paid the cheque. Josh left his car in the lot and they hailed a cab on 5th Avenue. He had a small apartment in the East Village above a shop that sold designer shoes. Josh made them a coffee, but they both knew they would not be sleeping much that night.

As they made love, he felt strangely disconnected, as though he were looking down upon himself. Then, when they finally drifted off into unconsciousness, it was only a half sleep. He could hear voices. He could make out the odd word, but none of it made sense.

A silvery light was beginning to filter through the blinds when Josh finally snapped into the waking world. Tania was asleep beside him. She lay on her side, her pale, naked form beautiful and vital in the pre-dawn. He slipped out of bed and went through to the living room. He switched on the TV with the sound down. Charleston had been hit bad, worse than anyone had feared. He watched the news report, feeling cold and numb. Then he dressed and scribbled a note for Tania.

Out on the cold pavement, the sun was coming up. Shadows cut between the buildings like shards of dark glass. Josh sat on a bench in Union Square, watching the joggers pass. A dog cocked a leg and pissed against a tree. The world continued revolving on its axis and moved a little further in its orbit around the sun. A flock of birds flew low overhead, the beat of their wings breaking the stillness. Slowly, his thoughts fell into place. What he should do seemed obvious. It had been obvious ever since he had returned from Tintara a few weeks earlier. Pulling out his cell phone, he dialled the number Mark Harrison had given him.

11

Hollywood Hills, Los Angeles

The truck was a blue Ford Ranger, a late model. 'Ace Pools
& Maintenance' was written in white lettering across the
doors on each side. In the cargo box at the back lay a
neat arrangement of metal trunks containing water filters,
chemicals and flexitubes. Alongside these was a chlorinator
in its box, a rolled-up pool blanket and a barracuda suction-
cleaning head.

The truck pulled up outside 19234 Sheoak Boulevard,
a hacienda built in the 1950s. The house had once been
owned by a now long-forgotten starlet. Apparently, two of
the Mamas and the Papas had met there at a party, and
Lenny Bruce once vomited on the doorstep.

The driver killed the engine and looked through his
aviators at the vanilla building. It was a huge property, at
least 10,000 square feet. The lawn stretching from the walls
to the road was an immaculate lush green, and a quaint
stone path wound up to the heavy studded-oak door. A line
of bay trees ran across the front of the house between the
ground-floor windows. The curtains were all closed, but even
from the street the thud of a bass drum and the crunch of
guitars from a cranked-up sound system somewhere at the
back of the house cut through the warm air.

To his employers, the man in the truck was known as
the Dragon. In their private universe in which they were
the Four Horsemen of the Apocalypse, it fitted perfectly.

Of course their favourite assassin should be known as the Dragon – a pseudonym for the devil, a name, like theirs, lifted from the Book of Revelation.

The Dragon glanced at the printout in his lap. It carried the face of a young man, the latest to cross the Four Horsemen. He scanned down the page, taking in the details. The Horsemen had used a contact in Switzerland to convince the head of a national bank to open a particularly precious vault. The vault had contained a box. In the box had been a single CD-ROM. The disk had been removed, and this simple action had given the Horsemen the green light to call in the Dragon. Now here he was outside 19234 Sheoak Boulevard, ready to remove a fly from the ointment.

Gordon Smith believed he was the luckiest man in the world. At school he had been the head nerd, bullied by the jocks and teased by the hot girls. Now they would all be laughing on the other side of their faces – he had posted his big news on Facebook and MySpace, along with suitable photos, just to make sure they would know.

A month earlier he had hit the jackpot. Aged 24, he had become the first to develop what he dubbed Ecofuel, an alternative to petrol he had formulated in his parent's garage in Spokane, 230 miles east of Seattle. Ecofuel could be produced without oil. It gave double the mileage of conventional gas at half the price, and produced only one-tenth of the atmospheric pollution. But there was something even better – the fuel could be used in conventional engines, so there was no need for expensive refits, no time lag until new cars hit the market.

Gordon was a bright kid – very, very bright – and he knew what he had discovered, the wonder of it, and the danger. He knew he was holding a gun to the head of the fuel industry, and that once the secret was out the oil companies would be really, really pissed. So he knew he had to tread carefully. He contacted a specialist New Jersey-based PR company, Nero Holdings, and explained his work to them. They were quick to see its potential. And it was Nero Holdings who had secured him a $25-million deal – silence money.

But Gordon knew he could trust the oil companies about as far as he could spit a goat. He placed a copy of all the data associated with his work in a Swiss bank vault and, through Nero Holdings, emailed every contributor towards his big pay cheque, stating that if anything should happen to him or his family, the secret of Ecofuel would automatically be released to the media.

The enormous house in LA, with its pool and celebrity connections, had come first, then the Porsche and top-of-the-range black Hummer, the Harley, the speed boat, the gold Rolex and the smaller house for his mother and father in a prissy Vegas suburb of their choosing. And now here he was, reclining in the hot tub, Fall Out Boy very loud on the expensive stereo a few feet away. And, snuggled up to him, one each side in the bubbles, were Crystal and Sophia, naked, their perfectly enhanced, perfectly tanned breasts bobbing on the hot water. Just above his shoulder, beyond the edge of the jacuzzi, lay a mirror with three fresh lines of the best Bolivian. He pulled the mirror towards him, plucked a hundred-dollar bill from under a crystal paperweight, and stuck his nose in the trough.

Gordon Smith was a happy man. He had no idea he had precisely two minutes and 22 seconds left to live.

The Dragon stepped out of the Ford. He was wearing a blue boilersuit and a baseball cap with 'Ace Pools' emblazoned above the peak. In his left hand he carried a metal toolbox. He strode up the winding path to the front door of 19234 Sheoak and pushed the buzzer.

For several moments there was no response. Then a voice came through the intercom – female, foreign accent. 'Yes? Who is it, please?' the voice asked, straining against the noise from out back.

'Pool man. Ace Pools,' the Dragon shouted back.

There was a click, the door swung inwards, and a tiny Puerto Rican woman stood on the mat. She was wearing an old-fashioned light-blue maid's uniform, clumpy trainers, her greying black hair tied back in a severe bun. 'The side gate's locked,' she said. 'Come this way.'

The maid turned and the Dragon stepped into the entrance hall, dropped the metal case on the carpet and grabbed the woman, one hand around her neck, the other hard across her mouth. With an expert twist, he snapped her neck between her C1 and C2 vertebrae. She slumped to the floor like a water-filled balloon.

The Dragon picked up the metal case and surveyed the hall. It was spacious, all marble and rare woods. Suspended from the ceiling was a huge chandelier. A pair of spiral staircases swooped upwards to a gallery. The thump of the music was louder now. He paced across the marble and opened a door into a long, wide corridor. At the end he could see daylight and the glimmer of Californian sun reflected on water. He walked along the corridor and carefully opened a sliding glass door.

The garden was huge. A gravel path led to the pool, and beside that was a jacuzzi sunk into the ground. As the Dragon emerged onto the path, three heads turned towards him, a young guy sandwiched between two peroxide blondes. The man looked puzzled, grabbed a small black object just beyond the edge of the hot tub, pointed it at a larger black box a few feet away and the music died.

The Dragon smiled and gave a little wave then pointed to his cap. 'Ace Pools,' he said jovially. 'You called about the filter?'

Gordon Smith's look of irritation slid away and he broke into a smile. 'Don't you mean, "You called about the filter, *sir?*"'

The Dragon looked down, shaking his head slightly, and smiled. 'Apologies,' he said, looking up. 'That's just what I meant . . . sir.'

Smith turned quickly to Crystal and then Sophia. 'Fuck, I love this shit!' The girls giggled. 'Okay, dude.' He glanced back at the pool man. 'Go right ahead, do your stuff.' He pressed a button on the remote and a new song burst from the stereo.

The Dragon walked slowly towards the pool. At one end, a set of three stone stairs led down to the pump housing. He sat on the top step, placed the metal case on the ground next to him, opened the latches and lifted the lid. The box was lined with grey foam. Nestled in the centre was a Magnum handgun, and beside it a silencer. He lifted the gun, pulled on the silencer and twisted it into place. Then he closed the box, stood and walked back towards the pool, the case in his left hand, the gun out of sight in his right.

As the Dragon approached, Smith turned from where he had been licking an erect brown nipple. He had no time to speak or to even lose his blissed-out expression. The Dragon fired a single bullet at the stereo and there was silence. He then turned the gun towards Crystal and squeezed the trigger. The Magnum bullet hit her between the eyes, and her pretty face froze. The bullet exited just above the nape of her neck, taking with it a chunk of skull and a cupful of grey-red slurry. She slammed backwards against the edge of the jacuzzi and slid under the water.

Sophia had spun in panic and was scrambling at the side of the tub. Moving the gun a few degrees to the side, the Dragon's next bullet hit her between the shoulderblades. A plume of blood sprayed across the hot water, which already was foaming with red. A second bullet smashed into the girl's neck, almost decapitating her.

Gordon Smith's face was cocaine-white, his pupils huge. They reflected the image of the Dragon, who was now pointing the Magnum directly at his forehead.

'You didn't really think you'd get away with it, did you, Gordon?' the Dragon said slowly.

'We had a deal . . . please –' Smith was shaking. Tears welled up in his eyes. 'I've got money. How much do you want?'

The Dragon gave him a disgusted look.

'Please – don't kill me,' Smith pleaded.

'Don't you mean, "Please don't kill me, *sir*?"'

Smith swallowed hard. 'Please don't kill me, sir,' he croaked.

The Dragon smiled. 'Fuck, I love this shit,' he said, as he pulled the trigger.

12

'You know the trouble with this place?' Josh Thompson observed, leaning back in his favourite armchair close to the pool table in the main recreation area. 'There aren't enough women working here.'

'How very socially aware of you, Josh,' Stephanie Jacobs retorted, turning away from the TV, which was showing a rerun of *The Sopranos*.

He laughed. 'Steph, you'll come out to dinner with me at the beach bar tonight, won't you?'

'Sorry, I have to wash my hair.'

'Ouch,' Tom sniggered.

There was a sound at the door, and a cheer went up from the five people gathered in the room as Maiko Buchanan walked in.

'Fuck! It's a Borg drone,' Tom Erickson yelled, wheeling over to Mai. Motioning that she should bend her head down, he quickly inspected her neck. 'Nope, can't see any bolts,' he said.

'Well, that's a relief!' Maiko laughed, and walked over to Stephanie, Pete, Josh and Mark.

'How're you feeling?' Mark asked.

'Great,' she replied instinctively. She rubbed her neck. The day before, she had volunteered to be the first of the group to undergo three hours of surgery to implant a set

47

of devices into her body. This was her first time up and about.

She was equipped with three enhancements. The first was a nano-processor planted just behind each eye, expanding her visual range dramatically. At the same time, it gave her far better vision in low light. The processor was so small that a million of them could fit onto a pin head, but it had the computing power of a conventional desktop. The second implant was a cochlear chip to enhance her hearing. Lastly, Maiko was implanted with a nano-processor in her brain stem. When needed, this controlled the release of a range of biochemicals that performed a variety of functions – pain relief, hunger relief, anti-motion-sickness, energy-boosting; even, in the direst of circumstances, voluntary euthanasia. They were triggered by the main computer centre at Base One but required a coded numeric sequence from the team member in the field.

'It's a weird sensation,' Maiko said, 'but the doc assures me it's just a matter of getting used to the stuff. And if I don't take to the implants they can be atomised remotely. It's pretty cool. I feel like the six-million-dollar woman!'

'Costs a bit more than that these days,' Mark retorted. 'And I believe you're next, Pete,' he added, glancing his way.

'I'm late already,' Pete said, jumping up rather enthusiastically. 'I'll see you in a couple of days.'

'Yeah, in all the colours of the rainbow simultaneously,' Tom sniggered.

'Don't worry, computer boy,' Pete shot back. 'I'll ask the doc to rig up a cyber interface so you can get nice and cuddly with the mainframe. With an I/O port right here, lad.' And he pointed to the middle of his forehead.

'Bring it on, dude! Bring. It. On.'

'Right,' Mark said as the door closed behind Pete. 'Mai, are you up to a flight simulation today?'

'I guess. It should be a doddle with these nanobots in my cranium.'

13

The four field members of E-Force were kitted out in their operational bodysuits. These were made from a 'smart' fabric, a blend of manmade fibres including latex and a polymer produced from ultra-fine strands of carbon called carbothreads. But the suits were much more than a clever fabric. Referred to as 'cybersuits', they were part-garment, part-machine, so light and thin the wearer was hardly aware of them. Across the chest was written E-FORCE, and under this the name of the team member.

Woven into the fabric were millions of nano devices and sensors that automatically adjusted the flow of liquids through microscopic tubes interwoven with the threads of the fabric. These cooled or warmed the wearer as necessary. The suit could also supply nutrients, blood and other bodily fluids through an almost invisible catheter. As well as this, nanobots in the suit communicated directly with the enhancements implanted into each of the field members of E-Force. Combined, these allowed the wearer to survive for weeks in even the most extreme environments. It also meant the team had no need for heavy equipment such as phones, laptops or sensor devices. Via the cybersuit, they were fully connected – wired to the internet with a connection speed of ten gigabits per second, thousands of times faster than the latest conventional connections.

The team was standing in Hangar C, the smallest of three at Base One. It was a vast empty space, except for a row of glass pods standing in a line stretching from one end of the 300-foot-long building to the other. The pods were cylinders fifteen feet in diameter and twelve high. They were each placed about five yards apart.

At one end of the hangar stood a control room raised about 25 feet above the ground on steel supports. It was accessed by a steel stair. The control room was very narrow, barely wide enough for two people to pass each other, but it was packed with high-tech equipment. A holographic view screen stood at one end, and there was a row of computer stations with their 3D displays projected in the air above virtual keyboards. The holographic image at the end of the room and the computer holoscreens showed the same thing – the four pods in the hangar.

'Okay. This is the set-up,' Mark said. 'Each pod is a mock-up of a fission reactor core, modelled on the reactor at Philli C on the Eastern Seaboard. It has an inner skin, a smaller cylinder, floor to ceiling. In our scenario, the core has gone critical. You have to go into the chamber between the inner and the outer cylinders and secure the three stabiliser devices there – A, B and C. These will control the core breach. An extra problem comes from the reactor's defence system, which will detect any alien presence. After 45 seconds it releases a toxic gas into the chamber. When this reaches a concentration of 0.400 parts per million, it's deadly. Once the third device is in place, the system will shut down and the defence matrix be neutralised. Have you got that?'

Pete, Josh, Maiko and Stephanie nodded in unison.

'Now, just to make it a little more interesting. One of the pods is real.'

'What?' Josh asked.

'Okay, not *real* real, but active. That is, the gas is real. Real deadly.' Mark stared at the four. 'Right. We're all cool with that?'

They said nothing.

'I'll take that as a yes.'

'One question.'

Mark looked at Maiko.

'Where will you be?'

'Tucked up nice and warm in the control room,' Mark replied, flicking a glance at the box on stilts at the far end. 'The code for the locks is 4321. On my mark . . . Go!'

Each of the four dashed to a pod, punched in the code and dived in. The doors swished closed, sealing them inside.

It was a tight squeeze between the inner and outer skins. Through the glass they could just see Mark striding towards the control room. The inner chamber was semi-opaque, changing colour constantly. Each of them set to work immediately. The alarm system would be kicking in in little more than 30 seconds.

Pete was the first to find the stabiliser marked Device A. He sized it up and found a catch on the side. It snapped open. Four small holes appeared and metal feet sprung out. Each was attached to a sucker pad. There was just enough space to twist the contraption round. He was about to fit it to the glass cylinder when, right on cue, the alarm went off.

The screeching sound reverberated around the hangar, but it was loudest inside the pods. Each member of the team had the sound instantly filtered automatically by the nano-processors in their cochlear implants.

The clock was now ticking.

Within ten seconds, all four team members had their first device locked into place. Mai was the first to the second device. She crouched down to pick it up. A computerised voice inside her right ear told her that the toxicity level in the chamber had now reached 0.100 parts per million! Still well within safe limits.

Twenty seconds later, Pete was screwing in the final sucker on Device B as Josh, Mai and Stephanie each dashed towards Device C.

'*Toxicity level 0.250 parts per million,*' the computer voice announced.

As Stephanie pulled one of the feet from the slot at the base of Device C, she began to feel queasy.

'*Toxicity level 0.325 parts per million.*'

Her fingers opened the catch and she depressed the release button for the four suckers. 'Damn!' she said aloud. 'What's happening? Is this a simulation or for real?'

Her words came through loud in the speaker in the control room.

'I've got the live one, haven't I?' she said without missing a beat, as she tugged again at the last foot to be released on Device C – it was stuck fast.

'Steph!' Mark's voice reached her ear. 'You've got the active chamber. Get your mask on!'

'Mask? What mask?'

'The mask – oh, for God's sake!' Mark turned to the operatives at the console beside him. 'She doesn't have her helmet. Unlock that door – now!'

The man nearest him stabbed at the virtual keyboard. Nothing happened. He hit the same sequence again. Nothing.

'What's happening?' Stephanie called through the communicator.

'We're opening up the pod, Steph. Don't worry.'

'It won't open,' the operative said.

'What?' Mark's mind was racing.

'Steph,' he said, making a supreme effort to keep his voice calm. 'We're having a problem opening the door automatically. I'm coming down to use the manual override. Can you get the third device up?'

'I'm trying . . .'

'Toxicity level 0.385 parts per million.'

At that moment, Pete Sherringham burst out of his pod, followed a moment later by Mai, then Josh. They looked pleased with themselves before noticing the fourth pod. A second later, they saw Mark running down the metal stairs. He was yelling to them.

Realisation hit them and they dashed to the door of Stephanie's pod.

Inside, Stephanie was choking, her eyes streaming, but her only hope lay in prising the fourth sucker pad out of its housing. She punched at the button repeatedly but it simply would not shift. Trying to suppress her panic, she looked around the narrow curving corridor searching for something to dislodge the foot of the device, but there was nothing.

She hit it again. Nothing. She could hardly see the button now, her eyes were filled with water. The nanobots in her suit were working overtime pumping her with stimulants to help her fight the effects of the gas, but there was only so much they could do.

'Toxicity level 0.390 parts per million.'

Josh was running towards a control panel set into the wall at the far end of the hangar. Pete found a wrench and raced over to the door of Stephanie's's pod, where Mai was vainly attempting to force it open with her bare hands. He reached the pod and started to smash away at the keypad to the side of the portal.

Mark reached the control panel at almost the same moment as Josh. 'Stand back,' he called. 'I know the sequence.' He began depressing keys on the numeric pad.

Stephanie was on the verge of passing out when the foot of the device suddenly sprung out. Shocked, she almost dropped it. It slipped to the floor. Steadying herself against the outer wall of the chamber, she pushed herself forward and held out the stabiliser, feet extended, ready to fix it into place.

'Toxicity level 0.395 parts per million.'

She could hear someone bashing at the door, muffled voices. The light in the chamber seemed to fade, then brighten. She began to lose focus and could not help her head falling forward. She caught herself.

'Toxicity level 0.399 parts per million.'

Her legs buckled and she fell back against the outer wall, the stabiliser tumbling onto her chest. She gasped and everything faded to a bleached and formless white.

14

83 miles south-east of Havre, Montana

Pestilence ran his hand along the withers of his favourite mare, Hermione, and whispered quietly in her ear. He and a stableboy had been up all night with the horse, helping her deliver a very large foal just before dawn. The spindly brown thing that had emerged from Hermione was already standing, albeit wobbly. She looked like a perfect clone of her mother.

Pestilence walked out into the orange glow of sunrise as morning broke over 100,000 acres of green. Screwing up his eyes and raising a hand to his brow, he could just see, coming in from the south, the black shape of a chopper. It began to slow, lowering towards the helipad 50 yards from the ranch. Pestilence could see two figures in the cockpit. Turning, he walked away towards the house to wash away the stench of the stable.

Twenty minutes later, Pestilence had changed into an immaculate pair of Levis, soft leather boots and a checked shirt. Striding into his library, he saw the Dragon sitting in an armchair close to the roaring fire. Without a word, Pestilence settled into the chair opposite and gazed at the fire. The two men were silent for at least 30 seconds.

'We congratulate you on the Hollywood Hills assignment,' Pestilence said eventually, without looking round.

The Dragon said nothing, staring into the flames.

Pestilence stood and took two steps towards a painting

of a black stallion to the right of the fireplace. He touched the corner of the ornate gold frame and the picture lifted. Inside was a metal panel with a line of three lights beside it. He placed his palm on the plate, tapped a keypad, and the panel slid to one side. Pestilence put his hand into the cavity and withdrew a cardboard folder. He closed the panel and lowered the picture, then returned to his armchair. Once seated, he handed the folder to the Dragon and looked into his face. 'Read,' he said.

The Dragon studied the contents of the folder carefully and Pestilence began to talk. 'Kyle Foreman,' he said. 'US senator, 43 at his last birthday. High-flier, very, very bright, and very, very determined. Tipped to become the 45th president. Extremely popular in the Senate, and with the public.'

'I've heard of him,' the Dragon said slowly, his faint accent just detectable.

'He's big on the environment. Formed OneEarth two years ago. It's become the fastest growing cross-party movement in history. As I said, he's popular . . . but not with us.' And Pestilence produced a cynical smile.

'What do you have in mind?'

Pestilence was staring at the flames again. 'How many men and women have you killed for us?' he asked, his eyes fixed on the ever-changing patterns of yellow and orange.

'Twenty-four.'

'Eliminating the good senator will be messy. He is very well protected, but we've given a great deal of thought to the matter, my . . . colleagues and I. Serious collateral damage will be unavoidable. How do you feel about serious collateral damage, my friend?'

The Dragon stared at him without expression.

'It could mean putting at least one zero on the end of your tally for us. How do you feel about *that*?'

The Dragon's face was an emotionless mask. 'When do I start?' he said.

15

Base One, Tintara

Stephanie's bleached and formless world began to regain colour and shape. But she couldn't regain consciousness. Instead, she was walking along Balmoral Beach on Sydney's North Shore. The sun was nothing more than a dome of pinkish red in the east, splashing dawn colours across the crisp white sand, but it was still hot. She was wearing an orange bikini and a sarong she had bought in Bali. Her long legs were deeply tanned and she had just had her blonde hair cut short.

A lock of hair fell from behind her ear and she pushed it back absent-mindedly. Someone was walking beside her. It was her husband, Ted. Her arm was linked in his. He was laughing at something she had said. At that moment, she loved Ted so much she thought she was going to burst.

In some ways, he was a typical upper-middle-class Englishman, stiff and formal, but he understood her, saw her every quality, her every fault – she worked too hard, gave him too little of her time, had no serious thoughts about ever becoming a mother. An athlete from childhood, she was obsessed with her weight, she over-exercised, and she was overcritical of him and his bad habits. She had been scarred by her impoverished childhood, her compulsive gambler of a father who had led them to ruin, debt collectors and holes in the roof. She knew Ted loved her despite those faults, her many faults . . . He had mended her, made her a better person.

Then the agony of recall flooded through Stephanie's brain. Ted was dead. Of course he was. He was very dead. His body had been smashed by a Taliban booby trap in the Barai Ghar mountains while he was fighting in the British SAS. She hadn't been allowed to see his body. It was in too many pieces, too much of it missing. But in the rain at RAF Brize Norton she had watched his flag-draped coffin as it came down the ramp of a Hercules. She had stood a hundred yards away with army dignitaries and Ted's relatives.

Stephanie opened her eyes and saw the ceiling imbued with a soft, warm light from an invisible source. The dread images faded fast. She moved her head and a pain flew across her eyes, making her gasp.

'It's alive!'

She turned towards the sound and Tom Erickson's face came into focus. She tried to sit up, but it was painful.

'I wouldn't,' Tom said. 'Take it easy, Steph.'

She ignored him and winced as she pulled herself up. 'What . . .'

'What happened? You came this close to the bright white light,' Erickson said, holding up his fingers a fraction of an inch apart.

She brought a hand to her temple as another stab of pain shot across her forehead. 'Oh yeah, the pod.' She looked around the room. 'So what you doing here, Tom?'

'Why not? I have an *excellent* bedside manner.'

Stephanie smiled. 'Where're the others?'

'Oh, the usual – out playing at being Mattel action figures,' Tom retorted with disdain.

'How long have I been unconscious?'

'Twenty-four hours, or thereabouts.'

'What?'

'It was pretty serious, Steph. Mark managed to get the door of the pod open with . . . oooh . . . *nanoseconds* to spare.'

'Nanoseconds? My goodness!'

'Think yourself lucky. You've missed out on the latest trial.'

'Which is?'

'I'm not really sure, but they're in the middle of it right now – out there somewhere.' He nodded towards the window. 'Make the most of it and go back to sleep. I know I would.'

16

A mile and a half away, Pete, Josh and Maiko were feeling overwhelmed.

It had started well. Earlier that day they had gathered at Camp Alpha, a cluster of small buildings at the north-east end of Tintara. The news about Stephanie was all good. She was on the mend and would be woken from her induced coma at 14.00. Meanwhile, the three of them had a new task to complete. With the soft lapping of the waves filtering through an open window in the meeting room at Camp Alpha, Mark had explained what they had to do.

'As you know, Tintara is a very small island,' he had said. 'But most of it's jungle, and it's very easy to lose something in that jungle. In this exercise, one of the technicians will play the part of a seriously injured civilian with no idea of survival procedures and no medical knowledge. He is trapped somewhere on Tintara. You have to find him and rescue him.

'Straightforward, right? Well, it would be – except for three things. One, you'll be up against the clock. You have 60 minutes to find the injured man and get him to the medical facility at Base One. Two, the only thing you'll have other than your cybersuits is a jungle knife – eleven inches of blackened carbon steel. And three, you'll need to avoid being eliminated from the exercise by any one of three Hunters who will be tracking you.'

'Hunters?' Josh had asked.

'Yep. This is a Hunter,' Mark had replied, lifting the cover from a spherical object about eighteen inches in diameter. 'They can move through the air, on the ground, even underwater. And they're fast. They're designed for rescue missions considered too dangerous for a human operative. They're equipped with sensors that can be programmed to seek out a target. In this exercise, they have been instructed to find three humans – two males, one female.'

'I see,' Mai had said. 'And what do they do if they find us?'

'You each have a sensor built into your cybersuit. If they are in range they can zap you and you're out of the exercise.'

'Kinda like paintball.'

'Precisely.'

'This way,' Pete said. 'To the clearing – I'm picking up a signal.' He ran ahead, Mai and Josh came up fast behind him. They reached a small gap in the undergrowth and crouched down.

'I'm definitely getting a connection,' Pete confirmed. He was looking at a small flexible screen wrapped halfway around his forearm, meshed into the fabric of his cybersuit.

They had been trying to get a link with the satellite for the past fifteen minutes. They needed to get a fix on the target. Sensors in their cybersuits were supposed to hook up to a satellite directly over Tintara. This would connect them to the mainframe at Base One, and beyond that to the internet. The problem was, Mark had either built in some interference just to screw them up, or there was a network problem that wasn't part of the exercise. Either way, it was impossible to get a precise reading.

'Okay,' Pete said, tapping at a soft pad beneath the screen. 'Something's coming through.'

Thousands of miles overhead, a satellite monitored the island and the surrounding ocean 24/7. This was primarily for defence, but it could also be used to locate anything bigger than a dime. It could also monitor the body heat of animals. Pete was trying to scan for a stray trace, the signature of a human hidden in a secluded part of the island.

He directed the detector on the satellite to zero in on the middle section of the island. That was where Base One was located. He could see the outline of the buildings above ground.

'Switch to infrared,' Mai said.

Pete ran his fingers over the keypad and the image instantly changed. The buildings disappeared, replaced by a smudge of light – the infrared signature of over 800 people and their machines. He guided the image away, and they saw a few dots of light close to the base, each of them moving along track roads. They needed to find a stationary signal somewhere off the main routes. Pete touched the keys again and the image shifted. He thought he saw a pinprick of light close to the southernmost tip of the island.

The screen died.

'Oh, hell!' Josh exclaimed.

'Too much of a coincidence to be a network problem,' Mai said heavily.

'It's irrelevant anyway,' Pete replied. He flicked off the screen and straightened up.

They all heard a whirring sound at the same time and spun round to see a Hunter just above the trees to the west, ten yards away.

There was nowhere to hide. The Hunter could detect them even if they were hidden from sight. But they dived into the undergrowth and started to crawl to an area of denser cover where it would find it harder to get a good shot at them.

They lay still in the damp vegetation. The Hunter came close and hovered overhead. Suddenly, a sharp cracking sound came from the sphere. It missed their sensor pads.

Josh was closest to the edge of the dense patch of undergrowth. Vines clambered over each other in tight knots. A huge beetle passed an inch from his face. The insect stopped, waved its antennae, then trundled off. Josh moved his hand half an inch and touched a hard, jagged object. A small rock. He worked the stone into his palm and gripped it tight.

'Mai, Pete,' he hissed, 'I'm going to try something. On three, scramble away from me in opposite directions, but for heaven's sake keep under cover. One – two – three!'

Josh sensed rather than saw Pete and Mai move away. Overhead, the sphere whirred. Josh glimpsed the machine through the undergrowth. It was hovering about ten feet above the vegetation. It spun towards Mai and then around 180 degrees to track Pete. Josh pulled himself up, and with all his strength he threw the rock straight at the Hunter.

The rock whistled past it. The machine spun round and fired at Josh. He dived into the undergrowth. The Hunter fired again and missed. Josh tripped and landed heavily against a boulder, winding himself.

The Hunter came back into view. Josh scrambled away but there was no cover. The machine came closer. It was no more than a dozen feet away when there came a loud clang, and it wobbled. Then he spotted Mai ducking down. He hadn't seen her throw the rock but her aim had been better than his.

The Hunter turned towards her, but then Pete sprang up and launched a rock at the device. It slammed into the sphere, knocking it aside. The Hunter emitted a high-pitched whistling sound and plunged to the ground.

Josh gave Mai and Pete high fives. 'Sharp shooting,' he said.

'Misspent youth,' Pete answered.

'So, what now?' Mai asked. She was panting from the exertion. 'Am I mistaken, or was there a trace to the south just before it went down?'

'I saw it too,' said Pete, suddenly excited. 'But it's a big area.'

'Hang on,' Mai said. 'We lost the signal, but the images should still be in the system's memory.'

'You're right,' Pete replied. He touched the pad on his arm and brought up the file browser. Scrolling forward, he found the final image just before the system had flicked off. They could see, to one side of the screen, an isolated, motionless infrared signature.

'Freeze that,' Josh snapped. 'There. What're the co-ordinates?' He brought up the map of the island on his own screen, keyed in the coordinates and matched it up with the signature. Then he glanced at his watch. 'Zero point three four seconds west. Let's go.'

The infrared signature was less than a hundred yards away, but between them and the target dense undergrowth covered a steep incline. The target appeared to be sheltered in a small cave at the top of a rocky outcrop. If the satellite was up they could have found the quickest path through the dense vegetation, but that luxury was lost to them.

They set off, using the map on Josh's screen to guide them. Five minutes later they had only managed to get twenty yards closer to the infrared signature.

It was approaching noon. The sun was almost directly overhead and the temperature on the ground was nudging 110 degrees with almost 100 per cent humidity. The cybersuits were keeping their bodies cool by circulating liquid nitrogen through the intricate network of capillaries woven into the fabric. But that luxury, too, was short-lived.

Mai was the first to notice. 'Hey, guys, stop a sec.'

Pete and Josh were a few steps ahead of her. They stopped

and turned in unison.

'Is it just me, or are you warming up too?'

Pete and Josh had been too busy slashing through the undergrowth with their jungle knives to notice. 'Now that you mention it,' Josh said.

'Oh, Christ!' Pete exclaimed. 'Don't tell me!'

'Another little gift from Mark, I think. No more thermal control,' Mai said.

Suddenly things got much worse. A subdued hum came from the three cybersuits and they flicked off simultaneously.

'What the –'

'The whole thing's down,' Josh snapped, staring in disbelief at the dead arrays, his screen blank on his arm.

'I bet you the only things working are the sensors for the damn Hunters,' Pete said.

Almost immediately they heard the familiar whir. A Hunter was directly in front of them, inside the foliage. They dived into the undergrowth, but it was too late. The sphere emerged from a tangle of vines no more than five feet in front of Mai. It fired, and an alarm sounded from the back of her cybersuit.

Josh and Pete were quick to respond. As the Hunter fired, Pete leapt up at the sphere, smashing his blade into the side of the device. The knife was sharp and heavy, and it sank at least two inches into the machine, crushing circuit boards and sundering components. The sphere emitted a low growl and fell like a stone, its lights flicking off.

Josh and Pete pressed on, while Mai headed in the opposite direction, towards a track that would return her to Base One.

It was exhausting work cutting through the foliage. They were sweating profusely, their cybersuits now useless and sodden. After ten minutes they stopped for a breather. Pete checked his watch. 'We've got nineteen minutes. It'll take at least ten to get the patient to the medical centre at Base One. Come on, man.' He helped Josh to his feet and they pressed on.

After two more minutes of slashing through vines and dense foliage they reached a clearing. From here they could see the jungle stretching like a green and brown fog hanging low over the rocky terrain. It was thickest to the north-east, thinning out to the south-west. In the middle of the thinner covering they could just make out a rocky hill. It was probably the highest point on the island. Half of it was covered with more dark undergrowth and two large acacias that were smothered with vines. Looking closely, they could see a rough, dark circle – a cave entrance.

They moved quickly through the clearing, all the while watching for the last of the Hunters. They made it to the first outcrop of rock unmolested, and slashed at the vegetation to find an opening in the trees. No more than 30 feet above them was the entrance to the cave.

'How long have we got?' Josh asked.

Pete glanced at his watch. 'Four minutes to reach the patient.'

Josh didn't answer but threw himself into the task with renewed gusto. He slashed at a web of slender vines that gave way almost as soon as the blade touched them, and suddenly they were through.

They were both panting, leaning forward with their hands on their knees. Josh was wincing. 'Stitch,' he gasped, as Pete looked at him. 'It'll pass.'

Pete put his hand on Josh's sodden back. 'It's right ahead – at the end of the path.'

Josh looked up to see a narrow opening between two jutting rocks, and beyond that the absolute black of a cave mouth.

For a few seconds they felt very exposed as they plunged into the gap between the rocks. They both knew it was a perfect moment for the last Hunter to strike, and they brandished their knives as they dashed forward. Once through the gap, they followed a path with a rock wall to their left. An impenetrable mesh of vines and lianas lay to their right. Six paces on and they reached the cave.

The cool of the shade felt like a panacea, but they had no time to enjoy it. 'We've got a minute, at best, to find him,' Josh said, stepping deeper into the blackness.

It took a few moments for their eyes to adjust, but gradually shapes materialised. There were large rock projections on either side. The floor was soft with a carpet of rotting vegetation. It stank.

Josh stopped for a second and leaned forward, his hand on his side.

Pete thought he looked on the point of collapse. 'You okay, man?'

Josh nodded weakly but couldn't speak.

They both heard a rustling sound from further inside the cave. A torch beam cut through the semi-darkness and they saw a figure standing on a shelf of rock. His features were obscured by the dazzling light.

The man stepped down to meet them, the torch bobbing. He switched it off. 'I'm so glad you've found me,' he said, lifting his hand. It held a small metal box. He took another step towards Josh and Pete and they finally saw the man's face.

'Mark!'

'Game over,' Mark said. He pushed a button on the device in his hand and the sensors woven into the back of their cybersuits went off. The sound reverberated around the rock walls.

'Great try, guys, but no cigar,' Mark said, handing them each a water bottle. 'And the moral is – trust no one!'

17

CIA headquarters, Langley, Virginia

The tall man in a grey suit and blue tie and wearing spectacles with Armani turtle-shell frames was seated at the head of a long, walnut table reading a report. His assistant – younger, shorter and in a black suit and grey tie – tapped on the glass door to the room and walked in. He strode the length of the room to the head of the table. The taller man indicated the assistant should sit.

'What is it?'

'This, sir. Just in from MI5.' The assistant slid a piece of paper across the smooth walnut.

The taller man read silently, then leaned back in his chair and removed his glasses. 'Sounds like horseshit to me,' he said, fixing his assistant with hard, black eyes.

'The Brits appear to be taking it seriously, sir. They've gone to orange.'

The taller man gave his assistant a sceptical look. 'And you think they know something we don't? Something planned on American soil?'

The younger man shrugged. 'There's more.'

The taller man's face was impassive. The assistant handed him another sheet of paper and the boss put his glasses back on. 'From the Bureau an hour ago,' the assistant said as his superior read in silence.

A minute passed and the boss placed the paper on the table. 'More speculation.'

'Perhaps, sir. But it comes from a field operative, Freddie Neilson.'

'Neilson? Well, that settles it. It is horseshit!'

The assistant allowed himself a faint smile. Neilson was famous in the FBI – and infamous among the conservatives in the CIA. Perceived as a hero by some and a fool by others, to say Freddie Neilson was no team player would have been like saying Bill Gates was comfortably off. But he had more scalps to his name than any other serving operative, and that was just about the only reason he had kept drawing a pay cheque from the Bureau.

'Apparently, Neilson was following his own leads, deep under cover. Wouldn't say anything to anyone about it, following his own agenda.'

'Yeah, that sounds about right. I've never understood why our friends at the Bureau suffered the man.'

The assistant nodded. 'Looks like he was onto something big, though, sir. He dropped out of sight three days ago – simply vanished. Then yesterday he filed this report. He was in southern California. Said he was close to the source. Asked for backup to be prepped for his next call in.'

'Ha! And?'

'Freddie Neilson's body was found washed up on the beach in Santa Barbara this morning.'

18

Base One, Tintara
E-Force training, week twelve

'Abort! Abort!'

'Okay, okay!' Stephanie brought her hand down hard on the joystick and threw herself back in the chair. 'I will never, ever get the hang of this thing!' she shouted into the helmet mic, so loudly that Mark and Maiko in the control room yanked off their headsets simultaneously.

'Okay, Steph. Take five.' It was Mark's deep voice coming through her comms.

Stephanie emerged from the simulator seething. She had been trying to land the Big Mac on a shelf of rock not much bigger than the base of the vehicle, and every time she had misjudged the altitude and slammed the VTOL aircraft down so hard that the undercarriage buckled and they plummeted 2000 feet into a digital ravine. 'I'm sorry, Mark,' she hissed, stomping towards the control room. 'I just –'

'Look – chill, okay?' Mark took her by the shoulders. 'I died at least a dozen times before I got it right.'

Maiko was at the door to the control room as Stephanie and Mark reached it.

'Your turn,' Mark said.

She was pulling on her comms headset when the central computer, known affectionately as Sybil, interrupted. 'Mark,' it intoned, in a soft female voice, 'perhaps you've forgotten

– the team are due to meet in Cyber Control at 15.00. Peter and Josh are on their way. Tom is there already.'

'Thanks, Sybil,' Mark said. 'I had forgotten.'

They reached Cyber Control a few seconds after Pete and Josh. The two men looked freshly scrubbed in new jumpsuits – the standard uniform for everyone at Base One. Made from polycarbon fibres, each suit weighed only a few ounces but was as strong as silk, with a similar texture. The two of them had just completed Survival Training Course 6M, one of the toughest – and messiest.

Tom gave Josh and Peter high fives as they came in. 'Good day at the office, guys?' he enquired.

'Can't complain, Tom. It must have been hell slaving over a hot keyboard all day,' Josh replied.

'Right, everyone,' Mark said. 'It's just the weekly check. How're we all feeling?'

'Apart from crashing six times today, just fine,' Stephanie replied.

Josh looked at her in amazement. 'You *still* haven't landed the Big Mac?'

'No, I haven't, smartass. I'm sorry to disappoint you.' Stephanie caught herself and took a deep breath. 'Oh, look, I'm . . . Not a good day.'

He had his hands up. 'Hey, I'm sorry.'

'Actually, there is something I want to pass on.' It was Tom Erickson. He was at a computer terminal. A holographic image floated in space in front of his eyes. At the apex of red and green converging lines was a paragraph of text. 'Sybil,' he said. 'Project the global map onto the big screen, please.'

Tom spun his chair round and the others turned as the wall behind them lit up.

'I don't want to panic anyone, but we've been picking up some strange intelligence traffic.'

'What does that mean, exactly?' Josh asked.

71

'Well, as you know, Sybil monitors all transmissions on the planet. Then, just like a search engine on the net, she sorts the stuff according to a set of pre-programmed criteria. The most useful sources are secret-service and military transmissions.' The screen lit up in clusters around Washington, London, Moscow and Beijing. 'During the past couple of days there's been increased activity from the US and European intelligence agencies. A lot of cross-talk. Sybil's picked up no fewer than 1800 communications between the CIA and MI5 since Tuesday. They obviously suspect something is about to go down.'

'Any idea what?' Pete asked.

'None at all. Either the spooks know and there's a complete security lockdown, or they've had a tip-off but nothing specific.'

'Okay,' Mark said. 'Keep monitoring it, Tom. The first hint of anything clearer, let me know.'

He was about to add something more when a technician came in. 'Sir?'

Mark approached the technician, who whispered in his ear. Mark looked grave. Turning to Maiko, he said. 'Mai, can I have a private word?'

They stepped into the empty corridor. Through a large window they could see palm trees swaying in a gentle breeze.

'What's up?' Maiko asked.

'It's a private matter, Mai. It's your mother. She's had a stroke.'

She stared at Mark, her expression blank with shock. Then she suddenly seemed to jolt into awareness. 'I have to go,' she exclaimed, looking around as if she was trying to find the exit there and then.

Mark fixed her with his eyes.

'You do understand, don't you?' Mai said.

Mark ran a hand over his forehead. 'Yes . . . yes, of course, Mai,' he said heavily. 'Leave it with me.'

19

At 2.54 pm Josh was woken from a deep sleep by the buzzer beside his bed. Only six hours earlier he had completed a 48-hour sleep-deprivation exercise.

'It's Mark,' came the voice at the end of the line. 'You'd better get to Cyber Control, fast.'

When Josh arrived, looking bleary-eyed, he found Mark already there. Pete entered a few moments later, then Stephanie, who had been down in the hangar getting instruction in how to use the Mole.

'What's happened?' Josh asked, as they gathered near Tom's computer module.

'About 30 minutes ago the CIA comms network went into overdrive,' Tom replied. 'Both the US and UK governments have gone to their highest alert levels. Neither have made it public yet.'

'Anything specific?'

'I'm trying. Sybil's analysing the comms. Everything's encoded, of course. I've got the system to pick keywords from the intelligence traffic. Here we go.' The holographic image shifted in front of Tom's eyes and he slid his fingers over the metal surface where the keypad was visible as a light projection on the desk. 'Here're the top three.'

Three lines of numbers appeared from the confusion of text.

'It's an RSA code,' Josh said, suddenly wide awake. He

felt energised by the fact that he could at last employ his knowledge of cryptography.

'Which is?' Pete asked.

'It's like the system used for credit cards,' Tom interjected. 'It depends on the level of encryption, but most of them are considered completely unbreakable.'

'Well, yeah, that's true for commercial transactions,' Josh added. 'The PIN number you use, or your bank password, is almost impossible to crack. But if you look at these rows of numbers, you can see they break up into smaller segments.'

'Tom,' Mark said, 'can you put them on the big screen, please?'

A few seconds later, numbers a foot high appeared on the wall.

'It's been estimated that to crack the very best of these codes it would take all the computers in the world – even working together – something like 12 million times the age of the universe,' Josh commented. 'But this doesn't look like a particularly complex one.'

'And we have one shit-hot advantage,' Tom added, patting the desk in front of him affectionately. 'The only quantum computer in the world.'

'Okay, Sybil,' Josh said. 'I think the spooks have used a third-level factorising equation to get these numbers. Which means we have to reverse the process. Let's take the first number cluster – 657609873. What do you make of it?'

All eyes were on the big screen. Then Sybil's synthetic voice cut through the quiet. 'Best fit is REHKTHY.'

No one spoke for a moment, then Tom laughed. 'Fantastic – that's C-3PO's mom, right?'

Josh sat down and ran his hands through his hair. He had dark rings under his eyes. He leaned forward, elbows on his knees, and peered at the screen. Then he stood up suddenly. The others looked on in silence.

'Sybil,' he said after a long pause. 'Good try. Let's look at the second number cluster – 6858876568.'

Another few moments of silence. Tom twirled a pen across the fingers of his left hand.

'Closest correlation is HYJJHHHKIO.'

Tom dropped the pen onto the console attached to his wheelchair.

'Okay,' Josh sighed. 'Sybil, the third numeric cluster – 7876345256.'

The silence was oppressive, then the computer voice rang out. 'SELL ONE GAS.'

'Oh, for Christ's sake!' Pete exclaimed.

'It's alright. It's an anagram,' Josh said. 'LOS ANGELES.'

Mark shot a glance at the cryptographer and nodded. 'So the spooks must know something big is about to go down in LA.'

'Yeah, but they obviously have no idea what it is, or clues to that information would have been imbedded in the encoded traffic we've picked up between the agencies. You haven't isolated any other keywords have you, Tom?'

'No.'

'Which means,' Josh continued, 'we have absolutely no idea what's about to go down either.'

Part Two

ENTER THE DRAGON

20

Senator Kyle Foreman stretched his long legs as best he could in the back of the Mercedes and watched the buildings flash by along Pico Boulevard. The morning sun was bright in a perfect blue sky. *I could get used to this place*, he thought to himself. Flying out of JFK only four hours earlier, he had left behind grey skies and rain. Sometimes he could barely believe LA and New York were part of the same nation. Whenever he flew into LAX, the City of Angels always felt like a foreign land to him, every bit as exotic as its name.

The car slipped into a short tunnel and he caught his reflection in the window – high cheekbones and square jaw, salt-and-pepper hair slicked back, large hazel eyes that spoke of his Italian ancestry. He looked weary. He had been working hard and it was showing. His skin was a little saggy around the eyes and there were new wrinkles at the corners of his mouth. He glanced down at the briefcase on his knees and tried to focus on the job ahead, but his mind kept wandering and it always returned to the same thing, Sandy. He hated leaving her right now. The timing could not have been worse. Only the night before, he had rushed her to Mount Sinai Hospital. It was a false alarm, but her due date was only two days away. The baby could arrive at any time.

He cursed his schedule. He had utter belief in his cause, but sometimes . . . Then reason prevailed. This gig had been booked more than eight months earlier. How could he have known?

Tonight's speech was to be the most important he had made, the culmination of two years of campaigning and dedication. He had been captivated by environmentalism three years earlier. Looking for a new direction in his career, he had found an immediate simpatico with what he quickly realised was the cause of the era. Environmentalism, as he often now said, was beyond politics.

Kyle Foreman's critics – and there were many, from all parts of the political spectrum – claimed that all he ever did was preach to the converted. He knew this was untrue and that in just two years his organisation, OneEarth, had grown from being a group of likeminded enthusiasts to a global campaign with over a million paid-up members. But even he had to admit that tonight's event was partly a show for the troops.

He was not doing all this purely for political impact, nor simply to enhance his profile. He sincerely believed in the cause, and he was a man who threw himself heart and soul into anything he felt passionate about. Now, at the age of 43, Foreman was at the top of his game, one of the most popular and successful members of the Senate, a man tipped to go all the way.

His had been a remarkable ascendency. Born into a poor family and brought up by his widowed mother in Ford Heights, Chicago, he had been forced by necessity to fight for absolutely everything he had achieved. Graduating from Yale *summa cum laude*, he became obsessed with succeeding as a politician because he believed politics was where the real action was. It was the arena in which he could do most to bring positive change to the world. He soon learned he possessed natural charisma and could communicate easily with people from all walks of life. Coupled with his massive, restless energy, these qualities set him on the road to great things long before the media made him famous.

Through the window, he could now see the California Conference Center, the massive complex of arenas and exhibition halls where, in less than eight hours, he would walk onto a stage to greet a thousand key supporters. He couldn't help but feel proud and excited, but at the same time he had a growing sense that his real place now was 2500 miles east – with Sandy in their upper eastside apartment.

The lead car pulled into the underground garage, Foreman's followed and the rear car came up to the bumper. Four CIA security agents surrounded the senator as he passed through a glass vestibule into an brightly lit reception area. A delegation of half a dozen officials from the Center met him. A member of his staff made the necessary introductions. It took another half an hour of glad-handing and backslapping before he reached his private suite on the top floor of the Hilton annex, which adjoined the CCC. Foreman threw his jacket onto the bed, loosened his tie and dismissed the two CIA agents who acted as his personal bodyguards.

Sitting up against the headboard of the bed, he dialled home. It would be lunchtime there now. There was a pause as the connection was made, then the comforting ring. Sandy didn't pick up. The senator felt an immediate ripple of anxiety. After a few more rings he put the phone down and redialled. It rang and rang. He stabbed at the disconnect button and called Sandy's cell phone. It could only mean one thing, he told himself, and let out a heavy sigh. 'I just knew this would happen.'

The cell rang five times before Sandy's message service kicked in. Foreman winced. Disconnecting, he threw down the phone, jumped off the bed and marched to the bathroom. He ran a bowl of cold water and threw two handfuls over his face, enjoying the shock of it.

The phone rang. He rushed back into the bedroom and snatched at the phone.

'Honey?' a voice said.

'Whoa – you had me worried there, Sand.'

'I was just seeing Marianne to her cab.'

'Of course, I forgot, your sister . . .' He was making a gargantuan effort to sound calm.

'So, no problem, okay?' Sandy added. 'Now, look. You get yourself nice and relaxed before your speech. And stop worrying!'

'Okay, boss,' he laughed.

'And, honey? Good luck.'

21

The Dragon surveyed the motel room. Four walls, a bed, a bathroom, and an arsenal of weapons. On the bed lay two M60 7.62 mm machine guns, each capable of firing 550 rounds per minute. Next to these was a box containing 1000 rounds of M61 armour-piercing shells. Towards the pillows lay two of the most powerful handguns in the world, his trusted Smith & Wesson Model 500 Magnum and an Israeli Army standard issue semi-automatic Mark XIX Desert Eagle .50 AE. Next to these rested a leather box containing six M67 fragmentation hand grenades, each with a 'guaranteed killing radius' of five yards. To complete the collection, propped up on a pillow, was an SAS favourite, a Fairbairn-Sykes No. 2 commando knife.

The Dragon was an ordinary looking man. He was 47 years old, with light-brown neatly cut hair, greying at the temples. He had a plain face, with a nose that was perhaps slightly too big, and watery pale-blue eyes. He was wearing a pale-blue shirt, cream chinos and conservative loafers that made him look like a college professor on vacation, or a middle manager on a mufti day. There was only one detail about his physical being that spoke of something else, something darker – a red tattoo of a coiled dragon on the inside of his left wrist. The dragon's tail ran back the length of his arm. It

83

had hideous black eyes and a lascivious, lashing tongue; the words Death, Conquest, Pestilence and War spewed from its mouth.

The Dragon's appearance may have been completely unremarkable, but the man's CV read like something from a Bond movie. Once upon a time he had been Igor Andrei Makanov, the son of Andrei and Lena Makanov. His Russian father had been sent to a Gulag in 1975, where he died from frostbite-induced gangrene. Lena was a Pole who had been only twelve when the Russians invaded her homeland. Igor had also been the brother of Angela and Ania, who, along with their mother, had died from malnutrition in Moscow. Igor, the youngest of the family, was the sole survivor. When he reached the age of seventeen he joined the army. He was later trained by Spetsnaz, the Soviet special forces.

With the collapse of the USSR in 1991, Igor destroyed all trace of his former life and relocated to America. He changed his physical appearance and severed all connections with his previous existence. He quickly forged links with the eastern-seaboard mafia families, who were happy to find work for muscle with no history. Searching for something more reliable, he headed south, where he became the personal bodyguard for the family of a Texan oil baron. When the youngest son of the head of the family was elected to high political office, his bodyguard went with him to Washington.

It did not take Igor long to cross the paths of the Four Horsemen and to acquire his new name. Now, after so many years, he had almost forgotten his birth name, but the memory of his family's suffering remained undimmed. He could not pin the blame for those horrors on any individual, but he knew that he would rather kill himself than ever be poor again. And because of this he had immediately clicked with the Four Horsemen, to whom the acquisition of money was everything.

The Four Horsemen demanded exclusivity, and the Dragon was happy to provide it. They paid him extremely well and he enjoyed his work. In ten years of service, he now had eliminated over two dozen people for them. The most recent had been the killings in the Hollywood Hills, but his CV was diverse.

One of the Dragon's earliest assignments had been Victoria Bramley, a lawyer working in the Department of Justice in Washington. The woman had stumbled upon some documents she would have been better off never seeing. The fact that Mrs Bramley was a young mother with two kids in preschool did nothing to dent his enthusiasm for his task, and he had completed it without fuss. Another prominent victim was Peter du Feu, an octogenarian congressman from Nebraska who had been sniffing around some elaborate financial operations planned by the Horsemen. He had enjoyed that assignment. Du Feu was a repulsive old weasel who smelled of death. The Dragon considered the job little more than euthanasia, almost a mercy-killing.

He was nearly ready. He placed the weapons in their various carriers, zipped up the bags and closed the latches. He had parked his anonymous, rented white Toyota close to the door of the motel room. In a few moments he had loaded the car, returned his room keys to reception and signed out as Michael Connor.

Now his adrenaline was starting to pump. Although he was over 300 miles from his destination, he was at last on his way.

22

A Red Hot Chili Peppers song was playing loud through the
stereo of the old VW campervan. Steve Marshall, his hair
shaved to a stubble, wearing ripped jeans and a vintage 1977
Led Zeppelin US tour T-shirt, was at the wheel and singing
at the top of his voice. Todd Evans sat beside him, his long
stoner hair tucked behind his ears. He was crumbling some
Lebanese blow onto a line of tobacco on a cigarette paper
placed precariously on a CD case.

In the back sat Dave Golding, playing a Nintendo DS,
a joint dangling from his lips. He had ultra-short hair and
wore round John Lennon glasses. Dave was rake-thin, a
fact accentuated by his baggy jeans and a 49ers sweatshirt
at least three sizes too big for him. He looked like a prisoner
released from a detention camp and hurriedly dressed
by liberating troops. The three of them were sophomore
students at Berkeley, and were travelling to Los Angeles
for Senator Kyle Foreman's speech at the California
Conference Center. They were serious OneEarthers at
Berkeley, handing out leaflets, chairing debates and
writing inspirational articles for the university magazine,
The Daily Californian.

The VW camper was Todd's, the spoils of a three-month
stint in his second term holding down two jobs – days at

Starbucks and evenings at Jerry's Steak and Chop House on Montgomery. Built in 1970, the camper was a piece of shit. It leaked oil, the carburettor filter needed cleaning every thousand miles, and it had two bald tyres. The best thing about it were the stickers on the rear window – 'No Blood For Oil' and 'Global Warming – It's A Hot Issue'. Some 150 miles out of Frisco all three students were quietly amazed they had got this far. The plan was to share the driving so they could get to the speech that evening. Later they would find some quiet lane, sleep in the van and head back to Berkeley at first light.

'I need a leak,' Dave said, tossing the Nintendo onto the seat beside him.

'Again!' Todd and Steve said in unison.

'Yes, again. I'm *terribly* sorry.'

A few minutes later they saw a small café and gas station just off the main road.

'Better get some gas anyway,' Steve said, eyeing the gauge. 'Fuck. This thing sure is a thirsty bastard.'

'She's an old lady, leave her alone,' Todd responded, patting the dash.

An attendant came out as the camper pulled into the station. 'Just some gas,' Todd said, jumping out the passenger side. 'I'll do the screen.'

'Don't tell me – students?' the attendant sighed. 'Counting the cents?'

'You got it, man,' Steve retorted. He grabbed the sponge and bucket of tepid water beside the pump. 'And I make no apologies.'

The attendant spat into the dust and pumped gas in silence.

Dave slipped out of the camper. 'You look pale, dude,' Todd said. 'You didn't tell us you got travel-sick, you pussy.'

Dave gave him the finger as he headed for the bathroom.

'So, Stevie,' Todd said coming round the back of the camper and draping his arm across his friend's shoulders. 'You missing Audrey already?' Then he pretended to cry and pumped his palm on his chest. 'Young lovers!'

'Oh, fuck off.'

'No, really,' Todd said, his face dropping to a mock serious look. 'I find it very touching. We should all have an Audrey.'

Steve shrugged Todd's hand from his shoulder and started to walk away.

'You don't reckon she'll be getting some of this tonight, do you, man?' Todd was making an obscene gesture with his fist.

'Maybe. Who knows?' Steve replied smoothly and reached into the camper to find his wallet. He needed some money but he also wanted to hide the look he couldn't keep from his face. Todd, as always, had hit a raw nerve. Steve had only been dating Audrey Delaney for six weeks, but he loved her so much he had begun to think that he was losing his mind. He hadn't been able to tell her. It was too soon. It would scare her off. And besides, he wanted her to say it to him first. He thrust his hand into his rucksack and surfaced with a handful of bills.

In the bathroom, with the door latched behind him, Dave was alone and sweating. He stood over the sink and splashed cold water over his face, letting it run down his neck and onto his chest. The face staring back at him in the mirror was that of a much older man. He looked down at his hands. They were shaking. He ran a basin of water and thrust his head in. The sounds of the world vanished and he imagined never surfacing. He could just die here, he thought. Then he pulled his head up and gasped. He dried his face and hair with a paper towel. Leaning against the mirror, he put his head between his outstretched arms and sobbed.

'Dave?' It was Steve, from outside the bathroom.

'You okay, man?'

'Yeah, cool. Be out in ten seconds.'

He heard a door close. Rifling through his pockets, he found the plastic container. On its side was a sticker from a pharmacy: 'Vicodin. 80 mg tablets. Strong Painkillers. Prescription Only.' He tipped two of the small white tablets into his palm and swallowed them dry. He washed his hands and splashed more water on his face before drying it with another fistful of paper towels. His hands were no longer shaking.

23

The VW campervan made it another 48 miles before breaking down. They had just passed the tiny town of Gorda with its Whale Watcher Café, white clapboard houses, flags and chintz curtains, when the temperature gauge started to climb rapidly. Just south of Gorda the van began to lose power. Todd, who had taken over the driving, let the old van glide onto a concrete bridge spanning Villa Creek and then steered off the road and onto a wide gravel verge.

'Great!' Steve said, jumping out. Todd popped the engine cover at the back of the van and followed Steve around.

'Fanbelt's gone.'

'Excellent.'

Dave eased himself out of the back seat and trudged around. 'What's the story?'

'Fanbelt's kaput.'

'Which means?'

'Which means the "old lady" won't go,' Steve snapped, glaring at Todd.

'So it's my fault?'

'I didn't say that.'

'Well, you implied it.'

'Whatever,' Steve slurred, turning away and pointedly studying the incredible view. A hundred feet beneath them waves smashed on rock, plumes of spray shot into the crisp afternoon air, water cascaded into the creek and back again. He turned back and was about to ask if either of them had any bright ideas when he saw a car crossing the bridge. It was a white Toyota. It slowed to a stop on the gravel just behind the VW.

The Dragon had been on the road for about 90 minutes and was already getting twitchy. It was a blend of excitement and expectation. He could taste blood in his mouth. But he had to be patient. Passing through Gorda, he thought of stopping at the Whale Watcher café, but decided against it. He had the driver's window down and the sun was warm on his skin. A short distance on, he approached the north end of the bridge over Villa Creek. A hundred feet away, off the road, stood a VW campervan with three figures behind it.

'Hey, guys,' he called through the window as he drew alongside. 'Trouble?'

One of the kids had his head under the bonnet, and another had turned from the view as he had pulled up.

'Yep. Fanbelt has snapped.'

The Dragon drove onto the verge immediately in front of the camper and stepped out. His feet crunched on the shingled road edge. He glanced at his watch. It was approaching noon.

The kids from the camper were a scruffy bunch. *Typical students*, the Dragon thought to himself. The one who had been poking around with the engine had grease on his hands. The Dragon offered his hand but when he saw the grease he withdrew it with a disarming grin. Todd smiled back. 'Sorry, dude. It's not the newest engine in the world. Leaks oil just a bit!'

The Dragon felt a twinge of hatred at the kid's familiarity. He had always hated the word 'dude'. 'Let's take a look,' he said.

91

Todd stepped back. Steve was over from the edge of the road and Dave hung back a little, close to the door of the camper. They watched as the Dragon bent low over the VW engine. 'I had one of these babies when I was at college,' he lied. 'Went everywhere in it. Where you headed?'

'LA,' Steve said.

'Yeah? Girlfriends?'

'I wish,' Steve replied. 'Kyle Foreman's giving a big speech at the CCC.'

'Is that right?' The Dragon's voice was strained as he yanked at something under the bonnet, his Russian accent just discernible. 'He's making quite a name for himself, isn't he? About time someone stood up and told it how it is.' He straightened up, the mangled remnants of the fanbelt in his hand. 'Yep, it's busted!' he said with a grin. 'I don't suppose any of you three have a tie? No, silly question.'

'Nope. No stockings either, dude,' Dave remarked from the side of the van. 'Although, come to think of it, Todd may have a secret he hasn't told us about.'

Steve laughed and Todd gave his friend a black look.

The Dragon felt his stomach tighten. The iron taste of fresh blood wormed around his tongue. 'I think I have something we could use,' he said and wiped his hands on a rag Steve had handed him.

Dave got back into the van and started to roll another joint. Steve stepped round and saw what he was doing. 'Jesus,' he said under his breath. 'Put that shit away!'

Dave looked nonplussed. Steve nodded towards the Dragon's back, and Dave hid the gear under the seat.

Reaching the Toyota, the Dragon pulled a metal box from under the front seat and opened the lid. Inside was a pistol – a Russian army Yarygin PYa wrapped in a piece of velvet. Beside it was a garrotte made from a length of piano wire with lightweight leather endpieces. He pulled out the garrotte, closed the lid of the box and pushed it back under the seat.

Back at the VW, Steve was in the passenger seat, Dave had returned to his Nintendo DS and Todd was again peering at the engine to see if there was anything else wrong.

The Dragon crunched his way slowly towards the van, the length of wire swinging beside his right leg. He caught a whiff of cannabis as he passed the sliding door of the vehicle and smiled to himself. Passing round the back of the camper, he saw Todd tugging a spark plug from its housing.

'Good idea,' the Dragon said, making Todd jump and bang his head on the engine cover.

'Shit!' Todd exclaimed. Bent over, he saw two polished brown loafers ahead of him. Straightening, he came eye-to-eye with the Dragon.

The wire was stretched between the Dragon's fists.

'It's not ideal,' he said, 'but it should get you to the next gas station.' And he crouched under the engine cover to slip the wire around the crank and the alternator.

Todd stood to one side, watching the man work. The Dragon was having trouble threading the wire around the water pump housing to one side of the alternator. He twisted his left hand around the spindle and caught the lower end of the wire where it was dangling beside the crank. Tugging it up, he pulled the wire tight and dexterously tied off the two leather ends.

As the Dragon pulled his hands away from the crank, his shirtsleeve rode up and Todd caught a fleeting glimpse of the tattoo on the underside of the man's left wrist. It was totally incongruous with the rest of the man's appearance, and Todd was shocked.

The Dragon straightened and snapped his head around. Todd was slow to compose himself but did his best. 'Fan . . . fantastic,' he said, taking a step back. A few feet behind him was the rail of the bridge, and beyond that the foaming water. A gull swooped low, gliding on a warm current of air.

A faint smile played on the Dragon's lips. He knew the kid had seen the tattoo, and he knew the kid knew he knew. For a second, he considered what fun it would be to slaughter the three of them. It would have to be done quickly, which would take some of the pleasure out of it, but it would be entertaining. The moment passed. The Dragon turned and walked to the side door of the camper.

Dave and Steve got out.

'Fixed,' the Dragon said.

'Cool! Thanks, man.'

'No problem. I think there's a gas station about ten miles further on. They should fix you up – to get you to LA, at least.'

The Dragon noticed a line of sweat above Todd's upper lip. With a wave, he paced back to the Toyota, started the engine and pulled onto the road, thinking with satisfaction that the kids he had just helped had only hours to live.

24

'You're *what?*' Simon Gardiner almost choked on his piece of steak.

Across the table, his elderly mother and father were smiling serenely. They were both white-haired, deeply tanned and wearing blue jeans, sweatshirts and sensible trainers. 'You heard me, Simon,' said Nancy Gardiner. 'We're cycling to the speech.'

Simon pushed his chair back and paced to the window, glancing at his wife, Maureen, who looked a little lost. He was a senior partner at Gardiner & Feinstein, one of the fastest-growing law firms in the city, and he was not used to being overruled – even by his parents. Those days had long gone.

'But you can't,' he insisted, spinning away from the vista of Wilshire Boulevard, a hundred or so feet below the driveway of the house.

'Why, Simon?' Marty Gardiner retorted sharply. 'Back home, we cycle everywhere. Since we had the RV converted to ethanol it's good for long distances, but we're not about to mess up our carbon footprint now . . . are we, dear?' He turned to his wife sitting calmly beside him, her hands in her lap.

Simon Gardiner was a man in thrall to his own self-image and social status. He hated his parents' RV – it was

95

too big to get in the underground garage and it messed up the lines of his garden. He didn't want to know what the neighbours thought of the thing stuck there on his drive. It had brought his parents down from rural Oregon the day before, and he would be glad to see the back of it. It was old, and a huge, ugly exhaust pipe and filter had been added beside the cabin, making it look like something out of *Mad Max*.

He returned to the table and leaned on it with both hands. 'Yes, Pa. But you might have noticed the roads are a little bigger here.'

'There's no need for sarcasm,' Nancy admonished.

Simon Gardiner shook his head and straightened. 'I give up,' he said, and walked out of the room.

Twenty minutes later the elderly couple had finished lunch without their son and had changed into identical red tracksuits and trainers, their cycling helmets in their hands and backpacks over their shoulders. Their hair was so white it looked almost as though it had been bleached with super-strong peroxide. Marty's was cut short at the back and sides, but swept across his head in a boyish style. Nancy still had a weekly 'do' at her local hairdressers, a traditional place that had changed little since the 1960s and where they still used the huge old-fashioned hair driers customers had to sit under.

The couple were now in their mid-seventies, and both were slender but robust. They radiated youthful energy and a sense of purpose. Each had dark-blue eyes that were as close in shade as to be indistinguishable. It was one of the things that had first drawn them together, a doorway to an intimacy that had lasted 42 years and become stronger as they had grown older.

Marty walked out to the RV, and Simon drew his mother to one side. 'Mom, you can't go through with this. It's insane.'

She surveyed her son's face with a mixture of amusement and affection. 'Simon, I'm not going to argue with you anymore.'

'Talk to her, will you, Maureen?' he implored his wife.

'I think their minds are made up, darling.'

'Yes, they are,' Nancy added. 'You know how passionate your father is about the environment. Can't you just drop it now?'

'So Dad's pushing you into this?'

'I didn't say that, Simon. I believe in the cause as well. It's just that your father lives and breathes it.'

Marty strode back through the front door. 'You ready, hon?'

Nancy snapped shut the clasp on her helmet and gave her husband the thumbs-up.

'Dad, before you go, I just wanted to give you something.'

'Heck. Can't it wait till we get back?'

Simon was already marching off down the hall to his study, so Marty followed him. Simon closed the door.

'What is it?' Marty Gardiner said in a rougher tone than he intended.

'Is there anything I can say to stop you doing this?'

The elderly man sat down in a leather chair facing his son's impressive mahogany desk. 'Look, son. I'm not a child. I understand what I'm doing. You forget that I grew up in this city.'

'Yes, Pop, but that was 50 years ago. It's changed just a little.'

Marty took a deep breath. 'Simon, your mother is a committed environmentalist. She totally believes in doing this.'

'So you're saying you're doing this for Mom? Because if you are –'

'No, not at all.'

'Look. How about I take you there? I don't give a fuck about my carbon footprint.'

Marty was shaking his head. 'You just don't get it, do you, son?' When Simon said nothing, his father went on. 'Look at yourself. You're overweight and overworked. You don't give a damn about yourself, let alone the world we all share. The way you're going, you'll be dead long before me.' He gave his son a stony look. 'Take heed, son, take heed.' And with that he walked out.

25

The Dragon parked the Toyota outside a four-storey apartment block in Glendale. It was a scruffy red-brick building in a back street. It hadn't been painted since it was built in the 1960s, and the garbage bins were overflowing onto a potholed alleyway running alongside the block. It smelt bad.

He took the stairs. There was no one around, but there was more garbage in the stairwell, and urine stains up the walls. It smelt worse than the alleyway. The man he was looking for was called Dexter Tate and he lived on the third floor. The Dragon had been here before, a week earlier, to make the offer.

Dexter was expecting him and opened the door before the Dragon knocked. A narrow hallway painted in a repulsive pinkish purple led to a tiny lounge with a couple of ripped armchairs, a low table covered with bottles and cigarette packets. In the corner stood a massive TV. A football game was in progress, Chargers versus Broncos.

Dexter threw himself into one of the chairs and nodded to the other. The Dragon ignored the invitation to sit. Dexter lit a cigarette.

'I would rather you didn't,' the Dragon said and snatched the cigarette, crushing it to pieces. Dexter sat to attention and started to protest but thought better of it.

'I assume everything's in order?' the Dragon asked, his Russian accent breaking through on the word 'assume'.

'Of course. So, you got the second payment?'

'All in good time, Mr Tate, all in good time. I would like to see the schematic. Talk me through your work . . . please.'

Dexter shrugged and pulled himself up from the chair. An IKEA cupboard that looked as though it hadn't been put together properly stood against one wall. Two of the shelves sloped. Dexter opened a drawer and pulled out a large roll of paper. He walked over to the table, pushed everything onto the floor and opened the roll. It was covered in lines, labels and typed numbers. It was a schematic of the California Conference Center in downtown Los Angeles. Dexter picked up a couple of bottles and placed them on the corners of the schematic to hold it down. Then he pulled one of the chairs up close to the table. The Dragon looked over his shoulder.

'The complex is huge.' Dexter ran his finger in a broad circle. 'This is the ground floor,' he said, pointing to one of the horizontal lines. 'Reception is here. There are entrances here, here and here, and four more at the other side of the Main Concourse.' He stabbed at the paper. 'The ground floor has two large auditoriums, Hall A and Hall B. One at each end. Tonight's event is in Hall A, over here to the west of the Main Concourse.' He paused for a moment to look up at the Dragon, who was staring at the schematic.

'There are three levels above the Main Concourse and Reception. A gym, indoor pool, small meeting rooms. There's a bar and restaurant on first. The whole place is bottom-heavy, though – there are six levels below ground, B1 to B6. B1 is administration: offices, storage facilities. B2 to B5 is all car park. B6 doubles as part car park, part major storage area. That's where they keep everything from spare light bulbs to twelve-foot-high video screens. There's a service lift at the back of the complex.

'Across the road from the CCC is a small mall with a Kmart, a bank, a cinema, a couple of eateries and a gas station. One thing you might find useful. A buddy at the local planning office got me the architect's plans for the complex and the buildings nearby. Not many people would ever have seen these. The shopping mall and garage across from the CCC were built at the same time as it, and they're all owned by the same company. Turns out there's a service tunnel from the Kmart that links up with B2 of the CCC.' He ran a finger across the paper. 'It's narrow, just big enough for a man to get through, and it's used to access electrical system nodes for the entire area. The main boards are just inside the CCC, here. I got in through the tunnel to position the devices, avoiding the security checks upstairs on the main level.'

The Dragon nodded. 'And where have you placed the devices?'

'One here.' Dexter pointed to a cupboard close to Reception on the Ground Floor. 'The other, larger one is here on B1, directly under Hall A.'

'I see. And security?'

'As tight as you'd expect, but the devices are well concealed and shielded, so no chemical leaks for the detectors to notice, and no smells. The dogs will pick up diddly-squat.'

'What about cameras? How did you . . .'

Dexter touched his nose. 'I have a friend who's a gifted cinematographer,' he smirked. 'Fucker should be working with Spielberg. He ran me off a DVD of empty corridors which I keyed into the system for the cameras covering the drop sites. The security guys were watching a movie for the whole 30 minutes I was in the building. Never knew I was there.'

The Dragon couldn't help smiling his approval. 'Very clever.'

'So,' Dexter said. He turned to look up at the Dragon. The barrel of a silencer attached to a Smith & Wesson Model 500 Magnum was two inches from his face.

'Up.'

Dexter's face was suddenly very pale. 'But I –'

'Not a word, please. Into the hall.'

Dexter Tate was rooted to the spot. 'The hall?' In a daze, he got up from the chair and began to walk towards the door. 'I don't understand,' he said, his voice fractured. 'What –'

'I use people only once. Dead men can't tell tales.'

'But, I wouldn't –'

'Stop.'

The Dragon walked past him towards the front door and turned. Dexter stared imploringly at the man in front of him. The Dragon felt nauseated, raised the Magnum and shot Dexter between the eyes. His head exploded, sending blood and grey matter to the ceiling and in great plumes along the walls.

The Dragon stepped over Dexter's body. He paced back to the tiny table and rolled up the schematic. Then he ripped the DVD player from under the TV and pocketed an iPod he saw lying on the IKEA cupboard shelf. He spotted Dexter's jacket slung over a stool in the kitchen just off the lounge. He yanked the wallet from the inside pocket, deliberately ripping the lining. Finally, he threw the low table at the TV screen. The image of the football game flicked off with a dull thud just as the Broncos quarterback took a snap.

With the scene left looking like a regular armed break-in – the sort of thing that happened a dozen times a week in this part of LA – the Dragon pocketed his gun, walked calmly back along the hall, left the front door ajar and headed back to his car. No one saw him leave.

26

The Dragon cut from Glendale Freeway south onto Hollywood, hitting the traffic full on. Cops were everywhere. A hundred yards ahead was a checkpoint. The Dragon glanced through his rear window. It was bumper to bumper, and there were no slip roads off the freeway before the checkpoint. He pulled the gun from his pocket and put it next to the Yarygin PYa in the metal box under the seat. He twisted the key and slipped it into the glove compartment. The other weapons he had already deposited at the lair opposite the CCC before visiting Dexter Tate.

The car in front of him was waved over to the hard shoulder by two motorcycle cops, and for a second the Dragon thought he would be allowed to drive on. But then he too was asked to pull over. A cop went to each car. One of them stood by the door of the Toyota and signalled to the Dragon to lower the window, then asked for his license. Without a word, he handed over the piece of plastic.

'Could you step out of the vehicle, please, sir?'

The Dragon complied. The cop frisked him.

'Pop the trunk, please.'

The Dragon leaned into the car and pushed the button. The trunk lock opened and the lid swung up. The cop walked round and glanced into the empty compartment.

'Are you carrying a weapon, sir?' the cop asked and stared straight into The Dragon's eyes.

The Dragon met his stare with just the right measure of nervousness. 'Er . . . no, officer.'

The cop went to search the inside of the car. As he ducked inside, he flicked a glance at the streams of traffic. 'What the –' He took a step back and saw his colleague running towards him, yelling into his radio as he went.

Passing the checkpoint, weaving between the cars, were two elderly people on mountain bikes. Each of them had signs attached to the backs of their saddles. One said '2 Wheels Good, 4 Wheels Bad', and the other 'Dump The Car – Take The Bike'.

In a moment, both cops were on their motorcycles, revving them up and pulling into the lines of traffic. The Dragon was as stunned as the policemen, but he found it much funnier. Beaming, he lowered himself into the Toyota and nosed back into the traffic.

27

Simon Gardiner was silent as he walked a pace ahead of his parents. They reached the bottom of the stairs leading out of the police station as the last rays of the setting sun broke through the distant palms lining the freeway. They could see the black silhouettes of cars and the haze of headlights.

'Your lack of smugness is irritating, son,' Marty said, half-seriously.

Nancy nudged her husband and gave him a withering look.

'Oh, don't worry, Dad, I feel *very* smug. Let's just view my callout fee as a down payment to cover putting me through Law School.'

'I suppose it had to come in useful some day!' his father retorted.

Simon led them to his Mercedes saloon.

'I'm pissed they won't let us have our bikes,' Marty snapped. 'Really pissed.'

'Oh, come on, Pa! What did you expect?'

'It's an infringement of our civil liberties. Why didn't you do something about it?'

'You forfeited your civil liberties when you decided to take your protest onto the city's freeways,' Simon replied tartly. 'You can have the bikes tomorrow. Now let's get home. Maureen's making a blackberry pie, apparently.'

Marty and Nancy looked at each other. 'We're going on,' Nancy Gardiner said.

Simon gave them both a frosty look. 'So what are you going to do this time? Walk along the freeway?' He suddenly felt furious. He loathed all this green nonsense. It was for hippies and layabouts. Somehow, though, his parents – of all people – had been corrupted by the 'pinkos' and trouble-makers.

Marty was about to snap back when Nancy raised a hand to stop him. 'It's not far, Simon. There'll be a bus on 6th Avenue.'

'Oh, for Christ's sake! Why? Why are you being so, so . . . pig-headed? What's gotten into you two?'

The elderly couple said nothing as their son glared at them, pulled the keys from his pocket and pushed the remote to unlock the car. 'Fine! Catch a freakin' bus. Have fun.' And he spun on his heel.

Simon Gardiner sat in his car for several minutes, trying to calm himself. His doc had told him not to get overexcited, to watch his blood pressure. Ever since his parents had turned up he'd done the exact opposite. He hit the steering wheel and filled the air with expletives. After a moment, he felt a little better for letting off steam. They had their hearts in the right place – he knew that. They were good people, just misguided.

Perhaps they're going a little senile, Simon thought, and suddenly an image of his mother and father 30 years younger flashed into his mind. They were going out for the evening and he had been left with his brother and a babysitter. His parents were dressed in their best and looked incredibly elegant – they were wealthy high-fliers, and very good-looking. He remembered thinking how he wanted to be just like his father when he was older, and how he would have a beautiful wife too – if not as beautiful as his mom, then close.

He took a deep breath, turned the key in the ignition and pulled out of the lot.

He saw them twenty yards ahead, walking arm-in-arm along the sidewalk. For a few moments they remained oblivious of him. He could tell from their body language that they were perfectly happy. It was almost as though they were enjoying the adventure. Then Nancy laughed suddenly, looked at Marty's profile, kissed him on the cheek and settled her head on his shoulder.

They heard the car and turned. He pulled up beside them, lowered the window and stuck his head out.

'You don't need to,' Marty said.

'I know that. But if you don't get in, I promise I will drive right around Los Angeles revving the engine at every stop sign until I drain the tank. My carbon footprint will be so big you'll see it from space.'

28

The nerves kicked in right on cue, 45 minutes before his appearance. Kyle Foreman knew the routine well and was pacing his room in anticipation. Three minutes later came a knock on the door. His personal assistant stuck his head into the room.

'Okay,' Foreman said, and straightened his tie in the mirror. 'Let's go.'

There was a uniformed cop with the CIA bodyguards in the corridor. One of the CIA men led, the other trailed at the back. After years in the spotlight Senator Foreman was used to security, but it never made him feel entirely safe. Like everyone else, he had seen the film of Kennedy having his head blown off from at least two directions. Years later, Ronald Reagan had almost bought it when John Hinckley, Jr, tried to make his day. There was only so much humans could do to protect him from other humans.

The hotel room was on the seventh floor of the Hilton, to the rear of the CCC. It was a twenty-storey structure that was always full. The elevator took them down to the third floor where the hospitality area was located. From there, he would be picked up in precisely 29 minutes and escorted across a glass-ceilinged bridge on the first level, to the CCC building itself. Another elevator would take him down one floor to the ground level, and from there, he would arrive backstage exactly three minutes before he was due to walk on.

In the hospitality suite Foreman found a small group awaiting him. The general manager of the CCC/Hilton complex shook his hand and a young woman in a tight black skirt and white blouse offered him a glass of champagne. He declined and asked for a Perrier with ice and lemon.

'No need for Dutch courage?' the general manager joked, taking a sip of champagne.

'Never before the show,' Foreman replied. 'But after . . . that's another matter.'

Foreman took a seat and thanked the waitress as she deposited his drink on a side table. The CIA guys stood by the door, while the cop paced the corridor outside. A black LAPD helicopter flew past the window and heads turned to watch it swoop away.

'Certainly looks like they're taking care of me,' Foreman said. He lifted his glass. 'To the security services!' He was smiling, but beneath the surface he felt uncomfortable, even more uncomfortable than normal just before an appearance. 'Now, ladies and gentlemen,' he added. 'If you don't mind, I have a few final checks to make on my speech.'

Foreman's assistant placed a gentle hand on the general manager's arm. The man got the message, handed his empty glass to the waitress and led his little group out into the corridor. 'Good luck, Senator,' he called back. Foreman glanced up and mouthed a silent 'Thank you' as his assistant handed him his speech and a red pen.

The best way to quell the nerves, he knew from experience, was simply to keep busy. But there was something extra tonight. Something he couldn't put his finger on. *Perhaps I'm just anxious about Sandy*, he tried to convince himself. But he knew that this was not the sum of it. What he was feeling ran deeper than mere anxiety. He had no idea where it had come from, and he was certainly no believer in any form of sixth sense, but the feeling was inescapable. The only word for it was 'foreboding'.

29

Nancy and Marty Gardiner made it to the CCC with just minutes to spare. At the door, an assistant saw them and bumped them up the queue, ahead of a group of three young guys. One of the kids, a tall young man with long hair tucked behind his ears, was about to protest, but his friend, a kid in very baggy jeans and a 49ers sweatshirt, kicked his ankle and he held his tongue.

They found their seats easily enough. Marty pulled a pair of ancient opera glasses from his backpack and handed them to Nancy. She put them on her lap for a moment as she extricated a plastic container from her shoulder bag. She removed the lid and fished around inside. Pulling out a sandwich wrapped in silver foil, she handed it to her husband. Then she replaced the lid, put the box back in the bag and picked up the opera glasses. All she could see was a black curtain across the stage.

Marty checked his watch. 'They don't look terribly organised,' he said matter-of-factly. 'They're bound to start late.'

'Relax, honey,' Nancy replied. 'It's not the army . . . and at least we made it on time.'

Marty smiled and patted her hand. 'Fantastic PB and J,' he said, and took another bite.

30

Precisely 338 feet away, the Dragon had also taken his seat, but he was considerably less comfortable. He was perched on a crate and was covered in camouflage netting. In front of him stood his two M60 7.62 mm machine guns. On the floor to his right he had placed his ammunition box. To his left was a leather box containing the six M67 fragmentation hand grenades. In the waistband of his trousers he had his trusty Magnum and the Mark XIX Desert Eagle .50 AE. In his jacket pocket he carried the Yarygin PYa.

He removed a small plastic unit from the pocket of his pants – a remote control. Between his feet was a squat metal box, on the top face of which was a row of lights. One of the lights was green, the others red. The Dragon ran his fingers over the keypad of the remote, punching in a numeric code sequence. One of the red lights turned green. He then depressed the 'enter' key and the remaining red lights turned green. He was ready.

31

The lights came up and Kyle Foreman strode onto the vast stage to tumultuous applause. He waved as he walked to the podium. Half the audience were on their feet. It took a full minute before he could calm the crowd into silence and return them to their seats.

'Good evening,' he said. 'I'm simply thrilled to see this place filled to the rafters, and I know many of you have travelled a long way to come here tonight. But, you know, it is yet another show of strength.' He stretched out his arms, as though he was embracing the audience. They cheered. 'I like to think of us as crusaders because, make no mistake, we are fighting a war. A war of ideologies. And I believe with all my heart that it is a war of right versus wrong. A war in which no blood will be shed, for sure, but a battle to the death nevertheless. The only way to save our planet is to engage in this fight – and to win it.' He hit the podium with the palm of his hand. 'The wrong-thinkers must not prevail. Our ideology is stronger.'

A massive cheer. People were on their feet again.

'I've prepared a short film I would like you to see,' Foreman announced, and suddenly the lights dimmed again before a huge screen lit up at the back of the stage. The film began with images of ice shelves falling into the

113

ocean, and moved on to some dramatic footage of wild weather. Foreman was speaking over the movie, a scripted commentary describing how mean temperatures had increased steadily and how levels of carbon dioxide in the atmosphere were directly responsible. A bar chart in primary colours appeared.

That was the moment the first bomb exploded.

The first thing anyone felt was the shaking. The room seemed to judder like a celluloid image caught in a projector. Many in the CCC thought an earthquake had hit. But then came the roaring sound, and the doors to the auditorium blew in, sending great chunks of wood and metal across the open space. A steel post soared through the air and smashed into one of three vast chandeliers. Thousands of pieces of glass cascaded onto the audience like hailstones. The lights went out and the auditorium erupted, instantly killing half the people there.

On the podium, Kyle Foreman saw the doors shatter and debris burst into the room. He dived to the side of the stage, seeing glass tumbling, blood spraying, severed limbs flying through the air. He fell from the edge of the stage and landed on something soft. Pulling himself to his knees, he looked down. A faint light coming from the nearest demolished doorway revealed the headless corpse of one of his bodyguards. Two seconds earlier the man had been standing at the side of the stage looking out towards the audience.

When a second explosion hit, Foreman dropped again. Covering his head with his hands, he scrambled under a table to the side of the auditorium. This explosion was much bigger. The room shook so hard he thought the ceiling would come down. A high-pitched sound came from a few inches above his head and he risked opening his eyes for a second. A crack an inch wide had appeared in the wall and was shooting up towards the ceiling. The room shook again and the sound of crashing masonry and glass mingled with the roar of the flames. Foreman heard screams and guttural moans as hundreds of people were incinerated.

Foreman glanced behind him and saw what he thought was a metal screen, but then he realised it was a steel sliding door. He threw himself into a small opening at one side of the door and tried desperately to slide it shut behind him. A fireball ripped through the auditorium, and even from behind the metal door the heat was searing. He was thrown backwards and slammed into a pile of plastic containers, sending them flying across the floor. Pain rippled along his arm.

The senator picked himself up and could just make out the contours of the space. It was a narrow corridor with a door at the far end. He stumbled towards it in the gloom, the heat from the auditorium still scorching his back. In the dark it was difficult to find the handle. His hand brushed against metal. He yanked at it. Nothing. It was locked.

His mind racing, Foreman grabbed for his cell phone. He could see from the illuminated screen that he had a very weak signal. Desperately, he stabbed at the keypad: 9, 1, 1. He heard the dial tone, then a click.

Foreman looked at the screen in disbelief. *Connection lost*, it read.

He dialled again. The words *No signal* appeared on the screen. He hit the phone with his fist and yelped in pain, then threw his arms down in despair. The screen light on the cell went out.

Foreman turned to survey the corridor, his eyes wild in the dark. He was sweating profusely, his breath coming in gasps. He could see no other exit. Ahead lay the inferno of the auditorium. Behind him a locked door. He hammered on the door in a futile attempt to break through by sheer willpower. Then he began to scream.

32

There were 32 satellites in total, each of them put into orbit seven months earlier. BigEye 1 through BigEye 32 had been launched in a single array from the Space Shuttle *Endeavour*. Now they formed a girdle around the earth at a mean altitude of between 22,330 and 22,335 miles. This altitude is known in the trade as a geosynchronous orbit, which is a fancy term for when a satellite orbits at the same rate as the planet turns. This means it stays in one position relative to the surface: it sort of 'hovers'. Between them these satellites could monitor 98 per cent of the planet's surface. And they were packed with some of the most advanced digital information collection and processing devices CARPA could offer; the sort of stuff that would not be seen in a conventional NASA or ESA satellite for at least two decades.

The BigEye satellites could detect any form of 'unconventional disturbance' on Earth. They could filter out, almost instantaneously, any 'registered' or 'legitimate' explosion, gas emission or radiation burst, and they could notify the ground crew of E-Force of any natural disturbance above a designated level. The moment an earthquake, a volcanic eruption, a bomb blast or a catastrophic gas leak occurred, a BigEye would know about it. The instant a serious gunfight broke out or a riot began, a BigEye would sound a warning.

But detection was just the beginning. A single BigEye, smaller than an automobile engine, possessed more processing power than the Pentagon. It could analyse the chemical composition of a gas leak in a building to one part in a billion. It could produce high-res 3D images of a dust mote from 22,000 miles up, and it could locate the heat from a human being five floors below ground. It could pick up the sound of a heartbeat.

BigEye 7 was positioned 22,334 miles above southern California when the bombs exploded at grid reference 34° 02′ 22.77″ N, 118° 16′ 03.93″ W, the California Conference Center in downtown Los Angeles. The first bomb blast was at 19.17.36 Pacific Standard Time, the second at 19.17.41. Travelling at the speed of light, the energy emitted from the blasts took about 0.12 seconds to reach BigEye 7's photoelectric detectors and gamma-ray receptors. Zero point six seconds later, the central processor array instructed the retro rockets to realign the satellite and the radiation detectors to focus on a circle half a mile in diameter with the CCC at its epicentre. Another 1.3 seconds passed before twelve of those detectors began to collect data. Information concerning chemical emissions and sound would take much longer to reach the satellites, but when that data arrived it would be added to the mix to give a fuller picture of what had happened.

The two explosions were 4.7 seconds apart, the second more powerful than the first. The detonation rate – the speed of the explosive wave-front – was 18,649 feet per second for the first explosion, and 19,989 feet per second for the second. The detectors aboard BigEye 7 quickly pinpointed the precise locations of each explosion. The first had been on the Ground Floor of the CCC, and the second on the Lower Ground Floor, directly beneath Hall A. First indications from BigEye 7's radiation detectors showed that the explosive material was non-nuclear. From the explosion profile and detonation rate, it was most probably a variant of HBX-1, a blend of TNT and RDX, a white crystalline substance often called hexogen and composed of calcium chloride and a wax dubbed D-2.

Even before a fireball with a measured mean temperature of 6960K ripped through Hall A – some seven seconds after the second blast – a warning signal was sent from BigEye 7 to Base One. With it was transmitted all the data gathered from the explosion sites up to that moment, a packet of just over 3 gigabytes of information. BigEye 7 then passed on a constant stream of updates as more data was collected.

Nine point two seconds after the second explosion, the first human beyond the immediate vicinity of the California Conference Center became aware that a catastrophic explosion had occurred in downtown Los Angeles. That person was Tam Finnegan, Technician 1st Class, at Base One, Tintara.

33

They were all gathered in Cyber Control. On the large screen was a map of Los Angeles.

'This is what we know so far,' Mark Harrison began. He was standing closest to the big screen and was wearing a black boilersuit and boots. He had been on a training exercise with Stephanie and Pete when he received the news. 'A BigEye has detected two large explosions at grid reference 34° 02′ 22.77″ N, 118° 16′ 03.93″ W. The first occurred eleven minutes ago at 19.17 PST. The second one came very soon after.'

The image on the screen changed as the computer zeroed in on the reference. A satellite image of downtown LA now filled the screen, and as the edges fell away the California Conference Center grew. Soon they could all see the large complex of buildings girded by the Santa Monica and Harbor freeways. There were two massive holes in the roof, and what looked like lunar craters all around the gutted infrastructure. On closer inspection, the gaping black holes were huge jagged openings in the metal roof pinpointing the epicentres of the explosions. All around the building lay concrete pillars, piles of twisted metal and a carpet of shattered glass. The image began to move again, focussing in on the building. They could see lumps of red and pink, and vaguely human shapes that were black as pitch.

119

Cyber Control was silent, apart from the hum and occasional click of one of the many machines in the room. Then Mark's voice cut in. 'Some of you may recognise this building. It is the California Conference Center. At the time of the explosion it was host to a special event, a speech by Senator Kyle Foreman, the founder of OneEarth. The hall he was speaking in has a capacity of 1100, and it was a sell-out – there was a queue outside the main entrance of the CCC.'

'Any idea of casualty figures?' Peter asked.

'It's not possible to say for sure. The local emergency services are on their way as we speak. We can only make an educated guess based on what we have from the BigEye.' He took two paces towards the main computer console, where Tom was positioned in his electric wheelchair. 'Sybil,' Mark said to the air, 'can we have the stats for the explosion, please?'

The female voice of the computer answered immediately, and at the same time numbers flashed up on the big screen. 'According to BigEye 7, the first blast had an explosive power of 18,649 feet per second. The second, 19,989 feet per second. Mean temperature at the epicentre of first blast was 6960K; for the second, 7180K.'

'Pete,' Mark said, turning towards him. 'You're the expert. What's that in English?'

Peter Sherringham shook his head. 'Not good,' he said, and ran a hand through his hair. 'Very bad, actually. Each blast was equivalent to about a ton of TNT. In the same ballpark as a very big airborne bomb used in Iraq.'

'Latest data from BigEye 7 suggests the first blast was equivalent to 0.9 tons of TNT, the second 1.2 tons,' Sybil confirmed.

'What about the type of explosive?' Pete asked, joining Tom at the console. 'Anything from the satellite, Sybil?'

'Preliminary spectroscopic analysis indicates the presence of at least 24 different chemicals. The most common are calcium chloride, a complex manmade wax, possibly D-2, and high levels of phosphorus.'

'Aye, it's an HBX explosive.'

'Which is?' Josh asked.

'A very powerful plastic explosive used by the military. A fistful of the stuff would produce blasts like these. It's practically odourless and easily hidden. Bloody perfect for this sort of operation.'

'Who uses it, apart from the military? Is it a signature explosive?'

'Yeah, it was a favourite of al-Qaeda. But the Chechen rebels used it too. Iraqi resistance forces dabbled with it. It's popular.'

Mark joined Pete and Tom beside the computer console. 'So what are we looking at in terms of damage?'

Pete shook his head, looking at his feet. He let out a heavy sigh. 'It's not going to be pretty, Mark. I'd put it at 90 per cent kill rate within a hundred feet of the blast. But of course there's no accounting for where the bombs were placed and what the structure of the Conference Center is like. Look at 9/11. Who could have imagined the towers coming down?'

There was another long silence. No one seemed to know what to say.

Then Stephanie spoke. 'Mark, what are you thinking?'

'That we're not ready.'

Peter, Josh and Steph all protested simultaneously.

'We've almost completed training. We know what we're doing,' Josh declared.

Mark raised both hands. 'I understand your enthusiasm. It's admirable, but we cannot risk –'

'Mark, don't talk crap,' Pete stated bluntly.

Mark looked stunned for a moment, then said, 'Okay. The emergency services are on their way. We can offer them assistance from here, satellite data, anything that will help.'

'That's horseshit, Mark, and you know it,' Josh spat. 'We could go into parts of the building the emergency services can't reach. We could ferry the injured to hospitals. We could put out fires, stabilise the roof, use our heavy lifting gear to rescue survivors. There's plenty to do, for God's sake.'

Mark whirled on him. 'Oh, right! You make it sound easy, Josh! Do you think I like turning my back on a disaster like this? Huh? You know as well as I do that if we go in unprepared we could do more harm than good. This isn't a game.' Then, with uncharacteristic venom, he added, 'Be grateful it's not your decision, my friend.'

Josh was bristling, but took a deep breath and kept quiet.

'The best thing we can –'

'Sir?' It was one of the technicians at the terminals.

Mark spun on his heel. 'Yes?'

'Priority red call, sir. It's Senator Mitchell.'

Mark took a few paces towards the big screen, which had now lit up with the visage of a man in his mid-sixties. White hair swept across his head. He had piercing dark-brown eyes and a small mouth. Senator Evan Mitchell had been Mark's most enthusiastic supporter in establishing E-Force.

'Senator.'

'You've heard, of course.'

'Yes.'

'What do you plan to do?'

'We're not ready to move. I'm sorry.'

'That is a pity,' Mitchell said. 'Have you taken a straw poll?' And he gazed into the face of each of the team, beginning with Josh, who still looked extremely tense.

'We're not a democracy.'

'No, I understand. It's just that I think you're going to have to be ready.'

'What are you talking about?'

'We've just traced a call made from Senator Kyle Foreman's cell phone. A call to 911. He's alive, or at least he was a few minutes ago. You have to get him out of there, along with anyone else you can save.'

No one spoke. Josh stared at Stephanie, who would not meet his gaze. Tom sat with his hands in his lap, a faint, unreadable smile playing about his lips.

'And this is not open to debate?'

'I understand your anxiety, Mark. Believe me.'

'But you want me to risk the lives of the team and the very real possibility we'll screw up on our first mission. What a great ad that would make.'

'That hardly sounds like the ringing endorsement your team deserves, does it?' Senator Mitchell looked around at the others again.

'You're twisting my words, Senator,' Mark responded. 'I have every faith in my team.'

'Excellent. So that's settled then. Keep me appraised, Mark.'

'Hang on,' Mark snapped. 'How on earth did you know Senator Foreman used his cell?'

Senator Evan Mitchell smiled briefly. 'Don't sound so surprised, Mark. I would have thought it was obvious. Kyle Foreman's a very important man. His phone has been tapped for at least a year.'

34

Mark Harrison lowered himself onto a stool close to Tom Erickson's workstation, crossed his legs, and folded his arms over his chest. After a moment, he looked at the team gathered around him. 'Well, that's that, then. We'd better get to work.'

'Mark –' Stephanie began.

He raised a hand. 'Enough has been said, Steph. But I just want you all to know, I have never doubted your abilities for a second. It's simply that this thing has never been tested. It's . . .'

'Risky?' Josh offered.

Mark shook his head. 'And then some.'

Tom brought a schematic of the CCC and the surrounding area up on the big screen. 'There are two parts to it,' he began. 'First, the 20-storey Hilton Hotel. From the BigEye images, it looks like it got off very lightly, just superficial damage.' Aerial shots of the tower with shattered windows appeared at one side of the big screen.

'There's a bridge on the first floor linking the Hilton with the Conference Center. Or at least, there was. It's collapsed. The other building is the CCC itself. It's a low, squat structure only four floors high, but spread out over a large area. However, there are six floors below ground. Mostly parking, but also admin and storage areas.

'There are six elevators serving all ten floors of the complex. It has four sets of emergency stairs, two at each end of the building.' Tom ran his hands over the virtual keyboard and a cursor indicated the stairs. 'There is also a large service lift, here.' A red cursor moved to the back of the building. 'This is for accessing the main storage area on B6, the deepest level of the complex. It runs directly from B6 to Ground, but does not go up to the other three floors.'

'Okay, Tom. What about the surrounding area?' Josh asked.

'It's smack in the middle of downtown LA, tucked up close to the junction of the 10 and 110 freeways. There's a large ground-level car park to the south-east of the main building. Directly opposite the main entrance is a low-rise mall, a Kmart, a Dunkin' Donuts and a gas station.'

'Well,' Mark said. 'As you know, we work with the emergency services whenever we can. We can see paramedics and firefighters have just been mobilised. The Los Angeles County operational coordinator will have been notified. Like everywhere, post-9/11, they'll have well-rehearsed procedures for responding to an incident like this. At least, I hope they do.

'Our orders are clear. We have to focus on the senator and whoever else is with him. Josh, you go ahead in a Silverback. Steph and Pete, you follow on in the Big Mac. We'll go through the equipment you'll need and get it on board ASAP.'

'What about Mai?' Stephanie asked.

'She'll be with her mother in Houston, I imagine. I'll contact her right away. If she's able to join us, I'll get her picked up. We have a base there with a Silverback on permanent standby. She should make it to LA about the same time you two get there.'

'Tom,' Mark added, 'I'll need the mayor and the emergency response coordinator.'

'They're going to be up to their necks in it.'

'I'm aware of that, but I must have their clearance. If there's any resistance from either of them, go straight to the governor. And if that fails, get Senator Mitchell to call the White House direct. Let's go.'

35

California Conference Center, Los Angeles

The first people to respond to the explosions at the CCC were those just beyond the blast radius who managed to escape injury and scramble for their cell phones. Most called their homes to speak to loved ones, but a few dialled 911. Information concerning the blasts was conveyed to the office of the disaster management area coordinator (DMAC), some two miles away from the explosions. Staff at the office had heard and felt the blasts, but it was not until they received the call that they knew for sure a major incident had occurred.

The DMAC was an old hand and had dealt with more than a dozen major incidents in LA since taking up the position over a decade earlier. He knew the emergency management system as though it were etched into his brain, and he flew into action. His first call was to the County Emergency Operations Center (CEOC), located some three miles away from his office. The staff there had heard and felt nothing, not only because they were further away from the explosions. Their building could shake off such effects in the way a super-tanker would react to the wake from a toy boat. After making his report, the DMAC placed his number two, the assistant management area coordinator, in charge. He was then driven to the CEOC.

The operational area coordinator (OAC) was called, along with the director of health services (DHS). They headed straight for the CEOC. En route, the OAC called the

Californian governor, the Area H fire chief, the police chief and the Community Emergency Response Team. Meanwhile, the DHS contacted the health authorities, who immediately put all local hospitals on red alert and mobilised scores of paramedics and the Red Cross.

At the CEOC, advisors contacted the chief administrative officer, the Department of Beaches and Harbors, the Department of Children's Services and the Department of Public Social Services. In that first wave of calls they also alerted the Department of Parks and Recreation so they could prepare areas for evacuees.

As soon as the governor heard the news, he called the Federal Emergency Management Agency, the Transportation Security Agency and the White House. After consultation with the President, White House staff contacted the Department of Homeland Security, the CIA, the FBI and the North American Aerospace Defense Command (NORAD), which had the second-largest satellite network in the world.

A chain of command was quickly established. Protocol dictated that this remain a local management issue unless a direct call for outside help was made. The federal government had been contacted almost immediately because no one could be certain the explosion at the CCC was an isolated incident. As the federal agencies swung into action, the chain of command in Los Angeles started to take shape. And on the ground – at the frontline – things began to move fast.

36

Methodist Sugar Land Hospital, Houston, Texas

The digital clock on the wall read 21:25. Outside, the night was shredded by city neon. From the eighth floor of the hospital, Maiko Buchanan could see all the way to George Bush Park, a distant smudge of darkness nestled in the urban glow.

It was very quiet in the room, just the steady wheeze of the respirator and the occasional click and whir of the machines keeping her mother, Eri, alive. Mai walked back from the window and sat in the chair beside the bed. She could only see parts of her mother's face, the soft pale flesh around the respirator mask, and her eyelids, almost translucent and flickering. Eri Kato's white hair, still luxuriant, lay across her left shoulder. There were two tubes running from under the right sleeve of her gown. They trailed away to shiny boxes beside the bed.

Mai held her mother's hand. 'You haven't had much of a life, have you, Mom?' she said quietly. 'And just when I was able to help, you go and have a stroke.'

Images were racing through Maiko's mind. Memories of her disciplinarian father, who had believed females should be married off at the earliest opportunity and should never work outside the home. Mai had started to resent him before she had reached her tenth birthday, and she had quickly realised the best way to get back at the man was to do the very opposite of what he expected of her. She was not going to follow the example of her mother and subsume her personality to his liking.

Maiko had excelled at school, won a scholarship to college and left home. Her father disowned her. Her mother was forbidden to see her again. But, of course, she had ignored this command. Eri and Mai would meet whenever they could, clandestinely, for almost five years. Mai had only gone to her father's funeral to keep her mother company. She'd been surprised at just how little she had felt as the coffin was lowered into the soil. She hadn't even felt relief – she had moved far beyond that.

It was probably another act of rebellion that had got her pregnant at college. The father of the child never knew he had played a role. And it was certainly more rebellion that had given her the strength to keep the baby, her daughter Greta, and to keep studying and to graduate with a GPA of 4.5, the best in her year.

That had probably been the hardest part – until recently. After obtaining a PhD, Maiko had joined NASA and risen through the ranks. By the age of 32 she had her own command mission aboard the *Discovery*. Yet as she was reaching her peak as an astronaut, her family was falling into disarray. She had married and divorced, and now found she had sacrificed far too much in achieving her goals ever to find a balance between family and work. Greta had begun to drift away when she hit puberty. Now Mai rarely saw her, and when mother and daughter did get together they could barely exchange a civil word.

There was a light tap at the door. The face of a young woman appeared. She had a puckish face, bunches of black hair and too much eye-shadow. She looked startled for a moment. 'Mom.'

Mai stood up and went to put her arms around her daughter. The girl stood like a piece of wood and Mai pulled back. 'Pleased to see me, then,' Mai said. Her voice was sad rather than sarcastic.

The girl was chewing gum. She shrugged. 'I didn't think you would bother.'

'What is that supposed to mean?'

Greta shrugged again.

'How did you get here?'

'Dad dropped me off.'

They walked over to the prone form lying in the bed.

'So why *are* you here?' Greta asked.

'She's my mother. What do you expect?'

'Thought you'd be too busy with Buzz Lightyear.'

Mai glared at her. 'If all you can do is insult me you can just go back to your *step*father's.'

There was a pained silence between them. 'Look . . .' Mai began.

'Save it, Mom. It's such a cliché – estranged mother and daughter bond over sick granny.'

'Why, you –' Mai stood up, fury etched into her face. A loud beep came from under her left sleeve. Instinctively, she pulled back the fabric. On her wrist was a metal bracelet, with a high-res screen that lit up like a beacon in the dim room. A face appeared.

'What the hell is *that*?' Greta exclaimed.

Mai ignored her, and with a supreme effort composed herself. 'Mark. What a pleasant surprise.'

'I'm sorry, Mai. I wouldn't have disturbed you, but –'

'What's happened?'

'Two bombs in a conference centre in downtown LA.'

'But we're not operational.'

'We are . . . as of three minutes ago.'

Mai swallowed hard. 'Okay.'

'We need you.'

She turned away from the screen, noticing the stunned look on her daughter's face, and felt the undertow of emotion. What lay there? Sadness? Resentment? Pity? She turned back to the tiny screen and nodded.

37

Fire Station 9, Los Angeles

Captain James McNally was 59 years old. He had been in
one of the first fire trucks to arrive at the World Trade Center
on 9/11, and that day he had seen dozens of his colleagues
die. A year later he had retired and moved to Los Angeles
with his invalid wife, Geraldine. But the boredom of early
retirement was killing him, so he joined the Los Angeles
Fire Department. Initially, his was a teaching role, but he
could never resist the smell of a fire and the power struggle
between man and nature.

The call had come into the station at 7.22 pm, and they
were out of there within 90 seconds, roaring through the
gates of Fire Station 9 and onto E 7th Street. It was smack
in the middle of Skid Row, one of the most deprived and
dangerous areas in Los Angeles. Even this early in the evening,
it was getting pretty funky. Station 9 was the busiest in the
country, dealing with 50 or 60 incidents a day, of which
only a few were fires. The crews at Station 9 were the last
defenders of the public, going in to mop up junkies or to get
smashed-up kids to hospital after the cops had given up or
were too busy with bigger business.

McNally watched the ramshackle shops flash by, the light
from the fire truck doing battle with the cheap neon. All the
trucks had left in convoy, with his in the lead. One of his
young guys was at the wheel. Freddie Bantelli was only 21,
with just a year on the job. He was still full of enthusiasm

and sincere in the belief that he could change the world. The word was that something really huge was going down; so maybe Bantelli would have his chance.

Captain McNally surveyed the small screen of the laptop fixed to the dash. It was part sat-nav, part feed to the internet, but in his old-fashioned way he felt more at home keeping in constant touch with the communications operator, a human being sitting in a control room.

At Main, they cut left, blaring the horn every few hundred feet. From a side street to the north they saw another truck heading towards them.

'That's from Station 14,' said Bantelli, nodding towards the vehicle, its lights blazing and horn blaring.

'Yep. Whatever's going down, it's big,' McNally responded. He turned to the radio. 'This is 9-Alpha. Got anything new for us, guys?'

'9-Alpha. What's your ETA?'

McNally glanced at the laptop. 'Six minutes.'

'Roger that. Incident is a multiple blast. Paramedics are right behind you. We expect high casualty figures. The structure of the CCC has been compromised. Advise extreme caution. I repeat, extreme caution.'

McNally knew precisely what the operator meant – there could be more bombs.

The operator was talking again. 'Looks like you'll be the first rig there, 9-Alpha,' she said. 'You'll soon have company. We're bringing them in from across the city, as far as San Fernando. Out.'

McNally whistled and turned to the other three men in the back of the rig, Gene Connor, Maney Steinberg and Raul Burgos. Their faces were flushed with excitement. Two helicopters roared overhead – LAPD – their searchlights sweeping across the glistening city.

Apart from the emergency vehicles, the streets were unnervingly quiet. One of the guys at the station said he'd felt the explosions. This close to the incident it must have seemed like a quake. Anyone with half a brain would have hunkered down.

They took Main all the way to Pico and hung a right, sweeping across the lanes, cars and trucks stationary or heading away from the CCC, east along Pico Boulevard.

They were only a couple hundred yards away now. The smell of burning was getting intense. McNally signalled to the guys in the back and they all put on their masks. He held the wheel as Bantelli did the same. McNally gave the operator an update.

Halfway through his report the truck came over the crest of a hill and they could see the incident site for the first time. 'Holy crap!' McNally said slowly. Then he fell silent as the operator babbled away. He had only ever seen anything like this once before. The memory of that day still burned in his brain, as hot as the fires he'd fought, the fires that had killed his friends and colleagues. 'Bastards!' he said quietly.

38

Base One, Tintara

The main hangar at Base One was foaming with human activity. At one end Ringo, one of the Silverback jets, was being made ready for its first operational flight. It was a small aircraft, 49 feet from the tip of its shapely nose to its tail, with a wingspan of only 27 feet. But it was incredibly beautiful, like a flying Ferrari or something designed by Philippe Starck. Each of the Silverbacks had been sprayed a distinctive colour. Ringo was a metallic auburn, John was black, Paul grey and George a deep blue. Each was coated with Camoflin, the high-tech material that confused cameras and camcorders.

A team of engineers in pale-green boilersuits was making final checks. One man was lying on the wing and peering into the sleek port engine. He adjusted something inside, carefully closed the engine cover and slid off the wing to the floor of the hangar. As he straightened up, he saw Josh Turner, kitted up in his cybersuit, striding towards Ringo.

'Ready to go, boss,' the engineer said. 'Good luck.'

Josh gave him an exaggerated salute and climbed a short flight of stairs. A panel in the side of the plane slid open, revealing three more steps up to the cockpit. The black Perspex-titanium canopy was levered upwards. Josh lowered himself into the padded seat. The panel on the side of the plane slid invisibly back into place.

Josh touched a sequence of keys on a virtual keypad to his left, and the canopy came down slowly, locked into place and let out a high-pitched hiss. He pulled on a lightweight helmet that covered his skull and ears like a swimming cap. Three thin wires hung in front of his face. The lower one, a tiny transceiver, came close to his mouth. The upper two were miniature projectors that displayed holographic images close to his eyes.

With the canopy closed, much of the noise from the hangar disappeared. Enclosed in this beautiful, sophisticated machine, the pinnacle of human technology, Josh felt empowered and protected. It excited him and he felt completely at home – almost a part of the machine itself.

In a way, this was more than just a feeling, because Josh was indeed interfaced with the Silverback. Nanobots that ran many of the plane's systems interacted directly with the nanobots in his suit, and they even communicated with those implanted in his ear, behind his eyes and in his brainstem. It was the closest anyone had come to genuine cyborg technology, a synthesis of human being and machine.

Josh surveyed the controls in front of him. The console was a single sleek piece of ultra-strong plastic. Imprinted into it was a collection of panels showing an array of lights and strips of colour. He ran his fingers over a virtual keypad and a holographic display appeared in front of him.

'Ringo's ready to roll,' he said into the transceiver.

'Copy.' It was Mark's voice from the control room. 'Opening roof.'

A moment later the vast roof of the hangar began to part. It was smooth and quiet, but surprisingly fast. Within ten seconds it had opened, revealing blue sky above.

'All systems green.'

'Copy that, Josh.'

'Initiating launch sequence.' His hands skittered over the virtual keys and he kept his eyes fixed on the holographic image now changing rapidly in front of him.

The twin engines under the wings of the Silverback began to hum. 'VTOL jets on green,' Josh said.

The plane began to lift. It slowly cleared the roof of the hangar. Then it appeared to hang in the air. Josh kicked in the main VTOL thrusters and the plane shot upward at phenomenal speed. Within seconds it had reached the first plateau of 10,000 feet. Josh then put the forward thrusters onto minimum power and the plane flew horizontally for a little over twelve seconds. It then started to climb vertically again. Three minutes after taking off from Base One, Ringo had reached its operation cruising altitude of 60,000 feet.

Pausing for a second, Josh sat back in his seat. 'Sybil?' he said. 'Play song selection 0891, please.' The opening notes of Lynard Skynyrd's 'Freebird' burst through his earpieces. Josh engaged the forward thrusters and gradually crept up the speed. Ninety seconds later he was rocketing towards the west coast of the United States at mach 10, heavy rock guitar reverberating through his cochlear implants.

Part Three

STATE OF EMERGENCY

39

California Conference Center, Los Angeles

When the banging started, Kyle Foreman was sitting on the floor with his back to the door, shaking from head to toe. He had no idea how long he had been there. All he could think about was Sandy – and the baby he would never see.

Shouts broke through the panic. At first, Foreman couldn't work out where the sound was coming from. Then he realised it was a human sound, voices and thumping on the door.

He pulled himself up and saw that the door had a glass panel above the handle. Through it he could just make out a shape on the other side. Then a face came into view. It was streaked with dirt and blood. A man. He was screaming something and coughing. Then, almost as though he was waking from a daze, Senator Foreman understood what the man was screaming. 'It opens from your side!'

'It's locked,' he shouted back. His chest was burning from the acrid fumes and he went into a coughing fit. Turning, he scanned the floor and the walls to see if there was anything – anything at all – that he could use to smash down the door. He could make out a shape to one side, and he crawled towards it on all fours. He was below the smoke but it was still getting into his throat. He had almost reached the object when he felt his stomach heave and he retched, feeling burning acid slither into his mouth.

Another effort and Foreman was there. It was a metal box. He cut himself on a sharp corner. Then, feeling around it

141

gingerly, he found a wire coming from one side. The other side had knobs and switches. Peering closely, he realised what it was – an amplifier from the sound system.

Crouching, Foreman picked up the amp and heaved it over to the door. 'Get back,' he yelled. He smashed the amp against the glass, which cracked but did not break. Foreman pulled back and again slammed the object forward. This time the glass shattered. Encouraged, he kept going, ramming the metal box against the wood of the door with all his strength. After four more blows, he was exhausted and feeling sick again. He paused, trying to breathe as little as possible.

Foreman watched as a small backpack flew through the opening. A leg appeared, then the rest of a man's body, a torso, an arm. He just fitted through the jagged opening, but cut himself on the splinters and shards of glass. He was a young, skinny guy with very short hair, wearing a pair of round glasses and a 49ers sweatshirt. One lens of his glasses was cracked. His bony face was filthy and he had a gash that ran from the bridge of his nose to his left cheek.

'I was trapped,' he was saying, 'in the john. Whole fucking place was shaking.' He was on the verge of hysteria. He bent down and pulled the backpack across his shoulders. Then he recognised Foreman. He started to say something but the senator took him by the arms.

'What's your name?'

'Dave,' the kid gasped. 'Dave Golding.'

'Dave. The passage your side. It's blocked, yeah?'

'Locked from the other side.' He nodded and gasped for air. 'A girder came down in front of it.'

Foreman looked back through the dim light towards the metal door at the end. 'There's only one way to go,' he said. 'Back to the auditorium.'

'But the heat –'

'We don't have any choice. Come on.'

The light grew redder as they approached the metal door. Foreman touched the door and recoiled. A searing pain shot up his arm. It was scolding hot. Yanking off his jacket, he bunched it around his palms and pushed on the door. It was stuck fast.

'Help me,' he said. 'Take off your sweatshirt.'

Dave did as he was told, wrapped the fabric around his hands and pushed as hard as he could against the metal sliding door. It gave, but they could feel the heat on their hands. Dave jumped back. Almost in tears, he was shaking his hands in pain. He bunched the shirt in his palms and they gave the door another push. It opened two feet. Just enough. A moment later they were on the other side.

Hall A was filled with smoke and the sounds of hopelessness – death groans. The only way they could move forward was to close their minds to it. They stumbled to the nearest wall, which was covered with cracks and smeared with blood. The only light came from the flames – reds, oranges, an occasional flash of purple.

They made it to the other side of the room. Foreman was trying to visualise where the room was in relation to the rest of the building. He had hardly noticed the Reception and the Main Concourse when he'd arrived earlier that day. All his thoughts had been focused on getting to his room, being alone. What a simpler life it once was.

'I need to stop,' Dave said. His breathing was laboured.

Foreman could feel the dust and smoke in his own throat. He leaned against the wall beside the kid. Two hunched shapes came out of the gloom, and Foreman and Dave saw they were an elderly couple. The woman was limping, and the man was supporting her and helping her along. Their clothes were shredded and blackened, faces cut and bloodied, and their white hair was flecked with purple from the glow of the fire.

143

As they reached the wall, the woman stumbled and fell forward into Foreman's arms. He and the elderly man managed to break her fall. The blood on her face was streaked with tears.

A few yards away, the wall had collapsed. There was a pile of smouldering rubble spread in a great jagged semicircle across the room. Underneath lay scores – perhaps hundreds – of bodies. From beyond the wall they could hear the sound of falling masonry, more moans, a gushing sound, water, steam. Looking down, Foreman noticed a small stream of water running from outside the room. It was pouring through the collapsed wall. At the edge of the rubble lay an industrial-sized water heater, its side ripped open. There was a terrible stink of burning rubber, charred hair and incinerated flesh.

The elderly woman looked up into Foreman's face and there was the sudden light of recognition in her eyes. She had a huge bruise on her left temple and small cuts all over her cheeks and under her eyes. He could see a sliver of glass protruding from the soft skin to one side of her nose.

'I think her leg is broken,' the elderly man said, his voice little more than a rasp.

'We've got to get out,' Foreman replied. 'There could be more bombs.'

The dread thought seemed to jolt the other three. Dave pushed away from the wall. 'Here,' he said, and took the old lady's arm and slung it over his shoulder. Foreman took the man's arm as gently as possible. 'Let me do this,' he said. He let the woman rest her weight on his shoulder.

They edged their way along the remains of the wall. 'Don't touch the water,' Foreman warned. 'It could be in contact with live wires.'

Picking through the rubble, they reached a point where the wall disappeared completely. They could see some of the Main Concourse. It was lit up from outside, and a few neon strips were still functioning. They hung from their wires and swung precariously, throwing wild shapes across the scene of devastation.

It was a massive space, at least 200 feet from end to end and almost as wide. It was obvious that the epicentre of one blast lay somewhere behind Reception. This area was completely obliterated, a ghastly black hole, strewn with rubble, girders, piles of wood and plastic, pieces of bodies. Clothing had been torn from victims and lay burning.

The air was a little clearer here but the fires were worse. Flames ran along the wall all the way to the auditorium and flickered up to the ceiling. Towards the main doors, whose frames were now twisted into jagged columns of metal, there were more lumps of charred flesh. A pair of jeans lay a few feet in front of them. Just visible in the flickering shadows were two red and white circles, stumps encased in skin-tight denim. The top half of the body was nowhere to be seen.

They saw movement ahead. Shapes formed out of the smoke and the irregular patterns of light. A young man and a young woman were leaning over two figures in the rubble. Dave and the senator lowered the elderly woman to the floor, and Foreman crouched beside her. 'What's your name, my dear?' he asked.

She looked up at his face and muttered something. He leaned closer. Her husband crouched on her other side. 'Her name's Nancy. I'm Marty Gardiner, Mr Foreman.' His voice was shaky.

'Nancy. You wait here a minute with Marty. We'll check out the main entrance.' He looked to Marty, who nodded. Foreman glanced down and realised his jacket was still wrapped around his hand. He unwound it, rolled it up and lifted Nancy's head, gently, placing the jacket under her.

Dave was walking towards the group of people a few yards ahead. Foreman went after him across the smouldering piles of rubble.

145

'Steve!' Dave exclaimed as he reached one of the figures. He looked down and saw Todd Evans on the floor. 'Todd!'

Todd's face was lined with pain. He nodded towards his arm and Dave could see it was covered with blood. A bone was protruding from the flesh midway between elbow and wrist, and his shirt was soaked with blood. Next to him lay a teenage girl. Her dress was ripped to ribbons and the front of it was crimson. Another young woman was crouched beside her, crying desperately.

Steve straightened up just as Foreman arrived. He did a double-take as he noticed the senator, but Foreman was already leaning over the young girl in the debris. She looked up at him, her eyes slightly unfocused. He took her pulse. Glancing at the other young woman, he said, 'Is she a friend of yours?'

'She's my sister, Jenny.'

'We have to get her out.'

Dave was at Foreman's side. 'Can you stand?' he asked Jenny.

She nodded weakly. 'I think so.'

'What's your name?' Foreman asked the other girl.

'Martina.'

'Okay, Martina. Stand back a second. Dave, you get Jenny's left side. On three.'

They lifted the girl and she swayed.

At that moment they heard a cry from behind them. Marty Gardiner screamed a terrible 'No!'

Foreman snapped back to Steve and Martina. 'You two – get a shoulder under each of Jenny's and find a way to the main doors. She'll die if she doesn't get attention immediately. Todd, you go with them.'

Foreman turned back towards the Gardiners, and Dave helped Todd to his feet. He stood up unsteadily and the pitiful little group staggered towards the doors.

It was slow going. The Main Concourse resembled a battlefield. Rubble was strewn across the expanse of marble floor. Concrete slabs lay beside jagged shards of glass, some sticking up like stalagmites. Others lay in treacherous sheets on the ground. Martina and Steve led the way with Jenny, and Dave followed with Todd.

Jenny stumbled and fell. Steve and Martina caught her just before she reached the ground, but as they dropped to save her, Steve gashed his side on a protruding metal rod partly encased in concrete. He screamed with pain and clutched at the wound, letting Jenny go. Dave dashed forward and just broke the girl's fall.

It took them a few moments to pull themselves together. Steve was crying with pain. They could see a red circle of blood spreading across his Led Zeppelin T-shirt. He could barely breathe, but somehow they all managed to reach the Main Concourse.

The framework of the main doors was almost completely obliterated. Only daggers of glass pointing at weird angles remained in the metal frames. Outside, they could see more fires burning. Debris peppered the broad stone steps that led down from the doors to a large plaza and a tree-lined street beyond. A huge jet of water from a burst pipe was drenching the floor near the doors, splattering across massive chunks of concrete and marble. One of the main supports close to the doors had collapsed and smashed to pieces. Several corpses lay pinned under the fragments.

'Come on!' Dave shouted. He stepped ahead, picking a way through the mess. Todd came up behind Steve and the two girls. Reaching the doors, they could feel the cool air of night.

Dave took a step back and went to help Todd move out through the doors. He felt a strange movement to his left, a jerking, a spasm. Turning, he saw blood spray into the air, and acting on pure, animal instinct, he dived to the floor.

As he fell, he saw Steve and the two girls shudder. Martina and Steve slipped away from the injured girl, who stood erect for a strange, timeless moment, her arms outstretched, beseeching. Then her legs gave way and she fell backwards in a pathetic heap.

Dave scrambled back, away from the doors, miraculously avoiding the bullets spraying the area, and pulled Todd down. 'Fuck!' he bellowed.

Todd landed heavily and screamed in agony, but Dave was oblivious to it. He dragged his friend back into the Main Concourse and out of the line of fire. Looking back towards the doors, Dave could see the three youths in their death throes, laying horribly contorted in a puddle of red that crawled outwards across the marble floor.

40

There were shards of glass and pieces of twisted metal a hundred yards from the CCC. Freddie Bantelli negotiated carefully. The road was covered with debris and slick with oil and water, and the air was filled with smoke and dust.

McNally instructed Bantelli to pull up ten yards from the mangled remains of the main entrance to the CCC. The captain opened his door. 'Wait here a second,' he yelled into the cabin. But Bantelli was already out of the truck and running around the front.

'Shit!' McNally hissed. Then he took a deep breath. 'Okay, Bantelli,' he called back. 'As you're out, check the main entrance. I'll guide the other trucks in. Don't – I repeat, *do not* – go beyond the doors. You got that?'

'Got it.'

'Fucking kid,' McNally hissed to the other three firemen. Two of them were adjusting the settings on their oxygen tanks, and Raul Burgos was reaching for the door handle. McNally looked over their heads towards the back of the truck. He had a torch in his hand and his helmet light on. He could see the first of the other Station 9 trucks slowing a few yards away. It was then he heard a burst of gunfire ripping through the sounds of destruction and mayhem.

Some sixth sense told McNally what was happening, no matter how unbelievable it might be. He heard one of the guys in the back scream, and he threw himself to the floor, gashing his knee on a sharp piece of metal. It sliced through his suit and he felt a surge of pain shudder up his leg.

'Stay here!' he yelled into the back, and ignoring the pain he crawled beneath the fire truck, quickly pulling his legs under the vehicle. He spun round on the ground to face the wreckage of the main entrance, and saw the soles of Bantelli's boots. He scrambled closer and crawled into a stream of fresh blood trailing away from Bantelli's body. The boy was shaking. McNally reached him a few inches beyond the undercarriage of the truck. The young fireman stopped moving.

Crawling out from under the rig, McNally managed to pull Bantelli's body into deep shadow between the fire truck and the shattered building, a gap of about three feet. He ripped off Bantelli's mask. The kid's face was white. He turned him slightly and saw that his back was ripped open from the nape of his neck to the middle of his spine, a mass of blood and bone protruding from under the remnants of his jacket.

McNally sat still, the ruined body of the kid draped across his lap. He closed Bantelli's sightless eyes. Only then did he hear the operator's voice. She was trying to keep calm but gradually losing it. '9-Alpha. Status, please? 9-Alpha, please respond!'

'McNally,' the captain said robotically. 'We have a shooter.'

41

'Connor!' McNally yelled into his radio. 'Get into the driver's seat and reverse out – *slowly*.'

The crew in the back of the rig had all heard the radio exchange with the operator. The shooter was high up somewhere on the near side of the fire truck. Engineer Gene Connor crawled to the front seat, keeping as low as possible, out of the line of fire.

The engine was still running. Connor slid into the seat and moved the shift into reverse with his body bent almost double, his head half under the steering wheel. The fire truck started to crawl backwards. Then a dozen rounds shattered the driver's side window. Following bullets passed through nothing but air until they arrived at the passenger's window, sending beads of safety glass outward onto the concrete. But two bullets hit Gene Connor's helmet, passed through it like hot pokers through butter and smashed into the door, taking large chunks of the fireman's brain with them. Blood cascaded down Connor's face and he fell forward, his foot jamming down on the accelerator.

The fire truck roared, its rear wheels screeching on the concrete. Then it suddenly jolted backwards and ploughed into a police car that was drawing to a halt immediately behind it. It kept going as if it had hit a toy car, gaining speed as it went. The police vehicle spun around 180 degrees, slammed through the mangled doors of the building and smashed into a girder dangling from the ceiling. The metal tore from the concrete above the car, and the upper end of the girder came loose at the joist. Twisting for a second on its single remaining bolt, the girder came down like a felled tree. The two cops in the car could see it all happen as if in slow motion. One of them reached the door handle and had even opened the door a fraction of an inch when the girder landed on the car, crushing the roof.

Outside the building, the fire truck had collided with the front of a companion rig. The engine of Connor's truck squealed like a spiked pig, its wheels spinning, sending up smoke and the stench of incinerated rubber.

Fifty feet from the truck, Captain James McNally was crouching beside his dead colleague and completely exposed to the shooter. Bullets ripped through the gaping windows and sent up sparks as they shattered their way through rubble and ricocheted from metal girders and posts. Keeping low, he crawled as fast as he could towards the stricken fire truck. The *rat-tat-tat* of shells hitting the floor and the remains of the wall of the devastated building followed him.

But McNally, it seemed, had nine lives. He reached the truck and was finally shielded from the shooter. Pulling on the door, he pushed Connor's corpse across the seat letting it fall into the space between the front seats. He killed the engine and the dreadful churning of wheels on concrete stopped. Keeping low, he looked into the back of the truck. Raul Burgos, who had been closest to the door, was obviously dead – a ricocheted bullet had hit him in the chest and ripped it open. Maney Steinberg appeared to be alive but unconscious – he had been thrown across the back seats and collided with an oxygen tank.

McNally crawled into the back as more bullets ripped through the cabin. He checked Steinberg's pulse and shook the unconscious fireman, slapping his face. 'Maney!' he shouted, and shook him again. 'We've gotta get out!'

McNally went out first, dragging the semi-conscious Steinberg with him. His biggest fear was that the shooter would hit the truck's gas tank. He was just trying to figure out how he could get away from the rig and reach cover when he heard fresh gunfire. 'Jesus Christ!' he exclaimed.

It was coming from the second rig. Moving to the back of the truck, between it and the building, McNally could just see three cops shielded behind a patrol car. They were taking turns to release a few rounds in the direction of the shooter before ducking down as the return fire came searing through the rancid night air. The cops were providing cover for the crew from the other truck to crawl out through the cabin.

The shooter unleashed a few more rounds towards the cops, then he sprayed the fire truck before flicking back to the cops again. But he was over-stretched. All four firemen made it safely behind the patrol car. McNally dashed towards the car, dragging Steinberg with him.

Three more patrol cars screeched to a stop behind the first one. Six officers scrambled out under the first car's cover and started firing in the direction of the sniper.

McNally was about to direct the firemen out of the shooter's line of sight and into the CCC when there was an incredibly loud roar from the plaza between the main road and the steps leading down from the entrance of the gutted CCC. It sounded like nothing on earth. They all spun round to see what had caused the noise, and for a second the gunfire ceased completely.

'What in the name of fuck is that?' McNally gasped.

42

Nine minutes after leaving Base One, Josh Thompson slowed the Silverback as he flew over the Californian coast at 60,000 feet. He brought the plane down to 20,000 feet, still a long way above the commercial air traffic coming into LAX, and checked in with Cyber Control at Tintara.

'You have airspace clearance,' a technician at Base One told him. 'All commercial flights across the country have been diverted or grounded. Emergency services have been notified.'

The devastated shell of the CCC lay directly below. Josh put on the close-range scanners, sweeping all electromagnetic frequencies, from radio waves in the low-frequency range, around 10 MHz, to gamma radiation with frequencies upward of 10 ExHz. Next he instructed the computer to filter out anything unrelated to the current situation at the CCC and its environs. The computer profiled the scene as a holographic image in his visor. Josh could see the fire trucks and police cars and the shootout taking place 20,000 feet below. It was all accompanied by the radio exchanges and live sound. He focused in on the shooter, who was located on the roof of a gas station directly across from the entrance to the CCC. But even with the technology aboard the Silverback, all he could make out was a hooded figure crouched over a machine gun.

Taking the Silverback down, Josh found a suitable landing site in the plaza close to the main doors of the ripped-open building. At the same time, he monitored the gunman on the roof. As the craft came down to land, he saw the shooter shift position, but he could still see almost nothing that might ID the man. A few dozen feet above the ground, the Silverback drew parallel with the roof of the gas station. The figure moved away from the gun, grabbed a bag and vanished from sight.

Josh decided to turn away from the assassin. His first priority was to get into the CCC and assess the situation. With a great roar from the engines, the Silverback touched down on the debris-covered concrete of the plaza. He shut down the engines and suddenly the aircraft was silent and still, sitting outside the CCC like Klaatu's flying saucer in *The Day the Earth Stood Still*.

He was removing his helmet and about to tell the computer to open the canopy when a voice broke through on 506 MHz, the radio frequency most commonly used by the LAPD. 'This is a designated emergency scene. Exit the aircraft with your hands up.'

'What?' Josh said aloud. Then he pulled his helmet back into place and tapped the virtual keyboard. 'Mark,' he intoned into his mic. 'I think I have a problem here. It seems the natives didn't know I was coming after all.'

For a moment there was only silence at the end of the line. 'Roger that, Josh. We've been trying to clear it but it's chaos down there. Leave it with me a minute. Out.'

'This is a designated emergency scene. Exit the aircraft with your hands up,' came the radio transmission again.

Josh looked out through the canopy. The building was a complete mess. Fires were still raging inside, flames licking up the exterior walls. There were bodies strewn everywhere, ripped asunder by the powerful blasts and thrown around like rag dolls. Outside the building stood a dozen fire trucks and at least another dozen patrol cars. But only a few figures were moving around. Josh realised the shooter must have had them pinned down.

'This is Silverback 4,' he said into the mic, transmitting the message to the sender of the police message and through speakers on the outside of the plane. 'I'm supposed to have clearance. I'm here to help.'

Silence the other end. Silence from Base One.

Josh flicked off the mic and swore loudly.

'There has been no official clearance for your aircraft. I repeat, this is a designated emergency scene. Exit the aircraft with your hands up,' came the police response.

Josh looked through the canopy and saw four officers approaching, sweeping their guns in front of them. Others were out of the patrol cars and leaning over the roofs of their vehicles to provide cover. One group kept their guns trained on the roof of the gas station. The rest were pointed at the Silverback.

'Mark?' Josh said, his voice betraying his growing exasperation. 'I need help here . . .'

'We're working on it, Josh. Bear with us.'

Josh knew he could simply sit tight. Nothing the LAPD could offer would so much as scratch the Silverback. But he had come here to do a job and he was being thwarted – by red tape, for Christ's sake!

'I'm going out there,' Josh announced to Base One.

'No, Josh. Don't do that –'

But Josh switched off his comms and was pulling off the helmet again. His finger hovered for a moment over the virtual keyboard, and after a second of indecision he unlocked the canopy and let it slowly pivot upwards.

Outside, the four cops stopped advancing and crouched down. They kept their weapons trained on Josh as he lifted himself free of the craft and began to back down the steps from the cockpit. Reaching the ground, he turned slowly with his arms raised. Two of the cops ran forward, grabbed his wrists and pulled restraining plastic strips around them. They led him to the nearest patrol car.

After telling his captors his name and purpose, Josh decided to say nothing more. The fire trucks were emptying now. Hoses were pulled into action as the fire crews dashed into the building. Two policemen ran over to the youths who had been gunned down just inside the concourse. Captain James McNally covered the bodies of his colleagues as they lay side by side close to the wall of the CCC. Then he joined the remainder of Fire Station 9 inside the building.

Josh was bundled into a patrol car and watched over by a single cop, a young man who looked like a scared rabbit. His blue shirt was soaked with perspiration. They were sitting in the front of the car and the cop had his gun level with Josh's left temple. The cop's hands were shaking.

Josh was growing increasingly concerned. But his concern was tempered with frustration. *We're all on the same side*, he kept telling himself. He was about to say something to the young cop when he saw another policeman approach the patrol car. By the look of the stripes on his sleeves, he was a senior officer. He ordered the rookie to go into the CCC.

'You're Josh Thompson,' the cop said.

'I believe so.'

'You're part of something called E-Force.'

'Correct.'

'What are you doing here? You can understand we're a little anxious.'

'If you know my name and where I'm from, I don't need to answer that.'

The cop sighed. 'Humour me.'

'Two more vehicles will be here soon, carrying my colleagues and specialised equipment,' Josh said. 'Our task is to rescue Senator Kyle Foreman, who we believe to be alive inside the building.'

The cop simply stared at him. 'FBI?'

'No. We're also keen to help the emergency services in any way we can.'

'Yeah, well, we need it,' the officer said wearily, looking at the cataclysmic scene beyond the window of the patrol car. 'And if that fancy looking thing out there is anything to go by –'

But before he could finish his sentence, an ear-splitting noise erupted from outside. The cop looked startled. Everyone was jumpy as hell. But then he saw a huge hamburger-shaped object lowering itself onto the plaza 50 feet from Josh's Silverback, and he relaxed a little. 'Looks like your buddies are here,' he said, stony-faced.

43

The Dragon had watched gob-smacked as Josh Thompson's Silverback came out of the night sky and settled on the concrete of the plaza.

Perching up here had been extremely risky, but necessary. His employers' instructions were clear. He had to make sure Foreman did not survive even if he escaped the impact of the blast. To make doubly sure, he needed to hamper the rescue operation in any way he could. The Four Horsemen were nothing if not thorough. The Dragon respected that.

His police scanner told him SWAT teams were minutes away and he had already decided it was time to go, but seeing the futuristic craft appear out of nowhere threw him off. He snatched up his bag and headed for the trap door at the back of the roof.

The key to any successful sniper mission was to prepare an escape route. The trapdoor had been left open for a speedy exit, but the Dragon was leaving at his own pace. Crouching low, he ran across the roof and quickly sank into deep shadow. He slithered into the opening in the roof and his feet found the rungs of a metal ladder. Once inside, he flicked on a torch and pointed it downwards. The light illuminated a narrow access way, but beyond the dissipated beam there was nothing but blackness.

The Dragon pulled down the cover and threaded the lock, clicking it into place and testing it. Next he moulded a knuckle of plastic explosive into the rim of the door, set a tiny pressure fuse and retreated down the ladder.

The access way led directly to the gas tanks under the station forecourt. A dozen feet below ground, an inspection channel a yard wide and two high ran between six chambers, one for each pump. Doors led off the inspection channel into each chamber, with windows at head height. The Dragon reached the foot of the ladder and saw the opening into the inspection channel directly ahead. Flashing the torch beam into the darkness, he could make out the curves of the first two chambers, one on each side of the inspection channel. He took three paces into the darkness. Peering in through the first window on the left, he could see the tank was half-full. The one on the right was almost empty.

It took just a few seconds for the Dragon to run the length of the channel. At the far end stood another ladder pinned to the wall. He climbed it, counting the rungs under his breath. Reaching the top, he flicked off his torch and pushed on the metal door above his head.

Clambering out into the stinking air, the Dragon carefully lowered the door back into place and crawled away to the cover of some bushes just beyond the perimeter of the gas station. Between him and the burned-out CCC stood a row of tall bushes that stank of burned vegetation. In their matted branches lay detritus from the blasts.

The Dragon could see just beyond the bushes to where the fire trucks and patrol cars stood, the devastated Conference Center their backdrop. Hearing shouts from close by, he watched as two Saracen assault vehicles rumbled past, their 7.62 mm turret-mounted machine guns pointed directly at him. But he was quite invisible, his dark form merging seamlessly with the night.

44

As the Big Mac landed on the concrete, billowing pink and purple fumes from the massive engines in its underside, two armoured Saracen assault vehicles rumbled onto the forecourt of the gas station. A 'Night Sun', a massive light, was mounted on each. They were switched on simultaneously, tearing twinned columns of light through the evening gloom. The lights swivelled towards the roof of the gas station, casting a blaze of white.

The SWAT teams in full body armour jumped out of the two vehicles and adopted classic defence–assault formations. Two men swung around 360 degrees, sweeping the scene. The others crouched low and ran for cover. It was a short dash to the stairs at the side of the gas station. The glass front of the building was smashed to pieces. Inside, the aisles had been shoved out of position and resembled a pile of dropped dominoes. Cans of drink and packets of potato chips and biscuits were scattered across the wet floor. A freezer unit at the back of the station was split open, a great plume of water from a burst pipe disgorging across the mess, pattering on the plastic containers and flowing out of the building and onto the tarmac.

The SWAT team ascended the stairs and emerged onto the roof, sweeping the area with their Heckler & Koch UMP 45s. Within seconds, eight men were on the roof and fanning out. At the leading edge of the roof they found a pair of M60 7.62 mm machine guns on tripods. Scattered around them were spent shells, hundreds of armour-piercing M61s.

The SWAT team leader radioed his commander and transmitted video footage of the scene to an operations centre in a van parked a mile away from the CCC. 'Scene has been vacated,' he reported.

The shooter had left not only the guns and spent shell cases, but also a crate, a box with his unused shells, and some camouflage netting. They searched around the edge of the roof, peering down into the darkness at the rear and the glistening, ruddy light at the front. There were no ropes, no ladders. Towards the rear of the roof the SWAT team leader found a rectangle of metal, two feet square. He tried to get his gloved fingers under the rim. He just managed it, but the door was stuck fast.

'Escape route located,' he reported.

A second later, the trapdoor rocketed into the air, taking the team leader with it. The explosion was small, but the explosive material had been configured precisely to localise the blast, sending the door skyward. The team leader, his body shattered by the force of the door hitting him, flew through the air. In his black assault uniform, helmet and night-vision goggles, he looked like a huge bat streaking across the roof and over the edge, onto the forecourt of the gas station. He landed in the water gushing from the station store and lay still in the fiery glow.

45

With professional calm, the Dragon watched the teams search the roof, waiting for his moment to move. When it came, the bang was almost disappointing, smothered as it was by the other sounds all around. But then he saw the black human shape soaring through the air over the front edge of the roof, and he belly-crawled through the undergrowth away from the scene of the disaster. Ahead lay a narrow verge of scorched grass, and beyond that a line of trees bordering the highway. Surveying his handiwork with a final glance, he sprinted across the grass verge to the road, and – with all eyes on the gas station – he slipped away unnoticed.

Two minutes later he reached his car. His cell phone vibrated in the breast pocket of his combat jacket. He pulled it out and read the message. *'Status?'*

He typed in *'Complete success.'*

A few seconds passed before another message appeared on the screen. *'Hold position.'*

46

Dave Golding thanked God he'd risked missing the start of Foreman's speech to pop some pills. If he hadn't been in the restroom when the bombs went off, he would surely be dead.

There was also the fact that the three Vicodin he had swallowed were all that prevented him from flipping out completely. Even so, they didn't stop him shaking as he stared around at the carnage. He was back with the senator, who was trying to comfort the old man whose wife had just died from her injuries. Todd's arm was in a really bad way. Dave had ripped up a T-shirt from his backpack and used it as a tourniquet, and had also improvised a sling. He then handed his friend a couple of Vicodin. Todd was so grateful and so distracted by pain, he didn't even ask where they came from.

'We can't stay here,' Kyle Foreman said.

'I'm not leaving her . . .' Marty Gardiner croaked.

'Mr Gardiner, I understand, but –'

'I can't.'

Foreman stood up. 'There could be more bombs,' he said quietly to Dave and Todd.

'We can't take the front,' Todd replied through clenched teeth. The Vicodin would barely scratch the surface of his pain, even when they kicked in.

'I realise that.'

'So . . . what?'

The senator did a 360-degree turn. Uniform devastation. Except . . . Looking closely, Foreman saw that the destruction wasn't actually uniform. The second blast had come from under the auditorium, but, he reasoned, the first bomb must have been hidden close to the reception desk. He could see this from the pattern of the debris – rubble, metal, plastic, body parts – which fanned out from there in all directions. But to the left of Reception and the gaping hole in the back wall, another concrete wall ran perpendicular into the Main Concourse. This had taken a hammering but hadn't collapsed, and behind it was a lobby and a set of elevators. He could see, just beyond them, an emergency exit sign.

Foreman knelt on one knee beside Marty. 'Mr Gardiner, I think you should come with us.'

The old man looked up for a moment, his eyes wet with tears. 'I'm not leaving her.'

'You can't stay here. The roof could come down. There could be another bomb.'

'I don't care.'

Foreman didn't know what to say.

'Forty-two years,' Marty murmured. He stroked his dead wife's hair. It was pure white, almost translucent. 'Not many marriages last a fraction as long. Certainly not in these godforsaken times. But this is my fault. I knew Nancy didn't really want to be here tonight. I railroaded her into the whole damn eco thing. I know it.'

Foreman touched Marty's arm. 'Mr Gardiner – may I call you Marty?'

The old man didn't take his eyes from Nancy's face.

'Marty, you can't blame yourself. You don't know for sure your wife thought that way.'

'Oh, I know. I knew, and I didn't say anything. I was too damn selfish. Too full of my own opinions. And now look what I've done.'

Foreman was trying to gather his thoughts. 'Okay, so let's say you're right. Why do you think she went along with it? Because she loved you, Marty.'

The old man broke down again, leaning in close to his wife's body. His shoulders shook as he sobbed.

'And you know what?' Foreman continued. 'She wouldn't have wanted you to stay here. Would she?'

Marty didn't reply. Foreman stood and walked over to the others, who were looking nervous and clearly wanted to move.

'I can't do any more,' he told them. 'Come on.'

They turned towards the back of the Main Concourse. Dave hitched his backpack and they started to weave a path through the rubble.

'Wait,' a small voice said.

They turned in unison to see Marty Gardiner in the same crouched position, with his wife's hand in both of his. He wasn't looking at the senator and the young men. It seemed like he couldn't break away from the woman he had spent most of his life with. 'You're right,' he added, still not looking up. 'You're right.'

He laid Nancy's hands across her chest, ran his fingers through her hair one last time, and eased himself up. And without looking back he picked his way over to the others.

47

The area around the elevators was the clearest part of the building. But even here lay marks of destruction. One of the three elevators had been open at the time of the blasts. The roof had come down on the two people inside, who were not moving. The doors to the elevator closest to the blasts were buckled and pitted. They looked like they would never open again. The elevator at the other end of the row appeared to be almost unscathed.

The four men walked past them towards the exit sign. It was flickering on and off, emitting a high-pitched whine as though it was about to blow. Dave tried the exit door, pushing on a pivoted horizontal rail. It wouldn't budge.

'It's either locked from the other side or something heavy is blocking it,' Todd groaned, and lowered himself slowly to the ground with his back to the wall. He sighed heavily.

Dave gave the door a kick. Nothing. 'If it's locked we'll just break through,' he said, and surveyed the floor.

A few yards away lay a section of metal beam about four feet long. Foreman, Marty and Dave tried to lift it, but it was incredibly heavy. Their combined strength could barely nudge it a few inches along the ground.

'Useless!' Marty exclaimed.

Then Dave saw something else – a metal pole about a yard long, half-buried under chunks of concrete. Marty and Kyle helped him pull the concrete away and Dave snatched up the pole, strode over to the door and hit it with three heavy blows close to the handle. The door stayed put. Three more ineffectual smashes and Dave changed tactic, ramming the end of the pole into the wood close to the lock.

After four strikes the pole finally went through the wood. With help from Kyle, Dave pulled the pole out. He widened the hole with the end of the length of steel, and in a few seconds they could see the exit door would be useless to them – behind it lay piles of concrete and steel. It was like a false door covering a concrete wall.

'Well, that answers that question,' Marty said.

Dave helped Todd to his feet and they returned to the elevator lobby. It was only then that they noticed the rectangular metal plate on the wall between two of the elevators. A simplified schematic of the building was etched into it. Todd lowered himself to the floor again while Dave and Foreman studied the diagram. Marty stood a few paces back, looking on.

'We're here,' Foreman said, stabbing at the diagram. 'Looks like there're emergency exits at the four corners of the building. Here, here, here and the one we've tried.'

'We can't even contemplate the front ones,' Marty said from behind them.

'No. And the other rear exit is right over the other side of the Main Concourse, which would be real hard to get to.'

They studied the schematic in silence.

'So what have we got?' Foreman said after a moment. 'There are ten levels altogether. We're on Ground. Three floors above us, six below.'

'My vote would be to go down,' Todd said from where he was sitting.

'Why?'

'Obvious, isn't it? The damage will be far greater up than down. It's unlikely you'd reach the roof, which is what you're thinking, right?'

Foreman and Dave were silent.

'He's right,' Marty interjected. 'Besides, even if you could get to the roof, the sniper could pick us off easy.'

Dave was scrutinising the diagram. 'Yes,' he said slowly. 'Yes . . .'

'What?'

'Well, look at the diagram. This spiral here.'

'What is it?' Marty asked.

'Access to the first level of the car park on B2. You see? B1 is admin – offices and storage. The five levels beneath it are all car park. The spiral represents the way into the car park from the ground level. And then you get between the lowest four floors by driving up and down these ramps in the centre of the level. Here, see?'

'So?' Marty asked.

'If we could get to B2, we could go up the ramp to the surface.'

'Alright,' Foreman said. 'I take your point. But isn't it academic anyway? How are we going to go up or down?'

'The elevator?' Todd said.

'You're insane!' Marty responded. 'The elevators are the last thing you use.'

'Well this *is* the last thing, isn't it?' Todd snapped.

'They're not going to work,' Dave exclaimed and stabbed at the button dismissively.

Nothing happened for a moment. Then they all saw the light over the door of the undamaged elevator start to blink on and off. They watched as the figure B5 flashed, then clicked off. B4 appeared, then B3. For several tense seconds they kept their eyes fixed on the clutch of LCDs in the strip above the door, expecting at any moment for the ascent to peter out because the lift had hit an obstruction. But it kept going. Amazed, they watched as G lit up and the doors opened.

48

'Shit, I hate elevators,' Dave said as the doors shut.

'Since when?' Todd asked, incredulous.

'Like you take a lot of notice. I always take the stairs at college. Don't trust these things.'

Kyle depressed the B2 button and the elevator began to move. Dave looked around, extremely uneasy. Todd was shaking his head, a mocking smile on his face.

'Oh, fuck off!' Dave exclaimed.

The elevator jolted and they heard a sharp cracking sound, then it stopped suddenly between floors. The lights went off and flicked back on again. Todd's smile vanished. Dave gripped the railing that ran around the interior wall. He caught a glimpse of his own terrified face in a mirrored panel.

Then the elevator dropped.

It seemed to fall forever. But it was in freefall for no more than a second. In that interval the four men in the elevator believed they were living through their final moments. There was no time to panic. They simply experienced a horrifying stillness, a sense of utter powerlessness. Their lives were stripped away. Everything became meaningless.

The elevator shuddered to a stop.

The jolt threw them around inside the tiny space. Foreman and Dave smashed together. The impact broke the senator's nose, and blood spurted down his shirt. Todd collided with the wall and landed heavily on his broken arm, making him

scream in anguish. Marty was propelled headfirst towards
the doors. He just managed to break his fall and quickly sat
up, dazed, his vision blurry.

There was a horrible creaking sound coming from the
centre of the elevator's ceiling. None of them dared move.

Foreman dabbed at his face with the sleeve of his shirt,
and soon the expensive Egyptian cotton was coated in
red snot. He slid to the floor, resting his back against the
wall, leaning his head back and pinching the bridge of his
nose.

Nursing his arm, Todd scrambled back against the opposite
wall, his face creased in pain.

Dave was shaking. His face was covered in sweat that ran
in rivulets down his filthy, bloodied cheeks. He was pulling
the backpack off his shoulders and rifling through the bag.
A moment later he had a small plastic container in his fist.
Surreptitiously he tipped a couple of tablets into his palm
and chewed them with practised ease.

Foreman slowly got to his feet and edged to the elevator's
doors. 'You okay?' he asked Marty, helping him to his feet.

'I guess.'

Turning to the two students, he repeated the question.
They nodded. 'Not much worse than I was,' Todd added.

Foreman looked at the keypad and then up at the electric
display above the door. It was flickering between B3 and B4.
'Anyone have a cell phone?' he asked, looking at each of
them in turn.

'Never owned one,' Dave replied.

'I had one,' Todd answered. 'It's back there.' He nodded
towards the floors above. 'In about a hundred pieces.'

Foreman glanced at Marty. The old man shook his head
and looked at the floor of the elevator, the muscles in his
face tightening.

The senator tugged at his own phone. 'This crapped out
earlier, so –' Glancing at the screen, he was startled to see it

was active. But a symbol in the top right of the screen told him the signal was practically nonexistent.

He keyed in 911. Nothing. Then, barely conscious of what he was doing, he called up his contact list and speed-dialled the first number. There was a long silence, then three clicks followed by an electronic whir. The light on the screen went out. Foreman lowered the phone to his side, stared at the floor and let out a heavy sigh.

'Kyle? Kyle – is that you?'

'Sandy!' Kyle screamed, pulling the phone up. He saw the word *Connected* on the screen, and a timer counting the seconds – *00:02, 00:03*. Then the phone died. No light, no signal, no sound – no power.

49

Of all the technological wonders available to E-Force from the work of CARPA, the Big Mac was perhaps the most impressive. It was a massive aircraft, and aspects of its design made it look like the great-grandchild of the B2 Stealth Bomber. It consisted of a giant disc referred to as a uni-wing. Above and below this were bulges, which in profile gave it the shape of a burger. The upper bulge housed the flight deck and ops rooms, while the lower contained the giant engines. The Big Mac worked on the same ram-jet principle as the Silverbacks, and like the smaller craft it was a VTOL aircraft capable of hypersonic speeds.

Stephanie Jacobs had piloted the huge craft from Base One and made a perfect landing outside the CCC, her failures in the simulator forgotten. She and Pete Sherringham unbuckled just as Mark came through on the comms.

'Had a slight hiccup with the police,' he began. 'News of your arrival hadn't gone right along the chain of command. It's okay now, though. Josh has talked to the ground commander and he's coming over to you to assess the situation and work out a plan.'

'What's the latest on Mai?' Stephanie asked.

'On her way. Should be with you in five.'

Ten minutes later, Stephanie, Pete, Mai and Josh were in the Big Mac's ops room. On a wall-sized video screen they

could see Cyber Control at Base One. Mark was in the foreground, and Tom was sitting beside him in his motorised
wheelchair. In the background they could see the holoscreens
and virtual keyboards of the workstations, and operators in
boilersuits manning the controls.

'Hi, Mai. We all really appreciate –' Mark began.

She raised a hand. 'Please, forget that. Where're we at?'

'The emergency services have swung into action. As you
all probably know by now, there was a shooter.'

'A shooter?' Mai hadn't heard.

'Obviously linked to the bombings, maybe the guy who
planted the devices. Anyway, that threat has passed, at
least for the moment. But it delayed things. Some of the
emergency crews were hit. Most are now in the building.
Paramedics are bringing out the injured.'

Through the windows of the Big Mac they could see
teams of doctors and nurses triaging the victims. A line of
body bags lay at one end of the plaza.

'Yeah, we can see,' Pete said, turning back to the screen.
'What's the state of the building?'

Tom looked up from the electronic pad attached to his
wheelchair, a laptop the thickness of a piece of card with
a holographic screen above it. 'Bad bits and less bad bits,'
he began. 'The overall structure is okay. The whole thing
isn't about to do a Twin Towers, but the environment of the
Main Concourse and Hall A, which took the full brunt of
the blasts, is extremely hazardous. Masonry and girders are
coming loose all the time and whole sections of roof could
come down . . . along with the three floors above them.'

'What state are the upper floors in?'

'Not good,' Tom replied. 'Huge structural damage. There's
a restaurant directly above Hall A on Level 1. Or at least
there was. It's taken a big hit. The east end of Level 1 and the
First Floor Reception were some way from the second blast
but took it bad from the first blast, which had its epicentre

behind the Ground Floor Reception. Most of the east end of Level 1 is a bar. It's pretty smashed up. Fortunately, there were very few people in any of these areas at the time of the explosions.

'Above these, Level 2 is almost all conference and meeting rooms. Every single window has been blown out, including a huge wall of glass at the front of the building. There's some pretty serious structural damage to the main support girders, but they should hold. There were only four people up there. They're all still alive, but we have no idea what condition they're in.

'On the top floor, Level 3, there's a pool and gym. The wall of the pool has fractured and water is leaking down through the CCC. Again, there were only a handful of people up there and they managed to escape down external emergency stairs to the rear of the complex.'

'What sort of casualty figures we talking about overall, Tom?'

Erickson tapped at the virtual keyboard. When he looked up, he was paler than usual. 'The big event was Kyle Foreman's talk. It was sold out and queues had formed at the front of the CCC since this afternoon. He's a popular dude.' He paused for a moment and took a deep breath. 'There were just over 1100 people in Hall A.'

In a corner of the big screen a strange-looking image appeared. It was a dark rectangle with a random arrangement of dots in red and orange.

'This is a thermal image from BigEye 7, which is directly overhead. It was taken about ten minutes ago. It shows that fires are still burning fiercely in Hall A.'

'Didn't the second bomb go off directly under it?' Mai interrupted. 'That's what I was briefed in the Silverback coming over.'

'That's correct. And as a result, almost everyone in the auditorium was killed.'

175

Tom's words fell like lead weights into the room. There was silence in the Big Mac. Its heavily insulated windows sealed out any sounds from outside.

'Analysis of the image suggests there are fewer than 65 people still alive in the room. And we have no idea how many of them are critically or even mortally injured. I think the rescuers and paramedics should get there soon, although it's heavy going and extremely hazardous.'

'Over a thousand dead,' Josh said, almost in a whisper. 'Gone . . . Just like that.' It was close to the death toll of the *Titanic*; one-third of the number killed on 9/11. 'We have to do something. We have to help the emergency teams.'

Mark looked up from an image of Hall A on the holoscreen next to him. 'Not our job.'

'Not our job?' Josh exclaimed. 'There may be hundreds still alive in other parts of the building. They may be trapped.'

'That's not what we've been sent in to do, Josh.' Mark glanced at the faces of those aboard the Big Mac.

'But with the equipment we have we could save a lot of lives.'

'Yes, and we'll do as much as we can. But we have a very clear objective.'

They were all silent.

Josh took a deep breath. 'Okay, okay. I know.'

'There are three dozen fire trucks, almost 60 ambulances and dozens of police units there already, or close by. Every hospital in Los Angeles is on high alert and every ER in the county is preparing for casualties. The air is thick with medical choppers and they'll soon be ferrying the most seriously injured to the nearest ERs. We'll offer every assistance we can. But our mission parameters are clear. We have to rescue Senator Kyle Foreman, who, it now seems obvious, was the prime target of this attack.'

'What's the latest on him?' Stephanie asked.

176

'We have two separate traces on his cell,' Tom replied. 'They were both fleeting. The debris is blocking the signal and his phone may have been damaged. The first call came from a point at the rear of Hall A very soon after the blasts. The second was just over 30 minutes later, from a point in one of the lower levels of the building.'

'A lower level?'

He called up the schematic of the CCC. 'We've pinpointed the call to one of the elevator shafts. Between B3 and B4.'

'He's stuck in an elevator?' Steph asked.

'Looks that way,' Tom said. 'We have infrared traces from BigEye. Foreman's with three other survivors. We're keeping a constant trace on them and will let you know immediately if there's any change.'

'Tom and I formulated a plan as you guys were en route,' Mark said. 'Pete, you take one of the Moles. You need to get down to B2 via the car park access.' He pointed out the spiral entrance ramp. 'From there you can get to the lower levels. The Mole will get you through any rock falls or other obstructions. Mai, Steph and Josh, I want you to find a way down via the Main Concourse. Questions?'

'Any sign of more bombs?' Pete asked. 'It would be nice to know.'

'I have a team conducting a detailed sweep, Pete. Nothing yet. But obviously . . .'

'And the structural integrity of the Main Concourse and Ground Floor Reception?' Josh asked.

'We're monitoring it from BigEye,' Tom replied, bringing up another image on the screen. It was a diagram of the four above-ground floors of the CCC – Ground to Level 3. It consisted of strips of grey and black. Superimposed on these were jagged lines in green, orange and red. 'The dark regions are the structural components of the building, and the coloured lines are stress features. Green indicates the safest, red the most dangerous. As you can see, the red lines are clustered around the area to the west of the Main Concourse, close to Hall A. It's the point where both bombs had an impact. This is the part of the building where Senator Foreman was before he and his companions took the elevator. It's undoubtedly the most dangerous part of the building. But I'm pretty sure collapse is not imminent.'

'Pretty sure?'

Tom looked up. 'Okay. Fairly sure.'

'This is getting worse by the second. Give me some figures.'

'There's a 50 per cent chance it will last more than an hour.'

50

The most senior member of the rescue team on the ground was the fire chief of Area H, Truman Maclenahan. He had a ruddy face, ginger hair and an almost comic handlebar moustache. Although he had grown up in the Bronx, he was proud of his Scottish heritage. According to rumour, he took it so seriously he organised private caber and haggis nights at his house in Palos Verdes and wore kilts in the privacy of his study. It was Maclenahan who insisted on a briefing with the E-Force team members before they set foot in the CCC. It was a reasonable request, but in Mark Harrison's eyes it was just a waste of vital minutes.

The briefing took place in an ops centre in a specially designed fire department RV-type vehicle, which was parked on a slip road just beyond the east wall of the CCC. It was surprisingly spacious, with a round table at the rear of the truck. On the wall, a screen relayed live images from the inside of the gutted building. At the front of the vehicle, a small team operated the computer systems that linked the van with the County Emergency Operations Center, which was across town. Sitting with E-Force were Maclenahan and his number two, Assistant Chief Gerome Roseley.

'I'll be honest with you,' the Chief said. 'I'm only allowing you into that building because I've been told to.'

'I understand your reticence,' Steph replied. 'But we can assure you our operation will not impede your rescuers in any way.'

Assistant Chief Roseley sniffed and glared at the four members of E-Force.

'That's precisely our grievance,' Maclenahan responded. 'There are a lot of injured people in there. My men are doing the best they can. Yet you insist on focusing on one individual, Senator Kyle Foreman.'

'Chief,' Josh said evenly, 'I appreciate what you're saying. Indeed, I, for one, am not totally convinced what we've been ordered to do is right. But those are our orders, and we have to follow them.'

'Whose orders?' Roseley asked, rather more aggressively than he had intended. 'Who do you represent?'

'I thought it had all been explained to you,' Mai said.

'Some ridiculous rescue organisation? It's a wonder you're not wearing capes.'

There was a silence for a moment. On the screen they could see the smoke and the debris, the remnants of human beings, charred bodies, fires burning, flames licking up the walls and across the roof. Fire Chief Maclenahan looked embarrassed. 'I'm sorry,' he said. 'Emotions are running a little –'

'Excuse me, Chief,' Roseley interrupted. 'You don't need to apologise for me. Yeah, sure, I'm emotional. I don't like seeing a thousand Americans incinerated. But these people aren't here to help us. They're serving outside interests, and I don't like that.'

'I'm sorry you feel that way, sir,' Steph replied in her most diplomatic tone.

She was about to go on but Fire Chief Maclenahan cut in. 'What exactly is your plan?'

Mai outlined what they had decided. She, Steph and Josh would try to reach Kyle Foreman and his companions, who were trapped somewhere between B3 and B4, by going through the Main Concourse. Pete would take a machine called the Mole directly into a lower level.

'Okay,' Maclenahan replied. 'That sounds like a plan. But I wish to make a request. You know I can't insist.' And he flicked a glance at Roseley, who looked like he was sucking on a lemon. 'I guess I have to simply appeal to you.'

'What is it?' Steph asked.

'We have reason to believe there are some survivors trapped in Hall A. Problem is, the techs believe the roof is about to come down. I have men in there, but it's slow going. I think it's likely the roof will collapse before they can reach anyone. Do you have anything on that ship we can use to support the roof? To buy us time?'

It was easy to see how Truman Maclenahan had reached his position. He was gutsy and self-motivated, but he also knew when to play the diplomatic card. It was a skill largely lost on Roseley, who snorted and folded his arms.

'I'm afraid –' Steph began, but Josh cut across her.

'The stabilisers.'

His three colleagues turned to look at him.

'How?' Steph asked.

'We used the stabilisers during training to contain the energy field inside the pods. If they were positioned carefully in Hall A, they could be set to repel each other and act in the same way as a metal strut holding up the ceiling.

Steph was nodding slowly.

'But no one outside E-Force could operate the equipment,' Pete said.

'What equipment? What're you talking about?' Maclenahan asked, his face screwed up. Even Roseley had looked up, suddenly interested.

'Steph, Mai and I could stick to the plan,' Josh snapped back to Pete. 'And you could help in Hall A, then make your approach to the basement.'

'It's not what we've been ordered to do, Josh.'

Maclenahan had his hands up in front of him. 'Could someone please explain?'

Stephanie sighed and was about to respond when Mai butted in. 'We have a way of stabilising the roof.'

'Then –' Roseley began.

'I think Josh is right,' Pete said, ignoring the assistant chief.

'But –' Stephanie started to protest.

'It's not what we've been ordered to do – I know, Steph,' Pete insisted. 'I'm sorry, but I can't obey those orders. For all we know, I could be wasting my time ploughing through the car park in the Mole. I could cause more damage. You could get to the senator long before me. Surely I'm just backup? You see that, don't you?'

'Yes,' Stephanie said. 'I get it. But who's going to convince Mark?'

51

'No! Absolutely not!'

Josh was talking to Mark Harrison using his wrist vidcom. Pete was back in the Big Mac, preparing to bring the machinery he needed down to ground level from the bowels of the giant craft. Mai and Steph were waiting for Josh close by the entrance to the CCC.

'Look, Mark. I don't have time for this.'

Mark glared back at him from the tiny screen. 'Now, you listen to me, Josh. We agreed –'

'Yes, but things have changed.'

'Not as far as I'm concerned.'

'Well, that's the whole point, isn't it, Mark? You're not here. We are. Pete can do this. He can be in and out of Hall A in the Cage in only a couple of minutes. It'll at least give the emergency services a chance to save lives without the whole ceiling coming down on them.'

Mark looked away from the camera that was transmitting his image some 1500 miles to Josh's miniature receiver.

'I have my orders,' he said finally.

'Yes, but you don't like them, do you?'

'No, I don't – but I will obey them.'

'That's your prerogative, Mark.'

'Josh.'

'Mark, we have to be allowed to make our own decisions on the ground. We have to, otherwise this whole mission will fail – every mission will fail! You have to extend us that respect.'

183

There was a faint crackle down the line. Josh stared at the top of his commander's head. Finally Mark looked up.

'You have fifteen minutes, Josh. Not a second more. I'll square it somehow.'

'Good call, Mark,' Josh replied, and snapped off the vidcom.

52

'We have to do something,' Todd protested. 'We could go down any minute.'

'Good at stating the fucking obvious, aren't you, Todd?' Dave snapped.

'Oh! Pardon me for breathing.'

'That's the trouble with you, dude, it's all me, me, me, isn't it? It's a wonder you don't get giddy watching the world revolve around you.'

Todd reddened. Enraged, he rushed across the two yards of the elevator, his good hand balled in a fist. But Dave was too fast for him. He sidestepped Todd's swing and landed a solid punch to the side of his head, knocking him away. He landed on his bad arm and screamed in agony.

Dave went to kick him in the guts, but Marty Gardiner got between them, holding Dave back with a surprisingly powerful grip. 'You might have five decades on me, son,' he said. 'But back in the day I was middleweight state champion. I could still flatten you, believe me.'

Dave went limp and slid to the floor, his back to the mirror. He buried his head in his folded arms. They could see his shoulders heaving and hear the sobs he was trying to keep back.

Todd shuffled to the opposite wall and nursed his arm. Lines of pain were etched into his lathered face. The bandage was wet with blood.

Marty tapped Dave on the shoulder. 'I think your friend

could do with a few more of those pills,' he said quietly, and flicked a nod towards the backpack. 'May I?'

Dave put his hand in the bag. 'Here,' he said, handing Marty the bottle. 'I've got another.' He glanced at Todd, who didn't meet his eye.

'Hold on.' It was Kyle Foreman. 'The bag – Dave?' And he held out his hand. The young man passed it over grudgingly. Foreman pulled a pen from his shirt pocket and stabbed it into the back of the bag, ripping open the nylon.

'Hey, man!' Dave protested. But the senator had completely disembowelled the backpack and was yanking at an aluminium pole about a foot long and three quarters of an inch thick. He pulled two identical poles free from the bag and tossed the remnants back to Dave. At the elevator doors, he rammed one of the poles into the tiny space where the doors met.

He half-turned. 'Dave – get the other one into the gap at the bottom of the door. I'll do the top.'

Dave stepped forward and picked up the pole from between Foreman's feet. He knelt down and tried his best to slip the metal into the narrow join. He couldn't get any leverage – the gap was too narrow.

'Yes!' Foreman exclaimed. He had managed to force the end of the pole between the doors. Leaning on it, the length of metal slowly bent. 'Damn it!' he hissed, then quickly removed the pole and stuck the bent end into the join. This time it kept its shape and a gap appeared at the base of the elevator door.

Dave set to work again. He pushed down at the fissure with all his weight, forcing an inch of metal into the space between the doors.

'Lever it left,' Foreman instructed.

They leaned on the poles and the doors opened an inch. Foreman got his fingers into the gap and yanked to left and right, straining with every ounce of his strength. Marty and Todd each went to a door to help.

The doors were not giving up easily. But with a gargantuan effort the four men managed to separate them enough for Foreman and Dave to step into the breach. They forced the doors back and into their recesses.

They stepped back, breathing heavily. Dave leaned forward, hands on knees. Marty rested his back against the wall. They were all painfully aware of a new creaking sound coming from the roof of the elevator. It was higher-pitched than before. They stood still and the sound stopped.

They had almost made it to B4. They could see the top of the opening where the elevator should have docked. It was about two feet above the floor of the elevator. It would have been enough to crawl through, but it was blocked. Foreman grabbed one of the aluminium poles and scraped at the blockage. Soil fell away into the elevator. Then a large piece of concrete crashed down.

They all felt the elevator rock. Todd let out a desperate cry that caught in his throat. 'Maybe not a good idea,' he gasped.

The senator ignored him and went at the blockage again. More soil, more small chunks of concrete. A tangled piece of metal slid onto the elevator floor. Then he hit something big and solid. Attacking a different section of the opening, he brought more wreckage onto the marble floor of the elevator. They watched it scatter across the shiny surface. A cylinder of reinforced concrete a foot in diameter and two feet long suddenly plunged from above the opening. It came to an almost silent stop, cushioned by the soil and small fragments beneath it. Then it fell forward with a crash onto the floor and smashed into a dozen pieces.

The elevator shook violently. They all heard the sound of metal grinding against the lining of the elevator shaft. Holding their breath, they strained to hear new sounds from the elevator cable above their heads.

Foreman looked back at the opening. The falling concrete had brought down a hundred pounds of soil with it. Now the way was completely blocked. The soil up against the elevator doors had been a tease. The opening was blocked by a single huge piece of concrete that had settled against the doorway on B4. There was no way on Earth they could move it.

'What now?' Marty asked.

'We just have to wait. Try not to move too much.' Dave responded.

'To hell with that,' Foreman snapped, glaring at the floor. He felt like a caged animal. He took a deep breath, lowered himself to the floor against the wall and leaned his head on his raised knees.

For several minutes no one spoke. Then suddenly Foreman's voice broke the silence. 'There'll be an access ladder. We'll have to go through the roof.'

The four of them looked up simultaneously. In the centre of the ceiling was a square hatch.

53

Marty was first up. Dave and Foreman made a stirrup with their interlocked fingers and hauled him aloft. He prodded at the hatch and it slid back easily. The others then hoisted the old man further and his upper body worked through the opening. He just managed to scramble through and onto the roof of the elevator.

Lying flat, Marty helped Todd up through the hole. But it wasn't easy. His injured arm made the process far harder. Perched on Dave and Foreman's palms, he almost lost his balance, started to fall, then caught himself. Marty leaned forward as far as he could. Todd grabbed the edge of the hatchway with his good, right hand and made it over the lip, twisting himself to get his body and one leg through the hole.

Todd surveyed the shaft. Looking up, he could see the elevator cables had snagged on a fallen girder projecting from the side of the shaft. The motion of the elevator had put a terrible strain on the cable, which was shorn, leaving the elevator dangling from a withered length of twined steel no more than an inch and a half in diameter and badly frayed. But on the wall furthest from the doors of the elevator, and running the entire length of the shaft, was an access ladder.

'Come on,' Todd yelled to Marty, and lay flat on his stomach. The old man did the same. Foreman helped Dave up inside the elevator and the two men on the roof leaned down. Three hands grabbed Dave by his shirt and then quickly under his arms. In a moment, he was through the hole and crouching on the roof of the elevator.

'Todd,' Dave said. 'Get onto the ladder. You can't do any more. It'll lighten the load on the cable.'

Todd didn't need to be told twice. Turning, he clambered onto the ladder and took two uneasy steps upward. He gripped the edge of the ladder with his good hand, never looking away from the wall in front of his nose.

'Right, Dave,' Marty said. Looking around him, he saw what he needed, a huge metal clamp where the cables ran through a hoop on the roof of the elevator. 'You lie flat, brace yourself against that metal thing. Hold my legs. I'll reach down into the elevator. Understand?'

Marty positioned himself over the hole. Dave twisted his body around the metal bracket on the roof of the elevator. With Dave gripping his feet, Marty then scrambled forward and down the hole. As he slid into the elevator his shirt sleeves rode up. He had muscular forearms. 'Fifty press-ups every morning,' he told Foreman, offering him a weak smile.

'Glad to hear it, buddy. You ready?'

Marty nodded. Foreman leapt up and tried to grasp at Marty's arms. He missed by half an inch.

'Again,' Marty said.

The second time, he made it. The senator was surprised by the strength of Marty's grip. Dave helped by pulling on the old man's legs, using the bracket on the roof for leverage. Foreman finally reached the lip of the hatch, and between them Marty and Dave got him under the arms and hauled him up.

Marty hopped onto the ladder and took a few steps up. He could see Todd a dozen or more rungs above him, halfway to B3. The boy looked extremely shaky.

'You okay, Todd?' Foreman called.

'Just.'

'Keep going up.'

Dave stepped onto the ladder and had just climbed a rung when the noise hit the four of them. It was like a thunderclap. Contained by the elevator shaft, it was tremendously loud.

Foreman leapt from the roof of the elevator to the ladder just as a steel girder tumbled end over end towards them. It smashed into the sides of the shaft, ripping away a section of the access ladder between B1 and B2. The ladder shuddered and those clinging to it felt it move an inch away from the wall, the support bolts straining and twisting.

The elevator's main cable came down a few feet behind the girder. It was a deadly coil of reinforced steel, slashing and weaving its way down the shaft like a giant cobra. The elevator simply fell away, a dead weight plunging downwards. It shuddered against the walls of the shaft, gashing a deep groove in the concrete. Hitting the ground, its walls buckled. Two edges of the roof broke loose and yawned inwards like the serrated lid of an opened tin can.

54

The principle behind E-Force's stabilisers was a simple
one. If two powerful electromagnets are placed one above
the other some feet apart, they can be made to attract or
repel. To keep the unstable roof up, the magnets could
be set to repel each other, just like the opposite poles of
a magnet. *It sounds simple*, Pete Sherringham thought as
he entered Hall A, *but these magnets must have some kick in
them*. It had taken CARPA scientists the best part of eight
years to develop that kick.

Wearing the Cage, Pete felt incredibly empowered. The
nickname was entirely accurate: it *was* a cage, but – like a
Volvo's chassis – it was designed to keep danger out, not
the occupant in. It was seven feet high and had a titanium-
carbon-fibre framework that was designed to shrug off an
impact force of half a million Newtons – equivalent to a
Steinway falling from a fifth-storey window. It also shielded
the wearer against fire and explosions thanks to blast-proof
windows made from specially formulated polycarbonate
resin.

Pete stood just inside the entrance to Hall A, aghast at
the destruction. Sure, he had seen it on the monitors, he
knew the stats, the number of dead. But experiencing it was
something else. The massive room was barely recognisable
as an auditorium. He saw shreds of chairs and the odd
square inch of fabric that once covered them. The podium
stood incongruously erect on the distant stage. These things

attested to the fact that, not so long ago, this room had been filled with avid supporters of Senator Kyle Foreman.

He took a step into the hall. At his feet were the remnants of a cloth banner. He could just make out the words: *No Blood For Oil*. It was soaked red, with a grey line of human viscera staining one edge.

The Cage was bulky, but Pete had spent many hours training at Base One and was able to pick a way through the rubble without making the ruins even more unstable. Ahead, he could see the main cause of the rescuers' concern. The eastern half of the roof – the section nearest the entrance to the hall, where it joined with the Main Concourse and Reception – was sagging badly. In places, steel beams had nose-dived through the concrete and plaster. Fire lapped at the ceiling, compromising it further.

Inside the main entrance to the hall, Pete turned hard right. Taking three paces, he found the source of the fire. He slid his fingers over the surface of a console and a thick stream of 'megafoam', a fluoro-protein fire-quenching compound, flew from four jets built into the front of the Cage. In a few seconds the megafoam had smothered the flames.

Sybil had calculated where the stabilisers had to go. Pete could see the spots from inside the Cage. It was an equilateral triangle, some 50 feet to a side. The first site was just a few feet ahead of him. With great care he cleared a path, using an angled plough at the front of the Cage and a grappling arm to lift heavy beams and boulders of reinforced concrete.

The stabilisers were larger versions of the ones the team had used during training. Roughly cylindrical, they were about a yard long and two feet in diameter. Each had a pressure pad at one end and weighed close to half a ton. The great magnetic coils inside them consisted of almost ten miles of copper wire. Each electromagnet was powered by its own energy source, which produced an incredibly powerful magnetic field using a technology known as super-cooled super-conduction. The electronic components of the electromagnets were kept at a temperature close to absolute zero, turning the metal cores of the stabilisers into heavy-duty attractors or repellers.

Reaching the first site, Pete fixed the ground stabiliser into place. Next, he took the second stabiliser from its housing on the outside of the Cage and levered it up to the delicate ceiling directly above his head. Taking great care not to compromise the ceiling further, he slowly eased the stabiliser against the concrete roof. With a small electrical pulse from the control panel in front of him, he sucked air from inside the pressure pad and the unit glued itself to the ceiling.

The path to the second site was almost clear. Pete side-stepped a pile of rubber pipes and, beside them, the remains of a workstation that had crashed through the ceiling and shattered into hundreds of pieces. Using the grappling arm, he moved aside yards of plastic air-conditioning duct.

He was soon at the second site. Repeating the attachment process, he secured the ground stabiliser and nudged the ceiling unit into place, sucked the air from the pad and withdrew. Lowering the grappling arm, he was about to turn towards the third site, some 50 feet to his left, when he heard a growling sound from overhead. A second later, the Cage rocked as a concrete boulder the size of a Harley-Davidson smashed into it directly above Pete's head.

Pete had been through all this in the simulators but nothing prepared him for the reality. He caught a glimpse of a concrete slab dislodging from the ceiling, and at the periphery of his vision he could discern the object falling through space. Then came the impact. He ducked down inside the Cage, and the instinct to run made him lean onto the control panel. The framework rocked backwards and forwards. But he had no need to worry. The Cage shrugged off the boulder like an armadillo being pestered by a mosquito.

Pete looked up and saw the hole where the concrete had been and felt a sudden stab of anxiety. 'Tom,' he said into his comms. It was the first time he had spoken since entering the devastation of the hall.

'Pete.'

'You saw that?'

'Yes.'

'Do we need to realign?'

'Give me a second.'

Pete scanned the ceiling. A new network of deep cracks had appeared overhead. He could see beyond the plaster and concrete clear through to the floor above. Some white fabric was flapping around. Suddenly the upper half of a man in a white shirt, his tie still knotted perfectly, flipped over and tumbled through the hole. A drop of blood spattered onto the blast-proof window at the top of the Cage as the man hit the floor of Hall A. His dead eyes stared towards Pete.

'Tom? Speak to me, man.'

'We're in luck, Pete. Sybil reckons just a minor adjustment will bring us back to the original level of stability. Place the third stabiliser three feet closer to number two, and reduce the angle to 54 degrees. Got that?'

'Loud and clear,' Pete responded. He retraced a couple of steps then moved left towards a huge hole in the floor of the hall, its edges ragged. Great chunks of concrete lay all around. Over everything lay a fine powder – insulation from a large water tank on the floor below had been thrown upwards and pulverised. Settled across the debris, it looked like orange snow. A fountain of water jetted upward from the tank, splashing across the lip of the crater.

Pete picked his way around the edge of the hole, reaching a point directly opposite. Two strides further, he reached the desired spot. It was then that he heard a low moan.

He tried to figure out where the sound was coming from but it stopped as suddenly as it had started. He forced himself to concentrate on the job in hand. He could not allow himself to be distracted. He knew there could be dozens still alive in this devastated room, but he couldn't drag them all out from the rubble. He could save lives by propping up the ceiling.

He quickly got the third ground stabiliser in place and was extracting the ceiling stabiliser from its bracket when the sound came again. A low moan, then a single word mangled by pain. 'Help . . .'

Pete paused for a second, the stabiliser unit poised a few feet short of the ceiling. Holding his breath, he strained to hear. *Where the hell was the voice coming from?*

Two yards away he saw a small arm poking from under a pile of chairs. It was moving. He didn't stop to think. One pace and he was beside it. The voice came again, pleading.

'Okay,' Pete said softly into his comms. The sound spilled from a speaker on the outside of the Cage. 'Lie still. I'll get you free.'

Pete's fingers darted over the control panel and a holographic representation of the pile of shattered wood and metal appeared. A thermal filter showed the body inside the mess. It was small, a child. The image glowed red and orange with life. A few more taps on the virtual keyboard and the computer had ascertained the correct order to remove the debris burying the child.

Pete lowered a grappling arm, lifted a row of three seats and placed them on the floor behind him. Turning back, he saw the child staring up at him, terrified.

'It's okay,' he said again. 'Lie still.'

He plucked up a steel strut as though it were a toothpick, then pulled aside a sheet of corrugated iron, a length of plastic piping and a rectangle of wood. The child, a little girl of about six, was uncovered.

'What's your name?'

The child was too terrified to speak.

Pete forced a smile. 'I'm here to help you. What's your name?'

'Consuela,' the girl said.

'Can you move, Consuela?'

The girl tried to move a leg, but nothing happened. She shook her head and started to cry.

'Consuela, listen to me, lass.'

The girl tried to stop sobbing.

'Consuela, this machine can pick you up and get you outside. But you have to trust me. You understand?'

The girl nodded.

'You just stay right there. I'm going to extend a metal arm. It's a very friendly arm. It won't bite.' He smiled again. 'I'll tell the metal arm to lift you very gentle, like, and then we'll turn round and go. You got that, Consuela? Is that cool with you? Great. Okay. Ready? Here we go.'

With the stabiliser still suspended above him, Pete used the second arm. It was red, could extend almost ten feet and had splayed 'fingers' at the end. Moving as fast as he could, but with great care, he eased the arm forward. The little girl recoiled. Her face was bleached with pain and fear. She had witnessed things no six-year-old should ever see.

'It's alright, Consuela. Lie still, love. Relax.'

Pete tucked the fingers of the grappling arm under the girl and lifted her slowly above the rubble. She could only move her head. Her eyes were wild and staring around her.

'Easy,' Pete reassured her. 'No probs, Consuela.'

Pulling the child close to the Cage, Pete swivelled the larger grappling arm up to the ceiling, sucked the air from the pad and left the final unit in its proper place.

'Tom – we are go,' he said into his comms.

'Copy that, Pete. Slick work, man. Now get the hell out of there.'

55

Fire Chief Truman Maclenahan was alone in the rear of the ops centre when his phone rang. It was Mark Harrison.

'Sir, I'm grateful for your cooperation,' Mark said. 'What's the situation with the shooter? You'll understand I'm concerned about my people going in there.'

The fire chief quelled his irritation. His people were in just as much danger. But, he recalled, these guys *were* helping him. 'Not a lot I'm afraid, Mark. The SWAT team-leader was killed. Booby-trap.'

'I heard. No sign of the perp?'

'No.'

'We have people here running scans on the area using a sat system, but we have no idea who we're looking for. Do you have forensics on the gas station roof?'

'Mark, I think you're forgetting we have a major incident here. Every resource I have is stretched –'

'I do understand.'

'If you did, you wouldn't be asking me.'

'Sir, with respect. My people – and yours – can't help anyone if they're shot through the head.'

Maclenahan stared around the room and sighed.

'Okay, what do you want from me?'

'Someone from the FBI will be up there imminently, yes?'

'I guess so.'

'This shooter's a pro. He and the bomber may well be the

same person. I imagine he was extremely careful with his prints, his DNA.'

'Yes, I imagine he was.'

'The FBI, being the FBI, will commandeer the evidence,' Harrison went on. 'But they could miss plenty that my people could spot. You have to spare someone to get me anything useful from that roof. I have a pilot still there after dropping off one of my team. He can get that evidence to me within half an hour. Can you help?'

56

There was only so much the Big Eye could detect. Tom did everything he could to filter out noise and to scan through the full electromagnetic spectrum in an effort to work out the best way for the team to get down to B3 or B4, but there was only so much he could do too.

Stephanie, Mai and Josh were kitted out. Their cybersuits were skin-tight, each a matt copper-bronze colour. At their waists hung utility belts containing a high powered halogen torch, a small laser cutter and a 50-metre length of super lightweight cord made from carbon threads. Alongside these high-tech devices they each had a pouch containing some old-fashioned back-ups – matches, a whistle and a Swiss Army knife.

The cybersuits would protect them for short periods from temperatures between –300 and +475 degrees Fahrenheit. They wore skin-tight helmets, and each carried a backpack only an inch thick made from almost weightless carbon-iridium fibres. This could supply them with oxygen for up to 24 hours. A chamber adjoined to the oxygen production tank could provide water and essential nutrients that could last a week. As well as these, the suit was fully integrated with their implants and had super-fast digital comms.

They were emerging from the Big Mac when Tom opened a link. 'This is the situation,' he began. 'We've ruled out the western emergency stairs. They're still too unstable. The elevator must have been a desperate choice. BigEye reckons your best option is the eastern rear emergency exit. I'm not sure why the senator didn't try it, but I guess they felt getting across the Main Concourse was too hazardous.'

'Okay, Tom. You got anything from BigEye about access?' Stephanie asked, leading the other two towards the ravaged front of the CCC. It looked like the stabilisers were holding up well in Hall A. Emergency workers were everywhere. Paramedics emerged bearing stretchers, and firemen were heading back into the hall with heavy lifting equipment and oxygen tanks on trolleys.

'Not much, to be honest. It's going to be a case of taste it and see.'

'Alright. Keep in touch, Tom.'

The Main Concourse was still ablaze. Material had fallen from the roof and this had fuelled the flames. The insulating material – which, according to Californian law, was supposed to be a fire-retardant – was not holding up too well. Lengths of fibrous material, insulation and plastic piping had tumbled through great gashes in the ceiling. They burned all too easily, filling the air with noxious fumes.

The Main Concourse had taken the worst of the blast. Very few people had been in the area but the explosions had gutted the inside of the CCC. Huge expanses of marble flooring had been ripped up in milliseconds and hurled through the air. They had smashed into the ceiling, bringing down concrete, steel, wood and plastic. With these had come human beings, many ripped to shreds, and computers, chairs, desks and filing cabinets. Papers were still fluttering down from a storeroom on Level 1. The marble and concrete and steel and wood had also blown outwards. The front of the CCC was barely standing. The doors and windows had gone, the lintels had collapsed. But the furthest point from the two blasts, the eastern wing of the complex, had suffered the lightest damage.

It took Stephanie, Josh and Mai several minutes to get to the far side of the Main Concourse. Picking their way through the devastation, they saw things that would remain with them forever. Raw dereliction, a remorseless stripping of humanity that would long haunt them at night.

Pete was waiting for them in the Cage at the emergency exit. He was manoeuvring a steel girder that had been lying across the door, picking it up as though it were a twig. He swung the grappling arm round and slammed it against the door. It disintegrated inwards and they could see a stairwell beyond.

'You're on your own now, guys,' Pete said. 'Good luck.' And he turned to the main doors.

They dove into the narrow passageway beyond the smashed door. It was pitch black. Powerful lights built into their helmets instantly flicked on. A stairway fell away to the right and twisted upward to the left. The air stank, a blend of fumes, incinerated plastic and the acrid smell of spilled chemicals. A pink-tinged smoke hung in the air.

Stephanie tapped at the keypad woven into the wrist of her suit. A small screen lit up and a few seconds later an image appeared – coloured bars and chemical symbols. 'Nasty,' she said. 'Sulfuric acid, hydrogen halides. Probably from foam insulation and glue. Come on.'

She led the way down the stairs then stopped so suddenly that Josh and Mai almost fell over her. At Stephanie's feet lay a body, face-down. Josh helped her gently turn it over and they crouched opposite one another over the prone form. The young man had asphyxiated, his face blue and contorted in a horrible grimace. He had one hand at his throat. His fingers were covered with dried blood, and some of them looked broken.

'I think he must have tried to get out through the emergency exit,' Mai said, 'but the girder Pete moved was too heavy. Must have been overcome by fumes, poor man.'

Stephanie straightened, exhaled heavily into her helmet and turned away.

Another turn of the stairs and they reached a door marked B1. Stephanie was about to try it when they all heard Mark Harrison's voice in their comms. 'Guys? We have an update on the senator and his companions.'

'Go ahead,' Josh replied.

'Looks like they're on their way out of the elevator onto B3.'

'That's good news.'

'Suggest you go straight down the stairwell and see if it's possible to get in through the emergency door. If not, we'll have to figure out something else.'

'Wilco.'

Mai was nearest to the stairway and she led the way. The fumes were growing worse. It looked as though a fire on a lower level was the source of the trouble. They ignored the exit into B2 and continued down. It was growing warmer as they approached the fire. Halfway down the stairs between B2 and B3, they could see orange fingers of fire slithering under the door into B3. Mai checked her wrist computer. The air temperature in the stairwell was nudging 180 degrees Fahrenheit.

They reached the door. The frame and the rim of the door itself was beginning to warp. 'There must be quite a fire the other side,' Josh commented. 'These are fire doors, designed to withstand temperatures up to about 250 degrees Fahrenheit. They're not going to last much longer.'

Stephanie was tapping at her computer and adjusted a micro-filter on her visor. Thanks to the nano-implants behind her eyes, she could view the door with her vision enhanced at either end of the visual spectrum. 'The stress lines look very bad,' she said. 'There's no way we can get through there.'

Josh peered down the stairwell. It was completely blocked

with rubble. 'The only way is up,' he said.

'Agreed. Let's go,' Stephanie replied, and led the way back up the stairs. She was talking into her comms as she ran. 'Mark – B3 is hopeless and the stairwell down from there is impassable. We're going to see if we can get into B2.'

A moment later they were back at the B2 emergency door. Josh took the handle, turned it and pulled. It was stuck fast. Crouching down, he surveyed the area around the lock. 'I'll try blowing it,' he said. 'Step back.'

He tapped at the keypad on his wrist. A fine tube slid from the cybersuit just above Josh's wrist. It was about two inches long and made from a carbon-nanotube composite, super-strong and super-light. He stepped close to the door, leaned back and pointed his hand a few inches above the lock. An intense blue light shot from the end of the tube. Josh slowly moved his wrist down, and there was a loud crack from the lock. The blue light snapped off and he grabbed the handle.

The door flew into the stairwell, sending Josh with it. He landed heavily at the edge of the stairwell and scrambled away as rubble cascaded through the opening. He leapt onto the handrail just ahead of the avalanche. Something caught his arm as he jumped and he felt a sharp stab of pain in his side.

Stephanie and Mai were standing a few steps up the stairs leading to the floor above. Stephanie reacted quickly, grabbing Josh's arm as he flung himself onto the rail. Josh hardly dared move as they watched the slurry tumble down the stairs.

Scrambling up the handrail, Josh kept a few feet away from the detritus flowing through the doorway, and landed with little grace a step below Mai and Stephanie. The pain in his side shot through him but he forced himself to ignore it. Between them, the two women managed to haul him up the stairs. Reaching the next turn, they could see down through the doorway. The cascade had almost stopped now, but the door was sealed. B2 was beyond reach.

'I need to stop a second,' Josh said, his voice pained.

'You're hurt,' Stephanie said and crouched beside him.

He was clutching his side. She felt the area gently and Josh almost jumped out of his suit when her fingers found a certain spot.

'I think you've broken a rib,' she said. Then, into her comms, 'Base One – Josh is injured. Please activate Conus, five mils. Nanobots need to be directed to left vertebro-sternal rib five.'

'Sybil's onto it, Steph. What's your status?'

'Door to Level B2 is impassable. Apart from Josh's injury, we're okay.'

'What's the plan?'

'We'll proceed to B1. See if we can get in that way and try to get down to B3 via an alternative route.'

'Roger.'

As they spoke, Sybil activated the nano-implant in Josh's brain stem, secreting the correct dose of painkiller into his bloodstream. At the same time, the computer ordered 35 million nanobots to make their way to Josh's damaged rib. It would take an hour for them to mend the break, but the painkillers would keep him mobile and able to cope.

The painkiller kicked in almost instantly. Made from a toxin found in the sting of the deadly cone snail *Conus victoriae*, it used a protein called ACV1, which quickly binds to pain receptors in the brain and shuts them down.

As soon as the toxin started performing its magic, Josh got to his feet. 'I love this stuff,' he said with a grin. 'So, what are we waiting for?'

Mai led the way up the stairs back to the emergency door on B1. 'What do you reckon?' she asked the other two as they met her in front of the door.

'I reckon it's our last chance,' Stephanie said grimly.

57

War was seated on the deck of his $50-million yacht *Rosebud* when he made the call to the other three Horsemen. *Rosebud*, which he had christened in honour of his favourite movie, *Citizen Kane*, was moored off Naladhu, in the Maldives. Powered by twin Bentley Marine gas turbines, the yacht boasted six luxury suites, each overlooking the ocean, an open-floor main deck 120 feet long, and a top-deck lounge with an electro-hydraulic retractable roof served by elevator. It could cruise comfortably at 40 knots.

The twenty crew members were all female and were forbidden to wear tops while on duty. Two of them were massaging War's massive neck as he lay on a lounger in the bright afternoon sun. His huge gut was glistening with suntan lotion. A trolley with a flat-screen computer had been wheeled beside him. Each of the other Horsemen was in a separate panel on the screen.

'Gentlemen,' War said, his eyes half-closed. He took a sip of his mint julep made from 60-year-old Kentucky bourbon. 'I hope I haven't called you away from anything important.' He chuckled and his chins wobbled. 'Only we have a problem.'

'What sort of problem?' Death asked. The wood panelling of his Washington DC office could be seen in the background.

206

'It appears our friend is still alive.'

The men on the screen stared at War impassively. They were not easily rattled.

'How can you possibly know that?' Pestilence asked. He was high above the Atlantic Ocean aboard a Hawker 400XP private jet.

'Communications are my business, remember? My people have picked up two separate cell phone calls from his private number.'

'Anyone could be using his phone.'

'Possible, but unlikely. Especially as the second call was to his wife.'

'So, the Dragon's work is *not* complete,' Conquest said, his black eyes surveying the others. He was in the back of a limousine being driven along Birdcage Walk in central London. It was four am, the streets wet with rain.

'I have instructed him to hold his position. Naturally, he is itching to complete his task.' War giggled like a child. The girls rubbing his neck smiled inanely. He bent forward on the lounger. 'A little lower,' he snapped at one of them. The other three Horsemen caught a glimpse of tanned breasts and, in the foreground, War's rolls of fat spilling over his skimpy trunks. 'I assume you agree he should move in,' War continued, raising his eyes to the screen.

'Of course,' Death said matter-of-factly. The other two were nodding.

'There is one other thing,' War added after a pause. He was relishing knowing things the others were unaware of, and he wanted to string it out as much as possible.

'Stop being so damn melodramatic,' Pestilence snapped.

War giggled, but hatred lay behind his wrinkled cheeks. He would love to have Pestilence's head in a vice, and to slowly tighten it until it split open like a watermelon. 'There is some strange group of rescuers at the site.'

'Rescuers?' It was Conquest, his face expressionless.

'My people report the presence of odd-looking aircraft at the CCC appearing out of nowhere. They're a small group, but they have technology no one's ever seen before.'

'What sort of technology?'

War gave a little shrug. 'I have no specifics.'

'Can you get images, video footage?'

'I'll try.'

'Where are these people from?' Pestilence asked.

'No idea.'

'What are they there for?'

War shrugged again. 'I just received the news myself.'

'This smells bad,' Conquest said grimly.

'Yes, I agree, it does,' Death responded. 'But we are in far too deep to back out now. The Dragon must proceed. And,' he added, glaring out of the flat-screen monitor, 'we must get everything we can on these "rescuers". You never know, gentlemen. We may acquire more from this operation than the removal of a nuisance like Senator Kyle Foreman.'

58

The four-way link with Washington, London and the mid-Atlantic cut out, and War ordered the girls to wheel his lounger into the shade. His second mint julep of the day stood on a silver tray beside him, along with a heaped plate of buffalo wings. The computer sat on the trolley beside the lounger.

War tapped at the keyboard and a set of images appeared. They were useless, shapeless blurs. He passed the pictures through an enhancement software package, but it did no good.

With a curse, he opened a video link to his contact on the ground close to the CCC in Los Angeles. His own image and voice were scrambled, so the recipient of his call had no idea of his true identity. The face of a young man appeared on the screen. His name was Jeremy Nichols, an English photographer for *The LA Times*. The tiny camera on his laptop distorted and fractionally delayed his image. Nichols had dust in his hair and his shirt was soiled. He had two state-of-the-art digital cameras around his neck. When he spoke, his voice was shaky with nerves and the trauma of what he had witnessed. 'What can I do for you?'

'What can you do for me? What can you do for me? You're a photographer, right?'

The young man said nothing and simply looked back at the scrambled image on his screen.

'You're a *professional* photographer, right, Mr Nichols?'

'What's wrong?'

War giggled. Through the distortion, Nichols could see

flesh vibrating. 'The images of the aircraft. They may as well be snaps of a blancmange at a kid's fucking birthday party. That's what's wrong.'

The young man looked confused. 'But that's impossible.'

'Didn't you look at them before you sent them?'

'No . . . I knew you wanted them fast so I emailed them straight over.'

'Look,' War said.

And the photographer stared at his screen, where one of the images was now visible.

'Oh.'

'Yes, oh. I think you'll agree they're not worth much to me, Mr Nichols.'

The photographer didn't seem to be listening as he studied the image on his screen. 'They're using some sort of distortion system,' he said to himself.

'What?'

'They have something that confuses the camera.'

'Oh, bullshit!' War exclaimed. He clapped his hands together and laughed loudly. 'That technology doesn't exist.'

'Well, it evidently does,' Nichols said, forgetting himself for a second.

War's face fell.

'If you had seen their aircraft,' Nichols went on quickly, 'you'd believe they could do anything.'

'Well, I haven't been able to see their fucking aircraft, have I?' And War burst out laughing again.

Nichols could think of nothing to say. War filled the silence by muttering to himself. 'So, they have image-distortion technology, do they? Well, that is very, very interesting.' After a moment he looked up at the screen. 'Okay, Nichols. You can fuck off now,' and he laughed so much he made himself cough. Then he broke the link.

'Image-distortion technology. I like that,' War said quietly. He drained his mint julep and chuckled. 'I *really* like that.'

59

California Conference Center, Los Angeles

The text arriving down the secure line to the Dragon's cell consisted of two short words: '*Move in.*'

From a kitbag on the back seat, he removed a dark suit, a white shirt and a brown tie. He pulled them on with slow, deliberate movements, placed his soiled fatigues in a plastic bag and double-knotted it. Next he pulled on a pair of latex gloves, removed the top from a jar of Vaseline, dipped his finger in and smeared some along his hair line, down his temples and across the back of his neck. He then took a lump of black rub-in dye and worked it into his hair. After applying four handfuls of the gloopy material, he combed back his hair, ran a couple of handy-wipes around his hairline to remove the barrier of Vaseline, pulled off the gloves and placed all the detritus into another, smaller plastic bag and double-knotted that.

The process complete, the Dragon studied his reflection in the vanity mirror inside the sunshade. Tightening his tie, he pinned a name badge to his lapel and was about to step out of the car when another text arrived. It read: '*Target is on B3.*'

The Dragon pocketed his Smith & Wesson and the Yarygin PYa and pulled a bag over his shoulder. It contained four M67 fragmentation grenades and a state-of-the-art micro-gasmask. Then he buckled on a concealed belt that held his sheathed Fairbairn-Sykes commando knife. Now outside the car, he leaned against the door as he reset his GPS tracker and waited for Kyle Foreman's location to appear.

The Dragon had always been a technophile. He had met the lab guys who worked for the Four Horsemen. He knew the level of sophistication of their surveillance technology. Foreman had been their number one target for two months, and preparations had been thorough. They knew he changed his cell phone and number every three weeks, but they had still been able to plant a microscopic bug into each of the phones the senator used. It allowed the tech guys to triangulate Foreman's position from his phone, even when it was not in use or the battery was flat. And they could transfer that information to the GPS system the Dragon now held in his hand.

A moment later, the data began to download. After a few seconds a red circle appeared on the screen of the GPS, showing that Foreman was moving east from the elevators on B3. The Dragon felt a ripple of excitement run through him. 'Beautiful,' he said aloud. Then he reached into his shoulder bag, removed a grenade, pulled the pin with his teeth, tossed it through the driver's window of the car and strode towards the road that circled the CCC. He didn't flinch as the car exploded behind him and he felt the heat from the blast on the back of his neck.

60

Josh, Stephanie and Mai entered B1 through the emergency exit door that led from the stairwell in the rear east corner of the CCC.

B1 was almost as badly damaged as the ground floor, especially in its western half, which was as smashed up as the auditorium directly above it. The second bomb had been planted here, inside an air-conditioning duct in the ceiling.

The lights were dead, but with their powerful helmet beams the corridor beyond was lit up pretty well. This was the main administration level, dominated by a U-shaped corridor with a warren of offices clustered around it. The reception area in the centre of the level was directly below the Main Concourse.

It was eerily calm. They could hear sounds coming from the western wing, the crackling of flames and cascading water, but they seemed far off. Most of the doors to the offices had been smashed to matchwood. From close by came the fizz of strip-lights ripped from the ceiling and still tingling with ionised gas and stray electric current. They were moist and deadly. The carpeted floor was sodden. The sprinklers had gone off, then the pipes had ruptured.

Five paces down the corridor, they almost fell over a woman in a business suit. Her body lay spread-eagled, with her head beside her. Her torso was drenched from the sprinklers, and her blouse pink with diluted blood. The cream carpet beneath her was now the colour of salmon flesh.

Most of the offices were deserted. Only a handful of people had been working down here when the bombs went off. It seemed unlikely anyone could have survived.

They advanced slowly along the corridor, then west towards the central reception area and the elevators. No more bodies. No one alive, either. Reaching the foyer, they saw the extent of the damage on the western side. Josh checked the temperature – it was over 180 degrees Fahrenheit. Without the filters in their helmets, the fumes would have been deadly. Flames were lapping along the corridor leading from the west wing to the central foyer. It was completely impassable.

'Our best hope was to get through to the west wing,' Mai said, an edge of despair in her voice.

'Damn it!' Josh snapped. 'And the main elevators are obviously out. Any bright ideas?'

'The air-conditioning ducts. They link up the floors.'

'Okay, but we know B3 on this side is ablaze around the emergency exit.'

'So we use the ducts to get one level down, to B2,' Stephanie said. 'Then we just have to hope there's another way down from there.'

'Doesn't sound encouraging,' Mai replied.

'Well, any other suggestions? This would be the time.'

Josh sighed. 'No, I don't have any. Mai?'

She shook her head.

'Right. You two stay here. I'll go and see if it's even possible,' Stephanie said confidently.

They chose the third office along the bottom of the U-shaped corridor. It seemed like a sensible choice – it was some way from the emergency exit, which meant that if the fire near the exit on B3 had reached the area directly above it, on B2, the air-con ducts this far west should still be alright. It was also some distance from the main area of devastation on the western side of the CCC. Josh radioed

Base One and informed Tom what they were planning, and he set to work finding a schematic of the air-con system for the complex.

There was a good solid desk on one side of the room. They slid it across the floor until it stood directly under a metal grille in the ceiling, which was just wide enough for a person to get through. Emptying a couple of metal filing cabinets, they heaved them up onto the desk and placed a chair on top.

Stephanie climbed up. The grille was held in place by four wing-nuts, one at each corner. She spun them loose, eased the grille out and handed it down to Mai. Stephanie heaved herself up through the gap and into the air-con duct.

The duct was a narrow square-sided channel, and Stephanie had to half-crawl, half-slither along the smooth metal surface. To her left, the duct led to another channel that ran above the main corridor. To the right, it curved away to the rear of the building.

'Base One,' Steph said into her comms. 'Do you have that schematic?'

'Just got it,' Tom replied. 'Sending it over.'

Steph looked at the flexiscreen on her wrist. A miniature version of the air-con schematic appeared, a complex mesh of coloured lines. Mai and Josh received it at the same time, and a much larger version was displayed on the wall of Cyber Control at Tintara.

'You're here,' Tom said, and a red dot appeared among the tangle of lines. 'You need to turn right. This will lead you to a point close to the elevator foyer. From there the duct splits. One channel goes up to the Ground Level. But from the BigEye image, it looks pretty smashed up. Another channel goes down to B2. There's no way of telling what you'll find there.'

'Copy that, Tom. I'm taking the right turn.'

Without her cybersuit, the task would have been completely impossible. The temperature in the duct was over 130 degrees Fahrenheit, and noxious fumes from the west of the building had found their way into the air-con system. The suit cooled Stephanie's body and filtered out the poisons, but clawing her way along the channel was still exhausting work.

It was a relief to reach the junction. She looked up and saw the channel blocked just a few yards above her head. Looking down, her helmet light lit up the channel. She could see where the down channel met another duct on B2 that ran parallel to the one she had just shuffled along.

'I'm at the junction,' she said into her comms. 'I'm going to lower myself on a wire.'

From her backpack she disengaged a narrow carbon-fibre wire with a pressure sucker at the end. She attached the sucker to the wall of the duct and eased herself over the side. The nanocomputers in her suit released the wire steadily, lowering Stephanie into the void between the floors. It took her just a few seconds to reach the air-con channel on B2. Touching down on the floor of the duct, she released the wire and it slithered back into her pack.

In the light from her helmet, Stephanie saw the channel stretching from north to south, to the rear and the front of the building. She looked at her flexiscreen. She could see that she was now on B2, the first level of the car park, and close to the main elevators. There were fewer outlets for the air-con on this level. The nearest was about 30 yards towards the front of the CCC. She turned into the narrow channel and headed south.

The weakened floor plate in the air-con duct was impossible to see. It had been caused by an exploding gas tank in the car park 30 minutes earlier. The tank had blown into hundreds of pieces that slammed around the car park, shattering car windows and punching great holes in vehicles.

Crawling forward, Stephanie leant her hands on the duct and a panel gave way. She tumbled forward. Her scream echoed around Cyber Control almost 1500 miles away, and in Josh and Mai's comms one floor above her.

61

'Steph!' Mai and Josh yelled in unison. On Tintara, everyone working in Cyber Control froze, hardly daring to draw breath.

Stephanie's reflexes were quick. As she tipped into the hole that had opened up under her, she scrambled to grab at anything solid. Her arms flailed and her suit caught on a piece of protruding metal. The carbothreads of the suit held fast, and with one gloved hand she just managed to grab the edge of the duct.

Below her lay twenty feet of air. This presented no real problem, but what did matter was the mangled pile of metal that carpeted the floor of the car park. Six-inch spikes of glass and coils of charred and jagged steel stuck up like deadly stalagmites. To make it worse, motor oil was burning all around the debris, sending up black billowing smoke and red flames.

'Steph – status?'

For a moment she was too stunned to speak. She just groaned. Then she brought her free arm up to improve her grip on the edge of the hole. The metal of the duct creaked ominously.

'I'm in one piece,' she said in a low, pained voice. 'Just. I've gone through the floor of the duct and I'm hanging on to the rim. Problem is, I can't get down. There's a fire directly below me and the floor is strewn with huge pieces of jagged metal.'

'Okay,' came Mark's voice from Base One. His eyes darted across the holoscreen above Tom's virtual keypad, where he could see the status of each member of E-Force. 'Steph, your suit has held. Are you injured?'

'I don't think so. But I can't get back up and I can't jump down.'

'Steph – I'm on my way,' Mai said. She was already clambering onto the filing cabinets. A second later she had pulled herself up into the opening of the air-con duct.

She moved faster than Steph had, and reached the junction into B2 a mere twenty seconds after entering the duct.

Dangling from the car park ceiling, Steph could feel herself weakening.

'Steph, we're releasing glucose boosters. You cool with that?'

'Sure am.'

Mark was about to speak, when Tom cupped his hand over the mic. 'Mark,' he said quietly. 'There's a micro-tear in her suit.'

Mark felt a spasm of fear shoot down his spine. He stared at the holoscreen and saw it – a rip, no more than a fraction of a millimetre long, in the arm of Stephanie's cybersuit.

'Steph,' Mark said, his voice booming through the comms. 'We have a problem.'

Mai heard Mark's words, and slowed for a fraction of a second. Then her training kicked in and she increased her pace. Whatever it was Mark was about to say, it meant she had to get there even faster.

'There's a micro-tear in your suit. Tom's onto it and the nanobots are already stitching it up. Our sensors tell us your suit is coping well, but what does it say on your screen? Can you see it?'

Stephanie fought back the terror. She could feel the glucose boosters doing their work. She could hold on, but what could she do about the tear? She tried twisting to see the flexiscreen on her wrist, but it was impossible.

'Can't see it,' she said.

'Mai – what's your status?' Mark asked.

Mai had her wire out and was attaching it to the inside of the duct. 'Almost there,' she replied, and slid down the wire to B2.

'Keep the wire in place, Mai.'

'Wilco that.'

A red light appeared on the holoscreen above Tom's virtual keypad. 'Shit,' he exclaimed.

Mark glanced at the figures darting across the screen, which each represented one facet of Stephanie's cybersuit. He could see the rip was being repaired at an incredible rate. But he could also see that the suit's temperature control was failing, and the methane levels in the air were increasing.

Hanging above the burning motor oil, the shards of metal and glass glinting in the blue light, Stephanie began to cough. Then she noticed her feet were warming up.

'Mark, I think there's a problem with the thermal control of my suit.' She coughed again.

Mai was within a few feet of the hole, moving forward with exaggerated care. The wire had played out behind her, but the tension was being automatically regulated. If she fell suddenly, it would hold her.

She reached the rim of the hole. The metal had severed along a join. As she approached the hole, Mai could see Stephanie. She looked like she was at the point of exhaustion. Under the plastic of her visor, her face was wet with sweat.

'Take my hand, Steph,' Mai said. Stretching forward, she could see the mess below, the ghastly spikes and the black smoke. Stephanie's eyes were ablaze in the beam from Mai's helmet light.

'I can't . . . I'll –'

'Steph. You have to take my hand. I'm wired up. It will easily take our combined weight.'

Stephanie couldn't move. Terrified, she had seized up. It was all she could do to keep gripping the rim.

The metal lip of the hole creaked, then it buckled. Stephanie screamed as she dropped six inches. Flames played against the soles of her boots.

Mai slid around the edge of the hole. The wire tightened, holding her in place. She looked down at Stephanie and could see her friend's gloved fingers clinging to the metal lip. Then she saw them begin to slip down over the buckled metal.

Mai's arm shot out. The metal beneath her gave way, coiling under itself, leaving only air directly beneath her. The wire reacted automatically. Mai had Stephanie's upper arm, gripping it tight. Stephanie let go with her other hand just as the metal lip tore away from the duct. She grabbed Mai's wrist.

Mai told the wire to retract slowly and they moved up through the hole, narrowly avoiding the jagged edge. They pushed on the walls of the vertical chute with their feet as the wire slowly raised them through the fumy air. Stephanie was coughing. Nanobots released oxygen into her helmet and she could breathe better. The glucose boosters helped her push against the walls of the duct.

In few moments they were inside the air-con channel on B1 and the air was clearer. Two more minutes crawling through the duct and they were back in the office, where Josh helped them down.

62

Foreman and Dave managed to scramble past Todd on the ladder so they could get to the lift shaft doors on B3. Between them, they wedged open the doors using the aluminium struts, which Foreman had slipped into his back pocket. He was first off the ladder, followed by Dave, and then they helped Marty and Todd over the lip of the opening onto B3.

The smell of smoke hit them and they started to wonder if it had all been worth the effort. Todd collapsed onto the concrete floor just beyond the doors, exhausted. He had lost a lot of blood and was growing weaker by the second. The senator bent down to take a look at his injury. None of them had any medical know-how, but a section of bone was protruding at least an inch through his skin.

'Todd,' Foreman said gently. 'We have to keep moving. Can you get up?'

'I'm fucked, man,' he replied. 'I can't feel my arm, and I'm so cold.'

Dave came over and crouched down, their earlier fight forgotten. 'We'll get you out of here, Todd. Just be strong, yeah?'

The four of them stared across the car park level, which was shrouded in smoke. It was packed with cars, but none of them looked the way they had when they'd been parked earlier that evening. Windows were smashed, and concrete supports and steel beams had flattened the roofs of at least a dozen vehicles. Others had popped bonnets or blown tyres. One four-wheel drive had rolled onto its neighbour.

'What now?' Dave asked.

'Good question,' Foreman replied with a heavy sigh. 'The smoke is thickest over there.' He pointed east, to the far side of the car park. 'You three wait here. I'll go take a look.'

Instead of heading straight across the car park, Foreman first veered left to check out the emergency stairs. A narrow paved path ran from the elevators to the exit, which was directly below the emergency door they had tried on the Ground Level. He didn't need to go the whole way. He could see from twenty yards away that it was blocked by a single piece of concrete that probably weighed a couple of tons.

The senator paused for a moment to get his bearings in the shrouded half-light. The smoke burned his throat. He yanked at his shirt sleeve, the hand-sewn seams giving with surprising ease. Covering his nose and mouth with the expensive fabric, he moved along the driveway, between the rows of decimated cars. Fifty yards on, he jumped suddenly as the alarm went off in a Toyota Prius. It was loud, amplified by the concrete all around. In a few minutes he had reached the centre of the level – four giant concrete columns, pitted and blackened with smoke, that stood on either side of the ramps leading up and down.

The smoke was thicker here, and Foreman started to cough. His eyes stung and watered. Then he saw reddish flames and a pink tinge to the fumes. The smell of burning plastic was overpowering. There was no way they could get out that way, even if the emergency exit that side of the level was clear.

He glanced back towards the elevators but he could no longer see his companions. For a fleeting second he had an almost uncontrollable urge to run, just run and never look back. Gazing at the ramp leading up to B2, he almost did.

The others would find their own way out. He saw Sandy's face and the imagined face of his unborn baby.

Foreman spun on his heel and ran back to the elevators. The shapes of Dave, Todd and Marty solidified through the smoke. They were sitting with their backs to the wall where the air was a fraction clearer.

'The far exit is impassable. That's where the fire is. But there's a car ramp, up and down. It's our best hope.'

Dave helped Todd to his feet.

'I'm okay,' he said shakily. 'I can walk.'

'The smoke's getting worse,' Marty said gravely.

'It is, and it's worse still over there,' Foreman replied, nodding towards the ramp. 'But there's no alternative. He ripped his other sleeve away and handed it to Todd. 'Use this.'

Marty tore at his own shirt sleeve and Dave ripped it in two. They covered their mouths with the cloth and followed Foreman into the thickening smoke. Then they all froze as they heard a loud series of explosions close by.

'Sounds like they're coming from the ramps,' Dave said.

'Not on this floor though,' Foreman noted. 'Come on!'

Rather than retracing his steps to the ramp, Kyle led them away from the elevators and towards the front of the building. The fumes were a little less suffocating there. They turned down the first aisle but stopped after only a few yards. A car had been pushed into the aisle and blocked the way. It was covered with glass and dust. Foreman led them between two other cars and they reached the second aisle. To their left and a few yards ahead a four-wheel drive was burning.

A car horn blared. They ran past it and saw a man's smashed head slumped on his steering wheel. One of his arms lay across the dash and protruded through the shattered windshield. His hand had been split down the middle to the wrist between his third and fourth fingers. Blood fanned out across the bonnet and was still dripping onto the concrete like leaking oil.

As he ran, the senator felt a growing sense of foreboding. They were doing something wrong. He had just seen something that wasn't right. Dave was next to him, then Marty. Todd was struggling along a pace behind.

'How you doing, Todd?' Dave called, glancing back without slowing his pace.

'I'm doing,' he gasped. His face was lathered with sweat, streaked black with soot and grime.

Dave dropped back. 'You can make it, man.' He went to put his shoulder under Todd, but Todd shook it off.

'No, I'll slow you down. I'm cool.'

A trunk lid lay in the middle of the aisle. Todd and Dave went around it different sides.

It was then that the burning car they had just passed blew.

63

Thick smoke hung low along the road that circled the CCC. The Dragon ran along the tarmac. Reaching the rear of the mall, he ducked into a small car park. The body of a man lay sprawled face-down on the concrete, his back a field of glass shards. For a second the corpse looked to the Dragon like some sort of macabre porcupine, and he laughed. This was the first victim of the evening's handiwork he had seen up close, and he felt not a scintilla of guilt nor remorse. His overriding emotion at that moment was contempt for the dead man, who had been fool enough to be in the wrong place at the wrong time.

He swung open a door at the loading bay at the back of the car park and found himself in a warehouse behind the Kmart. The place was deserted. He ran along a corridor, seeing no one. But he pulled out his Smith & Wesson just in case. He turned a bend and went through another door, and then he was on the shop floor.

The store had been closed for an hour when the bombs went off, so it had been empty. The front windows had been blown in, sending glass across the shop right to its rear wall. It crunched under the Dragon's boots. Once-neat shelves holding everything from paperback books to the latest toy robots were scattered randomly, flung around the space like a deck of playing cards flicked into the air.

The Dragon strode to the wall at his left. Close to the rear of the store was a door with a sign reading 'Maintenance'. It was locked, but one shot from the Smith & Wesson and the Dragon had smashed a hole above the handle, shattering the locking mechanism. He kicked the door in and it flew back, smashing against a brick wall.

Flicking on a light switch to the right of the doorway, he could see a narrow corridor. Storerooms led off left and right, and at the end of the passageway was a hatch in the far wall. It too was locked, but not for long. Switching on a torch strapped to his head, the Dragon pulled himself up into the opening and began to crawl forward.

The maintenance conduit was a little over a hundred feet long and lined with wires and dotted with junction boxes and larger units that bristled with cables. He covered the distance in 30 seconds and reached a metal ladder. It rose 25 feet, bringing him out into another tunnel.

The light from the torch bobbed about the walls of the maintenance passageway, illuminating more metal boxes, wires, thick ropes of multicoloured cable and glass-fronted panels. It was absolutely silent here. The Dragon felt cut off from human existence, a physical enactment of what he had felt in his heart and his shrivelled soul ever since he was a boy. It pleased him.

He knew from the map Dexter Tate had shown him that this conduit was only a couple of hundred feet long. It covered the short distance from the mall to B2 of the CCC, but with every step it felt as though the tunnel was growing longer and that he would never reach the end. It was hot and confined, and a lesser man – one without his years of training – might have panicked. But the Dragon kept his breathing steady and his pace even, and in less than two minutes he had reached the far end, a metal door that opened from the inside. It swung outwards, a few feet above the floor of B2.

He jumped down, the door slammed against the wall, and he leaned back against the opening. He wanted to breathe deeply, but the air was scorching and fumy. He removed the gas mask from his shoulder bag and pulled it on.

A few dozen yards to his left the Dragon could just make out the ramp leading down to B3 and up to B1. Here, in the eastern part of B2, the car park was ablaze from at least three intense fires. Two of these lay between him and the centre of the level, where the ramp was situated. A fierce fire was also raging to his right, at the eastern end of B2.

He pulled out the GPS and glanced at the screen. The red circle marking Kyle Foreman's position showed he was moving east from the elevators, towards the ramps. So the Dragon had no choice. If he was to intercept the target, he would have to get through the fires to his left. Only then could he reach the ramp and get down to B3.

He ran between the rows of cars, taking steady breaths filtered by the mask. He had to push north, towards the back of the CCC, to get around the more intense of the two fires, constantly aware that at any moment a car could explode next to him. He approached the ramp from the north and looked down to B3. There was no sign of Foreman. That was good. He jumped over a low parapet and landed on the tarmac slope.

Once he could make visual contact with Foreman, he would take him lower down, into the bowels of the building where he could deal with him unseen. The senator would end up just another charred corpse, most likely unidentifiable.

The Dragon lowered his shoulder bag to the floor. With deft movements he pulled out a grenade, tugged the pin away and flung it behind him. Then, as he ran down the ramp into B3, he tossed the remaining two grenades one after the other. They exploded two seconds apart, bringing huge chunks of masonry down onto the top of the ramp from B2 to B3 and showering him with dust. A moment later there was another crash from the top of the ramp as three vehicles landed on top of each other, sealing up the opening completely.

The Dragon leaned against a pillar, panting into his mask. He took one last clean breath, then ripped the mask from his face and tossed it into a pile of rubble nearby. Peering down at himself, he could see that his suit was covered with dust and stained with oil and dirt. That was good. He needed to look a little roughed up.

He tore at the sleeve of his jacket and then leaned down to rip his left trouser leg. Removing his commando knife from its sheath at his waist, the Dragon bent forward again. With a steady hand, he plunged the knife into his calf, carefully avoiding the major blood vessels. The result was a nasty-looking flesh wound that bled well but would cause no long-term damage.

Ignoring the pain, he pushed himself away from the wall, sheathed the knife, pocketed his gun and limped away to crouch behind a pile of debris to await the arrival of Senator Kyle Foreman.

64

The boom was ear-splitting and was followed by a rush of material shooting outwards. Marty and Foreman were blown off their feet and sprawled forward onto the concrete.

Dave was thrown onto a car to his right and ended up with his nose an inch from the shattered windshield. He felt a burning sensation in his calf. Looking down, he saw flames leaping from his trousers. The scene seemed to be moving in slow motion. Dave hit his leg with his bare hands. They stung and he yelped. It was burning fuel. He yanked at his backpack, saggy on his shoulders, and smothered the flames with it. Then he tore the fabric away from his leg.

It was only then that he saw Todd lying face-down, his body twisted horribly. A line of burning fuel from the exploded car was racing towards him. Dave slid off the hood and ran to his friend, screaming hysterically.

He grabbed Todd's leg and dragged him along the ground away from the stream of burning fuel. Marty and Foreman were just coming to. The senator pulled himself to his knees.

'Todd?' Dave was leaning over him. The boy's face was badly burned, his skin blistered from temple to chin. One eye was open but sightless, clouded in grey. 'Todd?' Dave shook him.

Todd started. He tried to look at his friend, but he seemed to be totally blind. He grabbed at Dave's arm and started to cry. He was trying to speak. Dave couldn't make out the words and leaned in closer, but Todd's head slumped to one side.

'Todd . . . *Todd*!'

Foreman and Marty were beside Dave, pulling him to his feet. 'Come on, we've got to go,' Marty was saying.

Dave felt as though time had stood still. He could see his friend's dead face, but it wasn't real. None of this was. He was going to wake up any moment and shake it off – a bad dream, nothing more. Marty's voice cut in, but Dave couldn't make out what he was saying. He turned and saw the old man's anxious face close to his. His mouth was moving but the words were soundless.

Dave felt himself propelled forward, strong hands gripping his arms. He was running, running without knowing why or where he was going. He felt the ground rise, the acrid air choking him as he gasped. He watched the ramp slide past, the concrete columns to left and right. They were close to the top of the ramp. They stopped and Dave heard Kyle Foreman swear. Marty made a loud choking sound in his throat.

Ahead of them lay three burning cars and a huge concrete slab from the caved-in ceiling. The way was completely blocked.

65

The Mole was one of the machines unique to E-Force. It was an astonishing piece of technology. It looked like a massive drill bit on tracks, and – as its name suggested – it was designed to burrow into the earth. But, although it did this with great efficiency, it could also withstand very high temperatures, allowing it to pass easily through fires.

Behind the drill was the one-man control centre, and behind that was a cylindrical capsule ten feet long and four feet wide. From the control centre the operator of the Mole had a 360-degree view of the surroundings via external cameras. Sensors in the machine's skin passed information about the external environment to the on-board nano-systems. The capsule behind the control centre was dubbed 'the Bullet' because of its shape, but it was also incredibly tough – blast-proof, radiation-sealed and resistant to almost every chemical known to humankind.

Pete Sherringham sat at the controls of the Mole, poised at the top of the ground-floor down-ramp that led to the car park on the eastern side of the CCC. He gave verbal instructions to the computer system and the machine edged forward, beginning its descent down the slope.

The walls of the ramp had been badly damaged by the blasts. Lumps of dusty concrete were strewn across the floor, and some of the tarmac had buckled. Pete drove down the first spiral and was soon parallel to B1. There was no off-ramp here, since the first parking level was on B2. He swung the

Mole around the next curve, and twenty seconds later he was at the entrance to the car park.

At first glance, the car park looked like a building site. Pete flicked on the Mole's powerful beams. They cut through the smoky gloom and the cameras charted the devastation. There were burnt-out cars and automobile parts scattered across the floor. Every windscreen had shattered. Great expanses of the ceiling had caved in. Huge energies had undone the work of many man-hours.

He pulled the Mole into the car park and paused for a moment. 'Anybody there?' he called through the external speakers. Nothing. The sensors in the skin of the Mole could pick up any sound from outside. Pete had the filter set to stream the sound of a human voice only. But nothing came through.

He moved forward, between the rows of smashed-up cars. A flame shot out from the shattered passenger window of a Cadillac CTS Sport and the engine exploded, sending the hood crashing into the ceiling before it cartwheeled along the aisle. It slammed into the Mole and rolled to a stop near the ramp.

The floor was slick with oil and water, but it meant nothing to the tracks of the Mole. Looking west, Pete could see the devastation was worse. Many of the cars had been ripped apart. At least a quarter of them had been upended. Nudging forward, in a few moments he had reached the top of the down ramp from B2 to B3. Where once the ramp had led smoothly down to B3, now the way was blocked by a massive pile of boulders, steel girders and a clutch of mangled vehicles.

Pete manoeuvred the Mole towards the lip of the ramp and stopped a few feet from the obstruction. The blockage was so complete that even with the powerful lights of the Mole, he couldn't see anything on the other side. He called through the speakers again, 'Is anyone there? The other side of this blockage?' Nothing.

'Base One,' Pete said into his comms.

'Yeah, Pete,' came Mark Harrison's low voice.

'Can BigEye get any detail down to B3?'

Mark looked at one of the technicians who shook his head. 'That's a negative, Pete. Too much interference. What's your situation?'

'I'm at the top of the ramp going from B2 to B3, but the way is completely blocked. I'm a little nervous about smashing my way through in case someone's alive the other side.'

'Any other way down?'

'Negative. The west end of B2 is smashed up so bad there's a danger the Mole could go right through the floor.'

'Well, you don't have much choice then, Pete.'

'Wilco.' Pete cut the link and surveyed his sensors. He could hear nothing around the frequency of a human voice. The infrared sensors were overwhelmed by the heat of the fires in the car park, so he couldn't separate out the body heat from anyone who might be the other side of the blockage.

Pete made his decision. The Mole started to move forward.

66

Base One, Tintara

A few minutes from sunset and the slowly descending orange sun lit up the expanse of the Pacific Ocean like a vermilion disco ball. Tom Erickson was in his private quarters overlooking the west of Tintara, the full splendour of the clear evening sky framed by his window. He had a console in his room that was almost as versatile as the one in Cyber Control, and from here he had complete access to Sybil, the quantum computer at the heart of the entire system.

As much as he had grown to love being part of the team at Tintara, Tom valued his privacy. It might have been something to do with the months he had spent at the Aldermont Correctional Facility, where his only friend had been his laptop. But now he had found a home, people he could identify with. Sure, he enjoyed teasing them, but he had never met a group of people he respected more. And now they needed him. This mission would fail unless he could find a way for the team on the ground to reach Senator Kyle Foreman.

'Sybil – bring up the schematic of the CCC, please,' he said. The holoscreen was aglow in front of his wheelchair, and the virtual keyboard was projected over his lap. The 3D schematic appeared two feet in front of his face. 'Music, please, Sybil,' he said, staring fixedly at the image.

'I have 3,257,419 individual pieces of –'

'Yes, Syb, baby, I imagine you do. Any Barry Manilow? Just kidding. Play . . .' He looked out at the sky now dominated by crimson and orange. 'The White Stripes, *Seven Nation Army* – loud, Syb.'

'Please specify –'

'Er, crank it up to eleven.'

'I'm sorry. That –'

'Sybil – volume nine. I'll let you know if it's wrong.'

The throbbing bass notes kicked in, then the drums, and Jack White's rasping bluesy voice. Tom pushed his head back against the rest of his wheelchair and closed his eyes. He tried to clear his mind and let the music wash over him. The heavier the sounds, the calmer he became.

Tom opened his eyes and looked at the schematic. At first glance it was just a maze of lines. He surveyed the ten floors of the building. Much of B1 was a mess, and B2 – the first level of the car park – was strewn with damaged vehicles, random fires and other hazards. A bad fire was raging on the eastern side of B3.

'Where's Pete, Sybil?'

A small dot appeared on B2. But Pete Sherringham's way was blocked. He was about to guide the Mole down through a major obstruction and it would take him a while to get through. Furthermore, there was no way of knowing where Kyle Foreman and the others would be by the time he got through. Tom had no choice – somehow he had to get Josh, Mai and Steph down there.

'Okay,' Tom said. 'Okay, so what now?' The music was good and loud and reaching a crescendo. 'Come on, man, think. *Think*!' He ran a hand through his long, greasy hair. 'What do buildings need? Electricity. Right. Gas. Right. Water. Sewage . . . Sybil – is there a schematic on the net for the sewage system of the CCC?'

A few seconds passed. 'Yes,' Sybil responded.

236

'Good. Can you superimpose it on the schematic of the building, please.'

A mesh of green lines appeared, linking the floors. They ran to a main artery to the east of the building, just below B6. From there, a thick green line extended eastwards. It was useless – the threads from the sewage channels from the building were no more than two feet in diameter. The main sewer in the area was four feet wide, but the compact CCC pipes didn't link to it until more than 50 yards east of the CCC. 'Damn it!' Tom exclaimed above the pounding music.

He stared out the window. The sky was turning purple and a few stars were beginning to appear.

'Sybil – superimpose all services to the CCC on the schematic.'

New lines appeared – yellow for gas pipes, black for electricity, red for mains water. None of them included maintenance conduits running to or from the CCC. There were no manholes or access tunnels big enough. But suddenly Tom had an idea.

'Sybil – can you find an image of the foundations? Either from BigEye or anything on the net?'

This time the delay was a little longer.

'BigEye can't reach that far down, Tom,' Sybil said. 'But there is an image of the site taken when the CCC was being constructed in 1996.'

'Alright,' Tom said. 'Bring it up, please.' He looked at the still image. It was a vast construction site. Three huge trucks in the foreground. Then he noticed something. 'What's that, Sybil? That opening at the far side of the foundations?'

'You could be referring to any of three different openings, Tom.'

'Sure. The one that's level with the top of the foundations. Top-left of the image.'

'That is a municipal drain. It was first constructed in 1934 to take rainwater to the ocean. It was decommissioned when the CCC was constructed.'

'Decommissioned? But not demolished?'

A pause. The image changed. The schematic of the CCC appeared: a new set of lines lay to the rear of the building.

'Close in, Sybil. Top-left corner of the foundations, please.'

The image changed again. The bottom left corner of the CCC took up the entire holoscreen.

'That drain, Sybil. Is there an entry point at ground level?'

The view transformed yet again, following the drain a hundred yards to the west of the building.

'It emerges here, at grid reference –'

'That's alright, Sybil. I can see where it comes out. And this is the $64,000-question, Syb. How close does it run to B6 of the CCC?'

'The closest point is at grid reference D17 on the image. Separation of drain wall and wall into B6 is 38.41 inches. Soil type: compacted rock, sand and clay.'

'Syb, baby, I love you!' Tom said.

67

For someone so young, the woman who called herself Francine Gygax – in homage to Gary Gygax, the creator of *Dungeons & Dragons* – had an almost invincible sense of self-confidence. She knew the men only by the collective name of the Four Horsemen – an epithet she thought rather ridiculous. But she didn't feel the slightest bit intimidated by them, and hadn't even bothered disguising herself on screen. The four men had, however. All she could see of them were blurred faces, while they could see each other clearly.

War was still on his lounger on the deck of the *Rosebud*, moored off Naladhu. The sun was hot and lemon rays danced on the calm water. Death was still in his Washington DC office, and Pestilence was aboard the Hawker 400XP, now closer to LaGuardia in New York. Conquest had arrived at his Mayfair penthouse, poured himself a generous brandy and was sitting on an antique cream sofa. It was 8.30 pm in LA, 11.30 pm in Washington, 4.30 am in London and 9.30 am in the Maldives. Francine was nowhere and everywhere. In cyberspace there are no time zones.

'You come highly recommended,' Conquest said, as four faces appeared on the huge screen on a wall of his apartment.

Francine produced a barely discernible smile. 'I would imagine I do. I'm the best there is,' she replied matter-of-factly.

Francine was twenty years old and had known great power for the past five. Five years that were a stark contrast to the first fifteen of her life. She had once been a shrew, an insignificant, plain young girl whom the other kids either ignored or verbally tortured. Now she understood how to manipulate. She knew the power she could exert, especially over men.

Blonde and statuesque, with jet-black eyes, thanks to extensive plastic surgery, Francine bore little resemblance to the mousy-haired, spotty teenager she had once been. War had been rendered almost speechless as Francine appeared on his screen. He felt a stirring in his loins and giggled to himself.

'I read the brief,' Francine said, concentrating on Conquest's distorted image. 'Looks like you need some help.'

Conquest bridled, but quickly brought his features under control. War was not so subtle and burst out laughing.

'You find something amusing?' Francine asked, turning her black eyes to the large wobbling shape on her screen.

War roared with laughter and gave a wink intended for his three cohorts. 'I love this girl,' he announced. 'She's giving me a hard-on.'

Francine's faint smile reappeared. Without looking down, her fingers flitted over a keyboard just out of sight. Suddenly, on the Horsemen's four screens in dispersed locations around the globe, War's face began to alter and it appeared out of the blur on Francine's screen. The plentiful flesh of his jowls and his thick neck began to vibrate. His lips trembled and he dribbled onto his massive white chest. His eyes started to bulge. Then, as quickly as it had begun to change, his face returned to something close to normal. But he looked drained and hideously pale.

The other three Horsemen were stunned. They had each seen many horrible things. They had each inflicted terrible pain upon others, but this was something new.

Death was the first to recover his composure. 'What did you do?'

'Oh, now, that would be telling.'

'I demand that you explain yourself.'

Francine fixed him with cold eyes and gave a nonchalant shrug. 'I don't respond to *demands*.'

'I'm intrigued,' Conquest interjected, his voice calm, placating. 'Humour us.'

She sighed. 'I simply sent your fat friend a few interesting visuals. Certain images can be, well, very *powerful*.'

Death glared at the girl, barely able to comprehend. 'You hacked into his computer?'

'I told you I'm the best. It wasn't difficult.'

Conquest glanced at War, who for the first time since he had known him was not seeing the funny side. The fat man looked petrified.

'Impressive,' Death said finally. 'But –'

'You have the brief,' Pestilence interrupted. 'As agreed, the first payment will be in your account in –' he glanced at the foot of his screen – 'a little under 30 seconds. The rest will be paid on successful completion of the project.'

Francine nodded.

'Any questions?' Death asked.

She had none.

68

They heard a voice – someone was shouting to them up the ramp. Marty was the first to turn. Through the haze he saw a dimly lit figure. His hands were cupped to his mouth and he was bellowing to them above the sound of fires and the groaning of concrete and steel. 'This way!' said the voice.

The man was wearing a dark suit. About average height, he had jet-black, greased-back hair. Now he was beckoning to them, urging them away from the impassable tangle of metal.

A few seconds later, they were back down on B3. The man was a dozen yards ahead of them. He was running down the ramp to B4. They followed blindly. There was nowhere else to go.

'Keep going,' the man called back to them.

They reached B4, then on to B5, and still the way was clear. The damage was far less dramatic here. They paused for a moment to catch their breath. Marty looked completely finished. He sat down for a moment. Dave collapsed next to him. He had a nasty cut across his forehead, and blood was running down his cheek. He lifted his T-shirt, dabbing at the wound, and saw an even worse gash along the inside of his forearm, a jagged rip from elbow to wrist.

Foreman reached the man first. 'Thank you,' he said, looking at the ID tag around the man's neck. He was CIA. 'Mr Goddard.'

'Please – call me Jerry. Glad to be of help, Senator. I was on a special security attachment to your group. You wouldn't have noticed me, I hope.'

'Watching over the security people?'

'Something like that,' Goddard said, smiling briefly, his teeth perfect. He was still wearing a knotted tie, his jacket buttoned. But the suit was soiled with oil and caked with dust. The left leg of his trousers was ripped from the knee down, and his calf was smeared with blood.

'I take it your cell is dead?' Foreman said.

'Lost it in the blasts.'

'So, what now?' Marty asked.

Goddard considered the old man. 'Have you gotten all the way down here from Ground Level?'

Foreman nodded. 'The bombs went off in the middle of my speech. The auditorium is totalled. There was no way out the front. Some crazy bastard with a semi-automatic was making that a little difficult.' He looked away and sighed. 'Why did you bring us down here?'

'I think it's the best chance any of us have.'

'How come?' Dave asked.

Foreman noticed the blood streaming down the young man's face. He walked over, pushed Dave's back gently and took a closer look.

'Part of my prep was to study this building inside out. It's not on the public maps, but there's a secondary service elevator that goes straight from B6 to Ground. B6 is where a lot of the heavy equipment for big shows and stuff is stored.'

Foreman looked up at Goddard. 'Where is it on B6?' he asked, helping Dave and Marty to their feet.

'Back of the building, smack in the middle,' Goddard replied, pointing down the ramp to the floor below.

'Will you be able to make it?' Foreman asked his two companions.

Dave nodded.

'Lead on,' Marty rasped.

Goddard walked ahead down the ramp, limping slightly. Foreman noticed that he walked with the trained caution of a law-enforcement officer. You could tell it a mile off.

The air was clearer down here and it was cooler. Every car was dented, their windows nothing but frames, not a windshield left intact. But quite a few ceiling lights were still working and cast a hazy glow. A stream of filthy water ran down the left side of the ramp, pooling in newly-made holes.

The ramp opened out onto the lowest level of the car park. This was different to the other four floors. Here only half the floor space was car park; the back, or north side of the building was a vast storage area. Ahead of them a wide corridor stretched into the gloom. They could just make out the end where it curved to the right.

They walked along the corridor, their footfalls echoing around the concrete walls. From behind them came the sounds of fires still burning out of control. To the left and right were wide roller-doors, like those used in warehouses. One was open. Goddard flicked a switch and the light came on, revealing a huge storage room.

They took a couple of steps inside. Wooden frames, partitions twenty feet wide, were stacked just beyond the roller-door. To one side of the room lay a row of massive stage lights. Beyond these were a pile of metal flight cases. On the other side of the room dozens of chairs were stacked, and on the floor beside these lay thick electrical cables and more lights.

They retreated back to the corridor. 'The service elevator is around this corner,' Goddard said, without slowing.

They reached the end of the corridor and turned.

The elevator doors were open. A man was slumped over the top of a huge cubic flight-case on wheels. From twenty feet away they could all see that the back wall of the elevator had ripped open, revealing brightly coloured wires and gun-metal grey cabling. A length of twisted steel protruded from the centre of the man's back, and his blood was dripping into a large red puddle on the elevator floor.

69

Base One, Tintara

'Sir?' the voice said in Mark Harrison's comms at Cyber Control.

'Dr Singleton.'

'I think I've found something important. Can you come to the lab?'

'Please tell me it's something I want to hear.'

'Not sure about that, sir. But it'll certainly interest you.'

'Swell,' Mark sighed and eased himself out of his chair. 'On my way.'

A few minutes later he was standing in Base One's laboratory with Dr Lucy Singleton.

'We had precious little to work with – just a few molecules of DNA scraped from one of the guns on the roof,' she began. 'I suspect it's from a hair that fell on the gun. Conventional analysers would need millions of times more DNA to get a result. Even so, the sample would have been useless if we couldn't match it up to anything.'

'But you have the Global Genetic Database.'

'Indeed we do.' Dr Singleton observed Mark Harrison over her glasses. She was in her early forties. She had a strong, intelligent face, her black hair pulled into a bun. She paced over to a console that was hooked up to Sybil.

Base One's quantum computer had complete access to one of the wonders of the 21st century. CARPA, in its wisdom, had created a database of every piece of genetic information known to humanity. It did not have the DNA profile of everyone on earth, but by combining the records of every police force in the world, every military institution willing to supply such information to the UN, every business institution that could be bribed to release its information, and every Western scientific organisation, CARPA had established a database of the DNA profiles of over five billion individuals, dead and alive.

'So who do we have, doc?'

'A certain Igor Andrei Makanov. Born in Moscow, October 1963. Soviet Army recruit, 1980. Blood sample stored and recorded, June 1984. DNA profile registered by CARPA in April 2005, using this sample. There are no more recent samples on file.'

'Soviet military training,' Mark said quietly.

'Special forces,' Dr Singleton replied, glancing at the holographic image. 'Spetsnaz, 1985 to 1989.'

'Extremely dangerous.'

'I guess so,' Dr Singleton said, 'except for this.' She touched the light keypad and the holographic image altered, and text scrolled down in front of their eyes. Mark Harrison read the next line. 'Died during training exercise, St Petersburg, May 1989.'

Exiting Dr Singleton's lab, Mark almost collided with Tom's electric wheelchair as it sped along the corridor.

'Just the man I wanted to see,' Tom said, and thrust a glossy print into Mark's hands.

'What's this?'

'A picture of the foundations of the CCC under construction in 1996. This –' and he tapped the glossy with a dirty fingernail – 'is a municipal drain built in the 1930s and left intact. It passes within a few feet of Level B6. It's a way in – and out.'

247

Mark stared at Tom for a moment, his face expressionless, then he gripped the boy's shoulder and smiled. 'I think it's time I got over there myself.'

70

Level B6, California Conference Center

Marty's face was pale as death. 'Oh my God,' he said quietly, and walked slowly back along the corridor. Dave stood motionless, his face buried in his hands.

'Jesus Christ!' Foreman exclaimed, one hand on his forehead. His face was creased with anxiety. He looked around as though a way out could be found in the very air. 'Right,' he said after a moment. 'We're running out of options here.'

'Sure are,' Dave said through his fingers.

'May I make a suggestion?' It was Jerry Goddard. 'We can't go back up the ramp – the smoke is too bad up there and more cars could blow. How about I go see if I can get back up to the elevator shaft on B5, get the door open and climb the access ladder?'

'That's basically how we got down to B3,' Marty said. 'But the access ladder was almost destroyed, and it was ripped from the wall above B3.'

'But it might be possible to get to B3 and then find another way up from there. If we can reach B2, we might be able to get up the entrance ramp to Ground.' Goddard looked at each of them. Apart from his injured leg, he seemed in the best shape of the four.

'But we've just come from B3.'

'I know, but there might be options from there.'

'How are you going to get to the elevator shaft on B5? You can't use the ramp, the smoke's too bad now,' Dave said.

'The emergency stairs. One of them must be passable. Might even be able to get higher than B5.'

'It's a plan,' Foreman said after a moment. 'I'm coming with you.'

Goddard shrugged. 'If you feel up to it, Senator.'

Foreman turned to Dave and Marty. 'Dave, we need to look at that arm. Let's get into one of the rooms along the corridor.'

They made their way back. Along the corridor they found a water fountain they had missed on their way down. Dave tried it. It was working. He bent his head down and took a long draught of the cold water. It had a metallic edge to it.

They returned to the room with the open roller-door. Foreman wandered off and came back a few moments later with an armful of white fabric. 'Tablecloths,' he said.

They ripped the cloths into strips and wetted a couple from the fountain. The tear in Dave's arm was deep but not life-threatening. Foreman bound it tightly with a damp cloth, then made a sling from another length of material. Then he cleaned the blood from the young man's face and dabbed at the cut across his forehead. Meanwhile, Goddard cleaned and bandaged the cut in his calf.

'We'll be back soon,' Foreman said to Marty and Dave as he turned towards the door.

The senator followed Goddard into the corridor and they set off in the direction of the ramp. The smoke was worse than before. There was no way they could get to the eastern side of the building. This meant they only had two chances. The emergency stairs at the back of the complex, and the ones at the front – both were on the western side. They headed for the stairwell at the back of the CCC.

They found a corridor to their right with more store-rooms, one or two with open roller-doors. Goddard led the way. The air became clearer with each step. More lights were working here. They took two turns, a left and then a sharp right, and found themselves at the door to the emergency stairs. It was shattered and half the staircase had been destroyed. It was impassable.

'Oh, swell!' Goddard exclaimed. 'The front stairs are our last chance.' He pushed back past Foreman and ran along the corridor towards the front of the CCC.

The two men emerged in the parking area of B6. It was as packed as the levels above, but most of the cars were in better shape. Goddard wove between them, with Foreman close behind. In a few minutes they had reached the front emergency stairwell. Goddard leaned on the door and pushed. It opened. Concrete steps led upward.

'Phew!' Foreman exclaimed.

Goddard turned. He had a gun in his hand, a Smith & Wesson Model 500 Magnum. He lifted it to waist height. Foreman looked at the gun, confused. Then he noticed Goddard's sleeve had ridden up to reveal a gruesome tattoo.

'Phew indeed, Senator Foreman. I'm afraid this is the end of the adventure. My name is the Dragon. I'm here to kill you.'

Part Four

GOING UNDERGROUND

71

California Conference Center, Los Angeles

Josh, Mai and Stephanie had just emerged into the night air through the shattered doors of the eastern side of the CCC when Mark's face appeared on their wrist screens. He was wearing a cybersuit, complete with flight helmet.

'Status?' he asked.

'Plan A's shot, Mark,' Josh said. 'The emergency stairwell below B1 is useless, and we can't get anywhere on that level – there's too much damage. We're running out of options. You're suited up?'

'I'm coming over,' Mark replied.

Josh raised an eyebrow but said nothing.

'Tom's just found a new option,' Mark continued. An image of the CCC's foundations appeared on the team's flexiscreens.

'How do we get in?' Mai asked.

'A ground level entrance about a hundred yards north of the complex. Here.' He sent them a map. 'Take the Pram . . . and you'll need the Sonic Drill. There's about a yard of earth between the drain and the wall of the CCC.'

'How do we know if we can get to B3 from B6?'

'No need. Pete's working his way onto B3 in the Mole – he's just picked up a faint trace of four people on B6. We're pretty sure it's Senator Foreman and the others. God knows how they got there. Just have to hope they stay put. Steph? What's the status of your suit?'

She tapped at her wrist and studied the screen for a second. 'The tear is almost fixed.'

'Yeah, copy that here. Sybil reckons your systems should be fully operational in a few minutes, but I think you should stay back at the Big Mac.'

'Wilco.'

The Pram got its name from a conversation between the designers that had turned ironic over a beer. Known officially as a High Speed Ground Transporter (or HSGT), it was about as far removed from a pram as any vehicle could get. Inspired by the hovercraft invented by Sir Christopher Cockerell in the mid-1950s, it was a sleek, low-profile transporter that skimmed along an inch above the ground. Capable of speeds up to 200 miles per hour, it was easy to manoeuvre and could carry six passengers and more than 2000 pounds of equipment.

With Mai at the controls and Josh beside her, the Pram shot from the exit hatch at the back of the Big Mac, swerved sharply to avoid a pile of twisted metal and concrete, then swung past Ringo and onto the slip road to the south of the CCC. Its powerful headlights cut through the gloom. The husk of the gas station – where the shooter had been – flashed past on their left. One of the underground gas tanks had blown, shattering the forecourt and reducing the building to rubble.

The road swept west and then curved north. Approaching the back of the CCC, Mai took the Pram across a well-manicured lawn now strewn with detritus. Sheets of paper whipped up by the breeze cascaded onto the windscreen. They tapped on the glass like impatient fingers before flying off into the night. A line of trees to the left was lit up by the white beams of the headlights. The trees were stripped bare. Paper and other debris had caught in the branches.

Mai pulled on the steering column and they swung a sharp right, slowed and drew to a halt. Jumping out, they could see the orange and yellow flames still licking the western wall of the Conference Center, and smaller fires dotting the horizon. A couple of yards from the Pram was a low brick wall. A concrete slope led down to a metal door.

They were each armed with stun pistols that could fire a narrow electromagnetic pulse that had a similar effect to the tasers used by police forces. Mai had a small med-kit on her shoulder and Josh carried the Sonic Drill, a device that looked like a bulky rifle. Made from a carbon-aluminium composite, it was extremely light, but a powerful generator at the business end produced a focused ultrasound beam in the range of 35 kilohertz. This could cut through almost any material with astonishing ease.

They reached the door. It was locked.

'Stand back,' Josh said, raising the Sonic Drill. With the device set to its lowest power setting, he fired a pulse. A foot-wide hole appeared where the lock and the handle had been. The door swung inward, limp on its hinges.

They flicked on their helmet lights, revealing a short, sloping corridor with a low, sodden roof. Green slime and moss hung down. They could see a narrow vertical shaft at the end. It was little more than a yard wide and had rungs cut into it. Mai led the way. She peered down the shaft, her helmet light illuminating the first twenty feet. Beyond that lay a featureless black.

It was unnerving in the shaft. Josh and Mai felt as though they were floating in space. All that was visible was concrete above and below, as far as their lights could break the gloom. They knew from the schematic that it was a deep shaft, descending to a depth of some 80 feet below the surface, but it felt as though they were climbing down hundreds of feet. They could see from their wrist screens that the temperature was dropping rapidly as they descended. The oxygen content of the air was also falling, and the moisture level rising.

Mai saw the concrete floor light up in the beam from her helmet. After a dozen more rungs she had reached the base of the shaft. She stepped aside to let Josh into the narrow space. Ahead, a low-ceilinged circular passage fell away into darkness. Water ran along the ground, gurgling into a hole close to the foot of the ladder. A few moments later they were standing in the drainage tunnel itself, their helmet beams lighting up swatches of curved wall.

The tunnel – which was once the primary drain of the city – was ten feet high and twelve feet wide. It ran under Los Angeles for fifteen miles, emerging just south of Marina del Rey. It had been decommissioned and superseded by a more modern pipe in the early 1990s, but a trickle of water still flowed along it in a shallow channel. Its walls were coated in slime, and it smelled of damp and rotting organic material.

Mai looked at her flexiscreen, which was glowing with a soft light in the darkness. She could see the schematic of the area. A little under a hundred yards to the east was the lowest level of the CCC, a black block on the display. The tunnel showed up as a narrow red line. It curved slightly north, then ran in a straight line east for more than 50 yards, before curving sharply south and almost touching the north-west corner of the CCC. After that, it ran along the edge of the building to the north-east corner.

'Base One? We're in the tunnel.'

'Copy that, Mai.' It was Tom. 'You can see on the schematic the tunnel gets closest to B6 exactly 12.6 yards along the north wall of the CCC. That will get you into the storage area – room B63. I can't tell what's immediately behind the wall there, so take care.'

'Okay. Where's Mark?' Josh asked.

'I'm aboard John,' Mark's voice came over the comms. 'ETA at emergency site in nineteen minutes.'

Josh led the way along the tunnel. The only sound was their own breathing and the faint trickle of water.

'I never even knew this thing existed,' Josh said into his comms.

'Don't think many people do,' Mai responded from a few yards behind him. 'But there's a complex web of tunnels and drains under Los Angeles, just as there is under most big cities. Over the decades, developers just built on top of what was already there. It's kind of tranquil, don't you think?'

'Maybe it is to you, spacegirl. You're used to being cooped up in confined spaces. It's not my favourite thing.'

'Josh Thompson! Not a weakness, surely? Not a chink in the armour?'

Mai could hear Josh sigh. 'Wish I hadn't said anything,' he said with faux-seriousness.

The way was almost completely clear, with just the odd pile of something unsavoury close to the trickling channel – organic waste and decaying wildlife that had somehow found its way into the drain. Josh and Mai made rapid progress, covering the hundred yards in under a minute.

As they approached the point where the wall of the CCC almost touched the rim of the tunnel, their flexiscreens showed their position. Mai walked ahead and stopped. Her helmet beam swept across the slime-covered wall of the drain.

'Right there,' she said, pointing to a spot at the centre of the light beam.

Josh swung the Sonic Drill from his shoulder. Pushing a button on the side, three retractable legs shot out and unfolded, before snapping into place automatically. He stood the device a foot from the wall, altering the height of the legs so that the barrel of the drill was level.

Suddenly, they heard a small splash of water, as though a foot had slipped into the channel running the length of the tunnel. It was followed by a tap, then a high-pitched whine.

They spun around towards the source of the sound. Josh almost knocked the drill over but caught it in time.

Mai was closest to the sound. Her hand shot to the stun pistol at her hip. In a second she had adopted the 'power stance' – left leg a little in front of the right, both hands holding the pistol at arm's length, her body turned slightly to the right. The light on her helmet cracked open the blackness.

Instinctively, they held their breath as they tried to detect the source of the sound. There was a sudden movement, a shape at the edge of the beam. Mai swung the stun gun. 'Who's there? Stop! I'm armed.' The shape vanished.

Silence for a second. Then another scrape. Josh flicked on a secondary light at his sleeve, allowing the beam to dance along the filthy wall of the tunnel. The shape reappeared and Mai fired. A rat the size of a tabby cat staggered into the pool of light, writhing in agony as the stun pistol sent an intense electromagnetic pulse through its body. The creature threw its head back, jaws open, eyes rolling. Then it seemed to crumple, its legs twitching as it died.

72

Kyle Foreman raised his hands. 'If this is some kind of –'

'Joke? No, no joke, Senator. I'm very serious.'

Foreman started to walk backwards slowly. His only hope was to stall him. 'Who sent you? What's all this about?'

The Dragon raised the gun. The point of the barrel was two feet from the senator's head. Foreman stepped back again and came to rest against a concrete pillar. The Dragon matched his steps and stood with his feet splayed, both hands on the gun.

Foreman caught a slight movement at the edge of his vision. Behind the Dragon a large chunk of concrete was swinging from a thin steel tube. The metal was bending, about to snap. He had to buy some time.

Then suddenly he knew what to do. 'Watch out behind you!' Foreman yelled.

The Dragon didn't so much as flinch. 'Oh, Senator Foreman, please! You insult me!'

Foreman saw the Dragon's finger moving back, the skin whitening as he pulled on the trigger. A line of sweat ran into his right eye, stinging.

The block of concrete crashed down, missing the Dragon by a fraction of an inch. He whirled around and Foreman seized his chance. He interlocked his fingers and with every ounce of strength in him he brought his fists down on the back of the Dragon's head, knocking him forward. He landed heavily on the jagged lump of concrete. The gun left his hands and slid across the floor of the car park.

In a blind panic, Foreman searched around for something he could use as a weapon. He grabbed at a piece of metal, a severed door handle. The Dragon was pulling himself up. Foreman swung the handle through the air, but the Dragon was too fast. One kick to the abdomen and Foreman was flying backwards. He landed on a pile of rubble and cried out as intense pain shot through him.

The Dragon was on top of the senator in a fraction of a second, one hand at the his throat, the other clutching the Yarygin PYa handgun he had pulled from his jacket. Foreman could feel the life draining from him. In desperation, he ran his hands over the floor beside him and touched metal, a pipe of some sort. He grasped it, brought it round and slammed it into the Dragon's head. The Dragon fell back, stunned, blood running from a wound just above his left ear.

Foreman found reserves of energy he had no idea he possessed and flung himself at the assassin. But the Dragon brought his arm up, smashing his elbow into Foreman's face. Both men fell backwards. The senator stumbled over a pile of masonry, almost tripping over the door handle he'd used earlier.

Grabbing it, he lunged forward again with all his strength. The Dragon was struggling to regain his balance, and the blow reached its target. This time the assassin went down like a sack of coal. Foreman brought the handle down again – hard – across the nape of the Dragon's neck, and then a third time across the top of his skull. The man fell forward and stopped moving.

For a couple of seconds Foreman stood gasping for air. He was covered in blood, sweat and concrete dust. He ran a hand over his eyes, but this only made it worse. He pulled a piece of cloth from his pocket, a remnant from the tablecloths he had used to bind Dave Golding's wounds. He spat on it and rubbed it over his eyes to clear away the grit and dirt as best he could. Then he dabbed at the wounds on his face.

He walked around the prone form of the assassin and picked up the Smith & Wesson Magnum. There was no sign of the Yarygin. The Magnum was heavy and felt unnatural in Foreman's hand. He had always hated guns. Bending down with the barrel close to the Dragon's head, he felt for a pulse. It was there – weak, but there.

What was he to do? The man was a trained killer, a professional. A wild thought flashed through Foreman's mind. He could put a bullet in the bastard's brain or, better still, smash his skull with a chunk of rock. He would be just another casualty. But even though this man had tried to kill him, and would have shot him without a second thought, the senator couldn't do it.

'Have to do something,' Foreman said aloud to the fetid air. Looking around him, he spotted a car stereo. It was smashed almost beyond recognition, but a bunch of coloured wires dangled from its back. He snatched it up and yanked at the wires. Crouching down, he pulled the Dragon's hands behind him and wound the wires around his wrists, knotting them four times. The metal shell of the stereo hung limp. Foreman remembered the man was wearing a tie. Tugging it free, he wrapped it tight around the assassin's ankles.

The senator stood up. Pain from a dozen different places screamed at him simultaneously. Everything seemed to hurt. He pocketed the Magnum and headed back to the storerooms at the rear of B6, his heart pounding so hard it felt like it would leap from his chest.

73

It took less than a minute for the Sonic Drill to cut a hole a yard wide in the wall between the drain and Level B6 of the California Conference Center.

'We're through,' Josh announced into his comms.

'Roger, Josh,' Tom responded from Base One. 'I still can't get a detailed fix on the location of Kyle Foreman or his party. And there's something else.'

'What?'

'We're picking up some pretty serious stress lines on B6. Must be loss of integrity up above, a knock-on effect. Advise extreme caution.'

'Wilco.'

Josh dismantled the Sonic Drill and retracted the legs as Mai went through the hole.

Room B63 was a large storeroom. They had to step over a huge plasma screen that had toppled over from the vibration caused by the drill. The ultrasound beam had been so precise the plasma screen was otherwise untouched, even though it had been resting against the wall.

Guided by the beam from his helmet, Josh found a light switch on the far wall. The fluorescent tube in the ceiling rattled into life. Against the side walls stood plastic containers with labels on their fronts. The boxes were covered in dust from where the ceiling and walls had shaken in the blasts. Josh wiped a label clean. 'Spare parts for audio visual equipment,' he said.

Mai paced over to a roller-door in the right-hand wall and bent down to the handle. It came up easily, opening onto a dark corridor. They could hear strange creaking sounds, and then a far-off scream. The air was hazy with particles of dust and smoke from the dozens of fires still raging in the huge complex.

Josh looked at a schematic on his flexiscreen. 'That corridor links to a passage with other storerooms off it. Beyond that there's a main corridor. We should take a right turn there. It'll lead us out to the car parking area and the ramp up to B5. We take a left after that, and we'll wind up at the large service elevator that goes straight to the Ground Level.'

'It's inoperable.'

'Yeah, but Foreman and the others might not know that. He may be close to it.'

'Okay, let's check it first.'

They took a left turn in the corridor outside B63. All the roller-doors were down. It was dark except for the beams from their helmets. They reached the main corridor and hung another left. A few seconds later they were standing in front of the smashed-up elevator and its dead occupant – the precise spot Kyle Foreman had been some twenty minutes earlier. They turned without a word and ran back along the passage.

'Guys?' It was Tom. 'Status, please?' There was an edge of urgency in his voice.

'We've checked out the service elevator. No sign of Foreman. Heading back to the corridor outside B63. Plan to press on into the main body of B6. What's up, Tom?'

'Hold your position.'

'Why?'

'BigEye has just picked up a hotspot close to your position.'

'A hotspot?'

'It's broken through the interference. Must be a very hot fire, perhaps a short circuit in the electrical system. According to Sybil, one of the storerooms contains gas tanks –'

The explosion threw them off their feet. Josh fell backwards onto a pile of empty cardboard boxes that had been left in the corridor, scattering them across the passage. The boxes cushioned his fall, but the wind was still knocked out of him. The Sonic Drill flew out of his hands. Before he could move, Mai landed on top of him, an elbow slamming into his face.

Mai pulled herself up, covered in dust. She looked down at Josh, who was holding his nose. She could see, through the mask of his helmet, that blood was streaming down from his nostrils.

'Josh? Mai? Status, please. Are you guys okay?'

They were too stunned to respond immediately. But Mai replied as she pulled Josh to his feet. 'I think we're okay.' She checked the screen on her wrist and Josh shook his head and lifted his arm. It ached. He looked down the corridor and saw the back end of the Sonic Drill protruding from a huge pile of rubble. The device was smashed to pieces.

'My suit's fine,' Mai replied.

'Josh?'

'I feel like my nose has snapped off, but apart from that . . .' Josh pulled off his helmet, coughing in the dense, fumy air. He ran his fingers under his nose and they came up bloodied. A couple of drops fell to the dusty floor.

'It's not busted, Josh,' Tom said.

'Well, that's good to know. Can't say the same for the Sonic Drill, though. It's pretty smashed up.'

'Put your helmet back on. You want some painkillers?'

'That would be nice. So what the hell just happened?'

'I'm sorry. We picked it up too late. You're so far down and with the electrical disturbances from the explosions –'

'What was it, Tom?'

'A gas tank at the other side of B6. Lucky you weren't closer.'

'We're going to take the main passage, see if we can find Foreman. And Tom? Next time –'

A loud rumble interrupted Josh. It started far off but grew louder, closer. Instinctively, Josh and Mai dived to the floor, covering their heads with their arms. The rumbling kept coming closer. Then, as quickly as it started, it stopped.

'Tom?' Josh said.

No response.

'Mark? Steph? Anyone? Come in?'

Nothing.

Mai and Josh stood up, the air around them even thicker with dust and smoke in the light from their helmets. Josh checked his wrist computer, tapping at the keypad. 'The noise came from beyond B63 . . . in the drain.'

Mai led the way along the corridor. A chunk of concrete the size of a fist shot down from the ceiling and landed an inch in front of her. Without missing a beat, she dodged a shower of pebbles and detritus and ran on. Josh was two paces behind her.

Room B63 was filled with smoke. Stumbling over rocks and pieces of tile and concrete, they reached the opening. Josh peered in. Thanks to his visual enhancements, he could see through the intense gloom. The tunnel was completely blocked.

74

Dave and Marty heard the boom of the tunnel collapsing. The far wall began to vibrate, the ceiling juddered and the roller-door started to move in sympathy. And then – a sudden stillness.

They looked at each other almost resignedly. Marty got up and walked to the door, straining to listen, but there was only an eerie silence from the corridor beyond. He sat down with his back to the wall and let out a heavy sigh. 'How's the arm, kid?'

Dave shrugged. 'Oh, you know. You?'

'My head's throbbing. And this air, the smoke . . .' Marty looked pained.

They had locked the shutter, although neither of them knew exactly why. Dave reached for his bag and pulled out the bottle of Vicodin. He emptied a couple of tablets into his palm and tossed them back.

'So what started you on those things?' Marty asked.

Dave gave him an angry look and shook his head. 'Does it matter?'

Marty looked away. A medley of sounds came from beyond the shutter. A loud creaking, as though the whole building was about to crumble to dust. From far off came the sound of falling debris.

'Couldn't cope with life, I guess,' Dave said suddenly.

'Yep, sounds about right,' Marty replied.

'And what would you know about it, old man?' Dave

snapped. He winced and grabbed at his injured arm. The cloth around it was drenched with blood.

Marty looked at the young man for a moment then laughed. 'I was in Nam,' he said quietly. 'Almost 45 years ago, but I remember it like it was yesterday. If you hear old-timers like me tell you it was pure hell there, you'd better believe 'em, Dave. I haven't been to hell – not yet, anyway – but I can't imagine it being any worse than Quang Tri Province in April '68. My three best buddies died the same day. Operation Pegasus, it was called. We were part of III Marine Amphibious Force, sent in to save a base in Khe Sanh. It was about to fall to the Vietcong. I made it back to Saigon without a scratch and was given leave. It was worse than the front. I was eaten up with guilt. Survivor guilt, they call it now. Probably suffer it again if we make it out of this place.'

Dave was studying the old man's face. It was grimy and he seemed to have aged ten years during the past hour. It struck him suddenly just how much living Marty Gardiner had over him.

'So what'd you do?'

'Same as half the US army – got smashed on bad local drugs, got so drunk I lost track of two whole days, and almost certainly did other stuff I'm glad I can't remember.' He gave Dave a pained smile, his teeth ridiculously bright against the smudged dirt over his face.

Dave looked at the floor and shivered. 'My parents died in a car smash,' he said. 'It was my fault. I'd gotten into trouble at college. Got mixed up with the laziest mother-fuckers in the year and nearly flunked my exams. My parents were on their way to see me and to talk to my tutor. Dad is – was – a professor at MIT, super-smart. My sister's a surgeon. So, no pressure,' he smirked.

'And you blame yourself for them getting killed in a car crash?'

'If I hadn't been such an asshole, they wouldn't have been coming to see my tutor, would they?'

Marty looked at him for several seconds, remembering what he had said only an hour ago, crouched over Nancy's dead body. It seemed as though only now the reality was sinking in. He had been in such a state of shock that he hadn't really processed the full horror of it all, and he knew the true pain of his loss would hit him very hard later – if he ever got out of this place alive. 'Some people think when you're time's up, it's up,' he said quietly.

'I've been through it all a thousand times in my head,' Dave went on. 'I can't shake off the feeling I was responsible for their deaths.'

'That's crap. Look, kid,' Marty said, and placed a hand on Dave's good arm. 'Hasn't this tragedy taught you anything?'

Dave stared at him.

'We have no control over anything. Oh, we might think we do. I chose to come here today. I persuaded Nancy to come. But when someone with his own agenda decides to put a bomb under the auditorium, I have no control. No more than you had control over the crash that killed your mom and dad. No more control than they had.'

'So the only one who had control today was the bomber?'

'No, not really. He, or she, couldn't control everything. Any number of things could have gone wrong for him. The cops could have spotted him before he pushed the button. The bomb might not have gone off. He could have miscalculated and killed himself in the blasts. None of us has control, Dave. We might think we do. We reassure ourselves we do. How else can we get through the day? We have to believe we're special, because the alternative is too horrible to contemplate.'

'But in that case, what's the point of doing anything? Thinking anything? What's the point of free will?'

'Because we have to keep going. What else can we do?'

'Makes no sense to me, Marty. Why be a OneEarth supporter if you believe you have no control?'

'Individually we have no control. But likeminded people can make things happen if they put enough energy into it.'

'So you reached this conclusion in Vietnam?'

'That was the start of it. I came back a wreck. I was an alcoholic for years. Then I met Nancy. She saved my life.'

'So you did have some control.'

'No. I lucked out, Dave. You see, that's the other great secret of life. Meet someone to love and who loves you.'

Dave was about to reply when they were both shocked by the sound of frantic banging on the roller-door. 'What the –' He leapt to his feet, shifting all his weight onto his good arm.

'Dave? Marty? It's me.' It was Kyle Foreman's voice.

Dave helped Marty up and between them they lifted the roller-door a couple of feet. Foreman swung underneath the half-opened shutter and they saw his face in the dim light. He was covered in dust, his lips cracked, his left eye puffy and bruised. Blood from his broken nose had started to flow again, forming two red tracks in the grey powder covering his face. He still had the Smith & Wesson in his hand.

'What's happened?' Dave said as he and Marty helped the senator straighten up.

'Pull the shutter down again,' Foreman snapped. He found the large padlock at the bottom of the sliding door, clicked it shut and pocketed the key.

'Where's Goddard?' Marty asked.

The senator leaned back against the door, panting for breath. He coughed and spat blood onto the dust-covered floor. 'He tried to kill me,' he said. 'He's an assassin.'

271

75

Aboard the Big Mac, Stephanie had just made a sweep of the area of B6, where it was thought Foreman and his companions were located, when her comms sounded. It was on 156 megahertz, the frequency commonly used by the US army.

'Yes?'

'E-Force? Major Larry Simpson, US Marines, requesting to come aboard.'

'What for?'

'We need your urgent assistance.'

She hesitated for a moment then clicked on the external viewer at the main door. She could see two men in fatigues. One was speaking into a small radio. The other was looking around, an M16 assault rifle over his shoulder.

'Sybil,' she asked the computer. 'ID check on our visitors, please.'

Sybil's quantum processors took less than a millisecond to scan the faces of the two men outside the Big Mac and check them in the E-Force database. 'Major Larry Simpson, US Marines, age 32, born –'

'Okay, Sybil. The other one?'

'Sergeant Vincent Paolomo, US Marines –'

'Thanks.' Switching on the external speaker, she said, 'Come aboard,' and opened the door.

The two soldiers came through the door and Stephanie took the elevator down to the lower deck. She met the marines in the main corridor. Close up, she could see they were covered in dirt, their faces blackened. They smelled of smoke and concrete dust. She took Major Simpson's grimy palm and he turned to introduce his companion. 'Sergeant Paolomo.' The other Marine nodded and shook Stephanie's hand, his face expressionless.

'May I see your IDs, please?'

'Sure.' Simpson took out his and Paolomo followed suit. They were credit-card-sized pieces of plastic providing name, rank, serial number and scrambled personal information. Stephanie studied them. Using her enhanced visual abilities, she checked across the wavelengths and picked up each card's authenticity strip – a line of ultra-thin gold, invisible to the naked eye, that ran down the edge of the ID.

'How may I help?' she said handing them back.

Simpson was gazing around at the smooth plastic walls of the Big Mac. 'One hell of a plane you have here, ma'am,' he said, appreciatively. 'A real beauty.'

Stephanie gave him a thin smile.

'We understand you have some pretty cool detection tools onboard.'

'What sort of detection tools do you need?'

'Sorry,' Simpson said smoothly. 'Specifically, we've lost track of a team of marines who went down to the lower levels of the car park about twenty minutes ago. They had orders to call in every five minutes with a status report. We haven't heard from them for the last two designated call-ins, and none of our heat-detection devices can trace them.'

'I see,' Stephanie said, looking from Simpson to Paolomo. 'Follow me.'

She led the way to the elevator. The doors closed behind them and it silently rose though the five storeys to the flight deck in the upper hemisphere of the ship. The doors swished open and they walked along a brightly lit corridor towards the Ops Room. At the end stood the door to the flight deck itself. Just before it closed automatically, the two marines caught a brief glimpse of the futuristic controls inside – sleek plastic panels and high-res holoscreens above rows of keypads.

The Ops Room was circular. The marines looked around it open-mouthed. In the middle stood a workstation, a single sheet of thin plastic on a steel pedestal. The panel was covered with lights that flicked on and off and skittered around the shiny surface. The walls contained large arrays of screens, each no thicker than a poster. There were three more workstations with holoscreens. Only one was activated – where Stephanie had been working. It showed a 3D representation of Level B6 of the CCC.

Stephanie walked over to the workstation. 'Which level were they on?' she asked and tapped at the controls. She turned. Simpson was standing six feet away, a 9 mm Beretta pointed at her head.

76

Sergeant Paolomo removed a miniature video camera from his pocket and began filming. When he was finished in the Ops Room, he strode into the corridor and headed straight for the flight deck.

'Shut down all systems, Sybil. Jacobs, S. Personal code 99697766#4,' Stephanie announced suddenly.

A faint purr came from one of the consoles in the Ops Room and the lights went out. The machines died and a faint emergency light came on, throwing a soft, creamy glow around the circular room. Paolomo paced back in, his M16 assault rifle at waist height and pointed straight at Stephanie.

Simpson sighed and took a small step towards her, the Beretta level with her forehead. 'Now, why did you go and do that?'

Stephanie said nothing. The major came so close that she could feel his breath on her face.

'Who are you?' she snapped.

'That would be telling, wouldn't it?' Simpson pressed the pistol against Stephanie's right temple. 'Let's just say my employer is intrigued by all this.' He swept his free hand through the air. 'Now, I know you people have some amazing stuff here, but I'm pretty sure you still bleed just like the rest of us. Am I right?'

Stephanie remained silent.

'I really don't want to blow your pretty little brains out . . . ma'am. But, if you don't let my friend here take his home movie, I'll just have to. Follow?' Simpson pressed the barrel of the pistol hard into Stephanie's temple, sending a stab of pain across her forehead. She could feel the man tensing up. She only had seconds.

'Sybil – reset, please. Jacobs, S. Personal code 99697766#4.'

'Very sensible,' Simpson said, and Stephanie felt the pressure on her head diminish as he pulled back the barrel a fraction of an inch. Paolomo raised his M16 as Simpson spun her around, yanked her wrists behind her and bound them with a nylon strap. He pulled it tight and locked it into place.

Turning her back around to face him, Simpson nudged her in the ribs with the Beretta. 'Get your ass on the floor. Back against that strut,' he said nodding to a steel column that ran from floor to ceiling. He ran another length of nylon cord around Stephanie's ankles and threaded the end through a self-tightening loop. He drew a length of cloth from his pocket and wrapped it around her mouth, tying it at the back.

Paolomo left the room and Simpson headed after him.

Stephanie managed to pull herself to her feet and hopped along the edge of the control panels until she reached the end. As she lowered herself to the floor again, she banged her head on the front panel of a workstation where it hung over its stand. She yelped, but the sound was muffled by the gag at her mouth.

Sliding along the floor, she reached a small door in the front panel of the stand. Bending low, she managed to nudge it with her chin and it swung outwards. Inside, stood a small cradle containing a set of delicate tools. Lying on her side with her back to the cupboard, she pushed her twined hands into the opening. She ran her fingers along the cradle of tools and finally slid out a screwdriver from its bracket. But before she could catch hold of it, it hit the smooth floor and rolled away noisily.

Stephanie held her breath, expecting Simpson or Paolomo to return at any moment. She thrust her bound hands back into the toolbox and felt the shape of a pair of clippers used to strip wire. She wormed her fingers around the handles and pulled it from its housing. Willing her heart to slow, and her fingers to do her bidding, she succeeded in twisting the clippers, bringing them level with the nylon cord about her wrists.

She was sweating now, and felt her fingers wet against the clipper grips. She pulled them in a fraction of an inch and was just about to hook the sharp edges of the clipper under the cord when she felt the grips slipping through her fingers. Gritting her teeth, she stretched as far as she could and just caught the clippers before they could crash to the floor.

At that moment Stephanie's mind was focused solely on the pair of grips clasped in her sweaty palms. Nothing else mattered. She had to turn the clippers, had to get them into position. Only then could she cut the cord.

Sweat ran down into her eyes, making them sting. She closed her eyes and turned her attention back to the clippers. She pivoted them under the cord, closed the handles, and squeezed with all her might.

The snap of nylon released the terrible pressure on her wrists. Stephanie pulled the clippers around, cut the binding at her ankles and yanked down the gag.

Rising to her feet, she took slow, silent steps along the edge of the control panel. Close to the door there was a small cupboard built into the wall. She ran a hand over a sensor pad beside it and it slid open. Inside, two stun pistols hung on magnetic grips. She pulled one out, checked its charge, then slithered along the wall towards the door.

She edged into the corridor with her back to the wall. Voices were coming from the flight deck. Two paces on and she reached the door. She pulled up the stun gun ready to fire, but just at that moment, Paolomo swung around with the video camera. Simpson turned at the same time, raised his gun and fired.

Stephanie dropped and the bullet flew over her head, ricocheting off the walls of the corridor. She sprinted back towards the Ops Room. Simpson was in the corridor. He let loose another round that hit the wall an inch from Stephanie's shoulder. She dove behind a bulkhead and held the stun pistol ready.

'Jacobs, come out. You're pinned down,' Simpson said.

Ignoring him, she took a deep breath and flew out from behind the bulkhead, blasting the corridor with her stun pistol as she ran. Keeping low, she dashed towards the next column along the passage, catching a glimpse of the two men as she ran. Paolomo had the M16 at his hip. Stephanie dove to the floor as the barrel of the assault rifle lit up and a stream of bullets burned through the air above her head. She lay still, spread-eagled, defeated.

She heard the two men approach, the silence broken only by the sound of their heavy boots on the metal floor.

'A slippery little bitch,' Paolomo growled. It was the first time he had spoken.

'You want to do the honours?' Simpson hissed.

Stephanie waited for the blast from the M16, but it never came. Instead, she heard the unmistakable sound of a stun pistol – two ear-splitting cracks that reverberated around the corridor, followed by gasps and the thump of heavy objects hitting the floor. She felt herself being lifted to her feet.

For a couple of seconds Stephanie couldn't see straight. Then she heard a familiar voice. Her sight cleared and Mark's face swam into view.

77

'Man, am I pleased to see you,' Stephanie said. 'How did you know?'

'Comms on the ground are down,' Mark replied, 'but your heart rate shot up to 130. Tom told me as I was landing and I guessed something must be up. I scanned the ship and saw the thermal signature from these two goons.'

'I don't get it. Sybil checked them out and their IDs are genuine. Can you believe it? They were filming the inside of the ship.' She bent down, removed the miniature recorder from Paolomo's pocket and pulled out the memory chip. 'I should have had Sybil scan them for recording devices.'

'Don't beat yourself up over it, Steph. We're all new to this. I'll get Tom onto it. I can't believe they were here in any official capacity.'

Stephanie and Mark bound the wrists of the two Marines. They were still out cold and would be unconscious for at least an hour. Then Stephanie led the way to the Ops Room.

'So, what's the latest?' Mark asked.

'I lost touch with Josh and Mai about ten minutes ago,' Stephanie said. 'There was a sizeable explosion on B6. According to the sensors, it looks like a gas cylinder went up – certainly not another bomb. It was some way from Josh and Mai's last known location, as well as that of Kyle Foreman's group. Tom spoke to Josh and Mai immediately after the blast, and they're okay. But Foreman and the others might have been caught by it.'

Mark nodded. 'Tom's working on comms,' he replied.

At that moment Erikson's voice came over the speaker. 'Hi, Steph. You okay?'

'Yeah, good, Tom. Mark came to my rescue. What's happening about the comms link with the others?'

'Working on it. It's a problem with the satellite. Should have it back online in a minute. There's something else.'

'What?' Mark snapped.

'That explosion on B6. It's brought down the roof of the drain.'

'Oh, wonderful! Just how bad is it?'

Tom sent over a blurred still of the tunnel taken from BigEye. It appeared as a 3D image on the holoscreen. 'It's at least 30 feet thick. Composed of rock, concrete, soil. The drain's structure has been severely compromised.'

They looked at the image and realised there was no way Josh and Mai could get the survivors out through the drain.

'Scan the length of the tunnel,' Stephanie said. 'North-east, away from the blockage. Is there any other exit?'

The image on the holoscreen shifted, pulling back and showing the length of the drain. The only pipes running to the surface were narrow drainage conduits, none of them more than a foot wide. 'Zilch,' Tom said.

'Alright,' Mark said, and sat down at the workstation.

Stephanie stood behind his chair. 'Where's Pete?'

'Last time I was in contact with him, he was trying to get down to B3,' Tom replied.

Mark tapped in Pete's call code.

'Pete? You there?'

For a second the line was completely silent. Then they all heard a faint crackle, followed by a burst of static.

'Mark – is that you, man?' It was Pete's unmistakable Geordie accent. The line was very weak and he was barely audible, but then it suddenly cleared and his voice came through crisp and loud. 'Thank Christ. I thought I was on my own for a second.'

'We had a comms failure on the ground. What's your status?'

'I'm in the Mole in the west side of B3. No sign of survivors. A few corpses, mind. Ramp down looks clear. What's the latest on Foreman?'

'He's on B6 now, with three others. Josh and Mai have gone down through a municipal drain, but there's been a cave-in and we can't reach them on comms.'

'So what now?'

'We're going to try to get through to them. But it looks like the only chance they have is to go up through the building after all. You say the ramp down is clear?'

'Well, down to B4 it is. After that . . . I don't know.'

'Okay, Pete, take the Mole down to B6 as fast as you can. Keep in touch. Steph,' Mark added, turning to her. 'This is what we're going to do.'

78

Stepping out into the corridor leading back to Room B63, Josh tried his comms again, but the silence down the line was oppressive. It was almost as though E-Force had ceased to exist. Mai looked at him but he shook his head. 'Nothing.'

They ran along the corridor heading south towards the main passage. As they turned into it, Mai glimpsed a figure in the distance. A fraction of a second later it was gone. Mai sped up and turned the next corner. She saw the person again, a tall man in a ripped white shirt and dark pants. Then he disappeared into the smoke.

'Hey! Stop!' she called, but the man had vanished.

'What is it?' Josh asked, stopping beside her, breathing heavily.

'Thought I saw someone.'

'What did they look like?'

'Tall, fit-looking, wearing dark pants and the remains of a shirt.'

'Could be Foreman.'

They walked along the corridor, stopping at each roller-door and listening intently. Their cochlear implants could detect the faintest of sounds, and the cybersuit computers filtered out any extraneous noise.

They reached the end of the corridor and turned right. Stopping at the first roller-door, they heard the sound of dripping water but nothing else. At the next door they stopped abruptly. Josh leaned in and immediately heard voices.

79

Kyle Foreman was leaning against the wall, trying to get his breath back, when he, Dave and Marty heard a rapping on the roller-door. They froze and looked at each other, fear etched into their features. Foreman lifted the Magnum and walked towards the door.

'Who is it?'

'Senator Foreman? Is that you?'

'Who is this?'

'My name's Josh Thompson. I'm from an organisation called E-Force. I'm here with my colleague, Maiko Buchanan. We've been searching for you. Can we come in?'

'Let me speak to your colleague.'

Maiko stepped up to the door. 'Hello, sir,' she said. 'This is Maiko Buchanan.'

Foreman glanced around at Dave and Marty. They nodded and he bent to unlock the door. A moment later Josh and Mai ducked down and entered the room.

Foreman stared sceptically at the two E-Force members. 'So, what's this all about?'

'We're –' Josh stopped talking suddenly and Mai dashed forward as Marty's legs crumpled under him. She was too late to break the old man's fall and he landed heavily on his side.

'Marty,' Dave yelled. He was at Marty's side instantly, lifting his head.

Mai knelt beside the old man and swung her med-kit off

her shoulder. She leaned forward and checked his breathing, then felt for a pulse. She looked up at Foreman and Josh. 'He's alive.'

Foreman stepped to the back of the room and returned with an armful of tablecloths. He rolled up a couple and placed them under Marty's head. Standing beside Josh, he watched as Mai placed a circular piece of plastic over Marty's mouth. There was a tiny tube attached to its side. The plastic clamped to Marty's face like a sucker.

'Oxygen,' she said to the others, without looking up. Then she pulled out an object the size and shape of a pen, with a disc about two inches in diameter at one end. She ripped open Marty's tattered shirt and placed the device vertically on his chest, moving it around slowly. It beeped and then produced a strange whirring sound.

Mai looked at her wrist. The screen was lit up, but only she could make out what was on it. She studied it in silence, then slowed the movement of the device over Marty's skin. Returning the device to the med-kit, she quickly pulled out another cylindrical object. It looked like a hypodermic but without a needle. She pressed it against Marty's neck and pushed a button on the side.

Dave pulled himself up. 'What's that?' he asked, darting a frightened look at Josh.

'She knows what she's doing,' Josh responded, crouching down. 'Heart attack?' he asked Mai.

'Looks like it. I wish Steph was here. There's not much I can do. I've given him a mixture of nitroglycerin and morphine to assist his blood flow. We need to get him aboard the Big Mac.' Mai tapped her comms control. 'Mark? Steph? Come in, please. Tom?'

Nothing.

Mai and Josh looked up as Dave started talking. 'Will he live?' he asked, his voice edged with panic.

'If we get him out of here quickly,' Josh replied.

Dave got to his feet and was shaking his head. 'I don't get this. What the fuck is going on? Who are you?' He looked as though he was about to lose it.

Mai stood up. Gripping the boy's shoulders, she looked him in the eyes. 'What's your name?'

'Dave Golding.'

'Dave, take deep breaths. We're here to help you. We'll get Marty to our ship as soon –'

'Your ship? What the fuck?'

'Look, it doesn't matter –' Josh began, but Mai stopped him with a stern look.

'Dave – listen, we're not from Alpha Centauri. We're just a rescue organisation.'

'But that shit . . .' he said, pointing at the plastic over Marty's face and the strange devices in the opened med-kit.

'We have some cool stuff, but we're human. Hit me, if you like!'

Dave was too far gone to even smile. He swallowed hard and slumped against the wall, then he began to rifle through his bag.

'Sir,' Josh said, turning to Kyle Foreman. 'We have to get out of here ASAP.'

Foreman nodded. 'Just point the way.'

'We have a problem. We came in through a drain that runs close to the building, but that explosion a few minutes ago brought the roof down.'

'Okay.'

'And we've lost contact with our base.'

Mai was trying her comms again. The screen was dead, but suddenly a voice came out of the receiver. Through the distortion, she could just make out Mark's rich baritone. 'Mai?'

'Mark!'

'It's good to hear your voice, Mark,' Josh said.

'We had a drop-out on the sat link,' Mark replied. 'I . . .' The line went dead again for a second. '. . . the Big Mac with Steph. W . . . happening?'

Twice more the connection cut out for a few seconds before settling down. Mai managed to bring Mark up to speed.

'So you've reached them? Good work. Put the senator on.'

'Hello?'

'Hello, Senator Foreman. This is Mark Harrison. What's your condition?'

'I've been better.'

'Sure, but you're fit enough to force your way out somehow?'

'I am. Dave is. But Marty's very bad.'

'Look, we're going to get you all out somehow. Josh, Mai? The blockage in the tunnel is at least 30 feet thick, but we're searching for a way through.'

'What about from the other direction?' Mai asked. 'North-east of the CCC? Aren't there any other exits?'

'Negative. Tom's studied the drain right back to where it starts. There are pipes but none bigger than a foot wide.'

'Great!'

'We need to attack the problem from two directions. I'm going to take the second Mole down to the tunnel and try to break through to your side. Pete's still in the other Mole and is coming down from B3. I'm going to send in a couple of Hunters. They can feed info back to Pete. Senator? How clear is the route down to B6? I assume you took the ramps?'

'Yes, we did, but the smoke was getting real bad.'

'That's no problem. The biggest difficulty will be if the recent explosion has blocked the way. It'll slow us down.'

'Mark, I'll go out to the main area of B6 to assess the situation,' Josh said. 'If we can meet Pete halfway –'

'There's something you should know,' Kyle Foreman interrupted. Josh and Mai turned to him as he spoke to the air, his voice carrying 1500 miles to Tintara. 'There's an assassin out there. Calls himself the Dragon. He almost had me just before the explosion. He was hit by some debris. I tied him up and took his weapon.'

There was a long silence over the line. 'I see,' Mark said at last.

80

The Maldives

War was still in a sullen mood. He had moved from the deck of the *Rosebud* and was slouched in a leather chair behind his desk, his eyes glued to a 60-inch flat-screen monitor on the wall of his office. He gave the other three a sour look.

Death spoke first. 'I'm growing concerned. My people tell me they haven't heard from the Dragon and can't reach him.'

'That *is* out of character,' Pestilence intoned, lowering his gin and tonic to the armrest of his chair aboard his Hawker, which was now 30,000 feet above Newfoundland.

'There is apparently a lot of interference on the ground. Residuals from the blasts, and radio traffic from the fucking emergency services.'

War giggled, finally snapping out of his bad mood. Death glared at him and he poked out his tongue. 'So what now?' he said.

'Have you learned anything more about this rescue organisation?' Conquest asked, directing his question towards War.

'I thought Little Miss Cyberspace was onto that.'

'It's going to take time.'

'Time is something we don't have in abundance,' Death said, fixing the other three on his screen.

'So, I ask again,' War said through a toothy grin, his lips hardly moving, 'what now?'

'The Dragon knows what to do if there's no contact after two call-in periods.'

'That's rather drastic, isn't it?' Death said, half to himself.

The other three looked at him, their expressions hard.

'Oh, I think it will be hysterical,' War said and giggled. 'But we are, of course, assuming the man is still alive.'

'Oh, he's alive,' Conquest retorted. 'I'd bet my last billion dollars on it.'

81

Base One, Tintara

Tom was on the balcony above Cyber Control. The doors
had opened automatically as he approached in his motorised wheelchair and rolled out into the balmy night. He
needed to get away from the hubbub at the workstations
down there. He needed some clarity. His laptop was still
linked to the mainframe, though, so he had full access to
Sybil and comms. Overhead, the sky was filled with stars,
the slipstream of the Milky Way a ribbon of a billion lights
set against the black velvet night.

He felt disturbed. The closest he could describe it to
anyone – other than a fellow cybergeek – was that he felt
like someone was looking over his shoulder. Not in the 'real'
world, but in cyberspace. His primary job these past few
months had been to develop Sybil further than the E-Force
engineers who had designed it. His specialty was hacking,
and that's what he had concentrated on – building defence
systems into the mainframe, as well as systems to detect
cyber-intruders.

His comms sounded and the interior of the Big Mac
appeared on his holoscreen. It was Mark and Stephanie.

'I've spoken to Josh and Mai,' Mark began. 'They're in
trouble. The cave-in has trapped them with Foreman and
two others, a young guy called Dave Golding and an elderly
man, Marty Gardiner. Gardiner's in a bad way.'

Tom nodded. 'Pete was in touch a few minutes ago. He's

not finding it easy either, even in the Mole. The structural integrity of the building is badly compromised and he's worried he'll kill survivors if he goes charging in. I've been trying to map the stress regions, but there's just too much interference. At least, that's what I think it is.'

'Okay. I've instructed Josh to find a way to get up from B6, try and meet Pete coming down. Meanwhile, I'm going to tackle the blockage in the tunnel.' He paused for a beat. 'There's another problem. Foreman was attacked.'

'Attacked?'

Mark told him about the assassin who called himself the Dragon.

'This is just getting worse,' Tom sighed. 'How's Steph?'

She came into view. 'Good, Tom.' She sent him a couple of images.

'These are the two goons who were filming the inside of the Big Mac. I'm really pissed off about it. I should have been more careful. The funny thing is, they seemed to know what they wanted, and where they were going.'

Tom looked puzzled but said nothing.

'Tom,' Mark butted in. 'I want anything you can get on these guys. Looks like they're genuine marines, but we need a lot more. Who they're working for is the number-one question.'

'Sure.'

'Keep us in the loop. Out.'

Tom took a deep breath. He called up the file on Major Larry Simpson. Text flowed down the holoscreen and he extracted the essentials.

Major Larry Harold Simpson

Age: 32

Joined the Marine Corps in 2008

Fast-track promotion; impeccable record

Decorations: Distinguished Service Metal, Bronze Star

Served in Iraq and Afghanistan. Special training for presidential bodyguard duties

Sergeant Vincent George Paolomo

Age: 25

Joined the Marines in 2004

Father is General Anthony Paolomo, presently Senior Advisor to the National Security Council

Tom raised an eyebrow at this last piece of information. He typed in an encrypted alphanumeric sequence, and a series of prompts flashed across his holoscreen. He responded to the prompts and in a few seconds he was into the US Marines database at its headquarters in Arlington, Virginia. He typed in Vincent Paolomo's serial number. A few seconds passed before a message came up. 'File *Unavailable.*'

Tom felt a tingle of excitement shoot through him. 'Well, isn't that just dandy?' he said to the warm night air. 'Right. Let's take a look at the good major, shall we?'

He returned to the database and ran his fingers rapidly over the keys, inserting Simpson's serial number. The display turned black. Then, to Tom's horror, a skull and crossbones appeared in the centre of the holoscreen. It flashed red and black. The computer was under attack.

'No!' Tom exclaimed. His fingers darted over the keys in a blur. With lightning speed, he keyed in a personalised firewall. It appeared as a set of interlocking chainmail fences in front of the skull and crossbones. The skull on the holoscreen smiled menacingly and appeared to move towards him. The chainmail shattered, its metal links flying apart.

Tom broke out in a sweat, his palms suddenly clammy. He kept typing, his fingers moving with phenomenal speed, his eyes darting across the holoscreen. 'Sybil, help!' he shouted. But there was no response. His mind in a whirl, he hit more strings of numbers and letters, then stabbed 'Enter'.

The skull and crossbones stopped moving. The smile faded. An old-fashioned cannon appeared on the screen. It fired a cannonball, and the skull and crossbones smashed into a thousand pieces. The screen went blue.

Tom was shaking, his mind racing. *That attack happened too quickly*, he thought. *Far too quickly*. Suppressing his panic, he typed in an alphanumeric code only he knew, a sequence he kept in his head. For several long, anxiety-filled moments nothing happened. Then out of nowhere a small figure appeared on the screen. It was a cartoon of Tom himself, except he was standing on two legs – athletic, powerful legs. It was his avatar, Tommy Boy, and he was armed to the teeth. He had a fuck-off assault rifle in his right hand, and at his waist hung a pistol with a massive barrel.

Tom took a deep breath. Now his avatar was on screen he knew he had stabilised the system – that he had a fighting chance. But he also knew the comms breakdown earlier that evening had been nothing to do with a failure of the E-Force network. Someone had broken into the computer system and gotten through his carefully constructed defence systems.

Tom's mind was racing, threads of half-formed thoughts coming together. He remembered what Mark had said. How had the assassin known where Kyle Foreman was? How had he got to him so easily? How did he even know the senator was still alive? And Steph had said that Simpson and Paolomo seemed to *know* what they wanted and where they were going aboard the Big Mac. There had definitely been a security breach. Someone, somewhere had been monitoring every move E-Force had made. They had been tracking every communication since the team had arrived at the CCC.

Tom was about to instruct his avatar when Sybil's voice

broke through the silence of the night. It reverberated around Base One, poured from every speaker at every computer workstation. But it wasn't the voice everyone on the base knew as Sybil's. It was androgynous, oddly weak and high-pitched.

Tom felt a fear he had never known before. It was paralysing, and filled his mind with dread, with a draining, cloying sense of hopelessness. Looking at the holoscreen, he felt a cold shiver pass through him as though fingers of ice were pulling at his heart. Another avatar had appeared and was walking towards Tommy Boy. It was a slim young woman in her twenties. She was wearing a frumpy tweed skirt, a turtleneck sweater and a string of pearls, her hair up in a bun. She looked like a librarian.

'You!' Tom exclaimed.

82

California Conference Center, Los Angeles

Mark drove the second Mole out of the holding bay of the Big Mac and tore along the tarmac towards the north-west of the CCC. Sixty seconds later, he passed the Pram and pulled up at the entrance to the drain. Setting the drill to minimum power, he nudged the Mole forward. It chewed through the rim of the doorframe as though it were tissue paper, then rumbled along the short passageway that led to the vertical shaft which dropped 80 feet down to the floor of the drain.

The shaft was less than four feet wide, while the drill of the Mole was seven feet wide at its base. Without hesitating for a second, Mark ramped up the drill speed, pivoted it downwards and started to burrow into the shaft. For twenty seconds he cut through the soil around the shaft, effortlessly chewing through its concrete lining. Just short of the floor of the shaft he slowed the drill, pulled the nose up, and steered the machine into the drain itself, churning up soil, concrete and chunks of rock as he went.

Setting the headlights of the Mole to max, Mark studied the tunnel ahead of him. There were huge cracks along the walls, and in several places jagged chunks of rock had pushed through. Running the camera images through a set of analysers, the onboard computer system built up a picture of the structural integrity of the drain. It didn't look good.

On his screen Mark could see thick and ragged red lines running the length of the tunnel, like blood vessels through flesh. These indicated the worst fault lines. They were bad enough, but there was also a latticework of fragmented orange lines clustered around them, representing only slightly less serious fissures. Together they showed that the mere presence of the Mole could cause more harm than good. Mark knew he would be safe whatever sort of disruption was caused to the integrity of the drain, but that wouldn't help him rescue the survivors trapped on B6. Problem was, there were no other viable options.

Following the path taken by Mai and Josh a short time before, Mark rolled forward, the tunnel lit up by the enormous beams of the Mole. Two minutes later the lights illuminated the wall of rock and soil that had sealed up the drain. The blockage stretched from floor to ceiling, sloping outward at its base.

'Steph – I've reached the cave-in,' Mark said into his comms.

'How does it look?'

'Not good. I'm going to run a full spectroscopic analysis. Out.'

He ran his fingers over the flat plastic control panel. Sensors on the exterior of the Mole probed the material of the blockage. The computer used infrared analysers, a petrographic polarising light microscope, a micro mass-spectrometer and a nuclear magnetic resonance spectro-meter to construct a data profile of the blockage. It then sent the information to the Big Mac to be processed.

'So what're we dealing with?' Mark asked after a few seconds.

Stephanie sent images back to the Mole. 'The obstruction has the following composition,' she began. As she spoke, Mark studied a histogram on his holoscreen. 'Composition of the blockage is 84.2 per cent soil originating from around the tunnel lining, 14.6 per cent concrete from the lining, and 1.2 per cent miscellaneous material, including water, organic substances and oxygen. The soil fits broadly into the Ardisol category. It's 38.5 per cent clay, 42.9 per cent sand, 9.7 per cent water and 4.6 per cent air. The other 4.3 per cent is made up of miscellaneous minerals and organic material. The obstruction depth varies between 27.4 and 32.6 feet. The average density of blockage is 5.67 pounds per cubic inch.' A coloured 3D representation of the obstruction appeared on the screen. 'The green areas are air pockets in the obstruction,' Stephanie concluded.

'Print that out for me, please, Steph,' Mark said.

A few seconds later he plucked a glossy print from the edge of the control panel. It showed the tunnel and the obstruction. The drain appeared generally cylindrical. On the far side of the blockage, there was about a hundred feet of clear tunnel leading to the hole Josh had made into B6 earlier.

'Alright, Steph, plot the fastest course through the obstruction which offers us the best chance of maintaining structural integrity – both for the blockage and for the drain on either side.'

'Course plotted,' she replied, and sent it over.

'What's the percentage risk to the structural integrity using this route?'

'Overall risk to blockage is 16.7 per cent. For the section you're in now, the risk is 11.2 per cent. For the eastern section, 30.9 per cent.'

'Is that the best we can do?'

'Yes. The alternative is a route that will take 59 per cent longer and only reduce overall integrity risk by an average of 1.3 per cent.'

The correct decision was obvious. 'Set the first course,

please, Steph,' Mark said without hesitating.

A moment later, the drill of the Mole began to scythe its way into the west face of the blockage.

83

Room B63, California Conference Center

Kyle Foreman pulled on the oxygen mask Josh had handed him. It was identical to the one over Marty's face. It weighed less than a gram and would give him air for 24 hours if needed. It clung to his face. Josh adjusted a tiny control near Foreman's chin and told him to breath deeply. 'It'll take a little getting used to,' Josh added.

'Are you guys armed?' Foreman asked, his voice distorted by the mask.

Josh patted a lump at his hip. 'Stun pistols. Not deadly, but effective.'

'Okay,' Foreman replied, removing the assassin's Magnum from his pocket. 'This Dragon character is a pro. I'll rely on this, if it's all the same to you.'

'But you said he was injured and tied up.'

'Even so,' Foreman replied.

Josh shrugged his shoulders. 'Well, let's go see.' He turned to the door and lifted the shutter.

'Josh?'

He turned to Mai, who was applying spray-on skin to Dave's wounded arm.

'Take care,' she said.

Josh flicked on his helmet light and handed Foreman a powerful halogen torch from his kitbag. The beams cut through the smoky air. They could see a dull orange glow coming from the fires in the main part of B6.

Foreman led the way. Turning right at the end of the corridor, they emerged into the wider passageway that led to the open area and the ramp in the car park section. They could see the fresh devastation caused by the exploded gas cylinder. A corridor leading to the north-east section of the floor was strewn with debris, and black smoke hung in the air. Through the smoke, yellow flames could be seen lapping the walls. The two men turned in the opposite direction, towards the emergency exit in the south-west corner.

The car park was swamped in a grey haze that hung about five feet above the ground. The cars were caked with dust and detritus, and the floor crunched underfoot.

'This way,' Foreman said, squeezing between two lines of cars. A second later he emerged onto an open area. It was strewn with chunks of concrete and pools of glass; there was dust everywhere. There was no sign of the Dragon.

'This is where I left him,' Foreman said. He crouched down to move away some of the rubble and spotted the car stereo – the leads from the back had been wrenched away. In the dust he could just make out patches of blood.

Josh drew his stun pistol from its holster. He gazed around the car park, but even with his enhanced vision he could see no sign of the assassin.

'Let's check out the emergency exit,' Josh said, and he clambered over the piles of shattered concrete and twisted metal. It was only a few paces away, and its door had been wrenched from the hinges. Josh approached the door from the side, his back hard against the pitted wall, the stun gun poised in front of his nose. Foreman followed him closely.

Sliding into the stairwell, Josh swung the gun around. A concrete staircase led to B5. It seemed clear, but it was impossible to tell for sure from here. Josh strained to listen – with his cochlear implants he could detect a man breathing from twenty feet away – but there was nothing.

They started to climb the stairs, crouching low and sticking close to the wall, out of sight to anyone higher up. The air was growing hotter. Josh was fine in his cybersuit, but Foreman was beginning to suffer. He was sweating so much that his ripped shirt was soaked, his hair dripping wet.

The door through to Level B5 was open a crack.

'I think we should keep going,' Josh whispered. 'See how far up we can get.'

Foreman nodded and wiped his face with the back of his hand.

'You okay?'

'Just hot.'

Josh looked at his flexiscreen. It told him the temperature was topping 120 degrees Fahrenheit, with 95 per cent humidity. Kicking at a pile of rubble, he picked up a foot-long steel pole and handed it to Foreman. 'Stay here, and keep your back to the wall. Don't go to the rail and don't go into B5. Is that clear?'

Foreman nodded and took a deep breath.

Josh dashed up the first flight of stairs, turned at the end, and then, keeping close to the wall, he took the second flight a little slower. The door to Level B4 was closed. He tried the handle but it was stuck fast. He checked his screen and could see that the door was pinned shut by a single beam of metal on the other side.

He stepped back and kicked the door. Nothing. Looking around, he saw a steel beam poking from a heap of crumbled concrete and brick. He pulled at it and it came loose. He stepped back and rammed the steel against the wooden door. It groaned on its hinges, but held.

Taking a deep breath, Josh launched the narrow girder at the door with all his strength. This time the beam ploughed straight through the wooden panels. Two more blows and Josh had punched a hole two feet wide in the door. He shoved the girder through the opening and knocked away the steel beam on the other side. It hit the floor of the car park with a dull thud.

A fire had recently burned itself out on B4. The cars close to the exit were little more than charred chassis. Josh checked his wrist. The temperature was nudging 200 degrees here. The air was a toxic blend of sulphur, carbon monoxide and vapourised hydrocarbons. More importantly, he could see that a ferocious fire was raging between the door and the ramp. Half the ceiling had collapsed. It was completely impassable, even in a cybersuit.

Josh ran back to the ravaged door, stepped over the piles of smashed wood, and began the descent back to B5. As he swung around the corner he looked down towards the door into the car park. Senator Foreman was gone.

84

'Shit!' Josh exclaimed under his breath. He stopped and listened, but all he could hear was creaking structure, the crackle of combustion, and water streaming down walls.

Creeping down the final steps, he tried to steady his breathing. He reached the landing, pinned himself to the wall and edged slowly towards the door. Taking a deep breath, he leapt through the opening, his stun gun sweeping the space just inside Level B5. He was alone.

He crouched low and headed along the gap between the first two lines of cars. At the third vehicle he heard a faint tapping sound and spun around. The Dragon appeared from behind a column.

He had his left arm around Kyle Foreman's throat, his Yarygin PYa handgun held in his right, with the barrel against the senator's head. Foreman's face was a picture of pain and terror, wet with perspiration, his pupils huge and dark. He had a fresh red bruise just under his left eye and a cut across his right cheek. Blood ran down to his chin. The oxygen mask still clung to his mouth and nose.

'Put the toy down, please, Dr Thompson.'

'How do you know my name?'

'Oh, I know many things,' the Dragon replied. 'My employers are extremely well informed. Now, I'll ask again. Put down the weapon.'

Josh didn't move. The Dragon thrust the gun forward and

303

shot the stun pistol out of Josh's hand. He yelped with pain as two fingers were dislocated at the knuckle.

'Why didn't you just kill the senator?' Josh said between gritted teeth.

'What's the hurry?' the Dragon smirked as he turned the gun back to Foreman's temple. 'Well, okay, I want you to see it, Dr Thompson,' he added. 'After all, you'll be meeting your maker immediately after Senator Foreman here.'

Josh heard something. But he couldn't figure out what it was or where it was coming from. The other two seemed oblivious to the sound.

'Oh, and there is something else,' the Dragon went on. 'I rather like the look of your suit. Might be a little large on me, what with your big muscles and all.' He sniggered. 'But it will come in very useful in getting out of this shithole.'

Josh caught a glimmer of light reflected off smooth metal. At the same moment, the Dragon heard a sound. He pulled Foreman to one side, the gun still pushed hard against his skull. He turned slightly to his left.

A Hunter came into view. It was hovering six feet above the floor. The Dragon glared at it, uncomprehending. Josh saw Foreman's eyes widen, his dark pupils lit up by the light reflected by the Hunter.

The machine moved two feet closer, then stopped. It swivelled in the air, scanning the scene, absorbing data. For a second it seemed as though the Dragon didn't know how to respond. He took a step back and came up hard against the wreck of a Ford Explorer. Its hood had popped and a haze of smoke hung over its engine.

Then the Hunter began to move again, heading straight for the Dragon and Senator Foreman. The Dragon slid the Yarygin away from Foreman's head and took aim at the Hunter.

But before he could fire, the machine let out a series of loud clicks, then a hiss. It wobbled, emitting a high-pitched squeal that froze the Dragon's finger on the trigger. The Hunter sped towards the two men, shuddered and plummeted, smashing into the engine of the Ford Explorer.

The car rocked as metal slammed into metal. Oil gushed from the engine and petrol splashed onto the concrete floor of the car park. It ignited immediately. The battery exploded, shooting boiling sulphuric acid into the air.

Stunned, the Dragon lost his grip on Foreman, who tore free, dropped to the floor and rolled away. Acid sprayed across the senator's left arm, burning through the fabric. But the Dragon took the full force of the flying yellow liquid. A great plume of the acid flew into his face. He screamed and dropped the gun. Blinded, he stumbled, tripped on a detached bumper bar and fell backwards into the burning fuel.

The Dragon went up like a Roman candle, his hair crackling and fizzing into black threads. He tried to clamber to his feet, but his hands slipped in the fiery liquid. He made it to a sitting position, an expression of abject confusion written into his features. Then he smiled resignedly. Looking straight into Josh's eyes, he shrugged. 'We're all dead. I've been busy . . . *boom*!'

Flames shot into the Dragon's mouth and his left eye melted onto his cheek.

Josh dove forward, grabbed Kyle Foreman and pulled him towards the doorway to the stairwell. He didn't stop until he had forced the senator to the first landing, down the stairs and around the corner onto the stairs leading back to B6. As they turned the bend, a huge explosion ripped through B5, sending a fireball into the stairwell. Josh jumped through the door to B6, dragging the senator with him.

The sound of the explosion reverberated along the shaft of the stairwell. It was followed by a weird silence. Josh pulled himself to his feet and leaned over Foreman, who was sprawled on the floor. The man's face was covered in dirt and blood. He opened his eyes, winced and tried to speak, but his mouth was too dry. He ran his tongue over his split and bloodied lips, tasting the iron. Grabbing at his left arm, Foreman recoiled as the acid bit into his palm.

Josh tore the fabric away. Underneath, the flesh was red raw. 'Can you walk, Senator?'

Foreman nodded. 'I think so.'

Josh helped him to his feet.

'We need to get that arm seen to,' Josh said. He spoke into his comms. 'Mai, we're heading back. One casualty.'

There was only silence along the line.

'Mai? Do you receive? We're on our way back.'

Nothing.

'Mark? Steph? Base One?'

Nothing.

Then Josh realised his suit had shut down. He pulled off his helmet and the stench of the fumes hit him. He coughed violently, then vomited into the dust.

Something had gone terribly wrong. That Hunter had crashed without warning, without anyone doing anything to it. And as he led Kyle Foreman back towards the storeroom, the Dragon's final words reverberated through his mind.

85

The slope down from B3 to B4 was surprisingly clear, but the air was rancid with a cocktail of very nasty fumes. It was unbearably hot. Inside the number one Mole, Pete Sherringham was comfortably cocooned at an ambient temperature of 70 degrees Fahrenheit. But the view through the external cameras displayed a barren scene of utter devastation.

As the Mole descended, Pete could see across B4 between the support columns of the ramp. Most of the floor was aflame, from the ramp right through to the western end of the building. To make things worse, part of the floor of B3 had collapsed into B4, making it impassable on foot.

At the bottom of the ramp, Pete immediately swung the Mole around, pointing the drill nose towards the down ramp to Level B5. At that moment a sheet of flame leapt across the ramp, igniting a river of oil and fuel that was running down the ramp to B5. A wall of blue and purple flames shot up, creating a corridor of fire.

Pete ignored it and pushed his way down the ramp. Then the Mole stalled. The onboard computer screen turned blue and the lights went out. The engine hummed for a few seconds, the note descending in pitch to a dull rumble. Then it fell silent. Two seconds later the emergency generator kicked in. A faint light flickered to life above the control panels.

Pete stared in disbelief at the array of useless plastic and metal at his fingertips. The control panels were blank, their lifeblood cut off.

'Base One,' he said into his comms. His voice was heavy. He didn't expect a response. None came.

86

Mark was in the number two Mole, twenty feet through the obstruction in the drainage tunnel, when his screen died. A second later the engines of the Mole shuddered to an ominous silence and his comms went down.

The backup generator sprung to life and Mark turned from the control panel to the Bullet, the module behind the drill. Its walls were curved and lined with bench seats. He walked over to one of the benches. There was just enough room to sit upright, his head less than an inch from the sloping ceiling.

He took a deep breath and leaned forward, his head between his knees. He looked to the back of the Bullet. There was a manual override to the back door of the Mole. What should he do? Wait to see if the power came back on, or climb out and see if he could dig through the obstruction with a shovel?

He looked at his wrist but his cybersuit was down too. That meant the whole system must be screwed, or at least a large portion of it – no power, no suits, no comms. 'God!' Mark exclaimed. 'I just knew something like this would happen. Interfering politicians thinking they know best. Fuck!'

He pushed himself out of the chair and, crouching down, made his way to the rear door. He turned a red lever to the right of the door and pulled on another next to it. Then as he pushed on the door the airtight seal hissed and the door eased smoothly outwards on its hinges. Mark grabbed a torch from the wall above the bench seat and shone it through the opening.

The powerful beam lit up smooth walls of earth, a twenty-foot-long cylinder, eight feet in diameter, freshly produced by the massive drill of the Mole. As the beam dispersed, it lit up the first few feet of drain wall. Beyond that lay a seamless black void.

87

Everywhere and nowhere

'Why so surprised?'

'Francine friggin' Gygax. I might have guessed.'

'Well, it's nice to see you too, Tommy Boy.'

Tom checked himself. He was still fully armed. She hadn't been able to touch his weapons. But what was the status of the system? Jesus! Almost everything down. He checked it out silently, fixing Francine Gygax with his toughest stare.

Sybil had been taken over. All comms were down – nothing at all was getting through to LA. Almost everything at Base One was frozen. The rest of the staff would be looking at blank screens and wondering what the hell had happened. As if on cue, someone came running onto the balcony to find him. He had just enough energy to shoo them away. He had plenty to contend with in cyberspace.

Tom gazed around. The two of them were floating in uniform blackness. He studied Francine. She really did look like a librarian, bespectacled and dressed in 'sensible' shoes and a skirt. Her avatar was as different to her as Tom's was to him. But then he noticed the tight knit top she was wearing. It didn't do much to disguise her large breasts. This was not the Francine Gygax he had known in 'real' life.

In the 'real' world Francine was blonde and blue-eyed – a 24-carat babe. Tom Erickson had met her when he was fifteen at a software convention in Minneapolis. She was seventeen and had already made the transformation from mouse to minx. They had stayed in touch, and hooked up occasionally in cyberspace to exchange ideas, challenges. Tom had met her again a year later at another convention in Detroit, where he'd taken her on in a game of *Interstellar Life*, a hardcore net-head's favourite. She had eaten him up and he'd never forgotten it. He knew she was keen, egotistical and brilliant, as well as totally amoral. She had actually congratulated him via email when he had pulled off his cyber-heist a year ago.

'So what's up, Francine?' Tommy Boy said.

'Oh, I'm in gainful employment.'

'So I see. So what's the deal?'

Francine smiled. She had a tooth missing, her left canine. 'Tommy Boy, I'd be shocked if you weren't able to put up a fight.' She eyed him carefully.

'Well, I owe my employers a duty of trust,' Tommy Boy replied with a smirk. Without warning, he drew a pistol from a holster at his side and fired. Francine vanished before the particles could reach her.

Then suddenly Tommy Boy was falling. There was no sense of time or space, no air rushing past, no sound at all. Tom closed his eyes involuntarily. Opening them a moment later, he found himself in a garden that stretched away to the horizon. It was carefully manicured, all neat hedges, beds of rose bushes and uniformly spaced rhododendrons. A bird flew low past his face and he ducked involuntarily.

A crash came from a few feet away. Tommy Boy spun around and there was a second crash – closer this time. He spotted Francine. She raised her gun as he dived behind a hedge. Clutching at his shoulder, he found his impulse rifle and rested its huge barrel lightly in his palm. He ran from the hedge, firing at the spot where he had last seen Francine's avatar. The flower bed vapourised and a tree vanished.

He saw Francine dash behind a wall and fired at it. Francine jumped 30 feet into the air. Tommy Boy swung the gun upward, just catching sight of a fluorescent net as it sailed down towards him. It shimmered menacingly but he just managed to spring away as it reached the ground and vanished. Francine was gone.

Tommy Boy walked slowly between two high hedges, sweeping his impulse rifle from left to right and back. It felt good to be walking again. He heard a sound, a creaking, but he couldn't focus on where it was coming from. He looked up and saw a huge cluster of black dots forming in the sky. They were growing larger.

Something hit him on the arm. He looked down at it. A small black worm slithered along his wrist and stopped. Another landed next to it. Then the pain came as the creatures undulated on his arm. Tom realised with a start that they were leeches sucking his blood. He felt two more spatter onto his face. He tugged at them, suppressing his panic.

He clicked his fingers and a golf umbrella appeared in his hand. It had a huge corporate logo, a Silverback poised above the words 'E-Force – We're There For You'. The leeches pattered onto the umbrella, some slithering to the ground at his feet, others clinging on desperately. He plucked the two leeches from his arm, tossed them to the ground and sped off.

As Tommy Boy ran, Tom felt the terrain change. Looking down, he saw the neatly swept path transforming into uneven rock. The leeches had stopped falling. He made the umbrella disappear and gazed around. The garden had gone, replaced by a landscape of ash and fire. Close by, a river of lava rippled in the haze.

Tom felt the heat slam into him like a wave. He stumbled and fell forward, cutting his hands on the jagged ground. The rifle left his hands and clattered across the rocks and into the lava, sizzling pathetically and exploding in a cascade of crimson and yellow.

Tommy Boy stood up. He was clad in a cybersuit, floating a few inches above the scorching ground.

Francine stepped out from behind a rock. She was lit up, flames in her hair. She smiled. 'You've grown soft, Tommy Boy. I thought Aldermont would have toughened you up, not turned you into a pussy.' Francine's smile vanished and a jet of flame flew out of her raised palm at incredible speed.

It almost had him, but he sidestepped the fire stream. Catching his toe on a rock, Tommy Boy stumbled again, coming down hard against a jutting outcrop of scorching hot lava. He stood up, swung around and raised his own palm outwards. A stream of ice shot out and met Francine's second fire-bolt mid-flight. Fire and ice met in a ball of steam.

Tommy Boy blinked. His opponent had vanished again. The lava had dissolved, replaced by a shining metal floor that stretched to the horizon, hard and featureless. He had a new pistol in his right hand.

A voice came from behind him. He spun around. Francine was there, a bazooka pointed at his head. 'Drop the gun, Tom,' she said, her voice brittle.

He tossed it to the ground.

His mind was racing. She had been at least one step ahead of him from the moment they had entered this cyber-reality, forcing him onto the back foot, and now she would destroy him. He had to think of something, anything.

For some strange reason Tom thought back to their other life, as teenagers at conventions playing nerdy games. He remembered how Francine always kept to the main hall and never went into the smaller gaming rooms where you could avoid the crowds. When they had done battle, she had refused to go into a gaming booth. They had played using headsets in the main meeting room, under powerful lights and with just a few fellow gamers watching. Then he remembered how jumpy she had been, even after she had won. How she had promptly left. That's when it came to him.

Tommy Boy held his hands up. Francine took a step towards him and lifted the bazooka to his head. He looked around and swept his hand in front of him, causing the floor to shrink. The horizon rushed towards them from every direction. Tommy Boy looked up, and four walls crashed into place. He mouthed a word and a rectangle of steel fell from the sky, thumping onto the four walls.

Francine glared at him. 'What are you doing?'

He ignored her and glanced over her right shoulder towards the wall behind. It started to move towards them.

'*What are you doing?*' Francine's face was frozen in panic.

She glared at the walls and they stopped moving. But the effort had distracted her. Tommy Boy grabbed the huge gun from Francine's small hands, spun it around and rested his finger on the trigger.

'I just remembered. Confined spaces – a no-no, hey, Francine? I know what an egomaniac you are, and although your avatar *looks* nothing like you, I kinda knew you would put as much of your mind into it as possible, claustrophobia and all. Mistake, baby!'

He pulled back his finger and Francine's body exploded into a hundred messy pieces.

88

California Conference Center, Los Angeles

The silence in the earth tunnel was even more oppressive than the darkness. It was hard to believe that such unspeakable horrors lay directly overhead. Mark crawled back to the opening into the drain and clambered down to the floor of the tunnel. He slid down the final three feet and almost went over in the slimy mess underfoot – a cocktail of mud, waste and filthy water.

Twenty feet along the tunnel Mark heard a clanking sound and froze. It had come from some distance away. He swept the space with his torch. There was nothing but tunnel walls, slime and darkness. The sound came again. Then a faint illumination appeared, close to where the Mole had ploughed into the drain from the shaft running down from the surface.

He turned his light off and crouched down close to the wall. He could just make out someone descending from the roof of the tunnel on what looked like a rope ladder. The figure was alone, but he could not see clearly. A torch beam cut through the black, running along the walls as the shape approached. Mark shielded his eyes and threw himself flat to the floor. The torch light ran along his body.

'Mark!' a voice called.

'Steph – thank Christ!'

He clambered to his feet, brushing away the clinging soil.

'The Mole's down too?'

'Yep. The Big Mac the same?'

'Yes. Looks like the whole system is offline. I don't know what the hell has happened.'

'You got out of the Big Mac through the emergency hatch?'

'Yeah. The manual override. How far into the barrier are you?'

'20.16 feet, to be precise,' Mark replied.

Stephanie handed him a long metal tube – a Sonic Drill. She had another slung over her shoulder. 'Not quite the Mole, but it seems the only option we have.'

He smiled at her. 'Good thinking, Steph.'

89

Pete gazed around the cramped interior of the Bullet at the back of the Mole. The emergency light cast a depressing sombre glow. His suit was down. That was to be expected. It was obvious that E-Force had suffered a complete system failure. Kneeling up on the seat that ran along one wall of the machine, Pete lifted a metal shutter covering one of four opaque panels made from glass doped with terbium and dysprosium, which made them strong enough to stop a Magnum bullet at close range.

What he saw made his heart sink. Blue flames surrounded the Mole, licking at the body of the machine. Normally this would be of little concern – the machine could travel through a furnace for an hour. But with the system down, coolant would no longer flow through the nanotubes under the outer skin of the vehicle. This would make it warm up with surprising speed, and then only the metal structure itself would provide protection from the searing heat.

The blue flames, Pete knew, came from burning fuel, and they would be particularly hot – around 3000 degrees Fahrenheit. He didn't need a thermometer to tell him that. He'd made a close study of the engineering details of all the machines used by E-Force. They were pretty sturdy pieces of technology. The shell of the Mole was made from maxinium, an alloy five times more resilient than the strongest titanium-steel composite. In its own right, it could resist heat, corrosive chemicals and high-powered impacts. But not forever. And he couldn't climb out. With his cybersuit not operational he would never make it through the flames.

How long did he have before the structural integrity of the Mole and the Bullet was compromised? He ran through the numbers in his head and was horrified by the conclusion.

He was sitting inside a pressure cooker. If the system stayed down, he had no more than four minutes before the hull started to heat up beyond the critical limit. Immediately after that, thermal energy would flow from the outer shell straight to the interior of the Bullet. Then Pete would slowly cook.

90

Everywhere and nowhere

Francine's gore was all over him. He shook himself and let
the mess slither away. A sound from behind made him spin
round. A young girl of about eleven was standing next to
him and smiling.

'Tom.'

He simply stared at her, uncomprehending.

'It's Sybil.'

Tommy Boy ran a hand over his forehead. Then broke
into a grin.

'We have to move fast. Everything's falling apart,' Sybil
added. 'Follow me.'

They were in a tunnel, lights running overhead, tarmac
underfoot. The end appeared as a silver disk that grew bigger
and brighter. Emerging from the exit, they were in a street of
old cottages. The cottages had thatched roofs, rose gardens.
It was a chocolate-box English village. The street was merely
a muddy track pitted with the marks of horses, piles of
steaming dung here and there. It stank – a rich country
smell of grass and animal odours.

Sybil walked ahead of him. 'This way,' she called back,
heading along a narrow garden path. On each side lay
flowerbeds filled with psychedelic arrays of exotic plants
that were quite alien to a real English country garden.

The door to the cottage swung open and Sybil walked in.
The hall was dimly lit by sunlight filtering through leaded

windows. A wooden staircase ascended to the first floor. Sybil immediately headed towards a lounge. Low oak beams ran over the ceiling, and the walls were whitewashed. There were more leadlight windows in deep recesses. Dried flowers stood in a vase inside an empty fireplace. Incongruously, the floor was scattered with small metal boxes. The closest one had a label that read '*Operating system*'.

'Quick, open it,' Sybil snapped.

Tom twisted the key and the lid lifted.

Sybil let out a deep sigh and walked over to another metal box. This one was marked '*Programmes A1–C4*'. Opening the lid, she let the contents flow over her. 'Whoa! That feels good,' she laughed, and scrambled to the next box.

Tom left her to it and walked through a low doorway into a dining room. A long, narrow teak table and six chairs took up most of the floor space. The table was stacked with more boxes.

He looked at the nearest one: '*Francine*'. He opened it and the information soaked into him. Francine had been free-lance for a year. This project was for a mysterious organisation, a group calling itself the Four Horsemen. She had known very little about them. They had their protocols cleverly guarded and resisted even her most determined efforts to break them. She had only seen the face of one of the four and knew no names other than their aliases – Death, Pestilence, War and Conquest.

Tommy Boy glanced along the table and read the labels on the boxes. '*The Dragon*', '*The CCC*', '*Money*', '*Plans and layouts*'. There were dozens of them. Then he noticed one marked '*The Four Horsemen*', and at last he realised where Sybil had taken him. He wasn't inside Francine's computer, he was in the mainframe of the Four Horsemen. Sybil had broken through into a system that had resisted Francine. He grabbed the box and put it in his pocket.

'Sybil?' he called through to the lounge.

There was no reply.

He lifted a couple of boxes. One was marked *'Political assassinations'*. Another was labeled: *'Foreman'*. Underneath this was another box. It was larger than the others, and as Tommy Boy read the two words on the lid a surge of excitement and fear rippled through him. *'Third Bomb'*.

He felt a rush of air behind him and spun around. A horribly corrupted version of Francine's avatar stood three feet away. She had been pieced together from the slivers and shards of the body that had been blown asunder by the bazooka. She was a hideous sight, dripping blood and oozing some obscenely pungent pus. An oily liquid dribbled from Francine's eyes and ran down the remnants of her face. She had a huge knife in her hand. It caught the light from the window in the dining room.

Francine lunged forward so fast that Tommy Boy had no time to defend himself. But then, an inch from his throat, the blade slipped from Francine's twisted, wet fingers. He threw himself to one side as her body collapsed in a squelching heap. There was a huge black hole a foot wide in her back.

Tommy Boy looked from the ruined form of Francine's avatar to see Sybil, now standing erect, a beautiful young woman in a business suit. A freshly discharged radiation weapon was in her hand.

'Thanks,' he said simply.

'You're welcome.'

91

Tom shook his head and tried to focus as the starlit sky over Tintara replaced the inside of the cottage. He glanced at his laptop, which was displaying the screensaver he always used – the Rolling Stones mouth with its red lascivious tongue poking out. Then, like a train speeding out of the night, reality hit him – along with the memory of what he had seen just before Sybil had saved his avatar existence. Two words reverberated around his brain – '*Third bomb*'.

'Sybil?' he snapped.

'Tom.'

'Status, please.'

'System is functioning at 45 per cent. I've diagnosed the operating network, backup systems, external feeds and comms. We've sustained serious damage to a number of key components. They'll take time to repair.'

'Details, please, Syb. How long? You saw that box too, yeah?'

'I did see it, Tom, and I'm doing everything I can. Processing systems here at Base One are coming back online now. The satellite network is functioning at 30 per cent of normal levels, but most of the damaged systems will be self-diagnosed and repaired within three minutes. Comms are down completely.'

'When will they be up?'

'Insufficient data for an accurate evaluation.'

'Sybil, please. Ballpark.'

'An hour.'

'Shit – can you open the box, the file?'

'It's on your screen.'

A schematic appeared on Tom's screen. It was a low-grade, 2D representation of the CCC. A light flashed close to the ramp on B6. It was the bomb. To one side of the screen Tom could see a digital timer – minutes, seconds. On the far right, tenths of seconds flashing past faster than he could follow them. It was obviously the countdown for the detonation. As he stared, the first number clicked down.

The bomb would go off in seven minutes.

92

California Conference Center, Los Angeles

Mai lifted the roller-door and stared at Josh in horror. He had taken his helmet off and his face was covered with sweat and dirt. Blood was running from his nose. Senator Foreman looked far worse. His shirt was in shreds, the oxygen mask was splattered with blood and oil, and his hair was slick with mess. He was clutching a piece of rag to his left arm, which was red raw. They limped in and collapsed against the wall.

Mai knelt beside Foreman and gently removed the rag. His arm was a swathe of red and yellow, the skin blistered. Pieces of shirt material and rag clung to the sticky wounds. Mai opened her med-kit and found a small plastic bottle. She wetted a ball of cotton wool and gently wiped at the acid burns on the senator's arm. He winced and she stopped for a moment.

'Hold still,' she said, and she plucked a small metal cylinder from a holder inside the med kit.

'What's that?'

'It's a Vasjet.' She pushed one end against a clear patch of flesh on his arm and depressed a small button at the other end of the cylinder. 'A needle-less injection. It sends a narrow beam of atomised liquid through your skin and the wall of the nearest blood vessel.'

'That's fantastic,' Foreman replied.

A second later, a blend of anaesthetic and antibiotic began to circulate around the senator's body. A few moments more and the anaesthetic kicked in, numbing the agony in his arm. Mai returned to cleaning the wounds.

'I can feel it working already,' Foreman added in astonishment.

'Mai, is your suit up?' Josh asked.

'Negative. Went off about two minutes ago.'

'Mine too. Comms?'

She shook her head.

'Marvellous. How's Mr Gardiner?'

'Not good,' Mai replied. 'I've made him as comfortable as possible, but I can't do a lot with just this med-kit.'

'So what's the situation out there?' Dave asked.

Foreman glanced up. 'Useless. No chance of getting out that way.'

Dave looked down, his eyes screwed up tight.

'What about the assassin?' Mai asked, dabbing at Foreman's blistered skin.

'Oh, we had a little tête-à-tête with the Dragon,' the senator said, looking up.

'Yeah, really nice guy,' Josh added. He walked over to the roller-door and pulled it down. 'I think the only chance we have is to get out the way we came in. We'll have to get into the tunnel and try to find a way through the obstruction.'

'Mark said it was at least 30 feet thick.'

'Yes, but he also said he was taking a Mole down there. We won't last five minutes out in the car park. If the fumes don't get us, the fires will.'

'What about Pete?'

'We have no idea where he is, Mai,' Josh said, a tint of desperation in his voice. 'With the comms down . . .'

'Yeah, you're right.'

'What about Marty?' Dave asked, looking up.

Josh strode to the back corner of the room, where there was still a pile of unused tablecloths. 'Dave, look in the corridor for a couple of lengths of metal, about so long.' He stretched his arms out. 'Failing that, look in the next open room. Make it quick.'

'Josh, you need those wounds looked at,' Mai said.

He waved her away. 'I'll live,' he said. He tossed the tablecloths onto the floor.

93

Pete eyed the flames beyond the window. It was starting to warm up in the Bullet. He glanced at his watch. Two minutes and the air would be burning his throat. Thirty seconds more and he'd be dead. He sat as still as possible, conserving his energy. 'Well, this is not the way I thought it would end,' he said aloud, laughing bitterly.

He thought back to all the dangerous situations he had been in during his career. He remembered GWII, the minefield a mile outside Basra. The armoured car ahead of his had hit a mine, sending the vehicle ten feet off the road, then they had come under attack from snipers. Four of his men had died in the blast and another had an arm blown off by shrapnel, but Pete had walked away untouched. Then there was Afghanistan and the incident that had seen him and the army go their separate ways. He should have died then, but he hadn't.

94

Base One, Tintara

Tom hit the control panel of his laptop and winced at the ripple of pain that shot along his arm. 'Sybil, we need comms. *Now!*'

'I understand, Tom, but that's a negative. I can't repair the network any faster than it's doing itself.'

Tom looked away from the holoscreen and stared at the wall. He suddenly felt completely useless. Back there in that alternate reality he had been empowered. He had functioning legs again, he could walk, he could run. Now, here in this dense, clumsy world of solid matter and the more prosaic laws of physics, he could do nothing. He couldn't even use his phenomenal intelligence. Every avenue was blocked. *I might as well be living twenty years in the past*, he thought, *not twenty years in the future*. All this wonderful technology at their fingertips and yet they were no better off than they had been before the invention of the internet – before radio, even.

'That's it!' Tom exclaimed. He looked back at the holoscreen, his face alight with hope. 'I'm a freakin' genius!'

95

California Conference Center, Los Angeles

Out in the corridor the fumes were far worse than they had been even a few minutes earlier. Dave had an E-Force oxygen mask clamped to his face. He was breathing deeply, but the acrid gases settling on his skin were burning and itching.

There was no sign of anything like the metal poles he was looking for on the floor of the corridor. He ran on ten yards and reached a roller-door. He pulled at it but realised it was locked. Crossing the corridor, he tried the first door on that side, but it was locked too. Then he saw a narrow cupboard door next to the shutter. Trying the handle, he found that it too was locked. He stood back and ran at the door, crashing into it with his shoulder. It shook but held fast. Then he kicked the lock with the flat of his boot. The wood shattered. One more kick and it swung inwards.

Dave had got lucky. Propped against the wall, he could see what looked like lengths of scaffolding for a lighting rig. Four of the poles were at least ten feet long, but after moving these to one side with his good arm, he found what he was looking for, a set of cross pieces about five feet long. He grabbed the first two, tucked them under his arm and headed back to the corridor.

Mai opened the roller-door and pulled it closed as soon as Dave was inside. She had been binding Josh's dislocated fingers with tape, and returned to finish the job and give him a shot of painkiller. Dave and Foreman set to work knotting together tablecloths. Dave laid the two poles on the floor and the two of them tied the cloth to the metal struts to create a makeshift stretcher.

'We'd better get going,' Dave said. 'The air out there is really nasty.'

Foreman and Mai lifted Marty onto the stretcher while Dave held up his drip. Then Mai clamped the last of the oxygen masks to her face and checked Marty's vital signs. Josh pulled up the shutter and led the way out. They made slow progress. The floor of the corridor was slippery and strewn with detritus. From the car park came the omnipresent orange glow of fire.

At the end of the passage they turned right, the beams from Mai's and Josh's torches scything through the cloying air. The fabric of their suits protected them from the condensing fumes, but the strips of skin between the edge of the oxygen masks and the necks of their suits tingled from the burning acid.

The main corridor was black with smoke. The torch beams fought the dark but it was impossible to see more than a few feet ahead. A dozen paces along the corridor they turned right. Ahead they could see closed shutters on each side of the passageway. Close to the end, on the right, was the roller-door to B63. Dave put the drip onto the stretcher beside Marty and knelt down. Using his good arm, he tugged on the shutter rim and pulled it up. Mai backed into the room and they lowered the stretcher to the floor.

In the far wall they could see the hole they had come through earlier. Taking deep breaths from their oxygen reservoirs, they made for the opening.

96

Even though the sonic generators of the drills did all the cutting work, driving a hole through the blockage was still exhausting work. And when their cybersuits went down Mark and Stephanie found the task almost unbearable.

It was filthy work. They were making a hole just over a yard square, and the drills were slicing through the soil as though it was air, but the machines were not designed to be used this way – they were meant to be mounted on stands and controlled remotely. Stephanie and Mark had them poised like assault rifles, and they vibrated so much it was almost impossible to keep hold of them.

The Sonic Drills shattered the soil into an ultrafine powder which would normally have dissipated, but in the confined space of the tunnel it filled the air with a dense cloud of tiny particles, making it impossible to see far beyond the end of the drill handle. With their cybersuits down, Mark and Stephanie felt the heat given off by the powerful drills almost immediately, and the miasma of dust and atomised soil shot through the inert filters of their suits like water through a sieve.

'How much further?' Stephanie yelled over the noise.

Mark glanced back. 'I'd guess another yard.'

A large chunk of concrete began to slither away from the top of the hole. They killed the drills immediately and jumped back. A beam about four feet long fell through the void and landed nose-down in the soil with a dull thud, before tipping backwards towards them.

Stephanie climbed onto the beam and pushed her Sonic Drill against the wall. Just as she was about to turn it on, she hesitated. A glimmer of light had appeared. Stephanie saw a tiny hole in the wall of soil and debris. The light vanished and then reappeared, brighter.

'There's a light the other side,' she said, turning quickly to Mark. 'Hello?' she shouted into the opening. 'Josh? Mai? Is that you?'

97

Pete felt as though he had dived into a pool of hot water. His skin was lathered with boiling sweat, and he had to wipe the moisture from his eyes just to see clearly. He estimated he had 60 seconds left before the heat inside the Bullet started to drain the life from him. Thirty seconds after that, he would be dead.

He hated this. It was not in his nature to lie down and die. He was a fighter, a battler – he had been all his life. This was the big one. If he did not fight now, he told himself, he would never fight again.

But what could he do? Pete wracked his brains for an answer. There was a solution to every puzzle – he knew that.

Then a desperate idea struck him. No, it was more than desperate, it was crazy. But then, what choice did he have? Even the craziest idea was better than just giving up. He reached under the seat and felt around. His hand came to rest on a small cylinder. He ran his fingers over its hot contours, the metal barrel and the nozzle at one end. He grabbed it and pulled it into view.

It was a miniature fire extinguisher. Pete's only option was to open the back door of the Mole and to run through the flames. If he could get through the fire he would put out his burning clothes with the extinguisher. He had no idea how intense the fire was nor how big it was, and he knew that once he was out there he would become disoriented almost immediately. But he kept coming back to the same argument – what was his alternative?

Kneeling down close to the back door, Pete touched the manual override lever and quickly jerked his hand away. It was scorching. The heat seared through the fabric of his suit glove. He bent down to look under the bench, searching for something he could grip the handle with, but there was nothing.

Time was running out. Pete could feel his breathing becoming laboured. He glanced at his watch. His time was almost up. He would just have to grab the handle and pray. He leaned forward, closed his eyes and thrust his hands forward, waiting for the agony to hit.

Suddenly the lights came on and a deep growl came from the front of the machine. Pete froze, his fingertips a fraction of an inch from the scorching handle. There was a hum and then a single loud note that started to ascend the scale. The control panels flickered to life, the screens came on and the voice of the onboard computer boomed through the inside of the Mole.

'Warning, warning – internal temperature critical. Immediate renormalisation essential.'

'Tell me something I don't know,' Pete muttered.

98

Josh's and Mai's cybersuits powered up just as they were manoeuvring Marty's stretcher into the tunnel.

'Thank Christ!' Mai exclaimed. They stopped for a moment and lowered Marty to the ground. Mai and Josh removed their oxygen masks and pulled on their helmets. It took only a moment for them to realise that comms were still down, but at least the suit coolant was working and the air-filters were operational.

They lifted Marty again and began to walk along the tunnel. Turning a bend in the drain, they caught their first glimpse of the blockage. It looked like a barricade from a battlefield, a huge mound of soil and concrete, twisted metal and pieces of plastic.

'Stop,' Josh said, his voice just audible through the helmet. He had a hand up, indicating they should stay quiet for a moment.

They all stood still, holding their breath.

'You hear that?' he asked Mai.

She nodded. 'Doesn't sound like the Mole.'

'It's a Sonic Drill. Actually, it's two.' Josh's cochlear implants were working hard to decipher the sounds.

They picked up the pace, and as they came closer Dave could hear the low hum of the drills. As they reached the blockage the sound stopped abruptly. They lowered Marty carefully to the floor of the tunnel. Dave hooked his drip onto a metal strut poking out of the barrier, while Mai crouched beside her patient. Josh clambered over the barrier to the area where the sound had been loudest.

Mai ran a sensor over Marty's chest. A series of coloured lights blinked in the darkness of the tunnel, and the device emitted a succession of bleeps. She checked the small screen on the top of the machine. Returning the sensor to the med-kit, she plucked out the Vasjet, replaced the cylinder containing the medication with another, and held it against Marty's bare chest, just over his heart.

Josh had stopped close to the wall of the tunnel. He was looking back towards Mai when they all heard a woman's voice calling to them. Josh scrambled up the wall of detritus and soil and quickly found the tiny opening into the blockage. He waved his torch across the opening, then lowered it. A return flash appeared.

Josh leaned in. 'Steph!' he shouted. 'Is that you?'

'Josh! Are you okay?'

'I am now that the cybersuits are back on.'

'Who's with you?'

'Mai and three survivors – Senator Foreman, Dave Golding and Marty Gardiner. Marty needs urgent medical attention.'

'Okay. We're no more than a yard away from you now. We're using the Sonic Drills. Suggest you stand back. We'll be with you ASAP.'

Josh clambered back down the jagged piles of soil, slipping in the slurry until he reached the floor of the drain. He began to tell Mai the news when the wrist of his suit emitted a bleeping sound, and Mai's went off at the same moment.

They both gazed down at the flexiscreens moulded on the wrists of their cybersuits. They knew immediately that normal comms were still down, but the computer in the suit had an emergency backup that allowed it to operate as a conventional computer hooked up to the internet via an internal modem.

In the grey darkness of the tunnel, the miniature screens were iridescent squares of intense light. Stretched across the brightness, Josh and Mai could each see a dark strip of letters appearing like a line of typing on a manual typewriter. It was an email giving them news that came straight from their worst nightmares.

99

Base One, Tintara

The message Tom had sent through the internet was succinct and uncompromising. *'There's a bomb on B6. It'll go off in under six minutes. Tom.'* Then he had typed in his E-Force ID serial number – 8683823567#5 – a code known only to the six team members. Hitting the send button, he spun his chair around. 'Jerome,' he said to the nearest technician, 'I need to speak to Senator Evan Mitchell immediately.'

The technician nodded and leaned over his virtual keyboard. 'He's not picking up, Tom,' he said a few moments later.

'Damn it! He has to. What's the number?'

The technician told him and Tom typed it in. Tapping a couple of keys on his own virtual keyboard, he pulled up a file on his holoscreen. He opened it and inputted a complex alphanumeric sequence. A moment later the holoscreen was filled with numbers and letters. The sequence flowed down in two columns. Tom thrust his cursor into the stream and plucked out a segment of numbers. A dial tone came from the speaker on his computer. There was no reply. Tom tapped at the keyboard again and a voice jumped out of the speaker.

'But Senator –' the voice said.

'No buts, Sam, no buts –'

'Senator Mitchell?'

'Who's that? We have a crossed line.'

'Senator. It's Tom Erickson, E-Force.'

'What?' the man named Sam interjected. 'Who the –'

'Tom?'

'T, O, M,' Tom intoned.

'Sam, I have to go,' Mitchell said.

'But –'

'Please, just hang up, yeah?'

There was a heavy sigh and a click.

'Alright, Tom. You have my attention.'

'There's another bomb in the CCC,' Tom said.

'What?'

'Another –'

'Okay, okay. Where?'

'On B6.'

'Any details?'

'It'll go off in –' Tom glanced at a digital clock to the left of his holoscreen – 'five minutes and 21 seconds.'

100

California Conference Center, Los Angeles

Captain James McNally had been ordered to lead a small group down the slope to the east of the CCC. It would take them from the Ground Level down to B2, the first floor of the car park.

Smoke billowed towards them as he and two others, Phil Lazardo and Julio Lopez, a rookie, descended the slope. They pulled on their oxygen masks but the smoke was so dense that they could see nothing further than a few feet beyond their noses. McNally led the way. His torch was as good as useless, its light swallowed up by the black fumes. A moment later he reached a clearer area.

'Over here,' he called through his radio, and he signalled to the other men. The smoke had cleared suddenly and they could see the devastated car park, cars ablaze and shrouded in dust and filth, the ceiling bowed from the weight of collapsed masonry on B1. 'Fan out,' McNally said. 'Phil, skirt along the north edge. Julio, you take the centre lane. We'll meet up at the ramp.'

Some of the electric lights were working, but they presented more of a hazard than a help as they swung loose on frayed cables, and it was hot. McNally made steady progress along the southernmost aisle between rows of demolished vehicles. There was no sign of life, which hardly surprised him considering the state of the place. All he could hear were flames crackling, the fizz of gas, the sound of falling debris.

341

Then he thought he heard something else. He stopped and held his breath. He strained to listen and heard the sound again – a banging.

Turning, McNally ran back towards the slope, then up the next aisle. The banging sound was growing louder, and then he heard two children yelling for help. At that moment a message came through from the Chief – a 10-33, which meant *'Get the hell out – now!'*

Then McNally learned the dread news: *'Another bomb will go off in four minutes, 45 seconds.'*

As he ran towards the cries, Phil burst in over the radio. 'Boss? Where are you?'

'Just get out. You and Julio. Head straight for the ramp.'

'But –'

'Just do it!'

McNally could see where the yells had come from. A BMW four-wheel drive stood at the end of a line. There were two faces at the rear windows, two kids, a boy and a girl, about seven or eight. They were hammering on the glass, their screams coming through a tiny air-gap at the top of the window.

McNally didn't hesitate. 'Get back,' he shouted, loosening the axe from his belt. He swung it at the door of the vehicle, creating a great gash in the metal panel that knocked the lock inwards. A second heavy blow shattered the lock. He grabbed the handle and pulled the door open.

McNally ripped his mask away from his face. 'Come on!' he yelled.

The kids scrambled across the seats towards him and he dragged them through the jagged doorframe. They were so petrified they could hardly move. McNally crouched down in front of them. The boy was the older of the two by maybe eighteen months. His sandy hair was matted to his face with sweat, his deep blue eyes bloodshot, his cheeks moist with tears and sweat. The little girl had her blonde hair in bunches and was clutching a toy dog.

'Okay, we're going to get out of here,' McNally said. 'What are your names?'

'Tim,' the boy said shakily. 'My sister's Juney.'

'Tim, Juney – you must be brave. You understand?'

They both nodded.

'The way out is over there. A ramp leads to the surface. Come on.'

He stood and pulled the kids to each side of him, an arm around their shoulders, guiding them on. They ran along the aisle. McNally checked his watch. Under four minutes.

He pulled his mask back on. He couldn't save anyone if he was overcome by fumes. They reached the end of the row of cars, and McNally saw Phil and Julio at the foot of the slope. The two firemen turned and saw them.

McNally waved and Phil started to move towards them, when an explosion directly overhead on B1 shook the whole building. McNally just caught sight of the ceiling buckling. Juney screamed and McNally grabbed the two kids, pulling them under the nearest car.

101

Pete was at the control panel of the Mole when Tom's email arrived on his wrist-screen. He spat out an expletive and responded immediately. 'Coordinates, Tom?'

The wait for the reply was agonising.

'Grid ref 9N, 6P, about five yards west of up-ramp on B6.'

Pete had swung the machine around in its tracks even before he had finished reading Tom's message. The Mole slid effortlessly through the flames that had been life-threatening only a few minutes earlier. Now the blue tongues of burning fuel slithered harmlessly around the outer skin of the machine.

The tracks of the Mole crunched over the concrete floor slick with oil and petrol, flattening piles of metal and wood. In a few moments Pete had manoeuvred the vehicle to the top of the down-ramp. He slammed on the accelerator and the Mole rocketed forward, picking up speed as it went. At the bottom of the ramp it spun on its axis and pointed west.

Pete braked hard. He scanned his control panel and tapped at the keyboard, and an image of the scene appeared on his holoscreen. His fingers flew over the controls, activating a set of sensors on the front of the Mole. They swept across the full spectrum of the space ahead.

Pete peered at the 3D image, searching for a 'bomb signature' – a unique cluster of colours on the screen. Suddenly he saw it – a small cylindrical device inside a plastic bag. A sensor just below the forward camera of the Mole detected the chemical profile of the object. It showed up as a bright yellow and purple shape. Below this was a stream of text: '*Steel casing, interior composed of a blend of calcium chloride, D-2 wax and phosphorus*'.

'Gotcha!' Pete exclaimed. He tapped at the control panel and a series of numbers appeared on the screen. He read the numbers and whistled. Six pounds of HBX – it was a bomb bigger than either of the first two.

He fired off another email to Tom as the Mole nudged slowly forwards, clearing a path through the rubble. '*Found bomb. Attempting defuse. Where are the others?*'

Tom's reply came a few seconds later. '*Copy that. Take care, buddy. Steph, Mai, Mark and Josh are in the drain with three survivors, including Senator Foreman. How big is the bomb?*'

'*Big enough,*' Pete typed back, and then he turned to the holoscreen. Pushing back his chair, he said to the vehicle's computer, 'Activate probe and position it directly in front of the Mole.'

The computer set to work. Pete heard a hatch opening and a whirring sound coming from the front of the Mole. Adjusting the external camera, he saw the probe resting on the cleared concrete floor. It was squat, a metal cube about a foot square, perched on tracks. On top of the cubic base was a cylindrical chamber that moved independently. A metal arm projected two feet ahead of it.

Pete leaned across the control panel and opened a metal box on the wall. Inside hung a soft plastic helmet. It was a synapse-cap, a sophisticated neural-feedback device. Covering the outside of the cap was a matrix of wires set into the plastic. The inside was lined with a dozen silver disks arranged in three rows of four. A patch hung down each side of the cap, and a strip of black plastic joined the patches. Pete pulled on the device. The patches covered his ears and the black strip ran across his eyes.

With the synapse-cap Pete could control the probe remotely. The sensors inside the helmet read electrical impulses in Pete's brain, and the onboard computer translated these impulses into instructions. This meant he could operate the bomb disposal probe by just thinking where he wanted it to go and what he wanted it to do.

The probe rolled forward and stopped a foot away from the bomb. Pete glanced at the screen. He had three minutes left.

A small metal rod descended from the probe's arm and stopped an inch from the metal casing of the bomb. Pete studied the screen above the control panel and then turned his attention to the black strip running in front of his eyes. The strip lit up with an image of the inside of the explosive device. The HBX was wrapped around a micro-detonator, which was hooked up to a timer and a power cell. Pete had seen something like this before – in Afghanistan.

Without hesitating, he extended a claw from the base of the remote arm and clasped the base of the metal cylinder. Pete instructed the claw to rotate anticlockwise. The metal spun in its casing, and a few seconds later the base of the cylinder had separated from the body of the device. Pete made the probe lower the disk to the floor. Two wires hung down from the opened base of the cylinder – one green and the other red. He directed the probe to extend its claw forward, and it started to move towards the green lead.

A crunching sound shot though the helmet, so loud that Pete almost fell off his chair. For a microsecond he thought the bomb had gone off, and that he was in some nowhere land suspended between life and death. But then he looked at the holoscreen and realised what had happened.

The probe stood motionless, its extension arm bent almost double. A lump of concrete two foot square had landed on the probe, crushing the upper part of the device

and twisting its base. One of the probe's tracks was buckled.
It would never move again.

Pete could not believe what he was seeing. He glanced at
the clock on the screen and felt a tingle of fear run down his
spine. The bomb would go off in less than two minutes.

102

The sound of falling masonry and steel was deafening. McNally clutched the kids to him and tried to shelter them. The car they were under rocked on its wheels, and for a horrible moment he thought it was going to flip over. But it stayed upright, and the shockwave finally screeched past.

McNally left it as long as he dared before emerging from under the car. The air was dense with white dust. The kids came out, coughing desperately. 'Here,' McNally said, crouching down and helping them each to draw breath through his mask. Then he stood up, pulled the mask back on and tried to see what state the exit was in.

McNally pulled Tim and Juney into the adjacent aisle, and then half-dragged them 50 feet onwards, towards the slope. It was only as they approached closer that they saw the way was entirely blocked.

Phil's voice came through McNally's radio. 'Boss? Boss? Are you there?'

'Are you okay, Phil?' McNally replied.

'We're fine. But you're sealed in.'

'You two get to the surface. I'll find us another way out.'

'Jim –'

'Do it, Phil! There's no time – just get the fuck out!' McNally turned to the kids. They knew nothing about the bomb, but they were terrified enough.

'We can't get out!' Tim cried. He rubbed at his sore eyes, succeeding only in pushing more grit into them.

348

'We'll find a way,' McNally replied as reassuringly as he could. He looked at his watch again. It told him they had two minutes.

'Why do you keep looking at your watch?' It was the girl, Juney.

McNally ignored her. Looking around, he tried to figure out what they could do. He tried to remember the exact layout of the CCC. He had studied the diagram on the laptop coming over from Skid Row. The ramp was useless – he knew that. It just went down. There were emergency exits at each of the four corners of the car park. He looked over the cars towards the north-east exit. It was shrouded in smoke, and he could see flames lapping up to the ceiling. A twenty-foot-wide arc of fire stretched along the car park running east to west, blocking the way.

McNally spun around and looked towards the slope again, and then on to the south-east corner. That exit was closer. He could just make it out over the car roofs. The sign was out, but he could see a white glass box with an E and a T. 'This way,' he shouted to the children.

He ran as fast as he could, dodging between the cars and checking every few seconds to see if Tim and Juney were keeping up with him. They passed the last row of cars and could see the exit ahead. It was completely blocked.

McNally felt his heart sink. He stopped and gasped for breath. He bent down, his palms on his knees. He glanced again at his watch. One minute and 24 seconds. He turned back towards the main body of the car park, controlling his terror, if only for the sake of the two young kids.

'Think, McNally. Think!' he said aloud. But there was nothing. What could he do? He looked at the two kids, their lathered, filthy faces, their desperate expressions. Juney started to cry. McNally pushed the front of his helmet back an inch and ran his fingers over his grimy forehead. There was only one way to go. One final, crazy hope. Although it was blocked by fire, they would have to try to reach the north-east exit.

103

Josh and the others stood well back as Mark and Stephanie punched a hole into the drain.

'We've no way of telling how close we are to the bomb,' Stephanie said, lowering her drill. Mark emerged from the hole behind her. They were both caked in dust and soil.

'But it's near enough,' Josh replied.

'There's only just enough room in the opening for the stretcher,' Mark said, taking the drip from Mai. 'We'll have to crawl into it. Steph, you get the other end.' He attached the drip to a nylon cord around the neck of his cybersuit, turned away from the stretcher and crouched to grasp the metal poles. Ducking low, he and Stephanie carried Marty into the hole. Dave, Josh, Mai and Kyle Foreman followed close behind them.

'Steph. You take the Mole,' Mark said as they emerged into the larger opening created by the machine. 'You'll have to drill your way out at the end of the drain. Once you get a few yards into the soil you'll be safe from any explosion. The Bullet is pretty tough anyway.'

Stephanie stepped into the back of the Mole and went straight to the control panel and prepped the vehicle. Marty's stretcher was laid along the length of the Bullet, between the bench seats. Mark slung the two Sonic Drills onto the floor beside the stretcher, retreated and closed the door. Stephanie locked it from the control panel, then slowly reversed out of the twenty-foot-long hole. The drain was just wide enough for her to do a U-turn, and she eased down on the throttle.

The others ran along the drain, watching the Mole speed off around a bend. Josh glanced at his wrist. They had just over 90 seconds to get as far away as they could. They reached the small opening that led up to the surface and saw that the Mole had gnawed its way through the wall of the drain, its back end already a couple of yards into the soil.

The chute to the surface had been mangled beyond recognition when Mark had come down from the surface in the Mole. But the ladder Stephanie had used was still hanging, its final rung two feet above the floor. The ladder was made from carbothreads and was incredibly strong.

Mark helped Foreman onto the rope ladder. 'How's the arm, sir?' he asked.

Foreman gave him a wry smile. 'You want me to pitch you a few balls?'

'I'll hold you to that, Senator. But right now I just need you to get up the ladder as fast as you can.'

Foreman gave Mark a salute and pulled himself up onto the bottom rung. Ignoring the pain in his arm, he clambered upwards.

Mai was second up, followed by Dave then Josh. Mark glanced at his wrist. Thirty seconds. He pulled himself up onto the ladder and started to climb.

104

Pete punched at the control panel and the rear door of the Mole slid open. He checked his suit. It was functioning normally, except that normal comms were still down. Crouching as he moved along the low-ceilinged gantry between the seats of the Bullet, he jumped out of the Mole, his feet crunching on the encrusted concrete.

It was eerily quiet. Even the crackle of fire and the constant drip of water from broken pipes had ceased. *The proverbial calm before the storm*, Pete thought as he dashed around the back of the machine and caught sight of the bomb.

Without wasting a second he ran to the end of the drill bit. The cylindrical bomb lay on a pile of concrete. Three-quarters of its length was exposed, where the probe had pulled away the plastic bag in which it had been wrapped. The base that the probe had unscrewed lay to one side, and Pete could see the two exposed wires.

He crouched down and stared at the device. Suddenly he was eight years in the past and half a world away. He and his 'bomb buddy', Matt Stevens, had been sent into a market in Kabul. The Taliban had planted a timed device in the main square, but British intelligence had discovered it before it could be detonated. The army had taken a consignment of the new Cutlass robot bomb disposal devices, but none had been commissioned yet and the nearest Wheelbarrow robot – the type they'd used since the 1970s – was 30 miles outside Kabul. They had to go in themselves.

The bomb had been small but powerful, four ounces of HBX in a tin box. A toy elephant sat on top of it. The explosive had a killing radius of at least twenty feet. Pete had sensed something bad about the device as soon as he saw it. Something was not right, but when Matt challenged him he couldn't offer anything tangible. It was just a gut feeling.

'Well, with respect, mate,' Matt had said, 'I'm going to go by what my brain tells me, not your gut!' And he had laughed good-naturedly, his hand on Pete's shoulder. Then he bent down to unscrew the top of the device.

Inside, the bomb had looked just as it should, just like the dozens of others they had neutered. 'We'll need the microdriver,' Matt said. Pete went to pluck it from his pocket, but it wasn't there.

'Bugger!' he'd exclaimed. 'Left it in the bag. I'll get it.' He ran back to the edge of the square where they'd left their kit by a low stone wall. Then he'd heard the *click* from across the 50 feet of dirt between him and Matt – he'd known what it meant in a millisecond.

With lightning reflexes Pete had dived behind the wall. The boom from the device had rendered him deaf for a month, and he'd spent six weeks in hospital. His ankles had been shattered because he hadn't made it behind the wall in time.

Pete's body had been relatively quick to mend but his mind had never really healed. He could never forgive himself for Matt's death. He could have stopped him, been more vocal about his misgivings. On top of this was a huge helping of 'survivor guilt'. Pete had only been saved by his own inefficiency. By rights, he should have been blown to pieces along with his friend.

All of this flashed through Pete's mind as he looked at the wires. And at that moment he had a bad feeling about this bomb – precisely the feeling he'd experienced eight years earlier in Kabul.

Pete was breathing hard, making the cybersuit work

overtime, and he could hear his own heart racing. A small tube extended from his wrist – a miniature laser cutter. He leaned forward ready to cut the green wire. In the corner of his eye he glimpsed the screen on his wrist and saw the numbers click by – 31, 30 . . .

Suddenly Pete felt preternaturally calm. The world around him seemed to vanish. He held his breath. Glancing at the counter on his flexiscreen, he saw the number change to 27. He knew what to do. He shifted his hand and sliced through the red lead.

The clock stopped at 26 seconds. Pete could hardly believe it. Something had told him that the wires were reversed in this device. He had no idea what it was – instinct, maybe – but he had made the right decision.

Then he heard a *click*. A thin disk of metal dropped inside the steel cylinder. Pete saw it fall, saw it come to rest above the lump of plastic material next to the timer and the detonator. The disk settled into a groove just visible above the explosive, and the clock flicked to 25.

Pete twisted round and sped back to the Mole. He had never moved so fast in his life. The Maxinium shell of the machine flashed past as he dashed towards the Mole's back door. He did not see the oil slick running beside the vehicle and hit it at top speed. His boots lost their purchase and he went over onto his back. For a second he struggled like a dying fly before he managed to twist around in the slurry and find his footing. He dared not look at his wrist. The only thing he could do was keep moving. Keep running until he reached the door of the Mole, or be blown to vapour by the HBX.

Pete grabbed the rim of the Mole and propelled himself into the Bullet, pulling the door shut behind him.

A flash came first, followed – a microsecond later – by the blast and the thunderous roar. Millions of newtons of energy, along with tons of concrete and steel, slammed into the Mole, sending it spiralling through the air.

105

McNally was just about to turn towards the north-east emergency exit when a flame shot up from a puddle of oil ten feet away. He recoiled, but as he moved his head back he saw a momentary flash of light to the far left of his visual field. He turned and saw the steel metal plate of a maintenance hatch. It was open, the door pinned back against the wall.

Without another thought he dashed to the hatch. Peering in, he saw the tunnel leading away into darkness. 'Over here!' he screamed, beckoning frantically to the kids.

McNally helped them up into the opening. 'Crawl forward as fast as you can,' he yelled, and he scrambled up the wall and levered himself into the hole. He knew they had only seconds. 'Move, move . . . Come on, we've got to go, guys!'

Without slowing he managed to catch a glimpse of his watch – nineteen seconds to go.

He heard the little girl yelp. 'Ow! I cut myself.' She began to cry.

'Okay, Juney, keep going, sweetie. I'll check it out when we get to the other end.'

But the girl had stopped. Her brother had reached her.

'Move, Juney,' the boy hissed.

She started to cry harder.

McNally caught up with them just as the bomb went off. They felt the walls of the maintenance shaft shake. Both children screamed, but the sound was drowned out by the roar of the explosion. McNally fell forward, pulling the kids down with him, and waited for the shockwave to hit.

The blast roared down the tunnel, a great plug of air sweeping dust and debris ahead of it. The force of it propelled the three humans in the passage forward. They crashed into the sides of the shaft and tried to clutch onto anything they could. The children rolled and turned head-over-heels, while McNally was knocked from wall to wall.

McNally thanked the Lord he had kept his helmet on as his head was smashed against the sides of the tunnel. He screwed up his eyes, covering his face with one arm and putting out the other to help break his fall. He felt himself crash uncontrollably against a bundle of cables. He made a grab for a loop of wire, but it ripped away from the wall. Then he felt a sharp pain in his back as he collided with a metal box. Tim's foot caught him in the neck and the boy's shoe smashed into his face.

And then suddenly they were falling, as though they had tumbled down a well.

McNally felt his neck spasm as he landed on a smooth metal surface. He could taste blood in his mouth. Then he heard two dull thumps as the kids landed close by.

106

Mark and the others were halfway up the ladder when the bomb went off. The roar was muffled by the solid earth between the blast site and the access chute. Then a second reverberation shuddered outward from B6 and along the drain.

At the epicentre of the explosion the wave-front moved at a speed of 23,947 feet per second, and the air around the blast had a mean temperature of 8378 degrees Kelvin. But by the time the wave-front ripped through the storage rooms and the outer wall of the CCC and smacked into the blockage in the drain, its impact was reduced by over 50 per cent.

The blockage, 30 feet thick, acted as a giant muffler. It absorbed 97 per cent of the kinetic energy from the blast and put a giant brake on the expanding gases. But the blast also blew the barrier apart and propelled the fragments west along the drain.

The three E-Force members, along with Dave Golding and Kyle Foreman, were some 40 feet up the air-conditioning duct as the material from the barrier crashed along the inside of the drain. The sonic boom – created by the explosive gases hitting tons of material in the blockage – was ear-bursting.

The majority of material from the barrier shot along the drain, gradually losing energy as it went. But some of it flew up into the escape chute. Mark, who was closest to the drain, could see a great cloud of dust and debris advancing up the hole. 'Don't look down!' he screamed above the roaring of the explosion. 'Press against the wall and keep your eyes shut tight!'

The material hit them like a giant wave crashing onto a beach, slamming them against the rock and soil of the churned up chute. The ladder swayed violently. Mark could just hear Dave yelling in terror above the screeching torrent that flooded over them. Then, shockingly, the noise stopped. But only for a second. The backdraft was even more powerful than the blast. As air was expelled from around the blast site, a vacuum was created and material was sucked in to fill the void. Everything that had crashed past them in the chute whooshed back down. Soil and lumps of rock cascaded onto their heads.

A chunk of concrete slammed into Kyle Foreman's shoulder. He screamed in pain and let go of the ladder with one hand, swinging out into the black chasm. His legs gave way and one foot slid between the rungs.

Mai heard the senator cry out. She shot a glance upwards and a stream of soil and dust fell onto her visor. She sprung up a rung, and with one arm wrapped tight around the ladder, she thrust out a hand and caught Foreman by his belt. He was writhing around in panic, but the terror energised him. He bent his body at the waist and shook off the stream of debris raining down on them, then caught the ladder with his hand and regained his footing. He shook his head and blood from a dozen cuts in his face splashed onto the carbothreads of the ladder. Ignoring the pain that screamed through his body, Foreman tugged on the next rung and hauled himself up.

Thirty seconds later they emerged into the concrete passageway that led up to the grassy area beyond the north-west corner of the CCC. The night was ablaze with reds and yellows from roaring fires. The air was filled with dust and smoke. Dave and Foreman drew heavily on the oxygen masks that clung still to their faces, then they collapsed onto the scorched grass.

Mark was the last to emerge. He scrambled over the lip of the chute and pulled himself onto the concrete floor of the passageway. His cybersuit was stained and covered with dust.

He strode up the slope towards Dave and Foreman and crouched down. 'Are you two alright? Senator, you took a nasty knock back there.' Mark could see that the remains of Foreman's shirt were ripped to shreds, and a large patch of fresh blood was soaking his left shoulder. The man's face was coated with blood and soil, making his eyes look almost comically white, like a character from a cartoon.

Foreman nodded slowly. His mouth was so dry and filled with dust that he could not speak.

'We're almost there,' Mark said, turning to check on Dave. The young man had clambered to his knees and was nursing his damaged arm. He looked up at Mark and let out a deep sigh. 'Man oh man,' he exclaimed, and slumped his head forward.

Mark helped Dave to his feet, and Josh and Mai got Kyle Foreman to a standing position with a shoulder under each of his arms.

'Mark? Mark? Come in, please.' It was Tom.

Mark could barely believe it – comms were back online. 'Yes, Tom,' he replied.

'Thank Christ! Where are you? The BigEyes can't get a visual from anywhere within twenty yards of the CCC.'

Mark talked as he assisted Dave across the grass towards the Pram. 'We're out. We have Senator Foreman and two other survivors. One with us, one with Steph.'

'Where is she?'

'In the number two Mole with Marty Gardiner. She should be hitting the surface soon. Have you heard from Pete?'

There was a heavy silence from the other end of the line.

'Tom? What's happened?'

'The last message from him was an email. He was going outside the Mole to defuse the third bomb.'

'Oh no!' Mark had stopped in his tracks.

'I can't see how he could have escaped the blast.'

107

Mark was on the flight deck of the Big Mac, where Josh and Mai were at the controls. A big wall screen perpendicular to the control panels showed a view of the area just beyond the ship. The sky was a mucky blend of grey haze and piercing firelight. The CCC had been gutted beyond recognition by the third bomb, and the western portion of the building had collapsed. It looked like a scene from the London Blitz.

Mai and Josh had spoken to the emergency services. Thanks to Tom's quick thinking, they had managed to get their teams to safety before the third device detonated. Only one fireman was missing. None of the rescuers had been below B2 at the time, so there was absolutely no news of Peter Sherringham. It was now over an hour since the final blast, and the E-Force team was beginning to fear the worst.

The door to the sickbay slid open and Stephanie walked onto the flight deck.

'How are they?' Mark asked.

'All asleep,' Stephanie replied, 'and all stable. Mr Gardiner was touch and go. Another five minutes and we would have lost him. He'll need surgery, but I think he'll pull though.'

'And the senator? He was pretty beaten up.'

'Severe acid burns to his left arm, broken nose, dislocated shoulder, two broken ribs and multiple lacerations. But he'll live.'

'And the boy?'

'He got off the lightest of the lot. Burns to his leg, lacerations to his arms and face, but apart from that . . . Anything from Pete?'

Mark shook his head. 'Sybil can't help. She's getting nothing from his suit – no locator beacon, no vital signs.'

Stephanie sighed and threw herself into a chair. She looked utterly exhausted.

'How about I take the Mole down there?' Josh said, spinning his chair around to face the others.

'Too dangerous,' Mark replied. 'That place is like a honeycomb.'

'Well, the Cage then?'

Mark was about to respond when Mai startled the others with a piercing scream. She had been staring intently at the holoscreen above the control panel. 'Close in, Sybil. *Close in!*' she bellowed. Jumping from her seat, she dashed to the main screen.

'What is it?' said Mark, moving beside her.

'This is unreal!' Mai said, her hands to her mouth.

The four of them were transfixed by what they saw. Sybil had zeroed in on a part of the CCC close to where the main entrance had once been. The area had been reduced to rubble. The doorframes and the entire front of the building had been blown away. As they watched, a human shape emerged from behind a pile of rubble, on top of which lay a huge metal frame of the letter C. It was one of the letters from the neon sign for the California Conference Center, which had once perched proudly over the main doors. The figure was limping and covered in grime and filth. But just discernible across his chest were the words '*E-Force*' and, below that, the name '*Pete Sherringham*'.

108

As consciousness returned, McNally tried to focus, but there seemed to be something wrong with his vision. He felt something clamped to his nose and mouth and heard a voice, but he couldn't make out the words. Then his eyes began to clear and he saw Phil's face swim into view.

McNally tried to move, but nothing worked.

'You're okay, Jim,' Phil said. He was smiling down at him.

McNally swallowed hard and managed to find his voice, a weird croak. 'The kids . . .' Then, as paramedics lifted him onto a stretcher, he saw them. Tim and Juney were also on stretchers, masks over their faces, liquid-filled tubes protruding from their arms. Tim gave him a weak smile.

'Broken bones, cuts and bruises, but they'll be good,' Phil said.

McNally felt a huge weight lift from his shoulders. Watching the ceiling drift past as the paramedics carried him out through the back of the smashed-up shell of Kmart, he could still smell the fires burning. It was a smell he knew all too well. He also knew that, after tonight, he never wanted to smell it again.

109

Josh and Stephanie were taking a well-needed rest. Mark was on the flight deck of the Big Mac, staring at the screen, which showed a view of the devastated CCC in the pre-dawn light. The fires had all burned out and the wreckage looked grey, a lifeless morass. A few emergency crews remained, picking through the rubble and ashes. A police helicopter circled overhead, its lemon beam sweeping across the jagged columns and twisted piles of concrete and steel.

Tom's face appeared on the screen. 'Morning, Mark,' he said. 'Thought you'd be asleep.'

'Nope. Steph, Josh and Pete are. Mai's just left for Houston. I obviously just didn't have a trying enough day!'

'When do you hope to leave?'

'I can't just yet. I'm waiting for a flight for Senator Foreman.'

'He's still with you?'

'He insisted. Said he was happy to wait and that there were many more urgent cases to deal with here.'

'How's Pete?'

Mark shook his head. 'A living miracle. No one would imagine he had been so close to a massive explosion. The nanobots are fixing him up. He has a couple of cracked ribs, cuts and bruises. It's ridiculous, really.'

'Testimony to the engineers who built the Mole.'

'Yeah, the poor machine is beaten up beyond recognition,

but the shell of the Bullet held. Pete was just thrown around inside. So, have you found out anything more?'

Tom frowned. 'Those guys are using some pretty sophisticated defensive software.'

'So you haven't.'

'I didn't say that,' Tom retorted. 'You're very privileged to have a living genius on call.'

'Okay, genius. Let's have it.'

'Sybil had broken into their system, but the files themselves were very well protected. I succeeded in cracking them – eventually. The owners don't have a clue I was there, of course, and they never will. I must give Sybil some credit for that. Once Syb and I had their defences opened up, I found out more about the marines who got aboard the Big Mac. It was a piece of cake to trace their connections.

'As expected, everything led back to one source – a group of four very influential guys. They call themselves the Four Horsemen, would you believe? Obviously some weird reference to the Bible. They clearly fancy themselves as Antichrists.' His expression darkened. 'Which is apt, I suppose. Seems they weren't content with killing a thousand innocent people in an attempt to get Senator Foreman. When they learned of us, they wanted to steal our technology into the bargain. Anyway, here's the info.'

As he spoke, a column of text appeared to the right of the screen on the Big Mac. Mark whistled as he read the information.

'Yeah, it goes right to the top – well, almost,' Tom remarked.

'And we've got a cast-iron case against them?' Mark asked.

'I can prove they have their paws all over the bombing and the assassination attempt. Their IDs are in the files, and there's a whole heap of comms records. Whenever they communicate with anyone outside the inner circle of four they use voice and image distortion software. But I've unscrambled the records. Here are the ugly bastards.'

Four faces appeared at the bottom of Mark's screen. He vaguely recognised two of them from newspaper articles, but he couldn't put names to them. They were obviously very powerful figures, but men who managed to remain almost completely anonymous.

'Alright, Tom. Good work. Leave it with me.'

Mark broke the connection and stood up from the control panel. He touched a patch on the wall and the door to the sickbay opened. Marty was still unconscious but Dave Golding was sitting at his bedside. Kyle Foreman was snoring quietly.

'How are you feeling?' Mark asked, surprised to see the boy awake. He pulled up another chair.

'I guess I'm okay . . . physically.'

Mark looked into the young man's face. 'The physical wounds always heal a lot faster than the psychological ones.'

Dave looked at his feet for a moment. 'What about Marty?'

'Steph reckons he'll make a complete recovery.'

Dave looked relieved. 'He's a good man.'

'Yes, and a tough one. You three never gave up.'

Dave looked at Mark and tears brimmed in his eyes, spilling over onto his cheeks. 'All those people . . .' he began.

Mark could say nothing. The door from the flight deck swished open and Stephanie walked in. She saw Dave's face, apologised and started to retreat.

'No, no, please,' Dave said, wiping his cheeks. 'Come in . . . I'm being a real wimp.'

Mark put a hand on the boy's shoulder. 'After what you've been through, that's the last word I'd use to describe you, young man.'

They all turned at a sound from the other bed. Kyle Foreman was pulling himself up on the pillows, looking dazed. Stephanie paced over to him. 'How are you?' she asked.

For a second the senator's face was totally blank, as though he had no idea who or where he was. He took a deep breath. 'A little muggy.' He glanced at the catheter in his arm, then around at Dave and Mark. 'Dave,' he said. 'And Marty – how is he?'

'Fine now, thanks to you two,' Stephanie said.

Foreman shook his head. 'You guys played your part. I don't know how to begin to –'

A bleeping sound came from the flight deck. Stephanie walked into the adjoining room and leaned over the control panel. A few moments later she was back in the sickbay, a big smile on her face.

'There's someone who wants to talk to you, Senator.'

He gave her a puzzled look.

'Sickbay screen, please,' Stephanie instructed the onboard computer. 'And raise the upper third of Bed 3 . . . 45 degree angle.' The screen on the far wall lit up and the head of Kyle Foreman's bed raised slowly. Stephanie helped him sit up.

The screen filled with the face of a woman.

'Sandy!' Foreman exclaimed.

'Darling . . .'

'My God! Where are you?' He had just noticed she was also in a hospital bed – she was wearing a green gown only partially covered by a silk Versace dressing gown.

'Where do you think?' Sandy replied, beaming. The camera pulled back and they could all see the face of a newborn baby, wrinkled and pink. He was wrapped in a blanket, asleep in his mother's arms. 'Meet Kyle junior,' Sandy said, as a tear of joy slid down her cheek to meet her smile.

110

Houston, Texas

The Lincoln Continental swept through the gates of Base Three, five miles from downtown Houston. An hour after sunrise, the sky was a bruised orange, as though it had been daubed by a young child with a dirty paintbrush. The road was awash with water and the wipers were working hard.

The driver had the radio on. Every station was abuzz with the latest news from the disaster site in Los Angeles. Reports claimed that more than a thousand people had died at the California Conference Center, and that hundreds more had been injured. The emergency services expected the death toll to rise, as many people were critical or still unaccounted for. As for who was behind the horror, no one had claimed responsibility. Fingers were being pointed at a spectrum of possible culprits, from al-Qaeda to nebulous groups of eco-terrorists.

Mai sighed and shook her head as she heard excited reporters describing the amazing rescue vehicles of a strange organisation called E-Force that no one had heard of before. The biggest tease for the newsmen had been the fact that any attempt to photograph or film the machines used by the organisation produced only shapeless blurs. E-Force, it seemed, had appeared out of nowhere. Nobody had any clear idea who was involved, or even if E-Force was a government body or the product of a mysterious philanthropic group.

Mai sat in the back of the car, letting the babble from the radio wash over her. She watched the buildings flash past, shrouded in rain. As she focused on the sound of water splashing against the undercarriage of the Lincoln, a menagerie of emotions vied for her attention. She was utterly exhausted, but more alive than she could ever remember being. She felt exhilarated to be part of E-Force. Only time would tell how the organisation would shape up.

What was to be their remit in the future? Although she was pleased they had been able to help the rescue services and had saved the lives of three good men, she knew they could do so much more. But then a darker voice in her heard told her that it wouldn't be her decision to make. It wouldn't even be Mark Harrison's. E-Force might be non-military and ostensibly apolitical, but that was an oxymoron. Could anything as important as E-Force remain apolitical for long?

The hospital reception area was quiet. A cleaner was polishing the floor, and a couple of young doctors walked by, studying their clipboard notes. Mai took the elevator to the sixth floor and walked along the brightly lit corridor. Reaching the door to her mother's room, she paused for a moment and took a deep breath, then turned the handle.

The room was in semi-darkness, the curtains still closed. Mai stood frozen in the doorway as two people came towards her, their heads bowed. It was Greta with Howard, Mai's ex-husband. He had his arm around Greta's shoulders.

They both looked up at the same moment. Howard's face was pale. He shook his head slowly, his jaws clenched. Greta glared at Mai, pulled away from her stepfather and pushed past her mother and out into the corridor.

Howard paused. 'I'm sorry,' he whispered, then he walked on.

Mai took a step into the darkened room and the door closed quietly behind her, blocking out the sounds of stirring patients in neighbouring rooms. She looked down at her mother. Eri Kato was tiny, a doll, her skin pale and shiny like waxed paper. The doctors had removed the respirator and the tubes.

Mai leaned over her mother's inert body and knew there was nothing left. No vestige of Eri remained. Mai ran a hand along the dead woman's cheek, feeling her skin. It was as soft as a newborn baby's. A tear fell from her eye onto her mother's lifeless face. Mai watched it slide onto the sheet and soak into the fibres.

111

Base One, Tintara
Two days later

Mark stared in silence at the faces of the two men on the screen. On the left was Senator Evan Mitchell. On the right, Clayton Franberger, the Secretary of State.

'It's hardly an appropriate time to celebrate,' Franberger said. 'But I think you and your team may congratulate yourselves on a job very well done.' He smiled. To Mark the man seemed like a rabid dog.

'Thank you, sir,' Mark replied dutifully. 'I'm proud of all of them.'

'And I understand Senator Foreman has already spoken to you to express his thanks.'

'He has, yes.'

The Secretary of State glanced at his watch surreptitiously. 'Well, once again, well done, Mark.'

'Sir, about our findings –'

'Findings?'

Mark glanced meaningfully at Senator Mitchell, who looked down for a moment and coughed.

'The Four Horsemen.'

'Yes, yes, the Four Horsemen,' Franberger said, fixing Mark with a hard look.

After a pause, Senator Mitchell spoke. 'We feel there is insufficient evidence to proceed.' He looked into the middle distance, unable to meet Mark's eyes.

Mark took a deep breath. 'I see. Insufficient evidence. Even though we have records of the men dealing with an assassin known as the Dragon. The man who planted the bombs at the CCC.'

'A dead assassin, Mark,' Franberger intoned. 'I think many would assume the man was operating alone.'

Mark looked directly at the Secretary of State and laboured to quell his fury. He was about to speak when Mitchell's voice cut in.

'Mark, I personally believe this Dragon was a solo operator with his own agenda. Perhaps we'll never know what that was. As Secretary Franberger has pointed out, the man is dead.'

Mark made to speak, but Mitchell went on. 'E-Force, on the other hand, is very much alive, is it not?' He paused dramatically to emphasise his point. 'And this mission has shown just how effective it is – how many lives will be saved in the future because your organisation exists.'

Mark looked away. He gazed at the banks of flashing lights and plastic control panels to one side of the screen. A thousand dead faces swam before his eyes. And then a steeliness gripped him. He swallowed hard and nodded. 'Very well,' he said.

Mark sat alone in the comms suite for several minutes. The only light came from the control panels and the holoscreen floating above one of the keyboards. Suddenly he felt very small. For all he had achieved, for all the resources at his fingertips, he realised – not for the first time – that he was nothing more than a cog in a giant machine. No, less than that – he was a worker ant, at the beck and call of truly powerful individuals.

But then, Mark told himself, those men are only as powerful as the people who elect them. It is the people who make them powerful. Their time will pass, and others will come along to replace them. Today he had been forced to do the bidding of politicians, men who would never get their hands dirty. He and the team had done their best and had saved lives, but he knew that in the future E-Force had to be better prepared and used properly.

E-Force was not simply a testing ground for CARPA's technology. More than half a century had passed since a group of congressmen, worried by the power handed to the military with the establishment of DARPA, had established the rival organisation. He knew that the idealistic days when the remit of CARPA had been to feed innovation into the everyday world of ordinary people had long passed. CARPA now had ambitions to claw back the billions of dollars it had spent over the years. And, of course, he knew that E-Force was an amazing advert for technological innovations at least two decades ahead of their time. But he and the other members of E-Force were not merely field-testing that technology so it could be sold on, and his team were not test dummies. That, he knew, was what the politicians and the holders of the purse strings would want. But he would fight them.

After today, Mark told himself, he would not kowtow to politicians. He had created E-Force, and he would do everything in his power to ensure not only that it survived but also that it worked in the way he knew it should.

He sighed heavily and stood up.

112

The E-Force team was gathered in Cyber Control, along with many of the crew from the hangars and the various operational divisions at Base One.

Mark was standing on a chair, holding a glass of champagne. A hush settled over the room. 'A few minutes ago, the Secretary of State pointed out to me that this was not a time for celebration,' he began. 'And he was absolutely right. More than a thousand Americans died two days ago at the California Conference Center, and many thousands more are grieving the loss of their loved ones. But amidst the pain and the heartache, there are things of which we should be proud, and for which we should give ourselves a collective pat on the back.

'We came through our first mission with flying colours. We achieved our goals – saving lives – and we proved ourselves very capable. This, then, is not a celebration but a time to reflect upon the positive aspects of the past few days.' Mark looked around the room at the faces of his team and allowed himself a flicker of pride. He knew that he had picked the perfect unit and that E-Force would achieve great things in the future.

'To E-Force,' Mark announced, raising his glass.

'To E-Force,' the gathering responded as one.

Tom's voice cut through the momentary silence as everyone downed their champagne. 'So does that mean these guys have to go back to training?' he asked with a wicked grin.

Mark's features stayed rigid as he looked around at the other field members of E-Force. 'No,' he said, slowly breaking into a smile. 'I think you should all take yourselves off on vacation . . . to a tropical island, perhaps!'

extracts reading groups
competitions books new
discounts extracts extracts
competitions
books new
events books
extracts new titles reading groups
interviews
events extracts events
discounts
new books events
events new
discounts extracts discounts
www.panmacmillan.com
extracts events reading groups
competitions books extracts new
reading groups
events
reading groups
books